THE ASYLUM

Johan Theorin

TRANSLATED FROM THE SWEDISH
BY MARLAINE DELARGY

Doubleday

LONDON · TORONTO · SYDNEY · AUCKLAND · JOHANNESBURG

TRANSWORLD PUBLISHERS
61–63 Uxbridge Road, London W5 5SA
A Random House Group Company
www.transworldbooks.co.uk

First published in Great Britain
in 2012 by Doubleday
an imprint of Transworld Publishers

A CIP catalogue record for this book
is available from the British Library.

ISBN 9780857521408

Addresses for Random House Group Ltd companies outside the UK
can be found at: www.randomhouse.co.uk
The Random House Group Ltd Reg. No. 954009

The Random House Group Limited supports The Forest Stewardship Council (FSC®),
the leading international forest-certification organization. Our books carrying the FSC label
are printed on FSC®-certified paper. FSC is the only forest-certification scheme
endorsed by the leading environmental organizations, including Greenpeace.
Our paper procurement policy can be found at
www.randomhouse.co.uk/environment

Typeset in 12/14pt Garamond by
Kestrel Data, Exeter, Devon.
Printed and bound by
CPI Group (UK) Ltd, Croydon, CR0 4YY.

2 4 6 8 10 9 7 5 3 1

MIX
Paper from
responsible sources
FSC
www.fsc.org   FSC® C016897

To Klara

Dear Ivan, is it possible to write a love letter to someone you have never met? I'm going to try in any case. I've only seen your picture in the newspapers, below those terrible, screaming headlines. Black and white photographs taken by the press to show 'Ivan Rössel, the crazed child-killer', or whatever it is they like to call you.

The pictures are harsh and unfair, but still I have spent a lot of time looking at them. There is something about the look in your eyes, so calm and wise and yet so penetrating. You seem to see the world as it is, and to see right through me. I would like you to be able to look at me in reality too. I would love to meet you.

Loneliness is a terrible thing, and unfortunately I have suffered my fair share of it over the years. I assume that you too must sometimes feel lonely, in your locked room behind the walls of the hospital. In the silence late at night, when no one else in the whole wide world is awake . . . It is so easy to be sucked in by loneliness, to be suffocated by it in the end.

I am enclosing a photograph of myself, taken on a hot, sunny day last summer. As you can see I have fair hair, but I like dark clothes. I hope you will want to look at this picture of me, just as I have looked at those pictures of you.

That's all for now, but I would very much like to write to you again. I hope this letter reaches you on the other side of the wall. And I hope that you will somehow be able to send me a reply.

Is there anything I can do for you?

I'll do anything, Ivan.

Anything at all.

PART ONE

Routines

Yet everyone begins in the same place;
how is it that most go along without difficulty
but a few lose their way?

John Barth, *Lost in the Funhouse*

1

CAUTION! CHILDREN PLAYING! Jan reads through the side window of the taxi. The words are printed on a blue plastic sign, and beneath it is the exhortation to DRIVE SLOWLY.

'Bloody kids!' the driver yells.

Jan is thrown forward. The taxi has swung around a corner and braked sharply in front of a tricycle.

A child has abandoned the trike virtually in the middle of the road.

The street is in a residential area in the town of Valla. Jan can see low wooden fences in front of white houses, and the big warning notice.

Caution! Children playing! But the streets are empty, in spite of the three-wheeler. There are no children here to necessitate caution.

Perhaps they are all indoors, Jan thinks. *Locked inside.*

The driver glances at him in the rear-view mirror. He looks close to retirement age, with deep lines etched on his forehead, a Father Christmas beard and a weary expression.

Jan is used to weary expressions; they are everywhere.

The driver had hardly said a word before the sudden outburst when he slammed on the brakes, but as the taxi moves off again he has a question for Jan: 'The hospital . . . St Patricia's . . . do you work up there?'

Jan shakes his head. 'No. Not yet.'

'Not yet? So you're applying for a job there?'

'That's right.'

'I see,' says the driver.

Jan lowers his eyes and does not respond. He doesn't want to reveal too much about himself, and he doesn't know what he's allowed to tell other people about the hospital.

The driver goes on: 'You know there's another name for that place?'

Jan looks up. 'No. What's that?'

The driver gives a little smile. 'I'm sure they'll tell you when you get there.'

Jan gazes out of the window at the rows of houses, thinking about the man he is soon to meet.

Dr Patrik Högsmed, senior consultant. His name was at the bottom of a job advert Jan found at the beginning of July:

CLASSROOM ASSISTANT / PRE-SCHOOL TEACHER
wanted at The Dell. This is a temporary post.

The wording below the heading was similar to many others that Jan had read:

You are a classroom assistant / pre-school teacher; we would be pleased to welcome a young man, since we are committed to the creation of a team which meets the criteria of equality and diversity.

As a person you are confident in yourself, and you are both open and honest. You enjoy music and play, and all kinds of creative activity. Our pre-school adjoins a green area, so you will also appreciate the value of excursions into the surrounding forest and countryside.

You will actively strive <u>for</u> a positive atmosphere at the pre-school and <u>against</u> all forms of abusive treatment.

Much of this applied to Jan. He was a young man, a qualified pre-school teacher, he enjoyed play, and had been something of a drummer in his teenage years – although mostly on his own.

And he didn't like abusive behaviour, for personal reasons.

But was he open and honest? That depended. He was good at *appearing* open, at any rate.

It was the contact details that made Jan cut out the advert: Patrik Högsmed, Admin Department, St Patricia's Regional Psychiatric Hospital, Valla.

Jan had always found it difficult to sell himself, but the advert had stared at him from its place on the kitchen table for several days, and in the end he had called the number below the senior consultant's name.

A deep male voice had answered. 'Högsmed.'

'Dr Högsmed?'

'Yes?'

'My name is Jan Hauger, and I'm interested in the position you're advertising.'

'What position?'

'At the pre-school. Starting in September?'

There was a brief silence before Högsmed responded: 'Oh yes, that position . . .' He spoke quietly and seemed distracted. But he continued with a question for Jan: 'May I ask *why* you are interested in this post?'

'Well . . .' Jan couldn't tell the truth; he had immediately started to lie, or at least to conceal things about himself. 'I'm curious,' was all he said.

'Curious,' said Högsmed.

'Yes . . . curious about the working environment and about the town. I've spent most of my time working in pre-schools and nurseries in cities. So it would be exciting to move to somewhere slightly smaller, and to compare the way in which a pre-school is run in that kind of place.'

'Good,' Högsmed had replied. 'Of course this is a slightly unusual situation, since the children's parents are actually patients . . .'

He had gone on to explain why St Patricia's Hospital had a pre-school: 'We started it a few years ago, as an experiment. The central idea is based on research into the critical aspect of a child's relationship with its parents in terms of the child's development

15

into a socially mature individual. Both long-term and temporary foster homes always fall short in some respects, and here at St Patricia's we believe it is extremely important for the child to have both regular and stable contact with the biological mother or father, in spite of the special circumstances. And of course, for the parent, this contact with the child forms part of their treatment.' The doctor paused, then added, 'That is what we do here: we *treat* the patients. We do not punish them, whatever they might have done.'

Jan had listened, and noticed that the doctor hadn't used the word *cure*.

Högsmed had concluded with a further question: 'How does that sound?'

Jan thought it sounded interesting, and had submitted an application along with his CV.

At the beginning of August Högsmed had called him: Jan had been shortlisted for the post, and the doctor wanted to meet him. They had agreed on a time, and then Högsmed had added, 'I have a couple of requests, Jan.'

'Yes?'

'You will need to bring some form of photo ID – your driving licence or passport, just so that we can be sure of who you are.'

'Of course, that's fine.'

'And one last thing, Jan . . . don't bring any sharp objects with you. If you do, you won't be allowed in.'

'Sharp objects?'

'Any sharp objects made of metal . . . No knives.'

Jan arrived in Valla by train – without any sharp objects about his person – half an hour before his interview. He was keeping a close eye on the time, but still felt quite calm. He wasn't about to climb a mountain; it was just a meeting about a job.

It was a sunny Tuesday in mid September; the streets near the station were bright and dry, but there were very few people around. This was his first visit to Valla, and as he walked out into the square he realized that no one knew where he was. No one. The senior consultant at St Patricia's was expecting him, of course, but to Dr Högsmed he was just a name and a CV.

Was he ready? Absolutely. He tugged down the sleeves of his jacket and tidied his blond fringe before heading over to the taxi rank. There was just one cab waiting.

'Can you take me to St Patricia's Hospital?'

'No problem.'

The driver might have borne a certain resemblance to Father Christmas, but he didn't appear to share his jovial nature; he simply folded up his newspaper and started the engine. But as Jan settled down in the back seat their eyes met for a second in the rear-view mirror, as if Father Christmas just wanted to check that his passenger was sane.

Jan thought of asking whether the driver knew what kind of hospital St Patricia's was, but it was obvious that he did.

They drove out of the square and into the street running alongside the railway line, and eventually turned into a short tunnel leading under the tracks. On the other side was a collection of large brick buildings that looked like some kind of hospital, with façades of steel and glass. Jan could see two yellow ambulances parked in front of the main entrance.

'Is this St Patricia's?'

But Father Christmas shook his head. 'No, the people in here are sick in the body, not in the head. This is the local hospital.'

The sun was still shining; there wasn't a cloud in the sky. They turned off to the left once they got past the hospital, drove up a steep hill and came to the residential area where that sign warned drivers about children.

Caution! Children playing . . .

Jan thinks about all the children he has cared for over the years. None of them were his own; he was employed to look after them. But they grew to be his, in a way, and it was always difficult to say goodbye to them when the job came to an end. They often cried. Sometimes he cried too.

Suddenly he catches sight of some children: four boys aged

about twelve are playing hockey by one of the garages.

Or is a twelve-year-old actually a child? When do children stop being children?

Jan leans back in his seat and pushes aside such deep questions. He needs to concentrate on coming up with clear answers. Job interviews are hard work if you have something to hide – and who hasn't? We all have little secrets that we would prefer not to talk about. So has Jan. But today they absolutely must not come out.

Don't forget Högsmed is a psychiatrist.

The taxi leaves the upmarket residential area and drives past several blocks of low terraced houses. Then there are no more buildings, and the landscape opens out into an extensive grassy area. And beyond it Jan can see a huge concrete wall, at least five metres high and painted green. Thin strands of taut barbed wire run along the top. The only thing missing is a series of watchtowers with armed guards.

An immense grey building looms behind the wall, almost like a fortress. Jan can see only the uppermost section, with rows of narrow windows below a long tiled roof. Many of the windows are covered with bars.

That's where they are, behind those bars, he thinks – the most dangerous individuals. Those who cannot be permitted to walk the streets. *And that's where you're going.*

He feels his heart begin to pound as he thinks about Alice Rami, and the possibility that she might be sitting behind the bars at one of those windows, watching him at this very moment.

Calm, keep calm.

Jan is a confident person, cheerful and pleasant, and he really *loves* children. Dr Högsmed is bound to understand this.

There is a wide steel gate set in the wall, but there is a no-waiting zone directly in front of it, so the taxi stops in the turning area. Jan has arrived. The meter is showing ninety-six kronor. Jan hands over a hundred-kronor note. 'Keep the change.'

'Thanks.' Father Christmas seems disappointed by his tip; four kronor won't buy any presents for the children. He doesn't get out of the car to open the passenger door.

Jan can fend for himself.

'Good luck with the job,' the driver says as he passes Jan a receipt through the half-open window.

Jan nods and straightens his jacket. 'Do you know anyone who works here?'

'I don't think so,' says Father Christmas. 'But most people keep quiet about the fact that they work up here . . . it means they don't have to deal with a load of questions about the inmates.'

Jan notices that a smaller door next to the wide gate has opened. Someone is now standing there waiting for him: a man in his forties with thick brown hair and round, gold-framed glasses. From a distance he looks a little bit like John Lennon.

Lennon was shot by Mark Chapman, Jan thinks. Why does he remember that? Because the murder brought Chapman worldwide notoriety overnight.

If Alice Rami is in St Patricia's, what other celebrities might be locked up in there?

Forget about it, says a voice inside his head. *And forget about Lynx too. Concentrate on the interview.*

The man waiting in the doorway is not wearing a white coat, just black trousers and a brown jacket, but it is perfectly obvious who he is. Dr Högsmed adjusts his glasses and gazes over at Jan. The assessment has already begun.

Jan looks at the taxi driver one last time. 'Will you tell me the name now?'

'What name?'

Jan nods in the direction of the concrete wall. 'The name of the hospital . . . What do people call it?'

Father Christmas doesn't answer immediately; he merely smiles with satisfaction at Jan's curiosity. 'St Psycho's,' he says eventually.

'What?'

The driver gestures towards the wall. 'Say hello to Ivan Rössel for me . . . He's supposed to be in there.'

The window is wound up and the taxi pulls away.

2

As he walks over to Dr Högsmed and shakes his hand, Jan works out that it is no ordinary barbed wire that surrounds St Patricia's psychiatric hospital – it is electrified. The strands of wire form an electric fence a metre high right on top of the wall, with glowing red diodes flashing on each post.

'Welcome.' Högsmed looks at him through his spectacles, without a trace of a smile. 'Did you have any trouble finding your way here?'

'No, not at all.'

The concrete wall and the electric fence remind Jan of some kind of old-fashioned zoo, a tiger enclosure perhaps, but on the gravel to the right of the gate he spots a little bit of everyday life: a bicycle rack, with ladies' and men's bicycles in a row, kitted out with baskets and reflectors. One of them even has a plastic child seat on the back.

The steel door clicks and is slid to one side by invisible hands.

'After you, Jan.'

'Thank you.'

Walking in through a prison gate is like taking the first steps into the mouth of a pitch-black cave. An alien, isolated world.

The door slides shut behind them. The first thing Jan sees is a long, white surveillance camera, with the lens pointing straight at him. The camera is fixed to a post next to the door, silent and motionless.

Then he sees another camera on another post closer to the hospital, and yet more attached to the building itself. A yellow sign by the road carries the warning CCTV CAMERAS IN OPERATION 24 HOURS.

They walk past a car park festooned with several more signs: one of them says AMBULANCES ONLY, another POLICE VEHICLES ONLY.

Now he is inside the wall, Jan can see the hospital's entire pale-grey façade. It is five storeys high, with long rows of narrow windows. Strands of some kind of ivy are creeping around the windows on the ground floor, like big hairy worms.

Jan feels slightly claustrophobic out here, trapped between the wall and the hospital. He hesitates, but the doctor leads the way, walking purposefully.

The path ends at a second steel door. It is closed, but the consultant swipes his magnetic card and waves to the nearest camera; after approximately thirty seconds, the lock clicks open.

They enter a smallish room with a glassed-in reception area, and yet another camera. The place smells of cleaning fluid and wet concrete – the floor has just been mopped. A broad-shouldered shadow is sitting behind the dark glass.

A security guard. Jan wonders if he is armed.

The thought of violence and guns makes him listen out for any noise from the patients, but they are probably too far away. Locked up behind steel doors and thick walls. And why should he be able to *hear* them? They're hardly likely to be bellowing or laughing or hammering on the bars with metal mugs. Are they? Their world is more likely to consist of silent rooms, empty corridors.

The doctor has asked a question.

Jan turns his head. 'Sorry?'

'Your ID,' Högsmed repeats. 'Did you remember to bring it with you?'

'Of course . . .' Jan rummages in his jacket pocket and holds out his passport. 'There you go.'

'You hang on to it,' says Högsmed. 'Just open it at the page with your personal details and hold it up in front of this camera.'

21

Jan holds up his passport. The camera clicks and he is registered.

'Good. We just need to take a quick look inside your bag as well.'

Jan has to unzip his bag and take out the contents in front of Dr Högsmed and the guard: a packet of tissues, a waterproof jacket, a folded newspaper . . .

'All done.'

The doctor waves to the guard behind the glass, then leads Jan through a big steel archway – it looks like a metal detector – and on to another door, which he unlocks.

It seems to Jan that the air grows colder and colder as they make their way further into the hospital. After three more steel doors they are in a corridor which ends in a plain wooden door. Högsmed opens it. 'So, this is where I hang out.'

It's just an ordinary office. Most of the items in the doctor's room are white, from the walls to the framed diplomas hanging next to the bookshelves. The shelves are also white, just like the piles of paper on the desk. There is only one personal possession on display: a photograph on the desk shows a young woman who looks tired but happy, holding a newborn baby in her arms.

But on the right-hand side of the desk Jan notices something else: a pile of assorted headgear. Five items, all well worn. A blue security guard's hat, a white nurse's cap, a headteacher's black mortar board, a green hunting cap and a red clown's wig.

Högsmed indicates the pile. 'Choose one if you like.'

'Sorry?'

'I usually let my new patients choose one of the hats and put it on. Then we talk about why he or she chose that particular hat, and what it might mean . . . You're welcome to do the same, Jan.'

Jan reaches out his hand. He wants to choose the clown's wig, but what does that symbolize? Wouldn't it be better to be a helpful nurse? A good person. Or a headteacher, who represents knowledge and wisdom?

His hand begins to tremble slightly. In the end he lowers it. 'I think I'll pass.'

'Oh?'

'Well . . . I'm not a patient, after all.'

Högsmed gives a brief nod. 'But I could see you were thinking of choosing the clown, Jan. And that's interesting, because clowns often have secrets. They hide things behind a painted smile.'

'Oh?'

Högsmed nods again. 'John Wayne Gacy, the serial killer, used to do voluntary work as a clown in Chicago before he was arrested; he liked performing in front of children. And of course serial killers and sex offenders are children in a way; they see themselves as the centre of the world, and have never grown up.'

Jan doesn't say any more, he just tries to smile.

Högsmed stares at him for a few seconds, then he turns and points to a pine chair in front of the desk. 'Take a seat, Jan.'

'Thank you, Doctor.'

'I know I'm a doctor, but please feel free to call me Patrik.'

'OK . . . Patrik.'

Jan thinks this sounds wrong. He doesn't want to be on first-name terms with the doctor. He sits down, lets his shoulders drop and tries to relax, glancing quickly at the senior consultant.

Dr Högsmed seems young to be in charge of an entire hospital, but he doesn't look too good. His eyes are bloodshot. Once he is seated behind his desk, he quickly leans back in the ergonomic office chair, takes off his glasses and opens his eyes wide, staring up at the ceiling.

Jan wonders what on earth Högsmed is up to, then he sees that the doctor has taken out a little bottle of eye drops. He squeezes three drops into each eye, then shuts them tight for a moment.

'Keratitis,' he explains. 'Doctors can be ill too; people sometimes forget that.'

Jan nods. 'Is it serious?'

'Not particularly, but my eyeballs have felt like sandpaper for the last week.' He leans forward, trying to blink away thin tears, before putting his glasses back on. 'As I said before, welcome to St Patricia's, Jan. I assume you know what the locals call this place?'

'I don't think I . . .'

The consultant rubs his right eye. 'Down in the town . . . the nickname people have come up with for St Patricia's?'

Of course Jan found out the name only a few minutes ago; it was going round and round in his head when he walked in, along with the name of the murderer Ivan Rössel, but still he looks around as if the answer might be written on the walls. 'No,' he lies. 'What do they call it?'

Högsmed looks slightly strained. 'I'm sure you already know.'

'Maybe . . . The taxi driver mentioned something on the way here.'

'Did he indeed?'

'Is it . . . is it St Psycho's?'

The doctor gives a quick nod, but still seems disappointed with the answer. 'Yes, that's what some outsiders call it. *St Psycho's*. Even I have heard the name a couple of times, and I don't always . . .' Högsmed breaks off and leans forward slightly. 'But those of us who work here *never* use that term. We use the correct name: St Patricia's Regional Psychiatric Hospital – or just "the hospital" if we're short of time. And if you are employed here, I would insist that you use one of those terms.'

'Of course,' says Jan, meeting Högsmed's gaze. 'I'm not keen on nicknames either.'

'Good.' The doctor leans back in his chair. 'And you wouldn't be working inside the hospital anyway, if you get the job. The pre-school is separate from the hospital.'

'Oh?' This is news to Jan. 'So it's not in this building?'

'No. The Dell is a completely separate building.'

'But what do you do with . . . with the children?'

'What do we *do* with them?'

'When they come here, I mean. How do they get to spend time with . . . with their mother or father?'

'We have a visitors' room. The children come in through a sally port.'

'A sally port?'

'There's an underground corridor,' says Högsmed. 'And a lift.'

He picks up several sheets of paper from the desk. Jan recognizes them: his application form. Attached is a printout from the criminal records bureau, showing that Jan Hauger has never been convicted of any kind of sexual offence. Jan is used to requesting this proof from the police; it is always required when someone applies to work with children.

'Now let's see . . .' Högsmed screws up his red eyes and slowly begins to leaf through the form. 'Your CV looks excellent. You worked as a classroom assistant in Nordbro two years after you left grammar school, then you qualified as a pre-school teacher in Uppsala, and you've had several temporary posts at various nurseries and pre-schools in Gothenburg. You're currently unemployed, it seems, and still living there.'

'I've only been out of work for a couple of months,' Jan says quickly.

'But you've had *nine* temporary posts in six years. Is that correct?'

Jan nods without speaking.

'And nothing permanent so far?'

'No,' says Jan, pausing for a moment. 'For various reasons . . . I've usually been covering for someone on maternity or paternity leave, and naturally they've always come back to work.'

'I understand. And this is also a temporary appointment, of course,' the doctor says. 'Until the end of the year, in the first instance.'

Jan can't ignore the faint implication that he is a restless person. He gestures in the direction of his CV. 'The children and the parents always liked me . . . And I've always had good references.'

The doctor carries on reading, and nods. 'So I see, they're excellent . . . from your last three employers. They all recommend you without hesitation.' He lowers the papers and looks at Jan. 'And what about the others?'

'The others?'

'What did the rest of your employers think? Were they unhappy with you?'

'No. No, they most certainly were not, but I didn't want to include every single positive—'

'I understand,' the doctor interrupts. 'Too much praise starts to look suspicious. But is it OK if I give them a call? One of the nurseries you worked at in the early days?'

The doctor suddenly seems alert and curious; his hand is already resting on the telephone.

Jan sits there in silence, his mouth half-open. It's all down to the hats, he suspects – he refused Högsmed's psychological test. He wants to shake his head, but his neck won't move.

Not Lynx, he thinks. *You're welcome to call the others, but not Lynx.*

He finally manages to move his head to indicate his assent. 'That's fine,' he says, 'but unfortunately I don't have the numbers.'

'No problem – they'll be on the internet.' Högsmed casts a final glance at the list of Jan's former employers, then keys in a series of letters on the computer.

The name of one of the nurseries from the early days. But which one? *Which one?* Jan can't see, and he doesn't want to lean across the desk to find out if it's Lynx.

Why did he include it in his CV?

Nine years ago! Just one mistake with one child, nine years ago . . . Is all that business going to be dragged up again?

He breathes calmly, his fingertips resting gently on his thighs. It's only lunatics who start waving their arms around when they're under pressure.

'Excellent, there's the number,' Högsmed murmurs, blinking at the screen. 'I'll just give them a call . . .'

He lifts the receiver, keys in half a dozen numbers and glances over at Jan.

Jan tries to smile, but he is holding his breath. Who is the doctor calling?

Is there anyone left from his time at Lynx – anyone who still remembers him? Anyone who remembers what happened in the forest?

3

'Hello?'

Someone has answered the phone; the doctor leans forward across the desk. 'Patrik Högsmed, senior consultant at St Patricia's Hospital . . . I'm looking for someone who used to work with Jan Hauger. That's right, H-A-U-G-E-R. He was with you on a temporary basis eight or nine years ago.'

Eight or nine years ago. Jan lowers his head when he hears those words. In that case it has to be one of the nurseries in Nordbro. Either Little Sunflowers or Lynx. Jan left the town where he grew up after that.

'So that was before your time, Julia? OK, but is there anyone who was there when . . . Excellent, if you could put me through to the person who was in charge back then . . . yes, I'll hold.'

The room falls silent again, so silent that Jan can hear a door closing somewhere down the corridor.

Nina. Jan suddenly remembers that the person in charge at Lynx was called Nina Gundotter. Strange name. He hasn't thought about Nina for many years – he has pushed all his memories from Lynx into a bottle and buried it.

The white clock is ticking away on the wall; it is quarter past two now.

'Hello?'

Someone is speaking to the doctor, and Jan digs his fingers into his thighs. He holds his breath as he listens to Högsmed once more introducing himself and explaining his reasons for ringing.

'So you do remember Jan Hauger? Excellent. What can you tell me about him?'

Silence. The doctor glances briefly at Jan, and carries on listening.

'Thank you,' he says after thirty seconds. 'That's very helpful. Yes, of course I'll pass on your regards. Thank you very much indeed.'

He replaces the receiver and leans back. 'More positive comments.' He looks encouragingly at Jan. 'That was Lena Zetterberg at the Little Sunflowers nursery in Nordbro, and she had nothing but good things to say about you. Jan Hauger was enthusiastic, responsible, popular with both parents and children . . . Top marks.'

Jan begins to smile again. 'I remember Lena. We got on very well.'

'Good.' The doctor gets to his feet and picks up a plastic folder from the desk. 'Let's head over to our own excellent pre-school . . . You do know that we use the term *pre-school* these days, Jan?'

'Of course.'

Högsmed holds the door open for Jan.

'The term *nursery* has become just as outmoded as *playschool*,' he says, before adding, 'And it's the same with psychiatric terms; they lose their acceptability over the years. Words such as *hysteric*, *lunatic* and *psychopath* . . . They are no longer used. We don't even talk about *sick* or *healthy* people at St Patricia's, we simply refer to *functioning* or *non-functioning* individuals.' He turns to Jan. 'Because who amongst us can say that we are always healthy?'

A difficult question, and one to which Jan does not reply.

'And what can we really know about one another?' the doctor goes on. 'If you were to meet a man walking along this corridor, Jan, could you tell if he was good or evil?'

'No . . . but I suppose I would assume that he wished me well.'

'Good,' says Högsmed. 'Trusting others is mostly a matter of how secure we are in ourselves.'

Jan nods and follows him through the hospital.

Högsmed is ready with his magnetic card once more. 'This is actually the quickest way to the pre-school,' he explains as he unlocks the door. 'You can go through the hospital basement, but it's a tortuous and not very pleasant route, so we'll go back out through the gate.'

They leave the hospital the same way they came in. As they pass the security guard's office Jan glances at the thick safety glass and asks quietly, 'But some of the patients here must be dangerous, surely?'

'Dangerous?'

'Yes – violent?'

Högsmed sighs, as if he is thinking of something tedious. 'Well, yes, but they're mostly a danger to themselves. Occasionally they might be violent towards others,' he says. 'There are of course certain patients who have destructive impulses, antisocial men and women who have done what you might call *bad* things . . .'

'And can you cure them?' Jan asks.

'*Cure* is a big word,' says Högsmed, looking at the steel door in front of him. 'Those of us who are therapists do not attempt to enter the same dark forest in which the patients have lost their way; we stay out in the light and try to entice the patients to come to us . . .' He falls silent, then continues: 'We can see patterns in the behaviour of those who have committed violent crimes, and one common denominator is childhood trauma of various kinds. They have often had a very poor relationship with their parents, with frequent instances of abuse and lack of contact.' He opens the outer door and looks at Jan. 'And that is why we run this particular project, the Dell. The aim of our little pre-school is to maintain the emotional bonds between the child and the parent who is a patient here.'

'And the other parent agrees to these visits?'

'If they themselves are well. And still alive,' Högsmed says quietly, rubbing his eyes. 'Which isn't always the case. We are not usually dealing with socially stable families.'

Jan refrains from asking any more questions.

Eventually they are back outside in the sunshine again. The doctor blinks in pain at the bright daylight.

They walk towards the high wall. It hadn't occurred to Jan before, but the air seems so pure on this autumn day. Dry and fresh.

'After you, Jan.'

The gate in the wall slides open and Jan steps out. *Out into freedom.* That's actually the way it feels as he stands there in the street, even though he could have left the hospital whenever he wanted to, of course. No guards would have tried to keep him there.

The steel gate closes behind them.

'This way,' says Högsmed.

Jan follows him, gazing across towards the outskirts of the town to the south. Beyond a wide, freshly ploughed field he can see several blocks of small terraced houses. He wonders what the owners of those houses think about the hospital.

Högsmed also glances across at the houses, as if he can hear what Jan is thinking. 'Our neighbours,' he says. 'In the past the town wasn't quite so extensive, of course, so the hospital was more isolated out here. But we have never had any problems with protests or petitions, unlike some other psychiatric units. I think the families over there know that our operation is secure . . . that the safety of all concerned is our number-one priority.'

'Has anyone ever escaped?'

Jan realizes this is a provocative question.

But Högsmed raises his forefinger to indicate the number one. 'Just one patient during my time here. It was a young man, a sex offender, who had managed to build a rickety structure out of fallen branches in one corner of the grounds. He simply climbed over the fence and disappeared.' Högsmed looks over towards the houses again and goes on: 'The police picked him up in the park that same evening, but by then he'd already made contact with a little girl. Apparently they were sitting on a park bench eating ice cream.' The doctor looks up at the electric fence on top of the wall. 'Security was tightened up after that, but I'm not convinced that anything nasty would have happened. Sometimes those who run away seek out children simply because they are looking for security. They are small and frightened inside.'

Jan says nothing, he simply keeps on walking along the track in front of the wall. He has guessed correctly; they are heading towards a wooden building north of the hospital. The Dell.

The wall curves away before they reach the Dell, crossing a grassy area before it disappears behind the hospital. There is only a low fence around the pre-school. Jan can see several swings, a red play-house and a sandpit, but no children. Presumably they're indoors.

'How many children do you have here?' he asks.

'About a dozen,' says Högsmed. 'Three of them are staying here on a permanent basis at the moment, for various reasons. Six or seven come during the day. Then there are a few more whose attendance is more sporadic.' He opens his folder and takes out a sheet of paper. 'We do have a small number of rules when it comes to dealing with the children. Perhaps you could read through them now.'

Jan takes the sheet of paper; he stops by the gate leading to the pre-school, and begins to read:

STAFF RULES

1) The children at the Dell and the patients at St Patricia's Regional Psychiatric Hospital are to be kept apart. This applies AT ALL TIMES OF THE DAY AND NIGHT, except for pre-arranged visits to the parent of a child.

2) Pre-school staff do NOT have access to any of the wards inside the hospital. Only the administrative departments of the hospital are to be visited by pre-school staff.

3) Pre-school staff are responsible for escorting the children through the sally port between the Dell and the visitors' facility within the hospital. The children are NOT allowed to go alone.

4) Under NO circumstances are staff to discuss hospital visits with the child, or ask questions about the child's parents. Such conversations are to be conducted only by doctors and child psychologists.

5) In common with hospital employees, pre-school staff are obliged to maintain TOTAL CONFIDENTIALITY with regard to all aspects of St Patricia's Regional Psychiatric Hospital.

There is a dotted line at the bottom of the page, and when Jan looks up he sees that Högsmed is holding out a pen.

He takes it and signs his name.

'Good,' says Högsmed. 'As I said, I thought it was best if you had a look at it before we go in. All pre-schools have their own rules and regulations, after all. You're used to that, no doubt?'

'Absolutely.'

But Jan has never come across any of these rules before. And the order from those in charge at the hospital is crystal clear:

Keep quiet about St Psycho's.

No problem. Jan has always been good at keeping secrets.

Lynx

Jan had started work at the Lynx nursery when he was twenty years old, the same hot summer when Alice Rami's debut album came out – the two events were linked in his mind. He had bought her record when he spotted it in a shop window; he took it home and played it over and over again. *Rami and August* was the title of the album, but August wasn't a person's name; it was her band, which consisted of two guys playing drums and bass guitar. There was a picture of them with Rami, two guys with black spiky hair on either side of her angel-white head. Jan looked at the picture and wondered if either of them was her boyfriend.

The following day he bought a cheap portable CD-player so that he could listen to Rami on his way to work at the nursery. The shortest route was through a dense coniferous forest; he ambled along the paths listening to her whispering voice:

> *Murder is always suicide;*
> *I kill you, I kill me*
> *Hatred can be called love*
> *then I know where I am with you.*
>
> *Life can be death*
> *and strength can be weakness,*
> *when lambs fill the trains every day*

Other texts were about power, darkness, drugs and moon shadows. Jan listened and listened all summer until he knew the words by heart; he felt as if Rami was singing to him. Why not? She even had a song on the album with the name 'Jan' in it.

In the middle of August a number of new children started at the nursery. One of them was special. A little boy with blond, curly hair.

Jan was standing by the entrance to Lynx when the boy appeared. He actually saw the boy's mother first; Jan thought he recognized her. A celebrity or an old acquaintance? Perhaps it was just that the mother looked older – between thirty-five and forty, quite old to have a child at nursery.

Then Jan caught sight of the boy – small and as thin as a rake, but with big blue eyes. Five or six years old. He had golden-blond hair, just like Jan had had at his age, and he was wearing a tight red jacket. He walked towards the nursery holding his mother's hand, but they went past Lynx and headed for the door leading to Brown Bear.

He thought they were an ill-matched pair: the mother was tall and slim, dressed in a light brown leather jacket with a fur collar, while her son was so small he barely came up to her knees. He was having to trot along with short, scampering steps just to keep up with his mother's strides.

The boy's outdoor clothes looked inadequate in the autumn chill. He could do with new ones.

Jan had opened the door of Lynx, on his way into the warmth with half a dozen children in front of him, but he stopped and watched when he saw the mother and child. The boy kept his eyes fixed on the ground, but the mother gave Jan a passing glance and an impersonal nod. He was a stranger to her, an anonymous classroom assistant. Jan nodded back and remained in the doorway long enough to see them walk up the slope and open the door to Brown Bear.

On the outside of the door was a dark-brown bear cut out of chipboard, and on the door Jan had just opened was a yellow lynx.

Two forest carnivores. Ever since he had started at the nursery the previous summer, Jan had thought the names sounded wrong; after all, bears and lynx were no ordinary animals. They were predators.

The boy and his mother had disappeared. Jan couldn't stand here in the doorway, he had work to do. He went to join his own group of children, but he couldn't forget the brief encounter.

The registers for all the nursery classes were held on the computer, and before Jan set off home accompanied by Rami's music, he sneaked into the office to find out what the new boy at Brown Bear was called.

He found the name straight away: William Halevi, son of Roland and Emma Halevi.

Jan stared at the three names for a long time. There was also a home address, but he didn't need to know that at the moment. It was enough to know that little William would be in the adjoining building all through the autumn, separated from him by only a short distance.

4

'Coffee, Jan?' asks Marie-Louise.

'Yes please.'

'A drop of milk?'

'No thanks.'

Marie-Louise is the supervisor at the Dell. She is between fifty and sixty years old, with light-grey curly hair and deep laughter lines around her eyes; she smiles a great deal and seems to want everyone around her to feel comfortable, whether they are big or small.

And Jan actually does feel comfortable. He doesn't know what he expected the pre-school to be like, but in here there is no hint of the high concrete wall just a few metres away.

After St Patricia's bare corridors and Högsmed's white office, Jan has entered a rainbow world where vibrant children's drawings cover the walls, where green and yellow wellingtons are lined up in the entrance hall, and where big boxes in the playroom overflow with cuddly toys and picture books. The air in here is slightly warm and heavy, just as it always is in a room where children have been playing.

Jan has been in many bright and clean pre-schools over the years, but the Dell made him feel calm as soon as he walked in. There is harmony in this little place – it feels *cosy*.

At the moment it is very quiet, because the children are having their nap in the snuggle room. This means that all the staff are free to meet.

There are three younger colleagues at the table with Marie-Louise. Two of them are women. Lilian, who has dark-red hair piled on top of her head, is about thirty-five. She has a sorrowful look in her eyes which she tries to hide; Lilian talks a great deal, moves nervously and laughs just a little too loudly. Hanna, who has straight blonde hair, is perhaps ten years younger; she is wearing a white blouse and pink jeans. Pretty blue eyes; she doesn't say much.

Lilian and Hanna are not alike, but they do have one interest in common. In the middle of their coffee break they go outside for a cigarette just on the other side of the fence surrounding the Dell; they seem to be very close. Lilian whispers something and Hanna nods.

As Marie-Louise looks out of the window at the two smokers, a small furrow appears between her eyebrows. Then they come back inside, and she is smiling again.

Marie-Louise smiles even more frequently at the fourth employee: Andreas. He doesn't smoke, he just takes snuff, and with his broad shoulders he looks more like a builder than a classroom assistant. There is something reassuring about Andreas; nothing seems to bother him.

Dr Högsmed is also sitting at the kitchen table. He began by introducing Jan, referring to him as 'the male candidate' – which gave away the fact that there was at least one other person under consideration for the post – but since then he has left the staff to do the talking.

But what can they talk about? Jan has just read the rules and regulations, and has no intention of breaking them, not today. So he can't ask any questions about the hospital, and he can't talk about the children. He searches for a topic of conversation. 'Who was St Patricia?' he asks eventually.

The doctor looks at him. 'A saint, of course.'

'But what did she do? Where did she live?'

The only response is silence and shaking heads.

'We don't have much to do with saints here,' says Högsmed with a grim smile.

The room falls silent again, so Jan asks Marie-Louise about working hours.

'The Dell is staffed around the clock at the moment,' she replies. 'We have three children who don't have placements in foster care for the time being, so they are staying here overnight.' She pauses. 'Would that be a problem for you, Jan, having sole responsibility for the children overnight?'

'Not at all.'

There is a tentative tapping on the kitchen window next to Jan, and when he turns his head he sees that it has begun to rain. Soon heavy drops are spattering against the glass. Beyond the curtain of rain he can just make out the wall and the hospital. He gazes out at the hospital until Lilian asks a question:

'Do you have any family, Jan?'

That's a new question. Is Lilian particularly interested in families? He gives her an involuntary smile. 'My younger brother is studying medicine in London, and my mother lives up in Nordbro. But I'm not married . . . and I don't have any children of my own.'

'What about a girlfriend?' Lilian says quickly.

Jan slowly opens his mouth, but Marie-Louise leans forward, her expression slightly troubled, and says quietly, 'That's personal, Lilian.'

Jan notices that neither Lilian nor Hanna is wearing a ring on her left hand. He shakes his head briefly. *No.* That could mean either that he's single, or that he doesn't want to answer.

'So what do you do in your spare time, Jan?' The question comes from Dr Högsmed this time.

'Oh, this and that,' he replies. 'I'm interested in music, I play the drums a bit . . . and I enjoy drawing.'

'And what kind of thing do you draw?'

Jan hesitates before replying – this is also beginning to feel rather personal. 'I'm working on a kind of comic strip . . . An old dream project.'

'I see . . . Is it for a magazine?'

'No. It isn't finished, far from it.'

'You'll have to show it to the children,' says Marie-Louise. 'We read to them a lot.'

Jan nods, but he doubts whether pre-school children will want to read his comic-strip story about the Secret Avenger. There is too much hatred in it.

Suddenly they hear a muted cry from the snuggle room. Marie-Louise stiffens, Andreas turns his head.

'That sounds like Matilda,' he says quietly.

'Yes,' Marie-Louise agrees. 'Matilda dreams a great deal.'

'She's got a vivid imagination,' Lilian says. 'She's always making up stories.'

That is all Jan hears them say about any of the children. They sit in silence around the table; it is as if they are waiting for more cries from the snuggle room, but nothing happens.

Högsmed rubs his eyes and looks at his watch. 'OK, Jan, perhaps you'd like to be heading home?'

'Yes . . . it's probably time.' He understands the hint – the doctor wants rid of him. He wants to hear what the staff think of the male candidate.

'I'll be in touch, Jan – I've got your phone number.'

Jan says his goodbyes, with a friendly smile and a firm hand-shake for everyone.

Outside the autumn rain has passed.

There is not a soul in sight by the wall as he walks out through the gate of the Dell. But St Patricia's itself looks almost alive; the rain has darkened the façade, and the hospital looks like a great stone colossus, looming over the pre-school.

Jan stops and gazes over at the hospital. At all those windows. He is expecting someone to show themselves – a head moving behind the bars, a hand placed against a pane of glass. But nothing happens, and eventually he begins to worry that one of the guards will spot him and think that a lunatic is standing there staring at the place. He sets off, with a final glance at the little pre-school.

St Patricia's enormous wall is eerily fascinating, but he must stop thinking about it. He must concentrate on the Dell, the little wooden building with its sleeping children.

Pre-schools are like oases of tranquillity and security.

He really wants the job, even though he is still feeling tense following Högsmed's scrutiny. *The hat test.* And even worse, the phone call to his former employer.

But what happened at Lynx is not going to happen at the Dell.

He had been young then, a twenty-year-old classroom assistant. And totally off balance.

5

After the heavy rain, the autumn air in Valla is cold and fresh. The town looks as if it is contained within some kind of cauldron; it lies below Jan as he walks back through the residential areas, across the railway and down into the centre where the streets are full of pensioners and teenagers. The young people are standing outside the shops, the elderly are sitting on benches. He sees dogs on leads and small groups of birds gathered around the rubbish bins, but very few children.

The next train to Gothenburg leaves in an hour, so Jan has plenty of time to stroll around. For the first time he wonders what it would be like to live in Valla. Today he is a visitor, but if he gets the job he will have to move here.

As he is walking down Storgatan his mobile suddenly rings. A chilly breeze is blowing up the street; he shelters by a wall and answers.

'Jan?' The voice is croaky and weak: his elderly mother. She goes on immediately: 'What are you doing? Are you in Gothenburg?'

'No, I've been . . . I've been for a job interview.'

He has always found it difficult to tell his mother what he is doing. It has always felt too personal.

'A job interview, that sounds good. Is it in town?'

'No, a little way out.'

'Well, I mustn't disturb you . . .'

'It's OK, Mum. It went well.'

'And how's Alice?'

'Fine . . . she's fine. Still working.'

'It would be lovely if you came up here some time. Both of you.'

Jan doesn't reply.

'A bit later in the autumn, perhaps?' his mother suggests.

There is no hint of criticism in her voice, as far as Jan can tell; just the quiet wistfulness of a lonely widow.

'I'll come up soon,' Jan promises, 'and I'll . . . I'll check with Alice.'

'Lovely. And good luck. Remember you have to be happy with your employer as well.'

Jan says a quick thank you and ends the call.

Alice. He happened to mention her name to his mother at some point, and slowly she has taken shape and become his girlfriend. There is no Alice in his life, of course, she was just a dream, but now his mother wants to meet her. Eventually he will have to tell her what the situation really is.

He carries on wandering around the centre of Valla and sees lots of imposing shop windows, but no church. And no churchyard either.

There is a very good local-history museum by the river, with a little café. Jan goes in and buys a sandwich. He sits down by the window and gazes out towards the bus station.

He doesn't know one single person in Valla – is that frightening or liberating? On the plus side, a stranger can start a completely new life, and choose which details to share if someone should ask where he comes from. The fewer answers the better. He doesn't need to say a word about his former life. Not a word about Alice Rami.

But it is thanks to his adoration of her that Jan is sitting here.

He first heard about St Patricia's Hospital at the beginning of June, when his last temporary post at a pre-school in Gothenburg was just coming to an end. It was quite an enjoyable evening; he was almost feeling happy.

He was the only man in a group of women, as usual. His

colleagues invited him out for a meal to thank him for his work, and he accepted. Afterwards he did something he had never done before – he asked them back to his small apartment in Johanneberg, a cramped one-room flat which he had taken on as a sublet.

What could he offer them? He rarely drank alcohol; he couldn't really cope with the taste.

'I think I might have some crisps at home if you'd like to come back with me.'

His five colleagues were delighted, but Jan had already begun to regret the invitation as he led them up the stairs and unlocked the door.

'I'm afraid it's not very tidy . . .'

'That doesn't matter!' they shouted, giggling and tipsy.

Jan let them in.

His diary was hidden in a desk drawer, along with his drawings of *The Secret Avenger*. So he had nothing else to hide, apart from the pictures of Alice Rami. If he had known about this visit he would probably have hidden those too, but as his colleagues walked in they saw the framed record sleeve in the hallway, of course, plus a concert poster in the kitchen, and the big poster that had been given away with a music magazine ten years ago, pinned up next to the bookcase.

It was a black and white picture of Rami, standing on a little stage with her electric guitar, legs apart, her spiky hair illuminated by the spotlights, the rest of the band like blurred ghosts behind her. Her eyes were closed, she was twenty years old, and she looked as if she was growling into the microphone. It was the only pin-up of her he had ever found, which was why he had kept it all these years.

One of his colleagues, a few years older than Jan, stopped to look at it. 'Rami?' she said. 'Do you like her?'

'Sure,' said Jan. 'Her music, I mean . . . Have you heard her sing?'

His colleague answered, her eyes fixed on Rami, 'I used to listen to her when the first album came out, but that was a long time ago. She never released a follow-up, did she?'

'No,' Jan said quietly.

'And now they've put her away.'

Jan looked at her. This was news to him. 'Put her away? What do you mean?'

'She's in some kind of mental hospital. St Patrick's, on the west coast.'

Jan held his breath. Alice Rami in a mental hospital? He tried to picture it.

Yes, he could see it. 'How do you know?' he asked.

His colleague shrugged her shoulders. 'I heard it somewhere a few years ago, I don't really remember . . . it was just gossip.'

'Do you know why . . . Why she ended up in there?'

'No idea,' she said. 'But I assume she must have done something stupid.'

Jan nodded without speaking.

St Patrick's Hospital. He wanted to ask more questions, but didn't want to appear obsessed with Rami. From time to time over the years he had joined various forums on the internet to search for news of Rami, but had never found anything. This was the best lead so far.

Then nothing happened; the summer drifted by and Jan drifted along with it, out of work. For several weeks he'd been scanning the local ads for jobs in pre-schools in *Göteborgs-Posten* and had found quite a few to apply for.

Then at the beginning of July the ad from the Dell had appeared. It was very similar to all the rest, but it was the address of the contact person that made Jan cut it out: Dr Patrik Högsmed, Admin Department, St Patricia's Regional Psychiatric Hospital in the town of Valla, just an hour by train from Gothenburg.

Jan read the advert over and over again.

A pre-school at a psychiatric hospital?

Why?

Then he remembered the rumour: Alice Rami was supposed to be locked up in 'St Patrick's Hospital, on the west coast'. St Patrick could be a distortion of St Patricia.

That was when he sat down and picked up the phone to call Dr Högsmed.

Jan had already applied for a dozen jobs at pre-schools in and around Gothenburg, without success. He might as well apply for one more.

6

Jan's telephone rings at quarter past eight on the following Thursday morning, while he is lying in bed. He crawls out and answers; there is a male voice on the other end.

'Good morning, Jan! Patrik Högsmed at St Patricia's here. Did I wake you?' The doctor's voice is full of energy.

'No . . . it's fine.'

His own voice is hoarse and slow; he slept heavily, with weird dreams. Was Alice Rami in them? There was definitely a woman, wearing a dark fur coat and standing on a stage, she had climbed into a big box . . .

The doctor brings him back to the present. 'I just wanted to let you know that we had a little chat after you left the day before yesterday, the staff at the Dell and I. It was a very productive discussion. Then I went back to the office and gave the matter some thought, and had a word with the hospital management. And now we've made our decision.'

'Oh yes?'

'So I was wondering if we could go over the terms of your contract now? With a view to you starting work here next Monday?'

Life can change so quickly. A day later Jan is back in Valla, his new home town. But he has no home here yet, so this afternoon he is gazing into a narrow hallway full of furniture and cardboard boxes. He is looking at a flat in a big apartment block, north of the town centre and to the west of St Patricia's.

A silver-haired old lady in a grey cardigan picks her way through the piled-up boxes; she is so small that they seem to be looming over her.

'Most of the people who live here are getting on a bit,' she says. 'Hardly any families with children, so there's no noise.'

'Good,' says Jan, making his way into the apartment.

'The rent as a sublet is four thousand one hundred,' the old lady says, looking sideways at Jan with a slightly embarrassed expression. 'I've hardly added anything to the original rent, so there's no point in haggling . . . but it is fully furnished.'

'OK.'

Fully furnished? Jan has never seen so much furniture in one flat. Chairs, cupboards and chests of drawers are piled up along the walls. It looks more like a storage facility than a home, and in a way that's exactly what it is. The furniture and the boxes belong to the woman's son, who is living in Sundsvall at the moment.

Jan opens a kitchen cupboard and sees rows and rows of bottles on the shelves – rum, vodka, brandy and various liqueurs. All empty.

'Those aren't mine,' the old lady says quickly. 'The last tenant left them behind.'

Jan closes the door.

'Is there a loft?'

'The grandchildren's bikes are up there. So, are you interested?'

'Yes. Maybe.'

He has already checked with the housing department in Valla; there are no empty apartments this month, and the waiting time for a rental contract that isn't a sublet would be at least six months. Under TO RENT in the local paper there was nothing but this furnished three-room flat.

'I'll take it,' he says.

After a late lunch that same day he catches the train back to Gothenburg, picks up his old Volvo from the garage and buys a few cardboard packing cases. Over the weekend he loads his own furniture on to a trailer and drives it to the local tip. Jan is almost thirty, but he owns very little, and feels an attachment to even less. There is a kind of freedom in not having too many possessions.

He moves into the three-room apartment and stows away as many of the old lady's boxes as possible; he tries to hide all the rubbish in the wardrobes and behind the sofa. Now he has a home of sorts.

He has brought with him his drawing board and the comic strip he calls *The Secret Avenger*, which is almost two hundred pages long. He has been working on it for fifteen years, but promises himself that he will finish it here in Valla. The finale will of course be a major apocalyptic battle between the Secret Avenger and his enemies, the Gang of Four.

Monday 19 September is a beautiful autumn day; the sun is shining on the trees and streets, and on the big concrete wall surrounding St Patricia's. At quarter past eight Jan passes through the gate for the second time and meets Dr Högsmed by the security guard's office in reception.

They shake hands. The doctor's eyes are clear now. Sharp. 'Congratulations, Jan.'

'Thank you, doct— Patrik. Thank you for having confidence in me.'

'It's not a question of confidence. You were the best candidate.'

They walk through all the locked doors, meet the head of human resources, and Jan signs his name on various documents. He is a part of the hospital now.

'Right, that's it,' says Högsmed. 'Shall we head over to your new place of work, then?'

'Excellent.'

They make their way out of the gate and into the road, but Jan can't help looking sideways at St Patricia's.

Högsmed gives him a short lecture: 'The institution was built at the end of the nineteenth century. Initially it was meant for those who were retarded, to use the terminology of the day, and later

48

it became a mental hospital where compulsory sterilization and lobotomies were carried out on a regular basis . . . but of course it's been refurbished since then. Modernized.'

Jan nods, but as they move away from the wall he can see the barred windows again. He thinks about Rami, then about the name the taxi driver mentioned: Ivan Rössel, the serial killer.

'Are all the patients on the upper floors?' he asks. 'Or are they in different parts of the hospital?'

Högsmed raises his hand to stop Jan. 'We never discuss the patients.'

'I understand that,' Jan says quickly. 'I don't want to know anything about a particular individual; I was just wondering how many patients there are?'

'About a hundred.' The doctor walks on in silence for a few seconds, before continuing in a slightly gentler tone of voice: 'I know you're curious about what goes on inside St Patricia's – it's only human. Not many people have been anywhere near a psychiatric hospital.'

Jan remains silent.

'There's only one thing I can say about what we do,' the doctor goes on. 'It's nowhere near as dramatic as people think. It's business as usual almost all the time. Most of the patients have suffered serious mental disturbances, with various kinds of trauma and obsessive-compulsive disorders. That's why they're here. *But*' – Högsmed holds up a finger – 'that doesn't mean that the hospital is full of bellowing lunatics. The patients are often calm and completely capable of interaction. They *know* why they're here, and they're . . . well, almost grateful. They have no desire to escape.' He falls silent, then adds, 'Not all of them, but the majority.'

He opens the little gate leading to the pre-school.

'I can tell you one final thing about the patients: a number of them have been involved in various kinds of substance abuse, and for that reason there is a strict ban on drugs on the wards.'

'Does that include medication?'

'Medication is another matter; that's all controlled by the doctors. But people can't be allowed to start self-medicating. And

49

we also have restrictions when it comes to using the telephone and watching TV.'

'So all entertainment is banned?'

'Absolutely not,' says the doctor as they approach the nursery door. 'There's plenty of paper, pens and pencils for those who want to write or draw, there are radios and lots of books . . . and we have a great deal of music.'

Jan immediately thinks of Rami with her guitar.

Högsmed goes on: 'And, of course, if the patient is a parent, we encourage regular contact with the child. Both the patients and their children need security and routine. This is often something they have lacked earlier in life.'

The doctor opens the door and holds up his index finger one last time. 'Fixed routines are critical in life. So you are doing a very important job here.'

Jan nods. *An important job with fixed routines.*

He can hear the sound of cheerful shouts and laughter through the open door, and he strides purposefully into the classroom.

He is feeling good now; he is calm. Jan always feels good when he is about to meet children.

Lynx

Jan used to have an apartment a few kilometres from the Lynx nursery, west of Nordbro town centre. There was an extensive park between the area where he lived and the nursery itself – several kilometres of coniferous forest, with rocks and low hills around a big lake with plenty of birds, all of which created the illusion of wild, remote countryside. He usually cycled to work, but whenever he had time he would walk through the forest, and sometimes he went for walks there when he wasn't working. He got to know the paths and tracks, and sometimes he turned off to climb on to an area of flat rock, gazing out at the lake and the birds.

One autumn morning as he was strolling to work he discovered the old bunker.

It had been cut into a hillside, with a view across the water. No paths or tracks ran past it, and at this time of year it was very difficult to spot; it resembled nothing more than a large heap of earth, hidden by branches and needles and sycamore leaves. But the rusty metal door stood invitingly ajar as Jan walked by, and it made him stop and scramble up the bank to take a closer look.

He leaned forward; it was pitch dark inside. The walls seemed to be a good twenty centimetres thick. The cement floor looked dry, so he got down on all fours like a potholer and crawled inside. The internal space was bigger than the concrete shell, as it had been dug out of the hillside.

Someone had been enjoying themselves in there, but not recently.

Yellowed newspapers and empty beer cans lay tossed in one corner, but apart from that the place was completely empty. There were actually a couple of windows, Jan noticed, but they were no more than long, narrow gaps just below the ceiling, almost completely blocked by earth and leaves. He guessed that the bunker had been used by the army as some kind of observation post – a relic of the Cold War.

He crawled back outside and stood on the slope. He listened. The wind was soughing gently in the trees. There was no sign of anyone at all.

Down below the bunker there was a flat, level expanse of gravel, partly covered by grass and undergrowth. There were no metal tracks, but it could have been the remains of an old railway line that had run along here decades earlier. Perhaps it had been used while the bunker was being built.

Jan clambered down and headed south. The gravelled track led to a narrow gap between two huge rocks. At the end of this gap there was a rusty gate; it was closed, but Jan managed to get it open. He walked up a gentle slope and found himself overlooking the lake about half a kilometre away, and suddenly he knew where he was. The children from Lynx had come up here on a little excursion last summer, just after he started work. No doubt they would be coming here again.

He stopped and thought.

The forest was dense here, but Jan found a path and walked a few hundred metres until he saw the nursery and the green fence surrounding the playground. The early birds from Lynx and Brown Bear were already there, playing outside. He saw little William Halevi sitting at the top of the climbing frame, raising his arms to show everyone that he was brave enough to let go.

William was a courageous boy; Jan had noticed this when the two groups were playing together. In spite of the fact that he was small and skinny, he would always climb the highest and run the fastest.

Jan looked at William, and thought about the bunker in the forest.

And that was how it began; not as a fully fledged plan to lure away a child in the forest, but mostly as a mind game. A pastime which Jan kept to himself.

7

'This is the timetable, Jan,' says Marie-Louise, pointing to the fridge door. 'We have to stick to these times every day. Sometimes we deliver a child to the hospital when we go to collect one of the others.'

He looks at the piece of paper. It shows a series of names, dates and times relating to handovers in the coming week.

At the top it says *Leo: Monday 11–12*. Then *Matilda: Monday 2–3*, and *Mira and Tobias: 3–4*.

It's only quarter to nine at the moment.

'We go with them,' says Marie-Louise, 'and we collect them. There are also special occasions when the other parent comes to visit, and in that case they go up together.'

Jan nods. *The other parent.* She is talking about the mother or father who is free. The one who isn't locked up.

He has met several of them already; they have popped into the cloakroom to deliver the children who do not live at the Dell. But are they the children's biological parents, or foster parents? Jan is not allowed to ask, of course. They are all neatly dressed men or women from the age of about thirty upwards. Some looked as if they might be pensioners.

He has stood in the cloakroom with Marie-Louise welcoming the children one by one. All the children who will be at the Dell today have arrived; there are eleven of them.

When children are dropped off there can sometimes be despair and lots of tears, as Jan well knows, while the parents can be exaggeratedly cheerful and talkative in order to hide their anxiety or embarrassment at having to leave their children. But here at the Dell the adults seem somehow subdued. Perhaps it is because of the concrete wall – the shadow of St Psycho's falls over everyone at the pre-school.

And the children? They are quite shy, for the most part. They smile and whisper and stare at the new person standing next to their teacher, wondering who he is. During all the years he has spent in various pre-schools, Jan has encountered almost exclusively children who are curious and wide-eyed. Children are subdued only when they are really ill. Unlike adults, they can never hide how they are feeling.

'Unfortunately you've missed our feelgood session today,' says Marie-Louise when she has finished showing Jan around.

'What's that?'

'It's something we do together as a team on Mondays. We just sit down for fifteen minutes and talk about how we're feeling.' She smiles at him. 'But you'll get the chance to join in next Monday.'

Jan nods without saying anything. He doesn't want to think about how he's feeling.

'So,' says Marie-Louise, 'are you ready to start work?'

'Absolutely.'

'Good.' She smiles again. 'I was thinking we might have story time.'

Jan has the honour of choosing a book from the boxes in the playroom, and he pulls out a slender volume from somewhere in the middle: *Emil in the Soup Tureen*.

'Story time!'

Jan sits down on a chair by the wall in the playroom, and the children stop playing and settle down on little stools in a higgledy-piggledy semi-circle. They are curious about him, but still quite wary. He understands them.

'OK, do you remember my name?'

No one speaks.

'Does anyone remember?'

The children stare at him in silence.

Eventually a little girl with only one front tooth whispers, 'Jan.'

She is sitting slightly closer to him than the others. Matilda – that was her name, wasn't it? She looks about five years old, with a centre parting and long, pale-blonde plaits.

'That's it – my name is Jan Hauger.' He holds up the book. 'And this is Emil – Emil from Lönneberga. Have you seen him before?'

Several of the children nod; he is starting to connect with them.

'Have you heard the story about the time when Emil got his head stuck in the soup tureen?'

'Yeees . . .'

'Have you heard it lots of times?'

'Yesss!'

'Oh, so maybe you don't want to hear it again?'

'Yes we do!' they shout.

Jan smiles at them. All your troubles disappear when you look into the eyes of a child. They absorb all the light in the world, and it shines out of them. He opens the book and begins to read.

The morning passes. Routines are important at the Dell. Marie-Louise seems to want as much order as possible, and the children feel the same. After story time everyone goes out to play. The children put on their coats and boots and go out into the playground, inside the metre-high fence. Almost half the group want to play tag, and Jan has to chase them. The last trace of shyness disappears, and they scream with fear and excitement as he chases them around the sandpit and the playhouse. The playground is not large, but it is very green; shrubs and grass are still growing in the mild autumn weather, and there is no tarmac and hardly any gravel in sight.

Jan can now see the hospital complex from a new angle. There is no wall at the back of St Patricia's, just a five-metre chain-link fence with a network of electrified wires right at the top.

'Chase me! Chase me!'

Jan carries on playing. He raises his arms like a real monster, chasing all the children who want to be chased. They hide behind the playhouse, and he creeps around pretending he can't find them – until he suddenly rounds the corner and bellows like a troll, 'Boo!'

It's fun; he is just as happy out here as in the playroom, but suddenly he turns to look towards the hospital – and realizes that someone is standing there staring.

Jan stops dead, and his smile disappears.

A tall, thin old woman is standing behind St Patricia's fence, dressed in a black coat. Skinny white legs are visible below the coat. She has a rake in one hand, and there is a pile of leaves at her feet. The other hand is clutching the mesh of the fence.

The woman is staring straight at Jan. Her face is pale, but her eyes are almost as dark as her clothes. Her expression is filled with sorrow, or perhaps hatred – it's impossible to tell.

'Jan?'

He gives a start and turns around; Marie-Louise is calling to him from an open window.

'Yes?'

'It's almost time for Leo to go over to the hospital; I thought you could come with me so that you can see what we do. Would you like to do that?'

'Yes, of course.'

Jan nods to her. Marie-Louise closes the window, and he glances over at the hospital again. But the woman behind the fence has disappeared. Only the pile of leaves remains.

The routines continue. The children come inside, take off their coats and boots and go straight to the playroom, where they sit down with a variety of games. Jan has always been fascinated by how disciplined small children can be when they know what they are supposed to do.

When everyone is settled, Marie-Louise looks at the clock. 'Time to go.'

She takes a magnetic key card out of a cupboard in the kitchen and leads the way to the cloakroom.

'Leo!' she shouts. 'Time to go!'

Beside the coat hooks there is a white door that Jan has not noticed up to now – or at least it hasn't occurred to him to wonder what lies beyond it.

Marie-Louise swipes the card and keys in a four-digit code, three–one–zero–seven, and the white door opens. 'My birthday,' she says. 'July thirty-first.'

Jan can see a steep stone staircase beyond the door. Marie-Louise switches on the light and turns around, holding out her hand and smiling. 'Right then, Leo – shall we go and see Daddy?'

Leo hasn't been playing outside. He is barely five years old; a slight child with skinny legs, dressed in little blue dungarees. He takes Marie-Louise's hand and walks down the stairs with her, one step at a time. Jan follows in silence.

'Could you close the door, Jan?'

The shouts and joyful laughter from the pre-school are cut off abruptly. The staircase is as silent as the grave. The walls seem to be made of the same material as the wall surrounding the hospital; any sound is muted down here.

Leo's little legs plod on down the stairs. Marie-Louise doesn't speak either; there is a palpable seriousness in the air.

After twenty steps they reach the basement level, and set off along an underground corridor with a concrete floor which is covered in a thin blue carpet. But someone has spent time trying to make the corridor look pleasant: the walls are painted a sunny yellow, and adorned with brightly coloured pictures.

Jan sees that they are pen and ink drawings. He couldn't have drawn them – they are too cheerful. Laughing mice swimming in a pool, elephants smoking great big pipes, walruses playing tennis.

It feels as if the animals are in the wrong place down here.

'Here we are,' Marie-Louise says all of a sudden. 'We've arrived, Leo!'

They have walked some fifty metres and are deep underground now, presumably beneath the hospital itself. To the right there is a white-painted lift door with a narrow pane of glass. But the corridor does not end here; it continues straight on for another eight or ten metres, then turns sharply to the right.

Marie-Louise opens the door of the lift for Leo, and he toddles inside.

Jan also takes a step forward, but she shakes her head. 'Leo wants to go up on his own,' she says. 'The children are allowed to do that if they want to.'

Jan nods. He feels tense, but he had hoped to get as far as the visitors' room. 'But we do go up with the children sometimes?'

'Oh yes,' says Marie-Louise. 'You and the child make that decision together.'

When the door is open Jan catches a brief glimpse of the lift. He sees a small metal chamber with two buttons marked UP and DOWN, next to another card reader and a red panic button. CCTV cameras? He can't see any on the walls or ceiling.

Marie-Louise steps into the lift, swipes her magnetic card and presses the button marked UP. 'Bye then, Leo!' she shouts as she closes the door. 'See you soon!' Her voice sounds even more exuberant than usual, as if she is trying to chase away a sudden twinge of unease.

Jan catches sight of Leo's little face looking out of the narrow window. Then the lift makes a clicking sound and begins to move upwards.

'OK, that's it, we can head back,' says Marie-Louise. Her voice sounds calmer now, and she goes on: 'Someone needs to collect Leo in an hour – perhaps you could do that on your own, Jan?'

'No problem.'

'Good.' Marie-Louise smiles at him. 'I'll set the little alarm clock in the kitchen to remind you when it's time. They send the children down from the visitors' room on their own dead on the hour, so it's important that we're here.'

They go back up the staircase, open the door and they are in the cloakroom once more.

Marie-Louise cups her hand around her mouth and shouts, 'Time for our fruit, everyone!'

Some of the children pull a face at the word *fruit*, but most come running, some of them pushing and shoving to get there first. Always a battle.

Everything is just the way it usually is in a pre-school.

But Jan looks at the moving hand on the wall clock several times. He can't help thinking about little Leo, all alone with his locked-up daddy.

8

There are no CCTV cameras at the Dell, which is a good thing of course. But Jan can't see a television either.

'A TV? No, we only have a radio in here,' Marie-Louise says seriously. 'If we had a TV we'd soon end up with a whole pile of cartoons the children would want to watch, and a passive child is an unhappy child.'

The children are having great fun in the playroom; they have laid out the thick crash mats on the floor and are pretending to be shipwrecked sailors drifting along on rafts. Jan joins in the game; it feels good after his subterranean trip.

He spots a notice in Marie-Louise's neat handwriting up on the wall. The children can't read yet, of course, but it appears to be meant for them:

Here at the Dell
. . . we always tell an adult where we're going
. . . everyone is allowed to join in when we are talking or playing
. . . we never say anything bad about anyone else
. . . we never fight or quarrel
. . . we never play with weapons.

Lilian is also playing with the children; they leap from mat to mat in order to escape from the sharks swimming in the sea. Just like Jan she joins in the game wholeheartedly, but from time to time he sees a shadow of sorrow pass across her face when she looks at the children.

After a while they sit down on one of the crash mats to recover; he wants to ask her if something is wrong, but Lilian gets in first: 'Are you settling in OK, Jan?'

It sounds as if she really cares.

'In Valla, you mean?' Jan needs to think about what he's going to say. 'Yes, although of course I've only just moved here. But it seems like a good place . . . Lovely surroundings.'

'What do you do in the evenings?'

'Not much . . . I listen to some music.'

'Haven't you got any friends here?'

'No . . . not yet.'

'Well, why don't you come down to Bill's Bar?' says Lilian. 'It's by the harbour, there's a good house band . . .'

'Bill's Bar?'

'I hang out there all the time,' says Lilian. 'There are usually a few people from St Patricia's there too. You'll get to know plenty of new people at Bill's.'

Should Jan start going to the pub and being sociable? He's never done it before, but why not? 'Maybe,' he says.

They carry on playing with the shipwrecked children until Jan hears the shrill sound of the alarm clock in the kitchen. Good, he has been waiting for it.

He collects the magnetic card, opens the basement door and heads down the stairs and along the corridor alone.

Nothing is moving down there. The pictures on the wall are still there, hanging in straight lines.

It is five to twelve and the window in the door of the lift is still in darkness; Leo has not been sent down yet.

Jan stops. *Go up in the lift*, he thinks. *Go up and have a look around inside St Psycho's.*

But he stays where he is, waiting for the lift for a minute or so, then he looks over towards the other end of the corridor. Over towards that sharp bend to the right. He is a little curious about what there might be around that corner. Another way into the hospital?

The lift has still not appeared, so Jan walks away slowly. He's just going to have a quick look to see where the corridor goes.

Around the corner the corridor continues for a little distance, and ends at a massive steel door. It is firmly closed, and has a long iron handle. Jan reads the words SAFE ROOM on a white sign next to the door. And underneath it says: *This door must be kept locked at all times!*

A safe room – Jan knows what that is. It's like an underground bunker.

A picture of little William comes into his mind, but he pushes it away and reaches for the iron handle.

It moves. It seems possible to open the door.

But at that moment there is a clicking sound in the corridor behind him. The lift door. Jan quickly lets go of the handle and hurries back.

Leo has been sent down via the sally port. He is trying to push open the heavy door, but can't quite manage it.

Jan helps him. 'Have you had a nice time, Leo?'

Leo nods without speaking; Jan takes his hand and they set off back towards the Dell.

'I think it'll be sing-along time soon. Do you like singing, Leo?'

'Mm.'

Perhaps it is Jan's imagination, but Leo seems a little more sub-dued than he was before his visit to see his father. Otherwise he looks exactly the same. No bleeding scratches on his face, no ripped clothes. Of course not – why shouldn't he look the same?

They have reached the foot of the staircase leading up to the Dell. Jan is ready with the magnetic card, but glances at Leo one last time and decides to risk asking a question: 'Was it nice seeing Daddy today?'

'Mm.'

'So what did you do?'

'We talked,' said Leo. There is a brief silence, then he goes on: 'Daddy talks a lot. All the time.'

'Oh?'

Leo nods again and sets off up the stairs. 'He says everybody hates him.'

9

During his first week at the Dell, Jan works from eight until five every day. And every evening he goes home to his dark apartment. He's used to it, he's always come home to a silent apartment, but this one isn't even his. It doesn't feel like *home*.

Sometimes in the evening he sits down at his drawing board and continues working on the Secret Avenger's struggle against the Gang of Four, but if he is tired he just flops down in front of the TV and stays there.

During the day he learns the names of the children, one by one. Leo, Matilda, Mira, Fanny, Katinka, and so on. He gets to know which ones are chatty and which ones are quieter, which ones get cross when they fall over and which ones start crying if someone happens to bump into them. Which ones ask questions and which ones listen.

The children have so much energy. When they're not under orders to sit still during assembly, they're always on the move, always heading off somewhere. They crawl, they run, they jump. Out in the playground they dig in the sandpit, climb and swing – and want to join in everything.

'Me too! Me too!'

The children fight for space, for attention. But Jan makes sure that no one is excluded from a game, that no one is nudged out of the group and ends up on their own, as he often did.

The group of children at the Dell feels harmonious, and it is easy to forget their proximity to St Psycho's – until the alarm clock rings in the kitchen and someone has to be taken to or collected from the lift beneath the hospital. But the trips along the underground corridor also become routine, in fact – although Jan does keep a slightly closer eye on Leo, whose father sounds somewhat paranoid.

On Wednesday morning the children go for a little outing into the forest which rises up behind the grounds of the hospital. They put on yellow high-visibility vests over their coats and go out of the gate in a crocodile. Many pre-schools insist that the children hang on to loops attached to a rope when they go on a trip, but here they favour the old method: the children hold hands, two by two.

Excursions into the forest always make Jan feel slightly tense, but he wanders along with Marie-Louise and Andreas between clumps of wilting bracken behind the school. They are very close to St Patricia's as they follow this little path – the fence is no more than ten metres away.

Marie-Louise leans towards him. 'We need to make sure the children don't get too close to the fence.'

'Oh? Why's that?'

Marie-Louise looks worried. 'It could trigger the escape alarm. There's a whole load of electronic stuff buried by the fence.'

'Electronic stuff?'

'Yes . . . some kind of motion sensors.'

Jan nods, looking over at the fence. He can't see any sensors, but notices that the fir trees have been planted very close together just inside the fence, perhaps to stop anyone looking in. Beyond the trees he can just catch a glimpse of gravel paths and a couple of low buildings inside the complex – yellow wooden structures that look quite new. Nothing is moving over there.

He suddenly remembers the woman in black, the woman he saw by the fence on Monday. Her dark eyes made him think of Alice Rami, but Rami is the same age as him, and the woman in black looked twice as old.

The children don't seem remotely interested in the fence; they lumber along in their thick autumn clothes, hand in hand, concerned only with what there is to see straight ahead of them on the path: ants, tree roots, odd bits of rubbish and fallen leaves.

There is a dull, rushing sound up ahead; it is a wide stream, full of swirling black water. It runs along the back of the hospital grounds like a moat, then curves away to the south and disappears along the fence. Jan wonders if the patients find the sound of the water calming.

The children tramp across a little wooden bridge with railings, then they head off upwards into the forest.

'Oh look!' It's little Fanny, three years old and right at the end of the line; she has let go of her friend's hand and stopped to stare at the ground beside the path. She is gazing at something that is growing there.

Jan stops too, and takes a closer look. Among the leaves beneath the tall trees he can see something that resembles little pink fingers, pushing their way up out of the ground. 'Oh yes . . .' he says. 'I think it's a kind of fungus. Pink coral fungus. It looks like fingers.'

'Fingers?' says Fanny.

'No, they're not real fingers.'

Fanny tentatively reaches out towards the slender pink fungi, but Jan stops her. 'Leave it, Fanny. I think they'd rather grow in peace . . . and sometimes they can be poisonous.'

The girl nods and quickly forgets about the fungus as she sets off to catch up with the others.

Jan watches her until she reaches her friends.

He breathes out and thinks of the children at Lynx, although he doesn't want to. A child can be lost in no time; all it takes is for the path to disappear between two big fir trees, and suddenly you can't see them any more.

But today there is no danger. The children from the Dell stick close together, the oak trees and birch trees are not as dense as in a coniferous forest, and of course the children are wearing their high-visibility vests, glowing bright yellow among the trees.

Marie-Louise keeps the group together by talking to the children.

She points out different kinds of leaves and bushes and explains what they are called, and asks every child a question.

But eventually she claps her hands. 'OK, play time! But stay where we can see you.'

The children quickly disperse. Felix and Teodor start chasing one another, Mattias runs after them, stumbles over a tree root and falls over, but quickly gets back on his feet.

Jan wanders among the trees, looking around and constantly counting the luminous jackets to make sure no one goes missing. He's on the ball, keeping an eye on things.

As he moves further away he hears laughter echoing through the forest and catches the odd glimpse of yellow between the trunks. Then he sees Natalie, Josefine, Leo and little Hugo standing in a huddle staring down at the path. Josefine and Leo are holding sticks and poking at the ground. When they spot Jan, they stiffen and smile, looking slightly embarrassed. Josefine meets Leo's eye, and they start to giggle. Suddenly they drop the sticks and race off, shrieking and laughing, heading into the undergrowth.

Jan goes over to see what they were playing with.

Something tiny. It looks like a little grey-brown scrap of material on the path. But it's a wood mouse. It is lying among the leaves with its mouth open, gasping for breath: it is dying. The soft, silky fur is flecked with blood. Jan realizes that the children were poking holes in it as part of their game.

No, not a game. A sadistic ritual, to experience the feeling of power over life and death.

Jan is on his own, he has to do something. He gently edges the soft body off the path with his right foot and searches for a big, blunt stone. He picks it up, raises it in both hands, and takes aim.

Thou shalt not kill, he thinks, but he hurls the stone down anyway. It lands on the mouse like a falling meteorite.

Done.

He leaves the stone where it fell and rejoins the group. They are all there, and he notices that Leo is still smiling and looking pleased with himself.

After almost an hour in the forest they make their way home, back across the bridge and along the fence.

When the children are all indoors and have taken off their coats, they are sent to wash their hands, and then it's time for Jan to accompany Katinka to the lift. She goes up to see her mother by herself.

Then it's story time. Jan chooses to read about one of the adventures of Pippi Longstocking, which includes her assertion that a person who is really big must also be really kind.

Afterwards he asks Natalie, Josefine, Leo and Hugo to stay behind in the playroom. He gets them to sit down on the floor in front of him.

'I saw you playing in the forest today,' he says.

The children smile up at him shyly.

'And you left something behind on the path . . . A little mouse.'

Suddenly they seem to understand what he's talking about, what he wants. Josefine points and says, 'It was Leo – he stamped on it!'

'It was poorly!' counters Leo. 'It was just lying there on the ground.'

'No it wasn't, it was moving! It was *crawling*!'

Jan lets them bicker for a little while, then he says, 'But now the mouse is dead. It's not crawling any more.'

The children fall silent, staring at him.

He speaks slowly: 'How do you think the mouse must have felt, before it died?'

No one answers.

Jan looks them in the eye, one by one. 'Did anyone feel sorry for the mouse?'

Still no reply. Leo stares back at him with a defiant expression; the others gaze at the floor.

'You poked that little wood mouse with your sticks until it bled,' Jan says quietly. 'Did anyone feel sorry for the mouse when that happened?'

Eventually the smallest child nods hesitantly.

'OK, Hugo, good boy. Anyone else?'

After a moment Natalie and Josefine also nod, one after the

other. Only Leo refuses to meet Jan's eye now. He looks at the floor, muttering something about 'Daddy' and 'Mummy'.

Jan leans forward. 'What did you say, Leo?'

But Leo doesn't answer. Jan could press him, perhaps even make him cry.

That's what Daddy did to Mummy.

Is that really what Leo said? Jan thinks he might have misheard, and would like to ask the boy again. But instead he simply says, 'I'm glad we've talked about this.'

The children realize they are free to go; they leap up from the floor and race out.

He watches them go – did they understand his point? He can still remember the telling-off he got from his teacher when he was eight years old; he was playing Nazis with his friend Hans and the other boys in his class. They had marched across the playground in straight lines, shouting 'Heil Hitler!' and feeling tough and power-ful – *they were actually marching in step!* – until a teacher came over and stopped them. Then he had mentioned a place they had never even heard of.

'Auschwitz!' he had yelled. 'Do you know what happened there? Do you know what the Nazis did to adults and children in Auschwitz?'

None of the boys knew, so the teacher had told them about the terrible journeys by cattle wagon and the gas ovens and the moun-tains of shoes and clothes. And that was the end of their Nazi games.

Jan follows the children out of the room; it will soon be sing-along time. Routines – he assumes there are just as many routines over at St Patricia's. Day after day, the same thing. Fixed times, well-worn tracks.

The children were not being evil when they tortured the mouse. Jan refuses to believe that children can be evil, even if he himself used to feel like a little mouse sometimes when he was at school and came across older boys in the corridor; he never expected any mercy, nor did he receive any.

Lynx

The week after Jan found the bunker in the forest he started to clean and prepare it.

He was very careful, and always waited until the sun had gone down before he left his apartment and strolled up to the hillside in the forest where the bunker was located. During the course of two weeks he went there three times with some rubbish sacks and a stiff brush concealed in a bag. He clambered up the slope, crawled into the bunker and swept the floor clean. He wanted everything out: dust, cobwebs, leaves, beer cans, newspapers.

Eventually there was nothing left inside but clear surfaces. He aired the bunker by leaving the metal door open, then took along a couple of air fresheners which he placed in the two far corners; they spread an artificial smell of roses throughout the place.

It was October now, and each time Jan went to the bunker there were more dead leaves on the ground. Slowly they piled up, making the concrete structure look even more like part of the hillside. When the door was closed and the old iron bolts had been pushed across, the bunker was very difficult to spot.

The trickiest part was trying to get the new stuff in without anyone seeing him, but he did it under cover of darkness, late at night, just as with the cleaning. He had learned to find his way through the trees to the hillside by now, and he didn't need any light.

He had found the mattress in a skip, but it didn't smell unpleasant, and when he got it into the forest he gave it a thorough beating to get rid of all the dust. The blankets and pillows came from a big store outside Nordbro; he had removed all the labels and washed them twice before arranging them on the mattress in the bunker.

The half-dozen toys he carried up in his rucksack came from a couple of other large stores. They were the kind of anonymous goods that were produced in factories in the Far East, and there had to be thousands and thousands of them around: a couple of cars, a cuddly lion, a few picture books.

The last item he acquired was large and quite heavy. ROBOMAN, it said on the box up on the top shelf among the fire engines, spaceships and ray guns. *Remote controlled! Voice activated! Record your own messages and watch ROBOMAN move and talk!*

The plastic robot could stand erect on a level floor and move its arms. Jan looked at it and tried to think his way back fifteen years to the time when he was only five – he would have thought Roboman was the best thing he'd ever set eyes on, wouldn't he? Better than a cuddly toy, almost better than a real dog or cat?

He stole Roboman. It was a bold move, but the aisle was empty and he quickly removed the robot and the remote control from the box and dropped them into a big carrier bag from another shop. Then he walked straight out. The girl on the checkout didn't even look at him. There was no sign of the security guard.

The robot cost almost six hundred kronor, but it wasn't the price that made him steal it. It was the risk that the checkout girl might remember the slightly unusual purchase if the police started asking questions.

Roboman? Yes, a young man bought it. He looked nice, trustworthy, a bit like a teacher. Yes, I think I could identify him . . .

10

Sometimes Jan thinks the pre-school is like a zoo.

It always starts late in the day, when everyone is tired: one of the children kicks off, and the others get dragged in. It's usually one of the boys who has some kind of manic outburst, suddenly becoming hyperactive and hurtling around the rooms, perhaps knocking down someone's carefully constructed tower of building blocks or trampling all over someone else's Lego house.

That's what happens at the Dell on Friday afternoon, when Leo suddenly decides to hit Felix in the face with a cushion. Felix hits him back, roaring at the top of his voice and with tears pouring down his face. Leo starts yelling too, and all at once the entire group is filled with fresh energy; the other boys start wrestling or fighting with cushions, the girls start screaming or sobbing hysterically.

'Quiet!' Jan shouts.

It makes no difference. The playroom turns into a blurred mess of agitated children, jumping around and making it feel like a cramped cage.

Jan is the only adult present, and he can feel a wave of panic beginning to rise in his chest. But he puts a stop to it; he breathes in and moves to the centre of the room. Then he raises his voice like a hell-and-damnation pastor: 'Quiet! Stop that *right now!*'

Most of the children stop dead, but little Leo carries on. His eyes are wide open and he is flailing around wildly with his cushion.

Jan has to move across and put his arms around him; he feels like a lion tamer. 'Calm down, Leo. Calm down!'

The little body is struggling in his arms; Jan holds on tightly until Leo stops wriggling completely. The beast has been tamed, but afterwards Jan is exhausted.

'I'm a bit concerned about Leo,' he says to Marie-Louise in the kitchen later, when they are doing the dishes.

'Oh?'

'There's so much anger inside him.'

Marie-Louise smiles. 'That's energy . . . He's got enough energy for all of us!'

'Do you know anything about his parents?' Jan asks. 'Are they both still alive? I think his father . . .'

But Marie-Louise shakes her head and dries her hands on a tea towel. 'We don't talk about that kind of thing, Jan. You know that.'

That evening after work Jan is sitting at home on the old sofa in front of the TV, trying to relax. But it's difficult. His neighbour on the other side of the wall is celebrating the arrival of the weekend with an early party; Jan can hear the sound of music and clinking glasses.

His first working week at the Dell is over. He ought to celebrate, but it doesn't feel appropriate somehow. It has passed quickly and has been easy, for the most part. He has done his best and taken his responsibilities seriously, and both the children and his colleagues seem to like him.

Jan has set up his old stereo; he puts on Rami's album and turns up the volume to drown out the noise of the party. His old favourite comes on: the ballad 'Your Secret Love', where Rami sings in her whispering voice:

> Go over your memories
> until you can see them
> floating by on the wind
> until you can hear them

Love or just a game
you will always miss
your most secret love
like a lost soul in the desert

The song seems to Jan to be about a love which is impossible. If they ever meet again, he will ask Rami if he is right.

If they meet again – to make that happen he will have to get into St Psycho's, perhaps through the basement. There is always a way into a building for the person who is brave enough.

He turns his back on the cramped room and looks out of the window.

There is not a soul in sight in the car park behind the apartment block, but it is full of cars. He counts eleven Volvos including his own, seven Saabs, two Toyotas and just one Mercedes. People have come home from work and gone indoors to join their families. Perhaps they are all sitting around the kitchen table, or in front of the TV. Perhaps they are busy with their knitting or their stamp collection.

But Jan is alone.

There – he has allowed himself to think the dangerous word, he has admitted his inferiority. He is *alone*, he is *lonely*.

He has no friends here in Valla. That is a cold, hard fact. He has nothing to do.

All he really wants to do is to sit here listening to Rami. But he still has boxes to unpack, and during the course of the evening he finds an old book containing drawings and newspaper cuttings. It's his diary from when he was a teenager; he used to write in it now and again, but sometimes there would be several months between entries.

He opens the diary, picks up a pen and writes down everything that has happened over the past couple of weeks, letting it all out: the move to Valla, the loneliness, the new job, and the dream that it will lead him to Rami.

He has stuck an old photograph on the front of the book. It's a Polaroid, slightly faded, but he can still see a blond-haired boy looking up in surprise from a hospital bed with its white sheets. It is Jan himself, aged fourteen.

11

After lunch on Saturday Jan goes down to the communal laundry room in the apartment block for the first time, and meets an old man. A white-haired neighbour whose beard is equally white is just leaving the room containing the washing machines.

Afterwards Jan realizes he should have spoken to him rather than merely nodding as the man walked past.

The man is carrying an old laundry bag over his shoulder, and as Jan glances at the fabric bag he can see that there are letters printed on it: T ICIA NDRY. There must be more letters, but they are concealed by the folds of the material.

Jan continues on into the laundry room. But suddenly his brain forms the words: *St Patricia's Laundry.*

Could that possibly be right? It is too late to check – by this stage the old man has already left the cellar, the door has closed, and Jan is alone with his washing.

When all his clothes are clean and dry he goes back up to the apartment and tries to make some more room, shifting boxes out of the way, cleaning up and pushing together his landlady's furniture. Then he eats yet another lonely meal at the kitchen table as darkness falls outside.

And after that? He goes into the living room and switches on the old TV. He sees dolphins swimming along beneath the surface of the water; it seems to be some kind of documentary. He settles down and learns that dolphins are nowhere near as nice and peace-loving as many people think.

Dolphins hunt in packs and often kill seals and other creatures, says the presenter.

Jan switches off the television after half an hour. The apartment is silent – but sounds are seeping in from elsewhere. Somewhere in the building someone is having another party. He can hear the thump of music, the loud slam of an outside door, loud voices and laughter.

Jan thinks about doing a little more drawing on *The Secret Avenger*; he is getting close to the end. Soon his hero must defeat the Gang of Four. Annihilate them.

The party continues, the laughter gets louder. In the end Jan puts on the stereo to drown out the noise, and gazes out of the window.

I ought to get myself a hobby, he thinks. *Or join an evening class.*

But what would he like to do? Learn French? How to play the ukulele?

No. After a while he switches off the stereo, puts on a black jacket so that he looks grown up, and goes out.

It is cold outside, and the street lamps have come on. It is quarter past eight. He can hear more music out here, echoing between the buildings. It's party time – for all those who have friends.

Come down to Bill's Bar, Lilian had said. *I hang out there all the time.*

Jan sets off towards the town centre. He wants to get to know his new home town, but what is there to see? Valla is a medium-sized Swedish town, with no great surprises. He passes a pizzeria, a Pentecostal church, a furniture store. A few bored teenagers are sitting around a table in the pizzeria; everywhere else is closed and in darkness.

A footbridge takes him over the motorway, and Jan is almost down by the harbour. He would really like to go down to the quay-side to feel the evening breeze coming off the dark sea, but the area is barricaded with gates and a fence which is almost as high as the wall around St Psycho's.

No, not St Psycho's. *St Patricia's.* Jan must stop using the hospital's nickname, otherwise he's going to end up saying it out loud sooner or later.

Beyond the fence there are a few small streets that could be regarded as the town's harbour area, but there is nothing romantic or adventurous about them. There are just low industrial units surrounded by cracked tarmac.

But there are several cars parked in front of one of the wooden buildings on the side nearest the town, and a welcoming red sign above the entrance says BILL'S BAR.

Jan stops in front of the sign. Visiting bars isn't something he enjoys. But even the loneliest of creatures is welcome in a bar as long as he behaves himself, so in the end he pulls open the heavy wooden door and walks in.

It is dark and hot inside; there's the heavy beat of rock music and muted voices. Shadows moving around one another, the sense that everything could just tip over. Bars are a kind of playroom for adults only.

All good children are fast asleep by now.

Jan unbuttons his jacket and looks around. He thinks of a line from a song by Roxy Music about loneliness being a crowded room. He can't remember when he last walked into a bar alone, because the feeling of being an outsider is always overwhelming in a room full of strangers, chatting and laughing together. Bill's Bar is just the same. Jan doesn't believe that everyone in there is the best of friends with everyone else, but that's how it *seems.*

He pushes his way over to the bar past heavy bodies that are unwilling to move. A lot of people have gathered in front of a small stage right at the back, where a local rock band is playing.

Jan hands over a note at the bar. 'A low-alcohol beer, please.'

The classic trick for a lonely person is to chat with the bartender, but he has already whisked away Jan's money and moved on.

Jan takes a couple of sips and feels slightly less isolated. He has company now – a glass of beer. The drinker's best friend. But he has hardly ever consumed alcohol, never got drunk – should he try it tonight, just to see what happens?

Nothing. Nothing would happen, apart from the fact that he would stagger home alone and feel terrible tomorrow morning. In a way you have to admire people who just get pissed and don't give a toss about the consequences; Jan has never been able to do that. He stays in control and is never going to end up unconscious in a swimming pool, like a rock star. Or in a psychiatric unit, like Rami.

The thought of her makes him glance around the bar, wondering about the clientele. He remembers what else Lilian said about Bill's Bar: *There are usually a few people from St Patricia's there too.* Security guards and nurses, he assumes.

Jan takes another sip of his beer. He can smell perfume in the air, and suddenly realizes he is standing between two women in their mid-twenties.

Tall and attractive. Time to act like a grown-up, but he feels like a boy.

The one on the right smells of rose petals. She is wearing a black sweater, she has long brown hair and is drinking something bright yellow. Their eyes meet, but she quickly looks away.

The one on the left has drenched herself in a mandarin-scented perfume; she is wearing a yellow top and a shiny gold jacket. A golden girl. She has green eyes and is drinking perry; Jan glances sideways at her and she actually smiles at him. Why is she doing that?

She doesn't look away, so he leans over and shouts, 'This is my first time here!'

'What?' she shouts back.

Jan leans a little closer. 'My first time here!'

'At Bill's?' she asks. 'Or in town?'

'Both, really. I moved here a few days ago. I don't know anybody . . .'

'You soon will!' she yells. 'You're going to have a brilliant time here! Loads of surprises!'

'Really?'

'Absolutely, I can always tell that kind of thing . . . Good luck!'

With that she turns and disappears into the crowd, like a deer in the forest.

So that was that. A short conversation, and as usual Jan found it difficult to make small-talk with a stranger, but he feels better now. People in here are friendly.

Carry on making contact, an inner voice encourages him. He gets another beer and moves away from the music.

Most tables are fully occupied. There is no room for him to join a group. He sits down at a free table on his own, drinking his beer and staring into space.

Congratulations, your new life starts here. But of course he has thought the same thing before. You can change your job and move to a new town, but nothing changes. You are trapped in the same body, the same dross in your blood, the same memories going round and round in your head.

'Hi Jan!'

A woman is standing in front of him; he looks up, but it takes a few seconds before he recognizes her. It's Lilian, with a bottle of beer in her hand.

At the Dell she has looked tired and worn over the past few days, but now there is a fresh energy about her. She is wearing a black, low-cut top and her heavily made-up eyes are shining, perhaps even glittering – that bottle is definitely not her first this evening.

'Do you like my weekend tattoo?' she asks, pointing at her cheek.

Jan takes a closer look and sees that Lilian has drawn something: a long, black snake writhing up towards her eye.

'Definitely.'

'It's not dangerous . . . It's not poisonous!'

Lilian laughs, her voice slightly hoarse, and sits down uninvited at his table. 'So you've found the best place in town?' She takes a swig of her beer. 'That was quick work.'

'Well, you told me about it,' says Jan. 'Are you here on your own?'

Lilian shakes her head. 'I was with some friends, but they went home when the Bohemos started playing.' She nods in the direction of the band. 'Sensitive ears.'

'Friends from work?' says Jan.

'Friends from work – now who would that be?' Lilian snorts and has another drink. 'Marie-Louise, maybe?'

'Does she never come here?'

'No chance – Marie-Louise stays at home.'

'Does she have children?'

'No, just her husband and the dog. But then she's everybody's second mum, isn't she? She's like a mum to all the kids, and to us. Fantastic . . . I don't think she's ever had a nasty thought in her entire life.'

Jan doesn't want to give any thought to what other people might think. 'So what about Andreas, then?' he says. 'Does he go out?'

'Andreas? Not much. He's got a house and a garden to look after, and a little wife. They're like a couple of pensioners.'

'OK,' says Jan. 'But Hanna comes here, doesn't she?'

'Sometimes.' Lilian looks down at the table. 'Hanna's the one I get on best with at work; you could say she's my friend.'

There is a brief silence. The music has stopped; the Bohemos seem to have packed up for the night.

'So Hanna is a good person?'

'Of course,' Lilian says quickly. 'She's a nice girl. She's only twenty-six . . . young and a bit crazy.'

'What do you mean, a bit crazy?'

'In all kinds of ways. She might seem quiet and reserved, but she has a very exciting private life.'

'With different men, you mean?'

Lilian presses her lips together. 'I don't gossip.'

'But she does come here sometimes?' says Jan. 'To Bill's Bar?'

'She comes with me sometimes, but she prefers the Medina Palace.'

'The Medina Palace?'

'The big night club here in town. It's almost as luxurious as St Patricia's.'

'You think St Patricia's is luxurious?'

'Absolutely – it's a luxury hotel.'

Jan looks at her with a blank expression; he doesn't know what she's talking about.

Lilian quickly goes on: 'Listen . . . Every room at St Psycho's costs four thousand per night. Four thousand kronor! Those who are in there don't have to pay, of course, but that's what it costs the taxpayer. Doctors, guards, cameras, medication . . . it all costs money. The patients don't know how well off they are.'

'And you and I work there . . . next door to the luxury hotel.'

'We do indeed,' says Lilian. 'Let's drink to that!'

Jan carries on chatting to her for another fifteen minutes or so, then stretches and fakes a little yawn. 'Time for me to head home, I think.'

'One last beer?' says Lilian, with a slow wink.

Jan shakes his head. 'Not tonight.'

Starting to party now would be a big mistake; he will be taking on extra responsibilities next week. On Thursday he will have a timetabled evening shift at the pre-school; for the first time he will be completely alone with the children.

12

'So how are you feeling, Jan?' asks Marie-Louise. 'Would you like to tell us?'

'Of course . . . but there isn't much to say, really. I feel fine.'

'Is that all? No problems fitting in with the team?'

'No.' Jan looks around the table at Andreas, Hanna and Lilian. 'No problems at all.'

'We're all very pleased to hear that, Jan.'

Monday's feelgood meeting for the staff takes place before the children begin to arrive.

This is Jan's first time. They are all looking at him, the new boy, but he finds it difficult to relax and talk at the same time.

'This is an important job,' he says. 'I'm well aware of that.'

They stop staring, and a few minutes later the feelgood meeting is over. Thank goodness.

Just before story time, Jan finds a sign of life from Alice Rami. Perhaps.

Little Josefine is helping him. She was one of the children who tormented the mouse in the forest, but Jan is trying to forget that incident, along with Leo's unsettling words about his father. And today Josefine is just like any other little girl: she is playing with a doll when Jan comes to fetch a book.

'Is there any particular story you'd like to hear today, Josefine?'

She looks up and nods, several times. 'The one about the lady who makes animals!'

Jan looks at her. 'What's it called?'

'*The Animal Lady*!'

Jan has never heard of it, but Josefine goes straight over to the book boxes, rummages through them and pulls out a thin white book, about the size of an LP record. She's right; the title is *The Animal Lady*.

'OK. Fine.'

The book is similar to all the others in the box, but there is no author's name, and the picture below the title is barely visible; it is just a faint pencil drawing of a small island and a slender lighthouse. It looks as if it is handmade; when Jan looks more closely he can see that someone has cut the pages and stuck them together with ordinary sticky tape.

He flicks through it. The text is written on the right-hand page. On the left-hand page there are pencil drawings, but like the one on the cover they are so faint they are hardly visible.

Jan is curious; he wants to read *The Animal Lady*. 'Come along, everyone!' he shouts. 'Story time!'

The children settle down among the cushions.

Jan sits down on the chair in front of them and holds up the book. 'Today we're going to read about an animal lady.'

'What does that mean?' Matilda asks.

Jan looks to Josefine for help, but none is forthcoming.

'Well . . . let's see.' He opens the book and begins to read:

Once upon a time there was a lady who knew how to make animals, and her name was Maria Blanker. Maria was very lonely. She had moved to a little island right in the middle of the sea, with a lighthouse that never flashed its bright light. She was living on the island in a little house made of driftwood.

Apparently someone lived in the lighthouse too. There was a name on the mail box: THE GREAT MR ZYLIZYLON. Maria could hear heavy footsteps echoing through the lighthouse every night as someone with big feet stomped up and down the stairs.

Maria wanted to be polite, and had knocked on the door of the lighthouse several times when she first arrived on the island, but she was actually quite pleased that no one opened the door.

Jan stops for a moment; he seems to think he recognizes the name Maria Blanker. But where from?

And the word *Zylizylon* sounds medical. Perhaps it's some kind of medication?

He looks at the drawing. It shows a little cottage with a tall lighthouse in the background. The house is pale grey, like driftwood bleached by the sun. The lighthouse is as slender as a matchstick.

'Don't stop!' shouts Josefine.

So Jan carries on:

The lighthouse never flashed its bright light because the ships didn't need it any more. There were tracks laid out all over the sea these days, so the ships never drifted off course. But there were no tracks near the lighthouse. Maria never saw any ships, and she felt even more lonely.

There were no animals on the island. Maria didn't like making them any more.

The next picture shows the inside of the cottage: a bare room containing only a table and a chair. A skinny woman with spiky hair and a wide mouth is sitting on the chair, the drooping corners of her mouth protruding like black twigs.

Instead Maria grew carrots and potatoes in the back garden. She drank taminal tea and looked for pretty pebbles on the shore. She still felt lonely, but she never knocked on the door of the lighthouse again. She didn't want to meet Mr Zylizylon, because the sound of his heavy footsteps on the stairs grew louder and louder every day.

The third drawing shows the thin, grey figure of the animal lady standing in front of the closed iron door of the lighthouse. The picture is so blurred that it is impossible to make out her face. Is she unhappy, or perhaps afraid?

At night Maria dreamed of all the animals she used to make when she was young and happy. People liked to watch her make them; they used to clap when the animals appeared from inside her clothes.

But the animals had got bigger and bigger, stranger and stranger. Maria had been unable to control them. In the end she had been too frightened to make them any more.

The fourth drawing is dark. The animal lady is sleeping in a narrow bed, like a grey shadow. Above her other shadows crawl and writhe around each other as they emerge from a dark tunnel in the wall.

The atmosphere in the drawing is menacing; Jan turns the page and carries on reading:

Then one day something happened that had never happened be-fore. While Maria was gathering pebbles down on the shore, she suddenly saw a ship on the horizon. It seemed to be coming closer, the waves nudging it nearer to the island. Maria realized it had come off track.

When the ship had almost reached the island, the animal lady saw that it was a ferry full of children. All the children were wearing blue helmets, and they had big cushions attached to their backs and tummies.

'I want a cushion on my tummy!' shouts Mattias.
'What's a horizon?' asks Matilda.
'It's where the earth ends,' Jan says. He turns the book around – this page isn't scary – and shows them the thin line beyond the ferry. He points to it. 'This is what the horizon looks like. Although it's just an illusion really; the earth doesn't end there, it's as round

as a beach ball. You know that, don't you? So the earth never ends, it just carries on until it comes back behind you . . .'

The children stare at him in silence. Jan sees that he has got himself all tied up in knots, so he carries on reading:

Eventually the ferry ran aground on the island. There was a horrible screeching, grating noise as it drifted on to the rocks. The children jumped ashore, but Maria was too scared to show herself. She had gone into her little house, locked the door and made herself a pot of really strong taminal tea. She could hear cheerful cries outside, but she drank her tea and didn't open the door.

This picture shows Maria cowering behind closed curtains; they have a chequered pattern which makes Jan think of the barred windows at the hospital. She is pouring hot tea, steaming and bubbling, into a big cup which is all the colours of the rainbow. But what is taminal tea?

'Hello?' a girl's voice shouted. Cautiously Maria peeped out, but the girl wasn't standing outside her door.
She was standing by the lighthouse.
And the lighthouse door was open.
For the first time since Maria came to the island, the Great Mr Zylizylon had opened the door of his big tower!
'Hello? My name is Amelia . . . is anyone home?'

This time the drawing shows what Maria could see through her window: a little girl in a thin dress standing in front of the black door of the lighthouse. But one thing distinguishes the girl from the other children, Jan notices. She is not wearing a helmet, and there are no cushions attached to her body.

The children are as quiet as mice. The atmosphere in the room is thick with anticipation.

Jan turns the page.

88

Through the window Maria watched as little Amelia walked up the steps to the door of the lighthouse.

'Hello?' she called again.

She took one more step; she was almost inside now.

Then Maria did something without even thinking about it. She raised her hand, closed her eyes, and quickly made a guardian animal.

Jan was expecting the children to ask what a guardian animal is – he doesn't know either – but no one speaks.

Maria could give anyone at all a guardian animal, but unfortunately she never knew what they were going to look like. So when Maria opened her eyes she saw that Amelia was being hugged by something that looked like a big frog. A yellow frog with long, hairy legs.

'Amelia!' shouted the frog. 'I haven't seen you for ages!'

The guardian animal gave Amelia another hug and quickly drew her away from the door.

Maria let out a long breath. She went and opened the door of her little house, just as the sound of heavy footsteps could be heard from inside the lighthouse.

'Come inside!' she shouted, pulling Amelia into her house. The guardian animal remained outside.

Jan turns the page, ready to read on. He scans the first sentence: *They heard a loud roar, and at long last the Great Mr Zylizylon came out of the lighthouse . . .* But before he actually reads it out loud he notices the drawing on the left-hand page, and closes his mouth.

This drawing is clearer than the others, with long, firm pencil strokes. It shows Mr Zylizylon stepping out into the daylight.

Mr Zylizylon is a monster. He is broad and hairy, and he has a leash around his thick neck. It is made of severed human hands. The monster has raised his arms and opened his wide mouth, ready to fall on the guardian animal, which is cowering on the ground in terror.

The children are waiting for Jan to carry on reading.

He opens his mouth. 'Then . . .' He tries to think fast. 'Then Maria the animal lady and her new friend Amelia went down to the ferry and all the children sailed away from the island. And Maria lived happily ever after in peace and quiet.'

He closes the book. 'The end!'

But Josefine straightens up. 'That's not how it ends!' she shouts. 'The monster eats up—'

'That's how it ended today,' Jan breaks in. 'And now it's time we had our fruit.'

The children start to get up, but Josefine looks disappointed. Jan keeps the book tucked firmly under his left arm as he hands out bananas with his right hand; when everyone is eating he slips away to the cloakroom and puts the book in his bag.

He wants to read the ending on his own. He's just borrowing it, he's not stealing it.

Back home that evening he flicks through *The Animal Lady* and looks at the words *Zylizylon* and *taminal*. Then he switches on the computer and looks them up on the internet. They both exist, and they are both drugs. Drugs that are used to suppress anxiety.

Then he thinks about the name Maria Blanker. Where has he heard it before? He gets out Rami's only album, *Rami and August*, and reads through the sleeve notes. He was right. At the bottom, after the usual blurb about which musicians played on the album and who produced it, there is one more line:

WITH SPECIAL THANKS TO MY GRANDMOTHER, KARIN BLANKER.

Suddenly *The Animal Lady* feels like a book he is going to have to read over and over again, until he knows the story by heart. He puts it down in front of him on the kitchen table and stares at the cover. Then he glances over at his box of pens and pencils.

Perhaps he won't just read it? He reaches out and picks up a Faber-Castell. A soft lead pencil. And he begins to fill in the spidery lines in the book, deepening the shadows. It feels so good that he carries on in black ink. Slowly the drawings become clearer, more detailed. The only things Jan doesn't touch are the faces; he decides to leave them looking vague and indistinct.

The work takes up the entire evening. When the ink has dried he can't help himself; he goes and fetches his watercolours and begins to do some careful colouring. The sky above the island becomes pale blue, the sea dark blue; Maria's dress is white and her frog has just a hint of yellow. Mr Zylizylon remains dark grey.

By midnight Jan has finished twelve drawings. He stretches his fingers and straightens his back; he has done a good job. *The Animal Lady* is starting to look like a real picture book.

Gradually he has become totally convinced that it was Alice Rami, sitting in her room behind the concrete wall, who dreamed up the story of Maria and the Great Mr Zylizylon. She might not want this to happen, but he is going to help her to finish it.

Lynx

The bunker was ready now, but there were still a few more things to sort out.

By the middle of October Jan had been at the nursery for almost four months, and had got to know the staff in both Lynx and Brown Bear. They were all women, and one of them was Sigrid Jansson. He knew that Sigrid was a cheerful and spontaneous classroom assistant who sometimes found it a little difficult to keep a close eye on the children. Sigrid was kind and pleasant, but her thoughts were often elsewhere. Whenever Jan spoke to her in the playground she was ready to chat, but rarely looked at the children.

At the weekly planning meeting, after the menus and cleaning rota had been discussed, he put up his hand and suggested a little excursion into the forest, a joint outing for the children in Lynx and Brown Bear. He also suggested a date: the Wednesday of the following week, when he knew that he and Sigrid would be on duty. He looked at her encouragingly across the table. 'Shall we sort it out, Sigrid – you and me? Make packed lunches and take the children out for a couple of hours?'

She smiled at him. 'Absolutely – brilliant idea!'

He had counted on the fact that she would react positively.

And Nina, who was in charge of the nursery, nodded her agreement. 'We need to make sure they're all wrapped up warmly,' she said, writing the excursion into the timetable.

Jan smiled in turn. The bunker was now clean and well

equipped; almost everything was prepared. He just needed to sort out the food.

But the next day he saw William's mother arrive at Brown Bear to pick up her son, and something trembled inside him. She didn't look at Jan, but he thought she seemed stressed and tired. Problems at work?

The weariness made her seem more human, and for the first time this didn't feel like just a mind game any more. For the first time, Jan hesitated. He would be risking his job at Lynx – but then again, it wasn't much of a job to lose. It was a temporary post, and he had less than two months left.

What was worse was the thought that he could harm a little boy, and he spent a lot of time brooding over that in the days leading up to the excursion. He made the final preparations up in the forest: he left the metal door of the bunker and the iron gate in the ravine wide open, and put up arrows made of red material, like a kind of paperchase along the hillside.

The bunker was going to feel like a hotel room – clean and cosy – and full of food and drink and toys. And lots and lots of sweets.

13

'Jan! Jan!' the children shout happily. 'Over here, Jan!'

Jan really likes the children at the Dell, and they have accepted him completely. Everything feels fine.

His first late shift starts at one o'clock on Wednesday afternoon and ends at ten in the evening. It almost feels like a practice for the night shift, when he will be alone with the three children who are staying at the pre-school all the time at the moment: Leo, Matilda and Mira.

Andreas and the children are out in the playground when Jan arrives. The temperature is only six degrees today, and Andreas has a thick blue woollen scarf wound around his neck.

'Hi there!' He is standing there with his hands pushed down into the pockets of his jeans, steady as a rock in the autumn wind.

'Everything OK?' says Jan.

'Absolutely fine,' says Andreas. 'We've been outside most of the time.'

They let the children play for another fifteen minutes or so, then they go inside where it's warm and hand out the lunch boxes which have been prepared over in the hospital kitchen.

Andreas stays on for an extra half-hour, but Jan doesn't want to ask why. Perhaps he's following orders from Marie-Louise; has she asked him to keep an eye on Jan?

Eventually Andreas leaves; the sun is low on the horizon. Jan is now solely responsible for the Dell.

But everything will be fine; he will take good care of the children.

First of all he gathers them together in the playroom. 'What would you like to do?'

'Play!' says Mira.

'And what would you like to play?'

'Safari parks!' Matilda shouts, pointing. 'Like over there!'

Jan doesn't understand until he grasps that she is pointing at the window and the fence outside. 'That's not a safari park,' he says.

'Oh yes it is!' Matilda says firmly.

She doesn't seem to connect her visits to the hospital with the high fence, and Jan decides not to tell her that there is a link.

The most important duties during the evening shift are to serve the evening meal, make sure the children brush their teeth, and put them to bed. So Jan makes cheese sandwiches for Matilda, Leo and Mira, gets out their pyjamas and asks them to get changed. It is pitch dark outside by now; the time is half past seven. All three children are quite tired, and they scramble into their little beds in the snuggle room without protest. He reads them a bedtime story about a hippopotamus who changes places with an ordinary man and finds himself looking after the man's little girl, then Jan gets to his feet. 'Goodnight everyone . . . See you in the morning.'

He can hear suppressed giggles once he has switched off the light. He waits for a moment, wondering whether to say something, but soon everything goes quiet.

Another evening duty is to air the building, so at eight o'clock he gently closes the door of the children's bedroom and opens the other windows wide, letting the cold evening air rush in.

Jan can hear music coming from outside, but it is not the thump of a disco beat from some party – rather the gentle, slightly melancholy sound of an old Swedish pop classic. It is coming through the window at the back of the pre-school, and when he looks out he can see a glowing dot in the shadows down below St Patricia's. The dot is moving up and down – someone is standing outside the hospital, smoking and listening to the radio.

The hospital is not full of bellowing lunatics, Dr Högsmed had said. *The patients are often calm and completely capable of inter-action.*

Is the smoker a patient or a nurse? Jan can't tell in the darkness.

He closes the windows. What can he do now? He goes into the playroom to have a look through the book boxes. Josefine had taken *The Animal Lady* from the middle of the box on the left; Jan kneels down beside it.

The Animal Lady has provided him with a task. This morning he completed the drawings on three more pages. When it is finished he will put it back in the box – but he wonders if there are any more handmade books in there.

Slowly he goes through each box, past *Pippi Longstocking* and *Grimms' Fairy Tales*. Right at the back he finds more thin books that look handmade; there is no author's name on them. Jan pulls out three and reads the titles: *The Princess with a Hundred Hands*, *The Witch Who Was Poorly* and *Viveca's House of Stone*.

He slowly turns the pages in each book, one by one, and sees that these too are handwritten, illustrated here and there with pencil sketches. Just like *The Animal Lady*, all of them seem to be sad tales about lonely people. *The Princess with a Hundred Hands* is about Princess Blanka, whose palace has sunk down into a bog. Blanka has managed to reach safety in one of the towers, but she has no control over anything except the hands of other people; she has to get them to do things for her.

The main character in *The Witch Who Was Poorly* is a sorceress sitting in her cottage deep in the forest, no longer able to cast her spells.

And the third book is about an old woman who wakes up alone in a big, dusty house, with no memory of how she got there.

Jan closes the books and puts them in his bag.

An hour later Marie-Louise arrives.

'Good evening, Jan!' She is wearing a scarf and a woolly hat. Her cheeks are glowing red. 'I had to dig out my winter hat! It gets really cold once the sun has gone down.'

She has a small rucksack with her, and in the staffroom she takes out her knitting and a book entitled *Develop Your Creativity*. She smiles at Jan. 'OK, I'll take over now. You can go home and get some sleep.'

When she pulls a black-velvet eye mask out of the rucksack, Jan asks, 'Are you going to sleep here?'

'Oh yes,' Marie-Louise says quickly. 'Of course you can sleep when you're on the night shift; that's fine . . . but you're not allowed to wear earplugs. You have to be able to wake up if anything happens.'

Jan is silent, wondering what could possibly happen, but she goes on: 'Sometimes the children wake up and need a bit of reassurance, if they've had a bad dream, for example. Never anything more serious – and even that doesn't happen very often.'

'OK . . . So how long do they usually sleep?'

'Some of them can be real sleepy-heads, but I usually get up at half past six when I'm on the night shift, and I wake them half an hour later. They have their breakfast, and the shift is over.'

Jan leaves Marie-Louise and the sleeping children. He goes out into the street and glances to the right. St Patricia's is just over there, like a big dark aircraft hangar behind the wall.

All of a sudden he stops; someone is standing waiting ahead of him in the street, a tall, dark figure – a man in a black coat, motionless under one of the oak trees lining the pavement. The light from the street lamps barely reaches him, and Jan can see only an indistinct, pale face.

They stare at one another. Then the man moves at last, waving some kind of thin rope he is holding in his hand.

Jan realizes it is a dog lead, and almost immediately the dog itself comes trotting out from behind the oak tree. A white poodle. The man bends down, takes out a little plastic bag and carefully scoops up whatever the poodle has left on the ground. Then they continue with their walk.

Jan slowly breathes out. *Get a grip*, he thinks as he sets off. There are no lunatics out here on the streets, just dog owners.

The buses into the town centre don't run at this late hour, but the night air is fresh and he enjoys the walk. It's only fifteen minutes to his apartment block; when he gets there, most of the windows are in darkness.

My home, he thinks, but of course it doesn't really feel like home. That will take a long time.

Then he notices someone smoking a pipe on the balcony two floors below his own. It's the white-haired man from the laundry room, the one who was (possibly) carrying a scruffy laundry bag from St Psycho's. The man sucks on his pipe and blows big white clouds into the darkness; he seems lost in thought.

Jan stops and raises his hand. 'Evening.'

The man nods and coughs out another cloud of smoke. 'Evening.'

Jan heads inside; he pauses on the second floor and sees that the sign on the right-hand door says V. LEGÉN.

Aha. So at least he knows the name of the pipe-smoker now, and which apartment he lives in.

He carries on up the stairs to the darkness of his own apartment, but he doesn't stay in. He quickly drops off his rucksack containing the picture books, changes his jacket and goes out again.

He's just going down to Bill's Bar for a little while. Perhaps he'll try to become a regular there – that's something Jan has never been before, not anywhere.

14

'Cheers!' shouts Lilian, raising her glass.

'Cheers,' Jan says quietly.

'Cheers,' says Hanna, even more quietly.

Lilian drinks the most, knocking back half the contents of her glass. 'Do you like Bill's Bar, Jan?' she asks.

'I do, yes.'

'What do you like about it?'

'Er . . . the music.'

They are talking loudly, almost the way they do to the children at the pre-school, in order to be heard above the house band. The Bohemos are made up of four youngish men in scruffy leather jackets, standing on a small raised stage. The singer's hair is pulled back in a blond ponytail, and he delivers rock songs in a hoarse baritone. The stage is cramped, but the band manage a few simple dance steps with their guitars from time to time without bumping into one another. Even though the people in the bar chat away through most of the music, they are still generous enough to give the Bohemos a brief round of applause when each number comes to an end.

Jan prefers Rami's whispering songs about loneliness and longing, but he still claps politely.

He raises his glass. The beer he is drinking tonight is stronger, and the alcohol has gone straight to his head like a rocket. His mind is floating free.

Right now it would be brilliant to be a regular here, but Jan doesn't have much of a talent for finding friends in pubs. He realized this earlier in the evening when he pushed his way to the bar without making eye contact with a single person. He finds it difficult to relax in the company of adults; it's much easier with children.

At least he got a friendly nod from the bartender when he went up for his second beer, and now his colleagues from work have joined him at his table. They just turned up and sat down: Hanna with her blue eyes, Lilian with her red hair.

Lilian empties her third glass and leans across the table. 'Did you come here on your own, Jan?'

He thinks about quoting Rami – *I am a lost soul in a desert of ice* – but instead he merely smiles. Mysteriously, he hopes.

'Oops, empty again.' Lilian gestures in the direction of the bar. 'Keep my seat, I'm just going for another.'

Jan and Hanna's glasses are still half full, but when Lilian comes back she has bought them another drink too. 'The next round's on you!'

Jan doesn't want to drink another drop, but he accepts the glass anyway. They carry on chatting, first of all about the Bohemos; according to Lilian they are definitely the best band in town, even if hardly anyone outside Bill's Bar has heard of them.

'They only play at Bill's as a hobby,' she says. 'They've got other jobs.'

'They work up at St Patricia's,' says Hanna. 'Well, a couple of them do.'

Lilian glances at her sharply, as if she has said too much.

'Do they?' Jan looks over at the band with renewed interest. 'At St Patricia's?'

'We don't know them,' Lilian says.

Jan is feeling good now; he buys the next round. And then Hanna buys three more bottles. The beer is flowing! That's OK by Jan. After all, he can have a lie-in tomorrow, before his night shift at the Dell.

But Lilian is drinking more than Jan and Hanna put together, and her head is sagging lower and lower. Suddenly she straightens up. 'Jan . . . lovely Jan,' she says, blinking tiredly. 'Ask me if I believe in love.'

'Sorry?'

Lilian shakes her head slowly. 'I don't believe in love.' She holds up three fingers. 'These are the three men I've had in my life . . . The first one took two years from me, the second took four, and I married the third one. And that ended last year. So now I've only got my brother. Just one brother. I used to have two, but now I've only got one . . .'

Hanna leans over. 'Shall we go home, Lilian?'

Lilian doesn't answer; she empties her glass, puts it down and sighs. 'OK . . . Let's go home,' she says.

Jan sees that Bill's Bar is closing up. The music has stopped, the Bohemos have left the stage, tables are emptying around them.

'Fine,' he says, nodding. 'Let's go.'

He keeps on nodding; he realizes he's actually drunk for the very first time, and his feet seem to have a mind of their own when he stands up. '*I am a lost soul in a desert of ice*,' he says, but neither Hanna nor Lilian seems to hear.

The air feels like the inside of a fridge when they get out on to the street, and the alcohol hits Jan over the head like a hammer. He staggers and looks at his watch; it's almost two o'clock. Late, very late. But he's free until nine o'clock tomorrow evening. He can sleep all day.

Lilian looks around and spots a taxi across the street. 'Mine!' she screeches. 'See you!' She makes her way unsteadily over the road, gets into the taxi and is gone.

Hanna is still standing there. 'Lilian lives quite a long way out . . . Where do you live, Jan?'

'Pretty close.' He raises his left arm and waves it vaguely towards the east. 'Over there, just across the railway line.'

'OK, let's head over there,' she says.

'What, back to mine?'

She shakes her head. 'No, just as far as the railway line. I'll walk with you. I'm heading in the same direction.'

'Great,' says Jan, trying to sober up.

They set off along the pavement, side by side, and after fifteen minutes they reach the tracks running past the town centre.

'This is where we go our separate ways.'

The sky above them is black, the railway line is empty.

Jan lowers his gaze and looks at Hanna. Her shining blue eyes, her blonde hair, her cool face. She is beautiful, but he knows he isn't interested in her – not in that way. But he carries on staring in silence.

'What's the worst thing you've ever done?' Hanna is asking him.

'The worst thing?' Jan looks at her. He definitely knows the answer. 'I'll have to think about that . . . so what's the worst thing *you've* ever done?'

'Lots of things,' says Hanna.

'Name one.'

She shrugs her shoulders. 'Being unfaithful, letting friends down . . . The usual stuff, I suppose.'

'Oh?'

'When I was twenty I slept with my best friend's fiancé, in a boathouse. She found out and broke off the engagement . . . but we're friends again now. Kind of.'

'Kind of?' says Jan.

'We exchange Christmas cards.' She sighs. 'But that's my problem.'

'What is?'

'I let people down.' She blinks and looks at him. 'I expect to be let down, so I get in first.'

'OK . . . Thanks for the warning!'

He is smiling, but Hanna isn't. Silence falls once more. Hanna is beautiful, but all Jan wants to do now is sleep. He turns and looks over at the apartment block where he lives. No doubt they're all fast asleep now, all those good people. Like the animals, like the trees . . .

'So what about you, Jan?'

'What?'

Hanna is staring at him. 'Do you remember the worst thing you've ever done?'

'Maybe . . .'

What did he actually do, that time at Lynx? Jan tries to remember. But the buildings are tilting around him and he seems to be feeling even more drunk, and suddenly the words just come out of their own accord: 'I once did something stupid . . . at a nursery in my home town. In Nordbro.'

'What did you do? What did you do, Jan?'

'I was looking after the children, it was my first temporary post, and I made a mess of things . . . I lost a child.' Jan stares down at the ground, smoothing out an uneven patch of grass with his foot.

'You lost a child?'

'Yes. I took a group of children out into the forest, along with a colleague . . . the group was much too big, really. And when we set off home we didn't have the right number of children with us. One boy got left behind in the forest, and it was . . . it was partly my fault.'

'When was this?'

Jan keeps his eyes fixed on the ground. *Lynx.* He remembers everything, of course. He remembers the air in the forest, just as cold as it is tonight.

'Nine years ago . . . almost exactly nine years ago. It was in October.'

Don't say any more, he thinks, but Hanna's blue eyes are gazing intently at him.

'What was the name of the boy?'

Jan hesitates. 'I don't remember,' he says eventually.

'So what happened in the end?' Hanna asks.

'He was . . . everything was fine. In the end.' Jan sighs and adds, 'But the parents were absolutely devastated, they just broke down completely.'

Hanna shrugs. 'Idiots . . . I mean, it was their kid who ran off. They hand over their precious little ones and then expect us to take all the responsibility. Don't you agree?'

Jan nods, but he is already regretting his confession. Why did he tell her about Lynx? He's pissed, he's a drunk. 'You won't say anything about this, will you?'

Hanna is still looking at him. 'To one of the big bosses, you mean?'

'Yes, or to . . .'

'I won't say anything, Jan. It's cool.' She yawns and looks at her watch. 'I need to go home . . . I've got to get up early for work in the morning.' She stands on tiptoe and gives him a quick hug. A little bit of warmth in the night. 'Sleep well, Jan. See you at work.'

'OK.'

He watches her set off towards the town centre, like a blonde dream figure. Alice Rami is also like a dream to Jan – she is just as vague and indistinct as a poem or a song. All girls are like dreams . . .

Why did he tell Hanna about Lynx?

Jan's head slowly begins to clear, and with clarity comes regret.

He shakes his head and unlocks the door. Time to sleep, then work. He's behaved like an obedient dog for two weeks, and now it's time for his reward. A night shift all by himself up at the Dell.

15

'This is the emergency telephone,' says Marie-Louise, pointing to a grey phone on the wall in the staffroom, next to Jan's locker. 'All you have to do is pick up the receiver and wait, and it rings through automatically.'

'Where to?'

'To the main security office by the entrance to the hospital. They're on duty around the clock over there, so someone will always answer.' She gives Jan a slightly embarrassed smile and adds, 'Sometimes it's nice to know that there's somebody not too far away at night . . . although I'm sure you'll be fine here, won't you?'

'Absolutely.' Jan nods and straightens his back so that he looks alert.

Marie-Louise runs her hand slightly nervously over her throat. 'Obviously you must ring them if anything happens, but we've never needed to do that up to now . . .' She quickly turns away from the emergency phone, as if she would prefer to forget about it. 'So, any questions?'

Jan shakes his head. Marie-Louise has gone through all the routine procedures twice, so he is well prepared. And stone-cold sober. He felt quite shaky when he woke up this morning after the night in Bill's Bar, but he's fine now.

It is the Friday evening of his second week at the Dell, and his first night shift – his first night shift ever, in fact. He is on duty from nine thirty in the evening until eight o'clock on Saturday morning, but he has been told that he doesn't need to stay awake all the time. There is a sofa bed in the staffroom and he can sleep all night, as long as he wakes up if one of the three children needs help or reassurance.

'Everything seems very clear,' he says.

'Good,' says Marie-Louise. 'Did you bring your own bedlinen?'

'I did. And my toothbrush.'

Marie-Louise smiles and seems satisfied. She has already put on her coat and her woolly hat, and she opens the door to face the darkness outside. 'In that case I will wish you a peaceful night, Jan. Hanna will come and take over in the morning, and I'll see you tomorrow evening. Goodnight!'

The door closes. Jan locks up behind her and looks at the clock. Twenty past ten. There isn't a sound inside the Dell.

He goes into the staffroom and makes up the narrow sofa bed, then he has a sandwich in the kitchen before brushing his teeth.

But these are just the routine tasks he's *supposed* to carry out; the problem is that he doesn't feel the least bit tired. What else can he do? What does he *want* to do?

Check on the children.

Quietly he pushes open the door of the children's bedroom, and listens to their soft breathing in the darkness. Matilda, Leo and Mira are fast asleep in their beds. Even Leo is lying completely still. According to Marie-Louise, none of the children normally wakes until it's time to get them up in the morning.

Normally. But when is anything ever *normal*?

Jan leaves the door ajar and goes into the dining room at the back of the school. He stands by the window looking out, without switching on the light.

St Psycho's is also virtually in darkness. Floodlights illuminate the fence, but the complex beyond is full of shadows. Grey shadows on the grass, black shadows beneath the fir trees. No one is outside smoking tonight.

The hospital itself looms up some forty or fifty metres away, and there are lights in only four of the windows up at the top of the building. It looks as if the light is coming from white strip-lighting in a corridor – just like the ones down in the basement.

The basement. The way into the hospital – although it isn't really, because there are locked doors down there too. And the door to the basement is also locked, of course.

Jan thinks about that door for a while. And the underground corridor, and the sally port. Then he goes back into the kitchen and opens one of the drawers. There they are, the magnetic cards. He picks one of them up.

Can he remember the code? Of course he can, it was Marie-Louise's birthday. He has delivered or collected a child on a dozen occasions and keyed in the code at least twenty times since he arrived at the pre-school. He taps it in again and swipes the card, and the lock clicks.

Open. So it works at night too.

The steep staircase looks like a precipice, or the mouth of a cave leading straight down into the underworld. It is dark down there, but not pitch black; a faint light is just visible along the corridor.

The light from the lift up to the hospital.

Jan hesitates and looks around furtively. The cloakroom is empty, of course – he locked the outside door when Marie-Louise went home.

He leans forward, reaches out and presses the switch. The strip-lights flicker and hum into life down below in the corridor. He can see the steep staircase clearly now, with the carpet leading towards the lift like a welcome mat. He can't see the actual door of the lift, but if he just went down four or five steps he would probably be able to see it in the distance.

Rami, are you there?

He moves down two steps in silence, then stops with his hand clutching the rail. He listens. There isn't a sound to be heard, neither in front of him nor behind him.

He moves down another step, then three more in quick succession. He can see the door of the lift now. The light in the little window tells him that the lift is down in the basement. It is standing there waiting for him.

One more step.

But he is finding it more and more difficult to move his legs. There is a mental barrier. He is thinking too much about the children, about Leo, Matilda and Mira; they are fast asleep in their bedroom and he is responsible for them, just as he was responsible for William nine years ago.

He can't do this. He glances at the sally port leading to the hospital one last time, then turns and goes back up the stairs.

When he reaches the cloakroom he closes the door behind him and checks to make sure it's locked. Then he turns off all the lights except for the nightlight in the hallway, and goes to bed. He shuts his eyes in the darkness and lets out a long breath.

But it is difficult to get to sleep. Impossible. Now it's dark it seems to Jan that the pre-school is full of sounds. Clicking, tip-toeing, whispering . . . Someone is lying there in the hospital just yearning, someone who wants him to come.

Alice Rami.

Jan closes his eyes, but she is gazing at him, her eyes glowing. *Come here, Jan. I want to look at you.*

He's not aware that he has fallen asleep until the alarm clock starts buzzing beside him. The display shows 06.15. It is still dark outside, but it is morning. He sees bare walls around him and realizes that he is in the little staffroom at the Dell.

Almost time to wake Leo, Matilda and Mira.

His first night shift is over, but there are many more to come, and as he gets out of bed he suddenly gets an idea about how he can go down into the basement at night without worrying about the children.

Baby monitors.

Lynx

It was Wednesday afternoon, and time for the outing from the nursery. When Jan and Sigrid set off with seventeen children, the time was twenty-five past one. That meant there were at least four hours left until sunset, which left a good safety margin. The group would be back by four at the latest.

The temperature outdoors was eleven degrees today, cloudy but with no wind. As they gathered outside the gate Jan noted that Sigrid had nine children from Brown Bear with her. Little William was one of the group; he was wearing a warm, dark-blue jacket with white reflective stripes, and a bright-yellow woolly hat.

Jan had brought eight children from Lynx. The whole group was made up of nine boys and eight girls, and it was quite difficult to count them when they were all together; as usual the children got excited as soon as they left the playground, and once they moved off the path and in among the trees they became even noisier. They kept on surging back and forth between the trees, screaming and jumping and leaping on top of one another. It felt as if they might just race off in all directions at any moment.

The children should have been walking in a crocodile, holding hands, but Sigrid was busy tapping away on her mobile phone, and didn't seem to notice how unruly the group was. Jan could see that she had received a text message with lots of exclamation marks, from a friend perhaps.

He made no real attempt to impose any order on the children.

He simply shouted, 'Come along, everyone!' and increased his pace.

The children kept up with him, and in less than quarter of an hour they had climbed the slope and were deep in the forest. The fir trees were more tightly packed here, and the path was narrowing.

'Do you know where we are, Jan?' Sigrid had switched off her phone and seemed to be looking around for the first time.

'Of course.' He smiled at her. 'I know my way around here pretty well. If we carry on we'll come to a clearing soon, and we can stop for our snack.'

And he was quite right; the fir trees gave way to a large, circular glade. Once they were back in the light, the children calmed down.

Their picnic consisted of cinnamon buns and strawberry juice. The children were quite tired by this stage, and it was comparatively easy to get them to sit down and eat together. But once the food was gone they all got a fresh burst of energy, racing around in the undergrowth, pushing and shoving and shouting at one another.

Jan looked at his watch: twenty past three. He caught Sigrid's eye and felt his heart pounding faster as he asked her, seemingly in all innocence, 'Shall we play for a little while longer before we head back?'

Sigrid was still full of life. 'Absolutely!'

'Well, why don't we split up?' suggested Jan. 'You play with the girls and I'll take the boys.'

She nodded, and Jan raised his voice and shouted to the boys, 'Playtime!'

He gathered them around him – William Halevi and the other eight.

'Quick march!' Like a sergeant in the marines he took command and marched the boys along the path, deeper into the forest.

16

They are small, made of white plastic, and they look just like cheap walkie-talkies. Electronic baby monitors. There are lots of different kinds, but the one Jan has chosen is called Angelguards. *Guardian angels.*

'This model is actually our top seller,' says the assistant. 'It's incredibly reliable, the nine-volt battery lasts for several weeks, and it transmits using a completely different frequency from mobile phones and radios. And it has an integral nightlight, which can also be used as a torch.'

'Excellent,' says Jan.

He is standing in a shop full of things for children: clothes, books and buggies. They sell every imaginable kind of protection and barrier and lock and alarm for little ones – ergonomic spoons and bibs that light up and little tubes to suck the snot out of a baby's nose – but Jan is interested in only one thing: the baby monitors.

'What's the range?'

'At least three hundred metres, in any conditions.'

'Does it work through metal and concrete as well?'

'Absolutely . . . Walls are no problem.'

Jan buys the Angelguards. The young sales assistant probably thinks he is yet another anxious father, because he winks at him and says, 'These angels are set to transmit one way only, so you can hear the child, but the child can't hear you.'

'Brilliant,' says Jan.

'Is it a boy or a girl?'

'Oh, both . . . and they're different ages,' Jan answers quickly. 'I've got three.'

'And they're restless sleepers?'

'No, no, things are usually pretty quiet, but, I mean, you want to make sure they're safe, don't you?'

'Of course.' The assistant places the Angels in a bag. 'That will be three hundred and forty-nine kronor, please.'

In the evening Jan cycles up to the Dell with the Angels in his rucksack. He wonders whether to show them to Marie-Louise – perhaps demonstrating them with the same enthusiasm as the shop assistant – but she would probably dislike them just as much as a couple of TV screens. So when he arrives at exactly half past nine he says nothing; he simply puts his rucksack in his locker and takes over from Marie-Louise.

Matilda, Leo and Mira are fast asleep tonight too, and Marie-Louise doesn't stay as long this time. Perhaps she is beginning to trust Jan.

'Did you feel tired today?' she asks.

'A bit drowsy.'

'But you slept well here last night?'

'Absolutely. So did the children.'

Marie-Louise goes off to catch her bus at quarter to ten, and Jan locks the door behind her.

The door leading to the basement is also locked, he notices.

Now he is alone again, alone with the children.

A light is showing in exactly the same four windows up on the top floor of St Patricia's as yesterday; he is certain it's a corridor up there with lights that are left on all night, just like the nightlight at the pre-school.

He stops gazing up at the hospital; he has a lot to do tonight. He tidies up the boots in the cloakroom, he listens to the sports programme on the radio (keeping the volume very low, so as not to wake the children), then he has a sandwich and a cup of tea in the kitchen for his supper.

But all the time he is thinking about today's major purchase: the Angels.

Shortly after eleven o'clock he takes them out of his rucksack and opens the door to the children's bedroom, which is in darkness. The children lie motionless beneath their small duvets, and Jan moves silently into the room. He stands still in the darkness for a minute or so, listening to the faint sound of their breathing. A reassuring sound.

Then he switches on one of the Angels, the transmitter, and hangs it on a hook on the wall between Leo's and Matilda's beds.

Leo moves slightly and mumbles something to himself, but doesn't wake up.

Jan creeps out of the room and switches on the other Angel, the receiver. The speaker on the front is small and round, and completely silent. When Jan holds it up to his ear, he hears nothing but a faint rushing sound. It rises and falls, like little waves gently lapping against the curve of a sandy shore. Presumably it is the children's breathing he can hear – he hopes so.

With the Angel attached to his belt he walks around the building, making up his bed and brushing his teeth.

Of course he could always try to convince himself that he has bought the Angels to help him monitor the children when he is asleep, but at quarter to twelve he takes a key card out of the drawer in the kitchen and opens the door leading to the basement.

He switches on the light, looks down the stairs and suddenly remembers a few lines by Rami:

> *Waiting, longing,*
> *the sound of a bell ringing,*
> *a glance, a word, a dance,*
> *you are there somewhere . . .*

Jan takes one step down the stairs. He's just going to go down and have a little look. He listens. Silence – even the Angel's little speaker is silent.

Calmly and cautiously he walks down the stairs and into the corridor.

No cameras here. Marie-Louise said there were no CCTV cameras down in the basement. He believes her. He is invisible. Jan's shadow glides along beneath the strip-lights, but he cannot be seen.

The brightly coloured animal pictures are still on the wall, but the one with the mice is slightly crooked. He quickly straightens it.

The lift is waiting, as if it has been summoned just for him. He stands in front of the door, thinking. What if he were to step inside, press the button and let the lift carry him upwards, straight up to the corridors of St Psycho's?

Do they have a camera by the door of the lift up there? Maybe, maybe not. If not, he could just go up and step out, see what happens. Pretend he got lost. Or that he's one of the patients . . .

But Jan doesn't open the door. He listens to the Angel, even turns up the volume, but it remains silent. He wants to whisper a faint 'Hello?' into the speaker.

You can hear the child, the assistant said, *but the child can't hear you.*

You can do whatever you like, thinks Jan. He walks past the lift and carries on along the corridor. He turns the corner and is faced by the second steel door, the wider one. The one that leads to the safe room.

He reaches out his hand, presses down the heavy handle – and it gives a bit. He grabs hold of it with both hands and pushes harder. Something clicks, and the heavy door is ajar: he can move it. It is stiff, but slowly it swings wide open.

The safe room inside is in total darkness. No windows.

Jan holds one arm out in front of him, cautiously feeling his way along the cold concrete wall. He takes one step into the room, still feeling his way, and eventually he finds the light switch. The strip-light on the ceiling flickers into life. He is standing at one end of a long, rectangular room, like a wide corridor – it extends some twelve or fifteen metres. This is where the patients will sit, if war comes.

Jan takes another step forward. But the next second a loud voice bounces off the bare walls.

'*Mummy?*'

Jan gives a start. The metallic cry is coming from the speaker attached to his belt; it sounds like a little girl's voice. Matilda, perhaps.

He holds his breath and listens. He doesn't hear any more cries, just a soft scraping noise, but if the children are waking up he can't stay down here.

His nerves are getting the better of him, but Jan ventures one last curious look at the safe room. It is almost completely empty, with a blue fitted carpet and white walls, but there is a mattress on the floor, along with a few pillows.

And on the left at the far end of the room Jan notices another wide door. It is also made of steel, and it is closed. Is it unlocked? He can't tell.

Who is waiting on the other side? Alice Rami? Ivan Rössel, the serial killer?

'*Mummy?*' Matilda is calling out again, and Jan turns around. He quickly closes the door of the safe room and hurries back along the corridor. Right now it feels as if coming down here at all was absolutely the wrong thing to do.

Two minutes later he locks the door leading to St Patricia's basement and goes straight to the children's room.

Jan opens the door and listens in the darkness. All is silent once more. He tiptoes into the middle of the room and stands there for several minutes, but none of the children move. They are fast asleep. He listens to their breathing and tries to calm himself, tries to slow his own breathing to match theirs, but it is difficult.

He ought to follow their example and get some sleep. It is ten past twelve.

He *will* go to sleep. Otherwise the risk is that he will stay up later and later, turning the day upside down.

But he doesn't really want to get into bed or to go to sleep. He is thinking.

It's a mind game, which is exactly how that business with William in the forest started. Jan is thinking about how he can get into St Psycho's, without anyone seeing him and without the children being affected.

17

The hour is late and as sluggish as treacle in Bill's Bar, but his recent shift pattern at the pre-school has turned Jan into a night owl. On his mornings off he has slept until ten, then in the evenings stayed up until well after midnight. A new lifestyle for him, but in spite of the fact that he hasn't touched a drop of alcohol, he is always tired.

The Bohemos have just finished playing after a whole hour of jamming, and Jan's glass of alcohol-free beer is almost empty. At the next table two young men are energetically discussing self-defence.

'What about a knife, then?' one of them says.

'A knife is a whole different ball game,' says the other. 'You can't defend yourself if he's got a knife.'

'No, I know that, but . . .'

'I mean, if you come at him with your fists he'll just slash them to bits.'

The first man laughs. 'In that case I'd better make sure I've got a sword!'

Jan doesn't attempt to join in the conversation, he just finishes his beer. There is no sign of anyone he knows in here tonight; no Lilian or Hanna. No one. He has no friends, and he is ready to go home alone. And sleep. Alone.

Suddenly a shadow falls over his table. 'Hi.'

Jan looks up. A man about his own age has stopped opposite him. A total stranger with black eyebrows and a blond ponytail.

No, come to think of it, Jan recognizes him – he's one of the Bohemos. The lead singer. He's taken off the leather jacket he always wears on stage, and is now dressed in a white cotton sweater with a towel looped around his neck. After a long evening under the spotlights both are drenched in sweat.

'How's things?' he says.

Jan doesn't quite know what to say, but opens his mouth anyway. 'Fine.'

The singer sits down at the table. His voice is slightly hoarse after the gig, but it is warm and friendly. He wipes his forehead with one end of the towel. 'We don't know each other,' he says. 'I know that . . . but it's cool.'

'Absolutely,' Jan answers uncertainly.

'But I've seen you,' the singer goes on. 'Have you seen me?'

'No . . . what exactly do you mean?'

'I've seen you through the fence, when I'm doing my other job. You've started cycling to the pre-school now, haven't you?'

Jan puts down his glass; he is slowly beginning to understand, and automatically lowers his voice. 'So you work at St . . . at the hospital?'

The man nods. 'Night security.'

'Sorry?'

'I work nights in the security department.'

Jan feels a shudder down his spine, and his pulse begins to race. He thinks about the underground corridor and the safe room, and suspects that he has been filmed down there. Filmed, or observed. He is waiting for a posse of guards to rush out and hurl him to the ground, grab hold of his arms, search him, interrogate him . . .

But the singer from the Bohemos is still sitting there smiling, apparently unconcerned. 'I know your name is Jan,' he says. 'Jan Hauger.'

Jan nods. 'And what's your name?'

'Rettig . . . Lars Rettig.'

'Right. A bit of a coincidence, meeting up like this.'

Rettig shakes his head. 'I know who you are. I wanted to meet you.'

'Why?'

'Because we need help.'

'With what?'

'To help those who are lost.'

'Lost?'

'The patients in St Psycho's . . . Would you like to help them feel better?'

Jan doesn't say anything. He shouldn't really be sitting here talking to a hospital security guard about their place of work – what happened to the confidentiality agreement? But he has begun to relax. Lars Rettig doesn't seem to be after him.

'Maybe,' Jan says. 'But what's it all about?'

Rettig doesn't say anything for a few seconds, as if he were planning a little speech. But then he looks around, leans forward and lowers his voice. 'It's about all the things we're not allowed to do. We're sick and tired of it.'

'Who's *we*?'

But Rettig gets to his feet without answering the question. 'We can talk more another time. I'll be in touch.' He nods encouragingly, and adds, 'You'll help us, Jan, I just know it. I can see it in your eyes.'

'What can you see?'

Rettig shoots him another smile. 'That you are ready to protect the weak.'

18

All the children are walking around clutching animals. It is cuddly-toy day at the Dell, and those who don't have a toy of their own are allowed to borrow one out of the basket. That includes the staff. So there are teddy bears and tigers and giraffes with wobbly legs in every room. Mira is carrying around a red and white striped snake, and Josefine has a pink elk.

Guardian animals, Jan thinks.

He has chosen a golden-yellow lynx. He found it in the basket, and when everyone else had taken what they wanted, he picked it up. It's quite a shabby lynx, but at least it doesn't smell.

'What's its name?' asks Matilda.

'This is . . . Lofty the Lynx, and he comes from the forest . . . a forest far, far away from here.'

'So why isn't he there any more?' Matilda wants to know.

'Because . . . he likes the children here at the Dell,' says Jan. 'He wants to see where you live . . . He wants to play with you.'

Leo is holding on to a one-eyed cat; he is clutching it so tightly that its body has become elongated and dented.

'What's the name of your animal, Leo?'

'Freddie.'

'And what kind of animal is it?'

'Don't know . . . but look!' He holds out his small clenched fist, and opens it.

On his palm Jan sees the cat's other eye: Leo has plucked it out.

Jan looks into Leo's face and wonders whether it is innocence or unhappiness he sees there. Jan doesn't know. He only knows that in some parts of the world it is not cuddly toys that children carry around, but rifles and machine guns.

How can he help the children? How can he help just one child, like Leo?

You are ready to protect the weak, the singer from the Bohemos had said. That may well be true, but there isn't much Jan can do.

Several of the children will be visiting the hospital this Monday too. Jan has begun to learn how the children react to these interruptions to their normal daily routine. Some of them, like Mira and Matilda, are happy to be seeing their parent, and get quite giggly as their little legs scamper down the stairs to the basement. Others, like Fanny and Mattias, remain calm as they make their way to the lift without speaking.

But there are also children who are very tense when Jan goes to collect them.

Josefine, the five-year-old who found the book about the Animal Lady, probably shows the clearest indications of anxiety. She always looks a little frightened when he goes to fetch her.

'All right,' she says quietly when he asks her how she's feeling.

He doesn't believe her. Not entirely.

This Monday Josefine is due in the visitors' room at two o'clock, and when Jan goes to pick her up from the playroom five minutes beforehand, she is busy building a Lego house.

'OK, Josefine – time to go!'

She doesn't respond; she just keeps on building her house.

'Come along, Josefine!' he says.

She still won't look at him, but silently gets to her feet. Without protest she follows him towards the stairs. Her pink elk is tucked underneath her arm; during assembly this morning she told everyone that his name was Ziggy.

Jan looks at Josefine and the elk, and thinks once more about the guardian animals. When they reach the underground corridor he asks, 'Do you remember that book about the Animal Lady, Josefine?'

She nods.

'But how did you know it was in the book box?'

'I put it there,' she says.

'I see . . . so someone gave it to you?'

'She gave me a few.'

'Who did?'

'A lady.'

They have reached the lift, and Jan stops. 'Would you like me to come up with you, Josefine?'

She nods again silently, and they step into the lift.

'Are you not feeling very happy?' he asks as they are travelling upwards.

Josefine shakes her head.

'Who are you going to see?'

'A lady,' the child says quietly.

A lady? Jan recalls that Josefine has been brought to school and picked up by several different people: sometimes a woman, sometimes an older man. Of course he isn't allowed to ask any questions about Josefine's family, but still he bends down and says, 'You're going to see your mum, aren't you?'

Josefine nods. And the lift stops.

This is actually the first time Jan has accompanied a child up to the visitors' room. He peeps out and sees a bright, clean room with a big sofa, parlour palms in pots, and a table with several children's books on it. But there are no CCTV cameras, as far as Jan can see.

The room is empty, but there is a closed door with a key pad at the other end.

'Out you come, Josefine.'

As Jan holds the door open she takes a tentative step into the room, then she turns around and whispers, 'Can you stay?'

He makes a sad face. 'I'm not allowed to do that, Josefine . . . unfortunately. You'll have to see your mum without me.'

Josefine shakes her head, and Jan doesn't know what else to say. The visitors' room is still empty, but he keeps his hand on the door of the lift. He doesn't want to leave Josefine alone.

There is a metallic click from the door at the other end of the room; it opens and a man in a pale-red nurse's uniform appears. It isn't Lars Rettig; this man is younger than Rettig. Shorter and more powerfully built too, with black hair cropped very close. He looks familiar.

Is he part of the security team who work the day shift? He reminds Jan of one of those fighting dogs that are ready to leap forward and sink their teeth into a tyre – or a throat.

His keys are attached to a thick belt around his waist, along with several white plastic loops. Next to them is a container which looks like a small metal Thermos flask. Handcuffs and tear gas?

The man takes three long strides away from the door and Jan tenses as if bracing himself for an attack; he almost jerks backwards.

But the man stops in the middle of the room and stares at Jan. 'Thanks,' he says.

Jan holds up a hand in acknowledgement, but doesn't move. He can see a shadow over by the doorway. Someone else is waiting on the other side – someone who doesn't want to step forward and show herself. A patient from St Psycho's, Jan realizes. Josefine's mother?

'Thanks,' the man says again. 'We'll take over now, that's fine.' His voice sounds mechanical, emotionless.

'Good.' But Jan doesn't think it's fine at all. His heart is pounding, his fingers are trembling. Security guards and police officers make him nervous.

He is almost convinced that Rami is Josefine's mother. That Rami is standing in the corridor, less than ten metres away from him. If he waits just a little bit longer he will see her, he will be able to talk to her.

But the guard takes another long stride into the room, his gaze fixed on the lift, and Jan has to go. He looks at Josefine one last time, gives her a reassuring smile and raises his voice: 'See you soon, Josefine. I'll come and get you. Do you remember my name?'

Josefine blinks. 'Jan.'

'That's it . . . Jan Hauger.'

He has said his name so loudly and clearly that Josefine's mother must have heard him. It feels as if this is important. Then he closes the lift door and goes back to the Dell.

His legs are shaking after his encounter with the guard, but his mind is full of Rami.

He is sure he was so close up there – so close to making contact with her at last, to being able to explain why things turned out as they did with little William, deep in the forest.

Lynx

'Shall we play hide-and-seek?' Jan asked.

It was the right time to make the suggestion now; he and the nine boys were out of sight of Sigrid and her group. The question sounded more like an order, and the boys didn't object.

'You're it, Jan!' Max shouted.

Jan agreed; of course he was going to be the one looking for them. But he wagged a finger at them and continued in the same firm tone of voice: 'Run away one at a time. I'll tell you which direction to go in. Then hide. You are to wait there until I find you, or shout to tell you to come out. Understood?'

The boys nodded, and he began: 'Max, you go that way.' He pointed to some boulders about twenty metres away, and Max turned and sped off.

'Not too far!' Jan shouted after him, then chose the next child. 'Paul, you go that way . . .' One by one he sent them off among the fir trees, but always in virtually the same direction.

In the end there was only little William left.

Jan walked over to him. He had never been this close to the boy before, and he crouched down so that he was on the same level. 'What's your name?' he asked, as if he didn't know.

'William,' the boy answered quietly, glancing away shyly; this was the first time Jan had spoken to him. To William, he was just another grown-up.

'OK, William . . .' Jan pointed. 'You can go in that direction, down that little path. Can you see the red arrow?'

William looked, and seemed to spot the arrow, almost a metre in length, which Jan had already fixed to the rocky hillside. He nodded.

'Follow all the arrows you see down there, William – and when they come to an end, that's where you hide. I think there's a fantastic hiding place there. Do you understand?'

The boy nodded again, and Jan placed a hand on his head.

'You won't need this,' he said, taking off the yellow woolly hat. 'We'll put it in your pocket.' Jan pretended to tuck William's hat into his pocket, but it was just a trick – in fact it stayed hidden in his clenched fist. 'Off you go!'

William turned and ran, scampering through the forest as fast as he could, just like the other boys – but in a completely different direction.

Jan stood up and watched him go. William had reached the first arrow and set off along the ravine, without any hesitation.

The forest was silent, but Jan felt as if he were standing in the eye of a hurricane. So many things could go wrong – a chaotic maelstrom of risks and potential misjudgements whirled around him.

Calm down, said an inner voice. *Just stick to the plan.*

He could hear the sound of drums. They were beating inside his head, beating and beating.

He took a deep breath. 'Stay in your hiding places!' he shouted. 'I'm coming, ready or not!'

That wasn't true. Jan didn't set off to search for the eight boys who had hidden themselves; instead he made his way through the undergrowth towards the ravine, where the ninth boy had disappeared.

William.

Jan broke into a run.

19

The main entrance to Jan's apartment block locks automatically at eight o'clock every evening; after that you need a key or an entry code to get in.

He has been back from work for a couple of hours by this stage; he has had dinner and settled down at the kitchen table with the picture books from the Dell in front of him. He has finished the first book, *The Animal Lady*; he has improved the illustrations and coloured them in. He wonders what Rami would think of the result.

He has made a start on the next book, *Viveca's House of Stone*. He is thinking about how to fill in the faint pencil drawings as he reads through the text.

Once upon a time there was an old woman who woke up one morning. What? What? What? she thought, because she was actually lying in a wooden coffin. She wasn't very strong, but she managed to lift up the lid and peep out. The room in which she found herself was big, with stone walls and a stone floor.

She shouted 'Hello?' into the silence, but no one answered.

She knew only one thing: Viveca. Her name was Viveca.

Jan reads the page twice, then begins to ink in the drawing. Viveca is a skinny woman with big eyes. Her head is sticking up out of a coffin.

It was several days before Viveca felt strong enough to get out of the coffin. Ooh. Aah. Aha! When she finally managed to push off the lid and get up, she saw a shabby dog basket on the floor beside her.

There was a label on the basket that said BLANKER, and in the bottom was a pile of grey dust and an empty dog collar. The dust was in the shape of a dog lying down.

Jan notices that the name Blanker is in this book too, just as it was in *The Animal Lady*.

He reads on, captivated by the story, as he goes over the thin pencil lines.

Eventually Viveca was able to leave the bedroom; the room next door was huge, with beautiful furniture, but everything was old and very dusty. A white wooden clock was hanging on the wall by the staircase, but when she looked at it more closely, she saw that there was something wrong with the hands. Tock, tick. It was going backwards.

Viveca moved into a hallway; there was an outside door, but it wouldn't open.

In another bedroom on the ground floor she found two more wooden coffins. They were neatly placed side by side, as if a married couple had decided to lie down in them. A man and a woman? No-no-no – Viveca didn't want to lift the lids and look!

Next to the bedroom was a closed door, and when Viveca opened it she saw a steep staircase leading down into the darkness. Cautiously she made her way down the steps, and found herself in a cellar. On the earth floor she found a pile of yellow bones. The bones of a monster. Ugh. She quickly went back to her room.

The days passed.

Viveca waited. Waited and slept. Every morning when she woke up, she felt a little brighter. She felt stronger, and when she caught her reflection in the mirror, she looked younger. And the hands of the clock kept on moving backwards, and in the end Viveca began to suspect what was happening in this house of stone:

Time was moving backwards!

Viveca suddenly realized that she would just keep getting younger and younger, and if she waited long enough, her parents would come back to life, and so would Blanker, her dog. She wouldn't be lonely any more.

But of course the same thing would happen to the big bones down in the cellar. Whatever it was, it would also come back to life.

Tock, tick, tock. The clock kept on going backwards.

One beautiful day Viveca woke up and looked at her hands, and saw that they were small and smooth. She was full of energy, and leapt out of bed. She had become a little girl again! She heard the sound of barking, and suddenly a golden-coloured retriever jumped up on to the bed and started licking her face. Blanker had woken up.

Her beloved Blanker!

Viveca was SO happy! She was no longer alone in the house of stone, and she hugged Blanker as tightly as she could.

But eventually she raised her head and listened. She could hear noises coming from the cellar. The clicking of bones.

Blanker growled. He ran over to the door and started barking. That wasn't good! Because Viveca could hear the sound of something big and heavy that had started to move down there . . .

At that point Jan's doorbell suddenly rings with a loud, cheerful tone. He gives a start and glances towards the hallway. *Who's there?* Jan has spent eight hours with pre-school children, and he wants his peace and quiet.

The bell keeps on ringing. He quickly hides the picture book in one of the kitchen drawers, then answers the door.

'Evening, Jan!' A blond man is standing there smiling. It is Lars Rettig from Bill's Bar, wearing his leather jacket. 'Am I disturbing you?'

Jan feels as if he has been caught out somehow, but shakes his head. 'No . . . no, it's fine.'

'Can I come in?'

'Sure. For a while.'

The evening chill from the street still clings to Rettig's jacket, and spreads through the hallway as he takes off his shoes and carries on into the living room. He has a carrier bag in one hand.

'Sorry to push in . . . I didn't want to stand out there drawing attention to myself.' He looks at all the furniture and boxes piled up along the walls. 'Wow, you've got plenty of rubbish.'

'That's not mine,' Jan says quickly. 'It's a sublet.'

'Right.' Rettig sits down on the sofa, still looking around. 'And you've got drums . . . Do you play?'

'A bit.'

'Cool.' Rettig's eyes flash: he has had an idea. 'You could come and do some jamming with us if you want. Our drummer in the Bohemos has just become a dad, so he can't always make the rehearsals.'

'OK,' says Jan, without even thinking. He feels a shiver of anticipation, but keeps the impassive mask in place: 'Perhaps I could come along and help out if you like . . . but I'm not all that good.'

Rettig laughs. 'Or else you're just being modest. But we can give it a try, can't we?' He takes something out of the bag. It's a steaming-hot kebab with bread, wrapped in foil. He looks at it hungrily, then glances at Jan. 'Want some?'

'No thanks – you carry on.'

Jan closes the outside door and stands in the doorway of the lounge. 'How did you know where I live?'

'I checked the hospital computer . . . Every employee's address is on there.' Rettig takes a bite of his kebab. 'How are you getting on at the nursery?'

'Fine . . . but it's a pre-school.'

'OK, *pre-school.*'

Jan doesn't say anything for a few seconds, then he asks, 'So you really do work at St Patricia's?'

'Indeed I do. Four nights a week, with lots of free time in between. That's when I play with the Bohemos.'

'And you're a security guard there?'

Rettig shakes his head. 'We prefer the term *care worker*. I work *with* the patients, not *against* them. Most of them are no trouble at all.'

'And do you see them often?'

'Every day,' says Rettig. 'Or every night, I should say.'

'Do you know their names?'

'Most of them,' says Rettig, taking another bite. 'But new faces come along at regular intervals. Some are allowed to go home, others are admitted.'

'But you know the names of the ones . . . the ones who've been in there a long time?'

Rettig holds up a hand. 'One thing at a time . . . We can chat about our guests, but first of all I want to know if you've decided.'

'Decided what?'

'Whether you want to help them.'

Jan takes a couple of steps into the room. 'I'd be happy to hear more . . . At Bill's Bar you said something about there being too many things you're not allowed to do.'

Rettig nods. 'That's what it's all about. There's too much bureaucracy at St Patricia's, too many rules . . . particularly when it comes to the closed wards. The daytime security team rules the roost up there.' He sighs gloomily at the thought of his colleagues on the day shift, and looks up at the ceiling. 'The patients are not allowed to write letters to whoever they like, and their post is checked. They're hardly ever allowed to watch TV or listen to the radio, they get searched all the time . . .'

Jan nods, remembering how he had to open his bag when he first went inside the hospital.

'You just get tired of all the supervision, that's all,' Rettig says. 'Some of us have been talking about this, and we think well-behaved patients ought to have a little more contact with the outside world.'

'Oh yes?'

'Through letters, for example. People write to the patients. Their parents, their friends, their brothers and sisters write to them . . . But the daytime security team stop the letters. Or they open them and have a good snoop . . . So we want to try and smuggle the letters in.'

Jan looks at him. 'And how would that work? Nobody from the pre-school is allowed into the hospital.'

'Oh yes they are,' Rettig says quickly. 'You are, Jan. You and your children.'

Jan doesn't say anything, so Rettig goes on: 'You're allowed to go up to the visitors' room, unsupervised. There are no cameras in there, no checks. And at night that room is completely empty. Anyone could go up and leave a bundle of letters in there . . . letters that could then be collected by me and taken into the hospital.'

Jan glances around sharply, as if Dr Högsmed is standing behind him in the apartment. 'And these letters,' he says. 'Where do they come from?'

Rettig shrugs his shoulders. 'From the people who write them. People send all kinds of stuff to the hospital, but most of it gets stopped. So I've got to know this guy in the sorting office in town, and he's started putting aside all handwritten letters addressed to St Patricia's. Then he gives them to me.'

Rettig looks pleased with himself, but Jan isn't smiling.

'So you don't know anything about these letters? You don't know what's in them?'

'Yes, we do,' says Rettig. 'Paper, paper with words on it . . . They're just ordinary letters.'

Jan's expression is doubtful. 'I'm not smuggling drugs.'

'It's not drugs. Nothing illegal.'

'But you *are* breaking the rules.'

'We are.' Rettig nods. 'But so did Mahatma Gandhi. For a good cause.'

Silence falls.

Jan clears his throat. 'Can you tell me a bit about the patients?'

'Which ones?'

Jan doesn't want to mention Rami's name, not yet. 'I've seen an old woman up there,' he says. 'Grey hair, dressed in a black coat.

She goes around sweeping up the leaves just inside the fence . . . I wondered if she works at St Patricia's, or if she's a patient.'

Rettig has stopped smiling. 'She's a patient,' he says quietly. 'Her name is Margit. But she's not as old as you might think.'

'Really? I've seen her standing by the fence, watching the children.'

'She's done that ever since the pre-school opened,' says Rettig. 'Whenever she's allowed outside she goes and stands by the fence.'

'Does she like children?'

Rettig doesn't answer at first. 'Margit had three children of her own,' he says eventually. 'She was married to a potato farmer in Blekinge . . . This was twenty-five years ago. Her husband used to leave the farm on Fridays and go into town to meet customers. But one day Margit found out from a neighbour that he had a room in a hotel in town, a room where he used to entertain his girlfriend . . . maybe several girlfriends. So she went to the gun cupboard and took out his shotgun.'

Jan looks at him. 'She went to the hotel and shot him?'

Rettig shakes his head. 'She took the children out to the barn and shot *them*. First of all the two oldest, then she reloaded and shot the little one.' He sighs. 'She's been locked up in St Patricia's ever since.'

The room is now deathly quiet.

Rettig has stopped eating. He shakes himself, as if he wants to forget what he has said, then goes on: 'But Margit is kept well away from your children, there's no need to worry . . . She's kept away from all children.'

Jan slowly opens his mouth. 'I don't think I wanted to know that.'

'Well, now you do know,' Rettig says. 'There's a lot we don't want to know about the people around us . . . I know way too much, personally.'

'About the patients?'

'About everyone.'

Jan nods slowly. He is thinking about the children's books hidden in his kitchen. He has secrets of his own.

'And it's only letters you want me to take in? Nothing else?'

'No drugs, no weapons, just letters,' Rettig insists. 'Think about it, Jan. I work there. Do you think I want people like Ivan Rössel to get their hands on drugs or knives?'

Jan stares at him. 'Is Ivan Rössel in there?' He recognizes the name from the newspapers and TV. And the taxi driver mentioned him too.

'He is.'

'Ivan Rössel the serial killer?'

'That's right,' Rettig answers in a subdued voice. 'We've got quite a few celebrities among the guests at our establishment . . . If you only knew.'

Alice Rami, Jan thinks. But out loud he simply asks, 'So when do you want an answer about the letters?'

'Preferably now.'

'I need to give it some thought.'

Rettig leans forward. 'There's a place down by the harbour; we use one of the rooms for our rehearsals. We can meet up there, do some jamming with the Bohemos . . . and afterwards we can have a chat. How about that?'

Jan isn't sure, but he accepts the invitation anyway.

'Come down there tomorrow, about seven. It'll be cool, as they say.'

When Rettig has gone and Jan has locked the front door, he immediately regrets his decision. Why did he agree to play with the Bohemos? He's heard them, and they're too good for him.

He glances over at his drums, wanting to sit down and practise right away, but it's too late at night. Instead he goes into the kitchen and gets out the four hidden books: *The Animal Lady*, *The Princess with a Hundred Hands*, *The Witch Who Was Poorly*, *Viveca's House of Stone*. He almost knows the stories off by heart now. He knows the princess shouts, 'I'm not unhappy, I just like *unhappiness*!' when she first arrives in the village, and he knows that the first symptom of the witch's illness is that her hair melts.

So why does he keep on reading the books, over and over again?

Perhaps he is searching for some kind of hidden message. If these are Rami's books, she must have had some ulterior motive when she asked Josefine to hide them in the pre-school.

And perhaps he finds a message in the end, because as he leafs through *The Animal Lady* for perhaps the fiftieth time, he suddenly sees a little patch of ink right in the bottom right-hand corner of the first page, below the text. There's nothing odd about that, but there is a similar mark on the next page, the same size and in almost exactly the same place. And on the next page.

Jan looks more closely; he has been concentrating on the pages with the pictures, and hasn't noticed this mark in the margin before.

It looks like a little animal. A squirrel?

He flicks through the pages, and the squirrel begins to move. It's an illusion created by the movement of the pages: the squirrel scampers along, all the way through the book.

He goes through the books over and over again, and eventually he gets them in the right order. The marks on the hundred or so pages of the four books form a short animated film. The black squirrel first appears in the bottom corner of the first page of *The Animal Lady*, then skitters up across the pages of *The Princess with a Hundred Hands* and *Viveca's House of Stone*, before finally disappearing into space at the top of the penultimate page of *The Witch Who Was Poorly*.

Jan stares at the squirrel's progress.

A sign. That's what it feels like, a sign especially for him.

20

The room where the Bohemos rehearse smells of sweat and dreams. It's not far from the harbour, just a few blocks away from Bill's Bar. The room is as bare as a scruffy youth centre – apart from the egg boxes. Hundreds of egg boxes have been stuck to the walls in order to reduce the echo.

Jan is sitting behind the drum kit, establishing the rhythm and being swept along by it at the same time. The Bohemos started with the classic 'Sweet Home Alabama', with a steady four-stroke beat which Jan was able to follow with no problem. That got them going, and now they have been playing old rock songs for almost an hour.

From time to time Rettig has turned around from his place at the microphone and nodded to Jan; he seems pleased. 'A bit softer on the snare, Jan!'

Jan nods and obliges. After all those years of sitting alone at home accompanying bands on his stereo, it's a strange feeling to be playing with real live musicians. He was a bit shaky at first, but he's getting better and better.

The drum kit he's using is an old Tama, not quite as good as his own; the skin on the bass and snare is worn and almost split in places. But it means he can be a bit less careful as he provides the backing.

'Good,' says Rettig. 'Tighter and tighter.'

Two other members of the Bohemos have turned up. The bass

guitarist is called Anders, and the rhythm guitarist is Rasmus. They are both about the same age as Rettig, and play without speaking. Jan has no idea what they think of the fact that he has taken over from Carl, the usual drummer; they haven't said a word to him all evening, just glanced over at the drums occasionally.

Jan wonders whether Carl, Anders or Rasmus are also care workers at the hospital.

At quarter past eight they stop and start packing away. The two other band members leave immediately with their guitar cases, but Rettig hangs around. Jan stays too; he knows that Rettig is waiting for an answer.

'You play well,' Rettig says. 'A bit of an African vibe going on there.'

'Thanks,' says Jan, getting up from his seat. 'I enjoyed it.'

'You've played in bands before, I assume?'

'Oh yes,' Jan lies.

The room is silent among all the egg boxes. Rettig walks over and picks up his black case by the door. He looks at Jan. 'Have you made a decision? About what we discussed yesterday?'

'I have.' He takes a moment. 'It's International Children's Day today, October fourth,' he says. 'Did you know that, Lars?'

Rettig shakes his head and starts to dismantle the microphone stand. 'Isn't it cinnamon-bun day?'

'That too,' says Jan. After another brief pause he asks, 'Have you got kids, Lars?'

'Why?'

'Spending time with children makes you wiser.'

'Probably. But I haven't got any kids, unfortunately,' says Rettig. 'I've got a girlfriend, but no kids. How about you?'

'No. None of my own.'

'Like I said . . . have you decided?'

'One last question,' says Jan. 'What do you get out of this?'

Rettig hesitates. 'Nothing, not directly.'

Jan looks at him. 'And *indirectly*?'

Rettig shrugs his shoulders. 'Not much. We charge a small

fee . . . a handling fee for delivery. Forty kronor per letter. But that's not going to make us rich.'

'And it's just letters?'

Jan has asked this same question several times, of course, but Rettig is a patient man.

'Absolutely, Jan. Just ordinary letters.'

'OK, I'll do it. I'll give it a try, anyway.'

'Excellent.' Rettig quickly leans forward. 'This is how it works. You get a package from me, and the next time you're on the night shift you take it into the hospital through the basement. At night, as close to midnight as possible.' He takes a sheet of paper out of his bag. 'But only on certain nights . . . This is the schedule; it shows you when one of us is working.'

'One of you . . . You and who else?'

Rettig lowers his voice. 'Carl, our drummer. He does the same job as me. OK, so between eleven and midnight you take the lift up to the visitors' room. Check that no one is in there before you open the door . . . but there won't be. You hide the envelope under the sofa cushions, then you go back to the children. They'll be asleep, I presume?'

Jan nods, thinking about the electronic Angels he has bought.

'Any questions?'

'Not about the delivery . . . But I would like to know more about the patients, as I said before.'

Rettig smiles wearily and puts his guitar in its case. 'The carers are not allowed to talk about those they care for. You know that, don't you?'

'What do they do up there?'

'Not much. They're waiting, just like the rest of us. We're all just waiting.'

Jan remains silent for a few seconds, then eventually he asks, 'I was just wondering . . . Is there anyone up there called Alice Rami?'

Rettig shakes his head; he doesn't even have to think about it. 'No,' he says. 'There's Anna and Alide, but no Alice.'

'Anyone called Blanker, then?'

Rettig considers for a moment before answering. 'There is a

Blanker . . . Maria Blanker.'

Jan leans closer. 'How old is she?'

'Not very old.'

'Thirty?'

'Maybe, between thirty and thirty-five . . . But she's pretty shy. She's on one of the women's wards, and she keeps herself to herself.'

The women's wards, Jan thinks. So there's more than one.

'Does she have a child at the pre-school?'

Rettig is taking longer and longer to answer. 'Maybe. I think she has the odd visit.'

'From a child?'

Rettig nods. 'A girl.'

'Do you know her name?'

Rettig shrugs and looks at his watch. 'I need to get home,' he says, placing his bag on the table. 'So, this business with the letters . . . When's your next night shift, Jan?'

'Tomorrow.'

'Perfect.'

Rettig takes out a large white envelope, several centimetres thick. It is marked in red ink: *S.P.* 'Can you deliver this?'

Jan takes the envelope and sees that it has been carefully sealed. He doesn't try to open it, but weighs it in his hands.

It is soft. A bundle of letters – nothing else? It seems so; Jan can't feel any hard objects or little bags of powder.

'No problem.' He smiles at Rettig, still trying to convince himself that this is a good idea.

21

Hanna Aronsson is working at the Dell the day after Jan's practice session with the Bohemos, and she is just coming out of the children's room when he walks into the cloakroom. She looks very tired, and quickly puts her finger to her lips when she sees him.

'*Ssh* . . .'

Jan realizes that she has only just got the children off to sleep. He waves to her and goes into the staffroom, quickly placing his rucksack in his locker. The rucksack containing the envelope; his secret mission as a postman.

Then he joins Hanna in the kitchen; she is busy unloading the dishwasher.

'Are they all fast asleep?'

'I hope so.' She sighs. 'They've been a real handful tonight. Bad-tempered and bickering non-stop.'

'Oh? How many of them are there?'

'Three . . . Leo, Matilda and Mira, as usual.'

There is an awkward silence; this always happens when Jan is alone at work with Hanna. It's easy to talk to the other staff at the Dell, but Hanna doesn't say anything beyond what is absolutely necessary.

Although of course there is something Jan wants to discuss with her, and after a moment he takes a deep breath. 'Hanna, what I said to you last week, when we were walking home . . .'

'What?'

'That I used to work at a nursery . . . and I lost one of the boys in the forest.'

She nods; he can see that she remembers.

'Did you . . . did you mention it to anyone else?'

Hanna's expression is blank, as usual. 'No.'

'Good,' Jan says.

It looks as if Hanna is about to say something else, or ask a question, but instead she puts away the last of the dishes and closes the cupboard doors. 'That's me done for today, then.'

'Fine. Do you have any plans for this evening?'

'I don't know . . . I might go to the gym.'

Jan could have guessed that Hanna was a gym bunny. She is slender but looks toned and fit. Not skinny like Rami.

Ten minutes later Hanna has gone home, and Jan has locked the outside door. Now he is alone in the Dell, and of course he has no TV or stereo – just the sound of all the rock songs he played with the Bohemos the previous evening echoing in his head. It was good fun; he wonders if Lars Rettig will invite him to play with the band again.

Maybe, if he carries off his task this evening.

The children are fast asleep, and there is nothing for Jan to do. It's going to be a long wait until eleven o'clock. He sits in the kitchen with a book, but often gazes out into the darkness, towards the hospital.

When it is quarter to eleven at long last, he fetches the thick envelope and both Angels from his locker.

He feels slightly foolish, but he still puts on his cycling gloves and wipes the whole envelope with a duster to make sure he hasn't left any fingerprints or strands of hair on it. Just in case Dr Högsmed finds it.

At five to eleven he switches on the Angel transmitter and hangs it in the children's bedroom, then he opens the basement door with the key card. The other Angel is attached to his belt and he is carrying the envelope in his left hand as he walks down the stairs and along the corridor, past the animal pictures.

The lift is waiting for him; he steps inside and presses the button. The metal chamber shudders and begins to move upwards.

Jan is not used to going up to the hospital without any children, and doing so in the middle of the night feels most peculiar.

The lift stops with a jolt. Jan checks through the window and sees that the visitors' room is in darkness. There is no sign of life.

Slowly, carefully, he opens the door a fraction. He waits, he listens, but there isn't a sound. Eventually he steps out on to the carpet. As always when he is inside St Patricia's he feels an all-consuming curiosity, a nagging desire to find out more.

The furniture in the room is a collection of angular shadows, but there is a small amount of light cast by the lift behind him, and from the pane of glass in the door leading into the main hospital. Jan peers through it and sees a long, deserted corridor. And the door is locked, of course – he won't be able to get any further this way.

All he can do is go over to the sofa, lift up the left-hand seat cushion, and tuck the envelope underneath as far as possible before rearranging the cushions. There. Job done.

With a final glance at the sofa, Jan gets in the lift and travels back down to the basement; he walks slowly up the stairs, then goes to the staffroom to make up his bed. But as usual he finds it difficult to get to sleep.

He's involved now. He's been working here for less than three weeks, and he's already a part of some kind of smuggling operation.

It's Rami's fault. If it is in fact Rami who is Josefine's mother, using a new name: Maria Blanker.

He lies awake in the darkness, wishing he had opened the envelope Rettig gave him. Were any of the letters for her?

Lynx

The clock was ticking. Of course Jan couldn't hear it as he ran through the forest, but he could feel the seconds racing by; time was passing quickly. He had so much to do in such a short period of time.

The high walls of the ravine rose above him, and he could see the second red arrow. There were no signs in the undergrowth to show that little William had passed this way – but then he couldn't have gone any other way.

Jan carried on through the open iron gate, then slowed down. He was out of the ravine now, and he stopped and gazed up ahead.

He had placed the final red arrow under a couple of heavy stones on the ground, some twenty metres beyond the end of the ravine. It was pointing up the slope, towards the open door of the concrete bunker.

William was nowhere to be seen.

Jan could feel the blood pounding in his ears like a bass drum as he clambered up the slope. For the last two metres up to the steel door he became a cat, slinking along without making a sound.

He reached the entrance to the bunker, bent down and listened. Yes, there was someone in there. He could hear a child snuffling within the concrete walls. Jan hoped he wasn't crying – and that he was just a little boy with a runny nose from being out in the cold.

Silently he reached out and slowly closed the door. Slowly, slowly . . . and when it was completely shut he shot both bolts across.

The previous evening he had hidden the robot's remote control in a plastic bag under a stone next to the bunker. He took it out and pressed the button, bringing the toy to life. He couldn't see it, of course, but he heard his own voice, distorted and metallic, echoing inside the bunker.

'*Wait here, William,*' said the robot's loudspeaker. '*Everything is all right, just wait here.*'

Jan put back the remote control and turned away. He climbed down on to level ground and raced back towards the ravine, grabbing the red arrow on the way. He screwed it up and tucked it into his jacket pocket, then did the same with arrow number two. He slammed the iron gate shut, and when he emerged from the ravine he removed the final arrow.

He was out of breath, but didn't slow down. Up the slope, the drums still pounding in his ears. When he reached the spot where the game of hide-and-seek had started, he looked at his watch. Three thirty-five. It felt as if it had taken much longer, but he and the boys had been playing for only ten minutes.

Suddenly he spotted a pale-green jacket between the fir trees. A little boy, crouching down in the undergrowth and trying to hide. Then he saw another of the boys slightly further away, then another.

He knew exactly where the boys were now. William was also in the right place. The plan was working; it was time for Jan to relax.

He smiled and cupped his hands around his mouth. 'I'm coming to get you! I can see you!'

22

Before setting off for his night shift on Friday, Jan picks up an empty coffee cup and leaves his flat. He's not going out this evening, just down two flights of stairs to visit his neighbour behind the door marked V. LEGÉN.

He can't hear a sound; he has rung the bell on two previous occasions, but no one has answered. He tries again.

This time someone is coming; then there is a rattling sound. Legén has put the chain on the door, but he opens it just a fraction.

'Evening,' says Jan, holding up the cup.

His neighbour doesn't say a word.

'My name is Jan Hauger . . . I live upstairs,' Jan goes on. 'I wondered if you could spare some sugar? I'm making a cake.'

Legén stares at him like a weary boxer facing his arch enemy. He's not in a good mood today. But he takes the cup and turns away. Jan silently steps forward and peers into the hallway.

It is dark and untidy, and it stinks of tobacco. The fabric bag he last saw down in the cellar is lying on the floor, next to the shoe rack. The text is clearly visible now: ST PATRICIA'S LAUNDRY. He was right.

Jan is wearing a satisfied smile when his neighbour returns with the cup half-full of sugar.

'Perfect. Thanks very much.'

He is about to carry on chatting; he was intending to point to the bag and say that he actually works at St Patricia's too, but

Legén simply nods and slams the door shut. There is a click as the key turns in the lock.

Jan goes back up to his flat and tips the sugar into the bin in the kitchen.

He cycles to the pre-school at around nine o'clock, thinking all the time about the envelope he left in the visitors' room on the Wednesday night. It should have been collected by now, and will have had some effect on the patients, although he isn't sure what that might be.

But nothing whatsoever has changed. The concrete wall is as solid as ever, the floodlights shine out and everything is just the way it always is when he arrives at the Dell. Lilian is waiting for him tonight, and she has already put the children to bed.

'Evening, Lilian.'

'How are you, Jan?' Lilian looks tired, but her voice is loud and brisk. Sometimes it seems as if the children are a little bit afraid of her, in spite of the fact that she enjoys playing with them. There is something tense yet fragile about her, Jan thinks.

'Fine, thanks,' he replies. 'Ready for the weekend?'

'Definitely.'

'Will you be out enjoying yourself?'

'I certainly will.' But there is no sense of anticipation in her voice. Lilian quickly pulls on her jacket, but she doesn't ask what Jan will be doing, and she doesn't wish him a nice weekend. She just gives him one last glance, then leaves.

Jan is alone again, getting ready for the night.

He checks on the sleeping children, then carries out the usual routines before getting undressed. He is in bed by eleven, but as usual he finds it difficult to get to sleep. The pre-school is too warm and stuffy, the sofa bed feels narrow and uncomfortable, and out there in the kitchen a key card is longing for him to come and get it out of the drawer. But not as much as he is longing to use it.

Jan sighs in the darkness. But he *is* going to stay in bed. He is *not* going to go down into the basement. There is no easy way into the hospital in any case, he knows that now. The door leading out of the visitors' room is locked. But Rettig must have a key, if he is able to go in and fetch the envelope Jan hid under the sofa cushions.

Have the patients received their letters yet? Presumably. Perhaps Lars Rettig is creeping around the corridors at this very moment, handing them out.

Jan turns over on to his side, still toying with the idea of finding a secret route into the hospital.

Perhaps via the safe room in the basement? It has two exits, and he doesn't know where the second one leads. He doesn't even know if it's possible to open it. It might lead straight into the hospital, or it might have been bricked up. But if he doesn't go down and try it, he will never know.

It's quarter to twelve. The children are asleep, and the key card is calling to him. St Psycho's is out there, like a huge mountain waiting to be climbed simply because it is there. Like Mount Everest. But many climbers have lost their lives on Everest . . .

No, it's better to think of the hospital as a cave to be explored. Jan has never heard of anyone dying in a cave, although of course it could have happened.

He makes up his mind. Throws back the covers and sits up in the darkness.

Just a quick look in the safe room, and then he'll be able to sleep.

Ten minutes later he is down in the underground corridor. The Angel is switched on and attached to his belt, he has turned on the light and walked down the stairs. The lift window is dark – the lift is up on the ground floor, but he doesn't press the button to call it down. Instead he carries on along the corridor, around the corner and all the way up to the steel door.

It is closed, and of course the sign is still there (*This door must be kept locked at all times!*), but Jan grabs hold of the big handle and opens it. He remembers where the light switch was, and flicks on the main overhead light.

The safe room looks exactly the same as when he peeped in last time. A fitted carpet, a few pillows, a mattress. No one has been in here. Or have they? The mattress is lying on the floor now – wasn't it propped up against the wall the last time he was here? He can't remember. There's an empty wine bottle – surely that wasn't here before?

There isn't a sound. Cautiously Jan steps inside. He leaves the door open and walks over to the other end of the room. There is the exit which might lead deeper into the hospital: another closed steel door with a long handle.

Jan grabs hold of the handle and presses it downwards. It gives perhaps a centimetre, then stops dead. He stands on tiptoe, tenses his arms and puts all his strength into trying to move the metal bar, but to no avail.

The hospital is not going to let him in.

He lets out a long breath, and suddenly he hears something. A sound. A faint vibration in the floor. A low whining noise is coming from the corridor, through the concrete walls, and at first Jan can't work out what it is, but then he recognizes it. The whine carries on, getting louder all the time.

It's the sound of the lift. The lift has begun to descend from the visitors' room; it's on its way down to the basement.

Jan lets go of the door handle. He listens intently.

The lift stops in the basement with a clicking sound. There is complete silence for a couple of seconds, then Jan clearly hears the sound of the metal door opening.

Someone steps out into the corridor.

23

Jan stays where he is, protected by the thick walls of the safe room. He doesn't move a muscle.

Make your mind up, he thinks.

All he did when the lift door opened was to reach out and switch off the light in the safe room, to avoid giving himself away. But ever since he has been in the same place, frozen to the floor.

He is standing completely still, just listening, with no idea of what to do. Every sound he can hear now is coming from the basement, bouncing around the sharp corners and echoing between the concrete walls.

He clearly hears the door of the lift close, and thinks he can hear footsteps moving across the thin carpet of the corridor. Quiet steps, gradually moving away.

Someone is calmly walking away from the lift and along the corridor.

Someone is on the way up the stairs to the Dell.

On the way up to the three sleeping children: Leo, Mira and Matilda.

Jan *must* move, and in the end he manages it. He turns around and takes one step towards the door. His shadow moves across the wall. Two steps. Three.

But suddenly the light in front of him goes out. The shadow disappears; the corridor is in total darkness.

Jan realizes what has happened: the person who came out of

the lift has now reached the top of the stairs, and switched off the light.

The door leading to the pre-school rattles as it opens, then closes again. The visitor from St Psycho's must have had a key card with him or her.

And now the visitor is inside the Dell. And Jan, who is responsible for the children up there, is trapped.

He has his own card and can get out of the basement, but that won't be enough. He needs a weapon. Something with which to defend himself and the children, anything at all. He gropes around in the darkness of the safe room, finds the empty wine bottle on the floor and picks it up.

A kind of club. He can grab the bottle by the neck and hold it up in front of him.

Out in the corridor it is almost pitch dark, with only a faint yellow glow from the window of the lift, and he gropes his way along the wall towards the stairs.

He has almost forgotten the Angel on his belt, but suddenly he hears muted, metallic sounds coming from the little box. Scraping sounds, then something that sounds like breathing. The sound of someone who has crept into the children's bedroom.

Someone is with the children.

Jan's heart begins to pound, he increases his speed.

Most of the patients in the hospital are not dangerous, that's what Dr Högsmed said. And yet right now he can't help thinking about those who are dangerous. About Ivan Rössel, the serial killer. And Margit, the old woman, with her smoking shotgun . . .

Fuck. Jan moves along with short, rapid steps, feeling his way. The concrete wall feels like sandpaper to his touch.

He hears a thud; he has knocked down one of the animal pictures, but he doesn't stop. All at once his shoe hits something hard. The bottom step. He climbs the stairs cautiously, one by one, until his hands brush against the door. But it's locked.

Jan will have to unlock it, but suddenly he can't remember the code. His mind has gone completely blank. Marie-Louise's birthday – but exactly when is it?

When?

He turns up the volume on the baby monitor and hears the sound of scraping footsteps, someone moving inside the room where the children are sleeping. A visitor from St Psycho's.

The code, what's the code?

Jan needs to think. He tries to relax, and gradually coaxes out the numbers; they pop into his head, one by one. Three, one, zero, seven. He fumbles in the darkness, keys in the numbers, swipes the card and hears the lock click.

Slowly he opens the door, the bottle raised in front of him. The small rooms in the Dell are silent now.

He takes two steps into the cloakroom, turns and sees that the door of the children's room is standing wide open. It was closed when he left. The hand holding the bottle is slippery with sweat.

Three children are sleeping in there – Leo, Matilda and Mira. He abandoned them. Holding his breath he moves as quietly as he can towards the doorway.

A room in darkness.

He peeps in, expecting to see a big black shadow looming over the beds, but he sees nothing.

Nothing is moving in there. The three children are safely tucked up, their breathing quiet and even. Jan tiptoes in and listens, but the room is small; there is nowhere for anyone to hide.

It's empty. So where has the visitor from the hospital gone?

Jan leaves the children, closes the door and switches on the light in the hallway. Then he goes from room to room, checking every corner, but he can't find any sign of the visitor.

Eventually he returns to the hallway. The outside door is closed, but when he presses down the handle he discovers it isn't locked. Someone has unlocked it and gone outside.

Jan opens the door and looks out, but there is no one in sight. 'Hello?' he calls out into the night, mostly to hear the sound of his own voice.

No answer. The playground is empty, the street beyond is deserted.

He closes the door against the cold, locks it and exhales. He looks at the clock: quarter past twelve.

There is one last thing he must do before he goes to bed: he must go down to the basement and hang the picture back on the wall. And of course he must replace the bottle – an empty wine bottle would be a little difficult to explain if Marie-Louise found it in the pre-school.

When he comes back up, he also jams a chair under the handle of the door leading to the basement so that no one will be able to open it from the other side – not even if they have a key card.

At eight o'clock the following morning, Jan goes home. The rest of the night was uneventful, when he finally managed to get to sleep. His heart was pounding as he lay in bed, but he felt lonely rather than afraid.

Our operation is secure, Dr Högsmed had said. *The safety of all concerned is our number-one priority.*

Jan has not found a way to get to Rami, not yet. But one thing he does know now: someone is using the pre-school as a sally port. As a way out of the hospital.

He hopes it isn't a patient.

24

The second envelope from Rettig is delivered to Jan that morning when he is back in his own bed. His mind has drifted off into a warm, soothing dream about love, but he is abruptly woken at nine o'clock. He can't work out why at first, but then it dawns on him that it was the clatter of the letter box.

He no longer remembers the dream; he might as well get up. When he peers out into the hallway there is an envelope lying there which looks familiar. This one is pale yellow, that's the only difference. But it is just as thick as the first one, with the letters S. P. printed on the front.

This time Jan does something he didn't have the courage to do last time: he opens the envelope. He takes it into the kitchen, places it on the table and studies the seal. It's ordinary transparent sticky tape – the kind you can buy just about anywhere – and that's what makes him begin to pull at it, teasing it away from the back of the envelope.

He hesitates for a brief moment. Is it wrong to open letters that shouldn't ever be delivered anyway? He pushes the question aside.

When he has removed the tape it is very easy to slide a sharp knife under the flap and gently work it open. He reaches inside and removes the contents.

Rettig wasn't lying. The envelope contains letters, nothing else. Jan counts thirty-four, in all colours and sizes. There are names on the front in pen or pencil, in different handwriting, all with the same address: *St Patricia's Hospital.*

Jan slowly looks through the names, and notices that one particular name comes up several times: Ivan Rössel. Rössel the serial killer has received nine letters altogether.

There are no other names on the letters that Jan recognizes. There is nothing for Alice Rami, or Maria Blanker.

Jan rubs his eyes and thinks. If he can't get in to see Rami, perhaps he can send a letter to her? What does he have to lose?

He has a set of stationery in one of the kitchen drawers. His mother gave it to him when he left home, with handmade envelopes and thick paper, but in ten years he has hardly ever used it.

He picks up a pen and stares at the empty sheet of paper for a few seconds, wanting to fill it with words. There is so much to say. But in the end he writes just one question: DEAR SQUIRREL – WOULD YOU LIKE TO GET OVER THE FENCE?

He signs his own first name. He considers adding his address, then realizes that Lars Rettig or one of the other care assistants will almost certainly see the envelope containing Rami's reply. If she replies. So he writes *Jan Larsson*, and his old address in Gothenburg.

Then he places the sheet of paper in an envelope, writes *Maria Blanker, St Patricia's Hospital* on the front, seals it and tucks it in among all the rest.

Jan has the package for the patients at St Patricia's in his rucksack when he arrives at the Dell the following day. He will be staying on for the evening shift; he will be alone with the children for three hours, which will give him plenty of time to nip over to St Psycho's when they have fallen asleep.

Everything seems quiet at the Dell, but when he walks into the staffroom he sees Marie-Louise sitting at the table with a strange man. He stops dead in the doorway, feeling a chill run down his spine. He suddenly remembers the events of Friday night: the unidentified visitor who emerged from the lift and walked out into the night through the pre-school.

But when he looks at the man properly he recognizes the glasses and the thick brown hair. And the mouth which rarely smiles.

'Hello, Jan. How are you?'

Dr Högsmed has come to visit. Jan almost expects to see a collection of hats in front of him on the table, just waiting to be picked up – but there is only a half-empty coffee cup.

He quickly forces a smile and goes over to shake hands. 'Fine thanks, Doctor.'

'*Patrik*, Jan.'

Jan nods. Of course he will never be able to think of Högsmed as anything other than *Doctor*, but he can pretend.

Högsmed studies his face. 'So, have you got the hang of all the routines?'

'Absolutely,' Jan replies. 'I love it here.'

'That sounds excellent.'

Jan's smile is becoming more rigid by the moment. He thinks about the letters in his rucksack. It isn't open, of course, but does Högsmed suspect anything? Has Lars Rettig been found out?

Eventually the doctor looks away and turns to Marie-Louise. 'Is he behaving himself?'

Högsmed sounds unconcerned, and Marie-Louise answers emphatically, 'Oh yes, we're very pleased with Jan! He's become a real favourite with the children, a real playmate.'

Jan hears the praise, but he still can't relax. He would prefer to slip away, out of the room and away from Dr Högsmed. When Marie-Louise asks if he'd like a coffee, he quickly shakes his head. 'Thanks, but I had one just before I came out. I get a bit shaky if I have too much,' he says, then adds, 'Caffeine, I mean.'

Then he goes off to join the children in the playroom. Behind him Högsmed leans over and quietly says something to Marie-Louise, but the children are shouting and laughing, making it impossible for Jan to eavesdrop.

'Come on, Jan!'

'Come on, we're going to build something!'

Natalie and Matilda draw him into the game, but he finds it difficult to chat and joke as usual today. He keeps looking over at the door, waiting to feel a hand on his shoulder, a harsh voice asking him to come for a little chat. An interview with the security team up at the hospital.

But it doesn't happen. When he glances into the staffroom a little while later, the table is empty. Högsmed has gone.

At last Jan can relax, or try to. He shouldn't go across to deliver the letters this evening – what if Dr Högsmed calls in again? But he doesn't want them sitting in his locker either.

The time passes slowly but at last it's evening. Most of the children are picked up, the staff go home. Jan warms up a stew with dill and potatoes for the three children who are left, then he reads them a story and eventually manages to get them to sleep.

By this stage it is quarter to nine. Rettig told him to go up to the hospital later than this, but Jan is too impatient. He has just about an hour before Andreas arrives to take over; that's plenty of time.

He waits for a little while, checks on the sleeping children one last time, then heads down into the basement with the Angel attached to his belt and the envelope hidden underneath his jumper.

Quickly, a postman has to work quickly.

The lift is waiting for him. He takes a deep breath and travels up to the visitors' room. Everything is quiet; it is deserted and in darkness. Jan quickly makes his way over to the sofa, lifts up the cushion and stops – there is already an envelope lying there. But it isn't the one he left a few days ago. This one is larger and thicker, and there are five words scrawled on the front: OPEN THIS AND POST CONTENTS!

A reply from St Psycho's. Jan stares at the envelope. Then he grabs it, tucks it under his jumper and puts the big yellow envelope in its place.

When Jan gets back to the Dell, everything is still perfectly quiet. Thirty minutes later the outside door opens. Jan gives a start, but it is only Andreas, cheerful and calm as usual. Andreas is a steady character, apparently with no worries in his life. 'Hi, Jan. Everything OK?'

'Everything's fine. All our little friends are fast asleep.'

Jan smiles and puts on his jacket, then opens up his locker and takes out his rucksack, where he has hidden the new envelope. He is full of anticipation; it almost feels like Christmas Eve.

'Good luck, Andreas. See you tomorrow.'

When Jan gets home he is still thinking about Dr Högsmed. He locks the door behind him and pulls down the kitchen blinds. Then he takes out the envelope and opens it.

Forty-seven letters come tumbling out – almost a full deck of cards of large and small letters, all neatly stamped and addressed to various people in Sweden, apart from two. One is destined for Hamburg, and one is going all the way to Bahia in Brazil. There is no sender's name on any of them.

Jan is fascinated; he lays out the letters in front of him like a game of solitaire. He moves them around on the kitchen table, studying the handwriting; some of it is very controlled and deliberate, some spiky and scrawled. Eventually he gathers them all up.

He is in charge of them now. He could throw them away.

When he is lying in bed an hour later, he wonders which patients have written all those letters. Ivan Rössel, perhaps. He got a lot of letters last time; does he reply to those who write to him?

And has Rami written to anyone? At least there is a letter from him up in the visitors' room, waiting for her . . .

Jan falls asleep and is quickly back in the same warm dream he had before. He remembers it clearly now: he is with Alice Rami. She and Jan are living together out in the country, on a farm with no fences of any kind. They are striding along a meandering gravel track, free and unafraid, with all of life's mistakes far behind them. Rami has a large brown dog on a lead. A St Bernard, or a Rottweiler. It is a guard dog, of course, but it's a nice dog, and Rami is totally in control of it.

Lynx

Sigrid walked into Lynx at twenty past four; Jan saw her out of the corner of his eye. They had been back from the forest for over half an hour by that stage, and the nursery was just in the process of closing.

Everything had gone well on the way home – apart from the fact that there had been sixteen children in the group instead of seventeen. But Jan hadn't mentioned it, and neither Sigrid nor any of the children had noticed that William was missing.

Personally, he could hardly think of anything else.

A short while ago he had taken a break, an apparently completely normal break to which he was entitled. He had popped out of the nursery for ten minutes and walked to the nearest postbox. It was three blocks away from Lynx, and on the way there he stopped in a dark doorway and took out William's hat.

The previous evening he had prepared a stamped addressed envelope. He pushed the hat inside, sealed the envelope and dropped it in the postbox. Then he quickly walked back to work.

When Sigrid arrived at the nursery Jan was standing in the cloakroom chatting to a woman whose name he couldn't remember at that particular moment – but she was Max Karlsson's mother, and she had come to pick him up.

Sigrid came over and interrupted the conversation, her voice low and anxious. 'Sorry, Jan . . . could I have a quick word?'

'Of course, what is it?'

She drew him slightly to one side. 'Have you got any extra children here?'

He looked at her, pretending to be surprised. 'No, we've only got four left; the rest have already been collected. Why do you ask?'

Sigrid looked around the cloakroom. 'It's William, little William Halevi . . . His dad is waiting over at Brown Bear, he's come to pick William up . . . but he's not there.'

'Not there?'

She shook her head. 'Is it OK if I just have a look around here, in the other rooms?'

'Of course.'

Jan nodded and Sigrid went into the nursery. Meanwhile Jan opened the door for Max and his mother and waved them off.

Three minutes later, Sigrid was back, biting her lip and looking even more worried. 'I don't know where he is . . .' She ran a hand over her spiky hair. 'I don't remember if William was with us when we left the forest . . . I mean, he was definitely there on the way up, I remember that, but I don't know if . . . I'm not sure if he was with us on the way back. Do you remember?'

Jan furrowed his brow, as if thinking deeply. He had a vivid mental picture of William running along the ravine, but he answered quietly, 'Sorry . . . I wasn't really keeping a tally of the children from Brown Bear.'

Sigrid didn't say anything. They looked at one another and she rubbed her face, as if she was trying to wake up. 'I'd better get back to his dad. But I think . . . I think we're going to have to call the police.'

'OK,' said Jan. He felt a hard icicle drop down somewhere between his lungs, spreading its chill right through his belly.

We're going to have to call the police.

It had begun. And Jan was no longer in control.

25

Like a criminal, a spy or a secret courier, Jan is careful not to run any risks with the letters from St Psycho's. He takes a long detour on his journey to work the next morning and quickly stuffs the whole lot in a postbox on a deserted street. *Good luck*. Forty-seven letters from patients, on their way out into the world.

Frost and patches of ice are starting to appear on the roads now; he will have to stop cycling soon if he wants to avoid skidding. It's lethal.

Small feet come racing up to him in the cloakroom when he arrives at the Dell. It's Matilda, and her eyes are shining. 'The police are here!'

She's joking, of course.

'Oh yes?' Jan says calmly, unbuttoning his jacket. 'And what do they want? Have they come to have a glass of squash with us?'

Matilda looks confused until he winks at her. Pre-school children can say just about anything; they find it difficult to distinguish between what is true and false, between reality and fantasy.

But the police actually *are* there. Not at the pre-school, but at the hospital. When Jan looks out of the kitchen window a quarter of an hour later, he sees a police car parked over by the entrance, with two uniformed officers walking along the inside of the perimeter fence. Their eyes are fixed on the damp ground, as if they are looking for something.

Only then does Jan feel a small beat of anxiety in the back of his mind. This always happens when he sees police officers, ever since what happened at Lynx.

Marie-Louise comes into the kitchen.

'What are the police doing here?' Jan asks.

'I don't know . . . something seems to have happened up at the hospital.'

She doesn't sound concerned, but Jan presses her. 'Has someone escaped?'

'I shouldn't think so,' says Marie-Louise. 'But I'm sure we'll find out tomorrow when the report comes out.'

She is referring to Dr Högsmed's weekly report. It comes through to the computer in the pre-school and Marie-Louise prints it out, but so far it has made very dull reading.

Jan waits, but there is no peremptory knock on the door of the pre-school. The next time he looks out of the window the police car has gone.

He starts to relax and forgets the visit, until it is almost ten o'clock and time for Felix to be escorted to the visitors' room. Marie-Louise comes over to him in the playroom and says quietly, 'No visits today, Jan – they've been postponed.'

'Oh?' Jan automatically lowers his voice as well. 'Why's that?'

'There's been a death up at the hospital.'

'A death?'

Marie-Louise nods, and whispers, 'A patient died last night.'

'But how?'

'I don't know . . . but it was obviously unexpected.'

Jan doesn't ask any more questions; he carries on playing with the children. Tag and hide-and-seek. But his mind is elsewhere. He keeps on thinking about the letters he left in the visitors' room last night. Love letters, but perhaps threatening letters as well.

Where does Lars Rettig live? What's his telephone number? Jan can't find him in the directory, and he can think of only one way of getting hold of him, so that evening after work he goes into town. First of all he calls in at Bill's Bar, but the Bohemos are not playing tonight.

161

Jan doesn't give up; he carries on to the place where they rehearsed the other day. The door is closed, but he can hear the sound of guitars coming from inside, and the beat of the snare drum. It makes Jan feel forgotten, excluded.

He knocks, but nothing happens.

Then he bangs on the door with the flat of his hand, but the music continues. In the end he opens the door and sticks his head inside.

The music stops. First the guitars, then the drums. Four heads turn towards him.

'Hi, Jan.' Lars Rettig has decided to acknowledge him, after a brief silence.

'Hi, Lars. Could we have a quick word, please?'

'Sure – come on in.'

'I meant . . . just the two of us.'

Jan feels as if they are all staring at him. The musicians behind Rettig have stopped in mid-movement; they are ready to carry on playing as soon as Jan leaves. Carl, the drummer, is a new face, but Jan thinks he has seen him somewhere before.

'OK,' Rettig says. 'I'll be there in a minute.'

The Gang of Four, Jan thinks. Perhaps the members of the Bohemos all work at St Psycho's.

He recognizes Carl now. The guard dog with the big jaws. He was the one who met little Josefine as she came out of the lift, with a canister of tear gas on his belt.

Carl is staring at the door, his expression grim. Jan moves back, but no doubt Carl has already seen him.

Rettig comes over. 'I haven't got much time, Jan, just a couple of minutes . . . Let's go outside.'

They walk along the deserted pavement for about ten metres before Rettig stops. 'OK, we can talk here.'

Jan finds confrontation difficult, but he pulls himself together. 'Who died last night?'

Rettig just looks at him. 'Who *died*?'

'We heard this morning, they said someone had died at St Patricia's.'

162

Rettig seems to hesitate, but eventually he replies. 'It was a patient.'

'A man or a woman?'

'A man.'

'One of the letter-writers?'

Rettig looks around, then leans closer. 'Don't mention the letters.' He smiles at Jan, but it is a tense smile.

Jan wonders if Rettig knows that he slipped an extra letter into the envelope, a message for the patient he thinks is Alice Rami. There is always that risk.

'I just want to know what this business with the letters is all about,' he says. 'Why they're important to you. Can you tell me?'

At first Rettig doesn't answer, but then he lowers his gaze. 'My brother is inside,' he says. 'My half-brother, Tomas.'

'At St Patricia's?'

Rettig shakes his head. 'Prison. Tomas is in Kumla, he got eight years for robbery with violence. And *he* would really like to receive letters, lots of letters . . . but most are stopped. And I'm not allowed to have any contact with him at all, or that's the end of my job.' He sighs. 'So I'm doing something on the sly for those poor bastards in St Patricia's instead.'

Jan nods. Perhaps this is true. 'But the person who died . . . was he one of the letter-writers?' he asks again. 'Or someone who got a letter last night?'

'No.' Rettig sounds weary as he replies. 'He was a paedophile who was in there because he'd been sectioned; he certainly didn't have any pen friends. He only had one friend left, and that was an extra head attached to his left shoulder. He was quiet and pleasant, but his extra head wasn't nice at all. Of course he was the only one who could see it . . . but he said it was the head that made him want to do things to little girls. He had no contact with anyone outside the hospital; even his lawyer couldn't bring himself to visit him, so he just got more and more depressed.'

'What did he do?'

Rettig shrugs his shoulders. 'Well, this morning he got a fresh burst of energy. He and his extra head managed to get into a room

163

without any bars at the window, then they threw themselves out, straight down on to the stone terrace from the fifth floor.'

'This morning?'

Rettig begins to move back towards the rehearsal room. 'Yup. We found him at half past six, but the doctor thought he'd probably jumped at around four. That's when the loneliness gets to us the most, don't you find?'

Jan has no answer to that; just hearing about the suicide is making him feel bad, as if it were his fault. 'I don't know,' he says. 'I'm asleep then.'

26

The concrete wall by the pre-school carries with it a feeling of hopelessness. Hopelessness and brutality. Sometimes Jan is filled with those feelings when he stares at the wall, so when he is out in the playground with the children he often looks across at the school's other neighbours, the rows of terraced houses.

Everyday life goes on over there – cars come and go, children walk to school, lights are switched on in bedrooms on dark mornings and switched off at night. The people in the houses have their daily routines, just as everyone in the pre-school does.

It is the middle of October, and dark clouds come scudding across from the coast. The children are playing outside, but suddenly icy raindrops begin to spatter the ground, and Jan quickly takes everyone into the playroom. It will soon be time for their health assessment anyway. Hanna Aronsson, who turns out to have trained as a nurse in the past, calls the children into the staffroom one by one and checks them over, examining their pupils and measuring their blood pressure and heart rate.

'Fit as fleas,' she says afterwards.

They gather in the snuggle room, where Marie-Louise leads the weekly suggestion session. The children always have lots of requests.

'I'd like a pet,' says Mira.

'Me too!' Josefine shouts.

'But why?' asks Marie-Louise. 'You've got your cuddly toys, haven't you?'

'We want *real* animals!'

'Animals that move!'

Mira looks at Marie-Louise and Jan, her eyes pleading. 'Please . . . please can we have a pet?'

'I want stick insects!' Leo shouts. 'Lots of stick insects!'

'A hamster,' Hugo says.

'No, I want a cat,' says Matilda.

The children are excited, but Marie-Louise is not smiling. 'Animals have to be looked after,' she says.

'But we *will* look after them!'

'They have to be looked after all the time. And what happens when there's nobody here?'

'Then they can live here on their own, in a cage,' says Matilda with a smile. 'We'll just lock them in with loads of food and water!'

Marie-Louise still isn't smiling; she shakes her head. 'Animals shouldn't be left locked up.'

That evening Jan is alone with two of the children, and they both fall asleep quickly. From this week it is only Leo and Mira who will be staying overnight; Matilda now has a foster family who pick her up at five o'clock each day. There is an elderly woman and a man in a grey cap; they seem friendly and reliable. Jan can only hope this is true. But how can you know? He thinks back to Rettig's comment on the patient who killed himself: *He was quiet and pleasant, but his extra head wasn't nice at all.*

We have to be brave enough to trust people. Don't we? Jan is very trustworthy – except for those few minutes at night when he leaves the sleeping children alone and takes the lift up to the hospital.

He does it again this evening, his heart pounding. The memory of hearing someone coming down in the lift and walking out through the pre-school lingers on, but nothing has happened since, and he is trying hard to forget that night.

His pulse rate increases in the empty visitors' room, because there is a new envelope waiting for him under the sofa cushions with the instruction OPEN THIS AND POST CONTENTS! Jan would like to open the envelope in the staffroom at the Dell, but he can't take the risk; it's twenty to ten, and any minute now Hanna will be arriving to take over.

Sure enough, she comes in from the cold at ten to ten.

'Everything OK?' Strands of blonde hair have escaped from beneath her woolly hat, and her cheeks are glowing; she seems unusually exhilarated.

Jan just nods to her and pulls on his jacket. 'They went off at about half-seven. Things are much calmer with just the two of them.'

He has nothing more to say to Hanna, and picks up his rucksack containing the hidden envelope – but suddenly he realizes he still has one of the key cards in his back pocket. He closed the door leading to the basement when he came back from the visitors' room, but forgot to return it to the kitchen drawer.

Idiot.

He turns around. 'I think I forgot something . . .'

'What?' Hanna asks.

But he is already in the kitchen.

'Did you forget to put back the card?' Hanna is right behind him, still wearing her leather coat and woolly hat. Her cheeks are not quite so red now.

'Yes . . .' Jan closes the drawer and straightens up. 'This afternoon, after the last handover.'

'I've done that too.'

Jan doesn't know if she really believes him, but there's nothing he can do about it. He wishes her goodnight and sets off home. At least he hasn't forgotten the envelope from the hospital; it is safely hidden in his bag.

As soon as he gets in his fingers rip open the envelope. His hands are trembling as he sorts through the letters on the kitchen table. It isn't nerves, but anticipation. He dare not believe that there will be a reply from Rami already, but—

Yes, there is a letter addressed to Jan Larsson, at his old address. Rettig has let it through, if he noticed it at all.

167

Jan picks it up and puts it to one side. He gathers up the remaining twenty-three letters and places them on the hall table; he will go out and post them late tonight. But first of all he opens his own letter.

There is just one sheet of white paper inside, with three sentences firmly printed in pencil, and no signature:

THE SQUIRREL WANTS TO GET OVER THE FENCE.
THE SQUIRREL WANTS TO JUMP OFF THE WHEEL.
WHAT DO YOU WANT?

Jan places the letter on the table in front of him. Then he fetches a sheet of paper and sits down to write a reply. But what should he call her? Alice? Maria? Or Rami? In the end he writes just a few short sentences, as neatly and legibly as possible:

I want to be free, I want to be a sunbeam you can hang a clean sheet on. I am a mouse hiding in the forest, I am a lighthouse-keeper in a building made of stone, I am a shepherd who cares for lost children.
My name is Jan.
I was your neighbour fifteen years ago.
Do you remember me?

That is all he writes for now; he can't send a letter to Rami anyway until it is time for the next delivery.

Rami must remember where they were neighbours, and when. She must remember those days in the Unit.

Jan has worn long-sleeved shirts and jumpers ever since. He pulls up his right sleeve now and looks at the faint pink lines following the veins. His own mark, his memory of his schooldays.

He could just as easily have pulled up his left sleeve; the razor blade has left long scars on both arms.

The Unit

The first thing Jan heard when he woke up was sorrowful music.

Slow guitar chords in a minor key. They sounded close, they were coming from the other side of the wall, and they just kept on and on. Someone was sitting there playing, the same simple chords over and over again.

Jan was lying in a bed, a sturdy bed with rough sheets. He opened his eyes and saw a broad bedstead made of stainless steel. A hospital bed.

The walls around his bed were high and white. He was in a hospital room.

He listened and listened to the guitar music, unable to move; there was no strength in his arms and legs. His stomach and his head were throbbing.

His throat remembered tubes – soft tubes worming their way down to suck out the mess in his guts. The taste of bile, the smell of sour milk.

That's what happens when you have your stomach pumped. It was terrible. His empty stomach was aching and felt like a balloon, pushing up towards his throat. He wanted to be sick, but he didn't have the strength.

He heard voices approaching, but closed his eyes and disap-. peared once more.

*

The next time Jan woke up, the guitar music had stopped. He closed his eyes again, and when he eventually looked up a tall man with long hair and a brown beard was leaning over him.

He looked like Jesus, dressed in a T-shirt with a yellow smiley on the front.

'How are you feeling, Jan?' His voice echoed in the bare room. 'My name is Jörgen . . . Can you hear me?'

'Jörgen . . .' Jan whispered.

'That's it, Jörgen. I'm a nurse here. Are you OK?'

He wasn't OK, but nodded anyway.

'Your mum and dad have gone home,' said the man. 'But they're coming back. Do you remember their names?'

Jan didn't say anything; he was thinking. It was strange. He could remember Mum and Dad's voices going on and on, but not their names.

'No?' said Jörgen. 'What about your name, then? What's your name?'

'Jan . . . Hauger.'

'Good – well done, Jan. Would you like to have a shower?'

Jan stiffened in his bed. *No shower.* He shook his head.

'OK . . . Try to get a little more sleep then, Jan.'

Jörgen floated backwards, away from the bed and out of the shimmering room.

Time passed. Jan heard a clicking sound. When he moved his head he could see that the door of his room was ajar. Something was moving out there. An animal? No. A pale face was looking in at him: a tall, slender girl of about his own age, with chalk-white hair and brown eyes. She stood there staring at him, her expression neither friendly nor malicious.

Jan swallowed; his mouth was dry. He tried to raise his head. 'Where am I?'

'In the Psych Unit.'

'In the what?'

The girl looked at him meaningfully. 'The Unit.'

Jan said nothing. He didn't understand. The girl didn't say

anything more either; she just carried on looking at him, then suddenly she raised her arms and pointed a little black box at him. There was a pop and a flash.

He blinked. 'What are you doing?'

'Hang on a minute.' She pulled a square of paper out of the camera, took two steps into the room and threw it down next to his pillow. 'There you go,' she said quietly.

Jan looked at the piece of paper, picked it up and watched as a picture started to appear. It was one of those photographs that developed itself, and he saw a pale face and a thin body gradually beginning to take shape. It was him, lonely and afraid in a hospital bed.

'Thanks,' he said. But when he looked up at the door, the girl had disappeared.

There was silence for a minute or so, and then the guitar began to play again.

Jan was feeling slightly better, and sat up. The main light was switched off and the blinds were closed, but he could see that the bed was standing in a small, bare room – almost a cell – with a desk and a chair on which his jeans and T-shirt lay neatly folded. His shoes were on the floor, but somebody had removed the laces.

His arms were itchy; he touched them and felt the bandages. They were wrapped around his forearms, as if he were an Egyptian mummy.

Someone had saved him and now he had woken up, even though he wanted to go on sleeping. Sleeping, sleeping, sleeping in the Unit.

The Unit?

He found out a couple of days later that it was an abbreviation, a nickname. At some point the full name, *Child and Adolescent Mental Health Unit*, had been shortened to save time.

Whatever it was called, the Unit was a place for those who were disturbed and those who were lost.

Lynx

Jan had led the small group of police officers and nursery staff straight up into the forest, but after a few hundred metres he had veered off, moving further and further away from the place where the game of hide-and-seek had started.

The officer in charge was standing on the path with his legs apart; Jan thought he had hard eyes. 'Is this where he disappeared?'

Jan nodded.

'You're absolutely sure about that?'

'Yes.'

The officer was at least one metre ninety, dressed in black boots and dark blue overalls. He had five colleagues with him. They had arrived in three patrol cars and parked on the road down below the forest.

William's father hadn't joined the search party; he had gone to fetch his wife. Jan had caught a glimpse of his face outside the nursery; it was stiff and terrified.

The police officer was still staring at Jan. 'So you had *nine* children when you started the game just here . . . and *eight* when you finished it?'

Jan nodded again. 'That's right. Nine boys to begin with.'

'Didn't you notice that one of them was missing?'

Jan glanced sideways, avoiding the policeman's gaze. He didn't need to pretend to be nervous now – he *was* nervous. 'No, unfortunately I didn't . . . The group was very boisterous, both when we walked up into the forest and on the way home. And this boy, William, he wasn't a Lynx.'

'*A lynx?* What are you talking about?'

'That's the name of my section of the nursery – Lynx.'

'But surely you were responsible for him today, during the excursion?'

'Well, yes,' Jan conceded, his expression resigned. 'Me and Sigrid.'

He glanced over at her. Sigrid Jansson was standing among the fir trees about ten metres away, her eyes red from weeping. When the police had arrived at the nursery and started to ask questions, she had more or less broken down, which was why the officer in charge had turned his attention to Jan.

'And when William went off to hide, which direction did he go in?'

'That way.' Jan pointed south. Even though the lake wasn't visible from here, he knew that it lay in that direction – in exactly the opposite direction from the one William had taken.

The police officer straightened up. He sent one man down to search in and around the nursery, then looked at the others. 'OK, let's move!'

The group spread out and began to search, but they all knew time was short. It was ten past five, the autumn sun had already set – it was dark and grey among the trees. In half an hour the light would fade, and in an hour it would be pitch dark.

Jan followed as straight a route as possible through the trees, appearing to search as carefully as everyone else. He called for William and looked around, but of course he knew they were searching in completely the wrong place. He shouted, but all the time he was thinking about how thick the concrete walls of the bunker were.

27

It's a few days before Rettig delivers another envelope to Jan. But by then Jan has met the nocturnal visitor to the pre-school.

The sun shines on these October days, and life is looking better and better; the shadows from the Unit and Lynx are slowly fading. In Jan's opinion he is a *totally* reliable colleague at this stage, popular with both the children and the other members of staff. The letters he smuggles into St Psycho's cannot alter the fact that he is an extremely conscientious pre-school teacher.

After all, he *likes* the children. Perhaps it is a sense of guilt, or the fear of being found out, that makes him work so hard for the *welfare and security of the children, building a solid foundation for lifelong learning* and *enabling them to develop into responsible and ethically aware citizens*, and all the other excellent aims he learned about during his professional training.

The other members of staff sneak out occasionally for a bit of fresh air or a quick smoke, but Jan remains with the children all the time. He jokes with them, listens to them, calms them down, dries their tears and sorts out all their little arguments. He spends a great deal of time with Leo, trying to gain his trust.

Sometimes when he is in the middle of a game he can see no difference between himself and the children. The years fall away, he is five or six years old and able to live completely in the present. No demands, no worries about the future, no anguish because of his loneliness. Just cheerful shouts and a warm feeling of total involvement. Life is going on *here and now.*

But sometimes he catches a glimpse of someone moving behind the perimeter fence at St Patricia's, and he abandons the game for a moment and thinks of Rami.

Rami the animal lady, Rami like an animal in a cage.

In a safari park the predators are enclosed together with the herbivores. But the difference between the dangerous animals and those that are harmless is always difficult to see.

The squirrel wants to be free, Rami wrote. And he wants to get inside St Psycho's to see her. He wants to talk to her, just like before.

'Jan!' the children shout. 'Look, Jan!'

Sooner or later one of the children starts tugging at his arm, and he is back in the moment.

It is afternoon, and the sun disappears behind the bare trees in the west. The autumn sky quickly grows dark. Jan has one last evening shift, then four days off.

He puts the children to bed and is due to be relieved at ten. When he happens to glance outside just before nine thirty, he sees a man and a woman walking along the street, side by side.

The woman is Lilian, but who is the man? They are walking so close together that they look like a married couple, but surely Lilian is divorced? Jan watches the man hug her outside the pre-school, then turn and disappear into the darkness.

In spite of the hug Lilian doesn't seem particularly happy when she walks in; she is frowning, in fact.

Jan is feeling very calm; he has devoted all his attention to the children this evening. 'Is it cold outside?' he asks.

'What? Yes . . . yes, it is cold. It's almost winter, after all.'

'Typical. I've got a few days off and I'm going away.'

'Great.'

Lilian doesn't ask where he is going; she seems stressed. She hangs up her coat in the cloakroom, looks wearily at the clock and then at Jan. 'I'm a bit early,' she says, 'but you can go if you want.'

Jan looks back at her. 'I could stay for a while.'

'No, you go. I'll be fine.' Lilian pushes past him and goes into the kitchen. The furrow in her brow is still there, and she hasn't asked a single question about the children.

Jan gazes after her for a long time. 'OK then,' he says eventually. 'I'll go.'

He puts on his jacket and shoes and takes his rucksack out of his locker with exaggerated movements, making sure she can hear him. It's almost like theatre. 'I'm going now . . . Bye then!'

'Bye.'

He closes the door behind him. It is very cold now the sun has gone, and as he walks away from the outside lights at the Dell, it is like wading into a deep pond; the playground is in total darkness. But his eyes slowly grow accustomed to the gloom, and out in the street he sees a figure dressed in a dark padded jacket and a black hood approaching from the bus stop.

The shadow is heading towards the pre-school. Towards him.

Jan moves instinctively to one side. He hides behind the play-house, waiting and listening.

He hears the rattle of the gate as it opens and closes. The front door of the pre-school opens and closes.

Jan steps out. The playground is empty. To the left of the play-house he sees the three swings, swaying gently in the night breeze. He goes over and sits down on the biggest one, which is made from an old tyre.

He pushes his hands deep in his pockets and waits. For what? He isn't sure, but he is warmly dressed and he can sit here for a while.

He remains motionless on the swing, gazing across at the hospital and the illuminated fence. From time to time he glances over at the windows of the pre-school, and once he sees Lilian dashing past in the dining room. She is alone; there is no sign of a visitor.

Quarter past ten. Nothing is happening. The lights begin to go out in the houses on the far side of the field as weary mums and dads go to bed. Jan shivers and gives himself a shake, but remains where he is.

Ten minutes later he is too cold, and he is starting to get tired of this. He is just about to make a move when the front door of the pre-school opens. Jan freezes. He sees a figure step out on to the porch.

It isn't Lilian; it's the visitor in the padded jacket and hood. A lithe figure moving quickly away from the building. The figure does not look over in the direction of the swings, but walks straight down the path and out through the gate. Jan hears the sound of heels clicking on the tarmac.

He gets up slowly and takes a few steps towards the gate.

The figure in the padded jacket has reached the first street lamp. It turns its head and gazes up at the hospital, and at the same moment a cigarette lighter flares into life – and Jan sees that the figure is his colleague, Hanna.

Hanna Aronsson. The youngest member of staff at the Dell, and the quietest. Since the evening when they walked home from Bill's Bar together, she has hardly spoken to Jan. And he has made a point of avoiding her, after telling her about Lynx and William that night when he'd had too much to drink.

Jan leaves his bike by the gate and silently follows Hanna down the street, staying out of the pools of light cast by the street lamps. She is heading for the bus shelter. She stops there, smoking her cigarette.

Jan stops too, fifty metres away.

What is he going to do? He needs to make his mind up before the bus comes, and eventually he walks up to the shelter, a tense smile on his face. 'Evening, Hanna!'

Her blue eyes look up and lock on to him. There is no answering smile. 'Jan.'

He stops a couple of paces away from her and lets out a long breath. 'That's it then – no more work for a few days!'

'Right,' says Hanna.

'So what have you been doing this evening?'

She carries on staring at him, but doesn't answer, so in the end he tries again: 'Where are you off to?'

Hanna drops the cigarette butt and stamps on it. 'Home.'

Jan lowers his voice, even though they are alone in the bus shelter. 'Have you been visiting someone at the hospital?'

She doesn't answer this time either. Jan hears a rumbling noise behind them; the bus into the town centre is approaching. When they get on, Hanna goes right to the back of the bus, glancing over her shoulder as if she wants to get away from Jan. But he follows and sits down next to her.

The bus is almost empty, but he speaks quietly. 'Can we have a chat first, Hanna? Before you go home?'

'What about?'

He jerks his head backwards, in the direction of St Patricia's. 'About what you do up there.'

28

Jan and Hanna end up at the Medina Palace, at her suggestion. The night club is in the cellar of the Tureborg, Valla's only luxury hotel, a towering structure of steel and glass which seems to aspire to being a real skyscraper. As pre-school teachers coming straight from work they're not exactly dressed for the occasion, and Jan actually has milk stains on his jumper after Matilda knocked her glass over during break. The suited and booted bouncer opens the door for them, but his expression is slightly dubious.

'Do you come here often?' Jan jokes.

'Sometimes.'

Hanna has already smoked two cigarettes since they got off the bus; she answers him quietly, looking down at the floor as they walk into the club.

Into an enormous playroom.

Jan has never been to a real night club, not even in Gothenburg, and when he sees the high, black ceilings adorned with long, curved pipes, and the cold metal surfaces of the walls, he knows he shouldn't be here. But there aren't many people in the club this Thursday evening. The music is just right – quiet enough for them to be able to talk, but loud enough to stop anyone eavesdropping.

Jan chooses a glass table in the corner – a secluded table for sharing secrets. 'What are you having?'

'Something with orange juice in it.'

Jan goes over to the bar. The selection is more upmarket than at

Bill's Bar; there is a range of cocktails, champagne, cognac . . . He goes back with two glasses of orange juice, but when Hanna takes her first sip, she looks disappointed.

She nods in the direction of the bar. 'I said something with orange juice *in it* . . . Can you go and get me a proper drink?'

'Like what?'

'Something to calm me down.'

Jan looks at her. 'You mean vodka or something?'

'Good idea.'

Five minutes later they are staring at their drinks in silence.

'So you crept up on me this evening,' Hanna says eventually.

'Well, I don't know about that . . . I thought Lilian seemed a bit tense when she arrived, so I waited in the playground to see if I could find out why.'

Hanna gazes down at the table. 'Did you know I was up at the hospital?'

'No, but I know someone has been there and then left via the school, so I've been wondering who it might be. Have you been up there often?'

Hanna takes a huge gulp of her drink, as if her vodka and orange juice was a health drink after a sauna. Jan takes a small sip of his.

'A few times,' Hanna says. 'I haven't kept count.'

'And how long has this been going on for?'

'Since May. I'd been working at the Dell for four months by then.'

'And Lilian knows about this?'

Hanna gazes at him with her blue eyes; she seems to be wondering how much to tell him, and in the end she says, 'Yes. I mean, we're friends, so she keeps an eye out for me . . . I only go up there when she's on nights.'

'No,' says Jan. 'You were up there one night when I was working. I heard you coming down in the lift. Then you went out through the Dell.'

'You're right . . . I was late that night.'

'And you were in the visitors' room at the hospital tonight?'

Hanna nods without speaking.

180

'What do you *do* up there?'

No reply.

'Are you meeting someone? Is it one of the guards?'

Hanna takes a couple of sips and peers into her half-empty glass. Then she changes the subject. 'I get so bloody tired of the kids sometimes. I enjoy the job most of the time, but when I've been with them for too long I start to get a bit panicky. They just want to do the same things, over and over again. Play the same games . . .'

Jan has never actually seen Hanna *playing* with the children; usually she just stands there watching them while they play on their own. But he smiles. 'Everybody feels like that now and again.'

Hanna sighs. 'I feel like that nearly all the time. I can't cope with hordes of kids, somehow.'

Jan sees the children from the Dell in his mind's eye. Cheery faces. Josefine, Leo and all the others. 'You should try to see them as individuals,' he says. 'They've all got their own character.'

'Oh yes? They sound like a troupe of monkeys to me. They spend all bloody day screaming; I'm practically deaf when I get home after work.'

Hanna empties her glass and an awkward silence falls.

Jan stands up. 'I'll get another round in.'

She doesn't object. When he returns with fresh drinks he wants to get back to the previous topic of conversation, so he looks around before asking, 'So do you know someone up at the hospital, then?'

Hanna hesitates, but then mumbles that she does.

'Who is it?'

'I'm not telling you. Who do *you* go to see?'

'Nobody,' Jan says quickly. 'Not one of the patients, anyway.'

'But you want to get to them, don't you? I mean, you were down in the basement that night when I came back . . . Why do you go creeping around down there?'

Now it is Jan's turn to fall silent. 'Curiosity,' he says eventually.

'Yeah, right.' Hanna smiles wearily at him. 'But there's no point in searching for a way in down there.'

'Oh? But you get through the sally port without any problems?'

She nods quickly. The vodka seems to be making her more

relaxed. 'I've got a contact. In the hospital, I mean. Someone I can trust.'

'A guard?' Jan immediately thinks of Lars Rettig.

'Kind of.'

'Who is it?'

'I'm not saying.'

This is like a game of chess, Jan thinks. A game of chess in a night club.

The music is louder now, and the place no longer seems quite so big. More people have arrived and begun to fill up the tables and the stools by the bar. It's only to be expected, of course; the Medina Palace is a night club, with the emphasis on *night* – people arrive late, and now they're here to stay. The night people.

But no one comes to join Jan and Hanna; they are sitting very close together now, as if they have been friends since childhood.

'You and I should trust each other too,' Jan says.

Hanna's blue eyes are cool. 'Why?'

'Because we can help each other.'

'In what way?'

'Well, in different ways . . .' Jan breaks off. He has grasped that Hanna might be able to help him meet Rami, but he doesn't know how.

Hanna's glass is empty. She looks at her watch. 'I've got to go.' She starts to get up, a little unsteadily.

'Wait,' Jan says quickly. 'Stay a bit longer. I'll get us another drink. Do you like liqueurs?'

Hanna sits down again. 'Maybe.'

'Good.' He dashes over to the bar; he is as fast as Rami's squirrel, and he comes back with four small glasses on a tray. A double round of coffee liqueurs, to save time. 'Cheers, Hanna.'

'Cheers.'

The drink tastes sweet and the world becomes even more noticeably wrapped in cotton wool. The beat of the music grows louder, and he leans closer to her. 'So what do you think of Marie-Louise?'

Hanna gives a little smile. 'Miss Control Freak,' she says with a snigger. 'She'd have a heart attack if that thing you told me about happened at our place.'

'What thing?'

'That business with the boy who disappeared in the forest.'

Jan gives a curt nod, but keeps his eyes fixed on the table. He doesn't want to talk about William, so he changes the subject. 'Is Lilian married?'

'No. She was, but it didn't work out . . . Her husband kind of got bored.'

Jan doesn't ask any more questions, but he wonders about the man who walked Lilian to work this evening. Has she got a new boyfriend?

Jan is quite pleased when there is a brief silence, because it means he can have another drink. He tries to pull himself together, and looks at Hanna over the top of his glass. 'Shall we play a game?'

Hanna empties her own glass. 'What kind of game?'

'A guessing game.'

'What about?'

'I'll try to guess who *you* meet at St Psycho's, and you try to guess who *I* want to meet up there.'

'St . . . We're not supposed to call it that.'

'I know.' Jan gives her a conspiratorial smile. 'OK, I'll go first . . . Is it a man?'

Hanna gazes at him tipsily, then nods. 'And yours? Is it a woman?'

Jan nods in return, and goes on: 'Is it someone from your past? Someone you knew before he ended up in St Psych— St Patricia's?'

She shakes her head. 'Did you know this woman?'

Jan nods and sips his drink. 'I met her before . . . years and years ago.'

'Is she famous?' Hanna asks with a smile.

'Famous?'

'Yes. Did people talk about her, did she have her name and her picture in the papers? Because of some crime?'

Jan shakes his head; he isn't lying. After all, Rami was never *famous* – not as a criminal, anyway. She wasn't very well known at all; as far as he is aware, she never appeared on television. He raises his glass to Hanna. 'And your friend on the inside,' he says. 'Is *he* famous?'

Hanna stops smiling; her gaze slides sideways. 'Maybe,' she says quietly.

Jan carries on looking at her. Suddenly another name comes into his head, a very well-known name, but it's such a stupid idea that he almost laughs out loud. 'Is it Rössel? Ivan Rössel?'

Hanna visibly stiffens – and suddenly it isn't funny any more.

Jan puts down his glass. 'Surely that's not who you're meeting up there, Hanna? Not Ivan Rössel? He's a murderer!'

She opens her mouth and hesitates briefly, then gets to her feet. 'I have to go.'

And that's exactly what she does, without another word. Jan watches her go, a straight-backed pre-school teacher with blonde hair, making a beeline for the exit.

He stays where he is, holding on to his glass. It's empty, but Hanna's second coffee liqueur is still standing there untouched, so he reaches out and knocks that back as well. It tastes horrible, but he drinks it anyway.

Then he gazes blankly into space, suddenly remembering what Lilian said about Hanna Aronsson: *She's young and a bit crazy, but she has a very exciting private life.*

A bit crazy? She must be, if she's sneaking into St Psycho's and hanging out with Ivan Rössel.

The child-killer.

That's what one of the newspapers called him, and another re-ferred to him as *Ivan the Terrible*.

What is Hanna doing with Rössel?

29

Ivan Rössel is smiling at Jan as if they are good friends. He has broad shoulders and black, curly hair that flops down over his forehead; he looks like a middle-aged rock star. He wears the satisfied expression of a man who seems to enjoy being photographed. Or a man who thinks he is smarter than the photographer.

The photograph was taken by the police, and it is on Jan's computer screen.

Rössel was not a rock musician when the police arrested him, nor a celebrity of any kind; he was a high-school teacher of chemistry and physics at a school here on the west coast. Unmarried and with no close friends. Rössel was popular with the pupils, but some of his colleagues found him arrogant and boastful at times.

His elderly mother has also spoken to a number of newspapers, describing him as 'a good boy with a kind heart'.

Needless to say, most of the articles about Rössel that Jan finds on the internet are concerned with the murders of young men and women allegedly committed by the teacher in various places in southern Sweden and Norway. He has been dubbed *the child-killer*, but in fact he is suspected of murdering teenagers. And his only conviction is for a series of arson attacks.

Rössel was a pyromaniac – or at least fires occurred remarkably frequently in houses and shops wherever he was living, and on two occasions people died as a consequence. Someone broke in at night, stole money and valuables, then set fire to the place.

It wasn't until Rössel had been arrested and sentenced to long-term psychiatric care for the fires and the burglaries that the police began to investigate another remarkable coincidence: the fact that several teenagers had been murdered or had vanished without a trace in the areas where Rössel had been living.

Many aspects of the murder investigation have been kept under wraps, but the newspapers keep on repeating the few details that were made public. Ivan Rössel was not only a teacher, he was also a great camping enthusiast. He owned a large, soundproofed caravan which he would set up in a secluded corner of some Swedish or Norwegian campsite early in the summer. There he would stay until the beginning of the autumn term, keeping himself to himself but undertaking lots of excursions in the area. A number of teenagers were found murdered in the vicinity of the campsites on which he had stayed, and one young man disappeared without a trace. Nineteen-year-old John Daniel Nilsson went outside for a breath of fresh air during a school dance in Gothenburg one evening in May, and never came back.

Jan actually remembers that particular case; he had been living in Gothenburg when John Daniel disappeared, six years ago.

Once Rössel had been locked up for the arson attacks, the police began to investigate the connection between him and the young people who had died or disappeared. But by that time Rössel's caravan had just happened to catch fire, his car had been scrapped, and any evidence was lost. And Rössel himself refused to admit anything.

There are many articles about Rössel's background and camping trips – hundreds of articles – but after reading half a dozen Jan has had enough.

Rössel is incarcerated, and St Patricia's seems to be the right place for him. Surely Hanna Aronsson can't be interested in such a disturbed individual? Or can she?

Instead Jan begins to search for another name on the internet: St Patricia's. But he doesn't find any pictures or long articles, just brief facts and statistics about the hospital from the Prison Service. And a link to St Patricia takes him in completely the wrong direction, to a website about patron saints. He learns that St Patricia was a nun, a member of the Order of St Clare in Stockholm in the fifteenth century. Patricia helped orphaned children, the sick and the old, and the poorest of the poor in the narrow alleyways of the city.

There are just a few lines about the saint, nothing more.

Jan shuts down the computer, stands up and starts to pack. He is going to visit his elderly mother and his childhood home in Nordbro for the first time in six months.

The smells at home are the same. The smells of his mother, her perfumes and pot-pourri. His father died three years ago, but the smell of his tobacco and his aftershave still lingers in the room; it has impregnated the walls.

Jan walks around among all the memories.

There is an old photo of Jan and his brother Magnus, three years his junior, on top of the TV. They are eight and five, smiling at the camera. Next to it there is a recent picture of Magnus as an adult in front of Big Ben, his arm around a girl. Magnus is studying medicine at King's College; he lives in Russell Square in London with his fiancée, who comes from Kensington, and he has a bright future.

Jan looks around the living room and notices that the parquet floor and the glass tables are thick with dust. 'You ought to do a bit more housework, Mum.'

'I can't do the housework . . . Daddy used to do the housework.'

Jan's mother always referred to her husband as *Daddy*.

'Couldn't you get someone in to do a bit of cleaning?'

'Out of the question – I can't afford it.'

His mother spends most of her time sitting in the shabby leather armchair in front of the television, huddled in her dressing gown and pink slippers. Sometimes she stands motionless by the window. Jan wants to get her moving, help her to make decisions, acquire new friends. She has spent too much of her life living through her husband.

Perhaps she is already bored with not having to go to work, only a couple of years after her retirement. She doesn't seem particularly pleased to have Jan home.

'Weren't you supposed to bring your girlfriend with you?' she asks all of a sudden.

'No,' Jan says quietly. 'Not this time.'

Of course Jan has no girlfriend to show around Nordbro. He has no old friends to catch up with in the neighbourhood either, so later that afternoon he takes a long, solitary walk through the town where he grew up.

As usual, on his way to the centre he passes the residential home where Christer Vilhelmsson is cared for along with the other brain-damaged patients, but it is windy and he is not sitting outside today.

Christer was in Year 11 when Jan was in Year 10, and since Jan is now twenty-nine, his schoolmate must be thirty. Time passes, even if Christer himself perhaps does not notice.

Christer was sitting outside on the patio just once when Jan walked past, on a sunny spring day four years ago. He was in a deckchair rather than a wheelchair, but Jan had wondered if he was actually able to walk. Even from the road, from a distance of some fifty metres, Jan could see that this twenty-six-year-old man was an adult only in physical terms. The blank expression and the way he constantly nodded to himself with his head slightly tilted to one side showed that time had gone backwards for Christer Vilhelmsson that night out in the forest. The car that had hit him in the darkness had hurled him into the ditch and back to his childhood.

Jan had stood there gazing at his former schoolmate for a minute or so; once upon a time he had been terrified of Christer. Then he had gone on his way, feeling neither joy nor sorrow.

When he reaches the main square he goes into Fridman's iron-mongery, as he has done a couple of times in the past. Torgny Fridman, the owner's son, has taken over, and this Saturday after-noon Torgny himself is standing behind the counter. He is a slim man of about thirty, with short, pale-red hair.

Jan goes towards the back of the shop to look at axes. He has no wood to chop, but still he picks up several different types of axe, weighing them in his hands and swinging them experimentally through the air.

At the same time he keeps glancing over at the till. Torgny Fridman has acquired a dark-red beard. He is standing behind the counter chatting to his customers, a family with children. He doesn't look in Jan's direction. Fifteen years have gone by, and Torgny seems to have forgotten him. Why should he remember? It is only Jan who remembers.

He picks up the biggest axe, which is almost a metre in length.

The bell on the shop door pings.

'Daddy!' A little boy in a white jumper and jeans which are too big comes racing in, hurtling towards the counter. Behind him is a woman, smiling broadly.

Torgny greets the boy with outstretched arms, picks him up and whirls him around. For a moment he is just a father delighted to see his son, not an ironmonger.

Jan stares at them for a few seconds. The axe is heavy, heavy and perfectly balanced. *Raise it above your head, higher, higher . . .*

He puts it down and leaves the shop without saying hello. He and Torgny were never friends, and they never will be.

The last stop on Jan's tour is Lynx.

The nursery where he worked as a twenty-year-old lies a couple of kilometres from the town centre. He wonders if he really wants to go there, but in the end he does.

The place is all closed up; it is Saturday, after all. He stops by the main door and looks at the wooden building; not much has changed. It is still coated with a brown oil-based paint, but it seems smaller than when he was last here. The painted lynx that used to be on the door has gone; maybe the name has been changed to something gentler now, like Wood Anemone or Mountain Hare. Or the Dell, perhaps.

So this is where he worked, all those years ago. In many ways he was still a lost child when he was at Lynx, even if he didn't realize it at the time. He wonders if anyone from those days is still here. Nina, the supervisor? Sigrid Jansson definitely isn't – she left at approximately the same time as him.

She was broken by that stage. During their last few weeks at the nursery they had avoided one another when they were out in the playground at the same time; there was a strange atmosphere every time Sigrid looked at him. Perhaps it was just a lingering sorrow over everything that had happened, but to him her silence seemed cold and dismissive, or possibly even full of mistrust.

He had often wondered if Sigrid suspected anything, if she had worked out how Jan had made his preparations on the day William disappeared.

Finally, before he goes back to his mother's house, Jan wanders down to the Nordbro pond. It lies below his family home like an almost circular cauldron, and Jan knows the black water well. At night it looks like dark blood.

Fifteen years earlier he was on his way to the bottom of that pond, on his way down through whirling bubbles to the final great coldness – until a neighbour jumped in and pulled him out at the very last moment.

The Unit

When Jan's parents came to visit him in the Unit, the words
attempted suicide hovered between them like a black cloud, but
they were never mentioned.

It was hardly possible to make any sort of conversation at all.
Jan lay beneath the covers, staring at his parents in silence. He
suddenly noticed that his brother wasn't with them.

'Where's Magnus?'

'At a friend's,' his mother said, adding hastily, 'He . . . he doesn't
know anything.'

'*Nobody* knows about this,' said his father.

Jan nodded. Eventually his mother went on, keeping her voice
low: 'We've spoken to your doctor, Jan.'

His father scowled. 'He wasn't a doctor, he was a *psychologist*.'

His father didn't like psychologists. At the dinner table the
previous year he had talked about a colleague at work who was
seeing a therapist, and had called it 'tragic'.

His mother chimed in, 'That's right, he's a psychologist. Anyway,
he said you'd be in here for a few weeks. Maybe four, or maybe a
little bit longer. Is that OK, Jan?'

'Mm.'

The room fell silent again. Jan suddenly noticed there were
tears running down his mother's cheeks. She quickly wiped them
away, just as his father asked, 'Have they spoken to you yet, the
psychologists?'

Jan shook his head.

'You don't have to speak to them, you know,' said his father. 'You don't have to answer any questions, or tell them anything.'

'I know.'

When had he last seen his mother cry? Probably at his grandmother's funeral the previous year. The atmosphere in this room was very similar to the atmosphere in the chapel, when they were all sitting there staring at the coffin.

His mother blew her nose and attempted to smile. 'Have you got to know anyone in here?'

Jan shook his head again. He didn't want to get to know anyone, he just wanted to be left in peace.

His mother didn't say much after that. She didn't cry any more, but she sighed wearily a few times.

His father didn't say another word; he just sat there in his grey suit, rocking back and forth on his chair as if he wanted to get up. From time to time he looked at his watch. Jan knew he had a lot of work, and wanted to get home. When he looked at his son, his expression was irritated and impatient.

That look made Jan nervous, it made him want to get out of bed and forget everything that had happened, just go home and be *normal*.

His mother suddenly raised her head. 'Who's that playing?'

Jan listened too, and heard the sound of soft guitar music coming from the room next door. He knew who was playing. 'It's my neighbour . . . Some girl.'

'There are girls in here too?'

Jan nodded. 'It's mostly girls, I think.'

His father looked at his watch again and got up. 'Shall we make a move, then?'

Jan looked at his mother. 'You go . . . I'll be fine.'

His mother stood up too. She reached out to touch his cheek, but her hand didn't quite get there. 'Yes, I suppose we'd better go,' she said. 'We haven't got long left on our parking ticket.'

Nobody said anything else until his mother turned back in the doorway. 'I nearly forgot . . . Somebody rang you yesterday, Jan. A friend of yours.'

'A friend?'

'He wanted to know how you were . . . I gave him the number of this place.'

Jan just nodded. A friend? He couldn't think of a single friend who might have phoned. Someone from his class? Presumably.

When his parents had left he felt as if he could breathe again. He sat up and slowly climbed out of bed. He went over to the desk and looked out of the window. There was a wide grassy area out there, wet after the winter – and beyond it a high fence with barbed wire along the top. He looked at it for a long time.

The Unit was no ordinary hospital, Jan realized.

He was a prisoner here.

30

Jan is back in Valla. He has cleaned his flat: he is expecting a visit from Hanna.

It was his idea to meet up this evening; when he went back to work at the Dell after his long weekend off, Hanna was also on duty, and when the staffroom was empty he stuck a note in her jacket pocket, with his address and a question: COFFEE AT MINE, 8 O'CLOCK? JAN H.

He didn't get an answer from her before he left, but bought bread on the way home anyway. She has to come – they have shared interests.

Shared secrets.

And Hanna rings his doorbell fairly punctually, at five past eight. She doesn't say much as she walks in, but Jan is pleased. 'I'm glad you came.'

'Thanks.'

Jan tries to relax; he leads her into the kitchen, makes tea and offers sandwiches. Then he makes small-talk about work, but eventually they get to the subject he really wants to discuss: St Patricia's. 'The women up there . . . Are they separated from the men?'

Hanna looks at him, her expression blank as usual. The air in Jan's kitchen suddenly feels thick and heavy, but it is still better to ask Hanna about the hospital than Lars Rettig. 'Yes,' she says eventually, 'there are a couple of women's wards . . . One secure and one open.'

'Are they close together?'

'Not exactly next door, but I think they're on the same floor.'

'And which floor is that?'

'The third, I think. Or the fourth . . . I've never been in there.'

Jan tries to come up with more questions, but suddenly Hanna has something to say: 'Tell me who it is, Jan.'

'Who what is?'

'The person in the hospital that you're in love with . . . What's her name?'

She is staring at him, but Jan refuses to meet her gaze.

'It's different,' he says.

'What do you mean, different?'

'Different from you and Ivan Rössel.'

Hanna slams down her teacup. Her blue eyes are cold. 'What do *you* know about how things are between us? You don't know anything, you don't know why I got in touch with him . . . How can you make a judgement?'

Jan looks down at the table. The atmosphere is suddenly icy. But he was right – it *is* Rössel she has met up with in the visitors' room.

'I'm just guessing,' he says. 'But you do like him, don't you?'

Hanna is still staring at him. 'You have to see the person beyond the crime,' she says eventually. 'Most people can't do that.'

'If you're sneaking in to see Rössel, surely you must like him?' Jan says. 'Even though he's done . . . bad things?'

It takes a while before she answers. 'I don't see him,' she says. 'The contact is through one of the guards. Ivan is working on a project to make the time pass more quickly in there . . . and I'm helping him.'

'With what? What's he doing?'

'It's a writing project. He's working on a manuscript.'

'A book?'

'Kind of.'

'What, like the memoirs of a murderer?'

Hanna's mouth tightens. 'He's a suspect. He's never confessed.' She sighs. 'He says his book will explain everything . . . People will realize that he hasn't done anything.'

195

'And he believes that?'

'Yes, he does.' Hanna's voice is more animated now. 'Ivan feels *really terrible* about how things have turned out; there's a much greater risk that he'll take his own life rather than anyone else's. Right now it's only my letters that are keeping him going . . .'

She stops, and Jan doesn't know what to say. The intense look in Hanna's eyes makes him uneasy; he doesn't really want to talk about Rössel any more.

Neither does Hanna, apparently. 'I have to go soon.' She looks at her watch, then at Jan. 'So are you going to tell me now?'

'Tell you what?'

'Her name . . . the woman you're seeing up there?'

Jan lowers his gaze. 'I haven't seen her yet.'

'So what's her name, then?'

Jan hesitates. He has two names to choose from – Rami or Blanker – but he decides on the least well known. 'Wait a minute,' he says. 'I'm just going to fetch something.'

He goes into the living room and comes back with the picture books: *The Princess with a Hundred Hands, The Animal Lady, The Witch Who Was Poorly* and *Viveca's House of Stone.* He puts them down in front of Hanna. 'Have you seen these before?'

Hanna shakes her head.

'They were up at the pre-school. They're handmade . . . so this is probably the only copy of each one that exists. And somebody must have put them in the book box.'

'Marie-Louise usually puts books in there,' says Hanna.

'Not these . . . I think one of the children was given them by their parent up in the visitors' room.'

Hanna leafs through the books, then looks up at Jan. 'Who wrote them?'

'She calls herself Maria Blanker,' he says. 'She's Josefine's mother . . . I'm almost sure of it.'

'Blanker . . . So she's the one you want to meet at the hospital?'

'Yes . . . Do you know who she is?'

'I've heard a few things about her,' Hanna says quietly.

'From Rössel?'

196

She shakes her head. 'From Carl . . . my contact.'

Jan recognizes the name, of course. The drummer from the Bohemos.

Hanna is still looking at the books. 'Can I borrow them?'

Jan hesitates. 'OK,' he says eventually. 'Just for a few days.'

She gathers up the books and gets to her feet; it's time to go home.

But Jan has one last question: 'Is Maria Blanker on the secure ward or the open ward?'

'I don't know where she is, I've never been inside,' says Hanna, before adding, 'But I should think she ought to be on the secure ward.'

'Why?'

'Because Blanker is psychotic. She's completely out of it. That's what I've heard, anyway.'

'Do you know what she's done?'

'She's dangerous.'

'Is she a danger to herself?' Jan asks. 'Or to others?'

Hanna shakes her head. 'I don't know. So you're going to have to go in and ask her.'

Jan smiles at the joke, but Hanna isn't smiling. 'I'm serious,' she says. 'There's always a way in, if you're willing to take it.'

'But everything is locked at St Patricia's.'

'One way is open.'

'And you know about this?'

She nods. 'I know where it is, but it isn't that easy to get through . . . Do you suffer from claustrophobia, Jan?'

Lynx

Being locked in wasn't all that bad, surely – not if you had plenty of food and drink, and you were warm enough? And a talking ro-bot to keep you company?

Jan convinced himself that this was true, over and over again, whenever he thought about William inside the bunker.

In fact, being locked up behind thick concrete walls could make you feel really safe and secure.

It was half past eight in the evening, and the police had called off the search for William half an hour ago. They had continued after darkness had fallen, using torches, but it had all been very badly organized, in Jan's opinion. And they found nothing. William had vanished without a trace; he could have stepped off the edge of the world.

Or at least disappeared from solid ground. The police had spent the last hour searching the long shore of the lake, and Jan realized they were afraid that the five-year-old had fallen in the water.

Lynx had become an assembly point for the search parties. But they were all tired now, and many of those who had been out looking for the boy were on their way home. When daylight came on Thursday morning, the search would resume, with increased manpower.

Jan had walked back to Lynx with an older police officer, who had puffed and panted his way through the forest. 'Bloody hell . . .

I hate this kind of thing. Let's hope he makes it through the night, but there's not much chance of that.'

'Well, it's quite mild at the moment,' said Jan. 'I'm sure he'll be fine.'

But the officer didn't appear to be listening. 'Bloody hell,' he repeated. 'I remember once a kid was found dead on a forest track . . . He'd been hit by somebody's car, then they'd hidden him in the forest, like a sack of rubbish.' He looked at Jan with weary eyes. 'You never forget something like that.'

When Jan got back to the staffroom he suddenly heard a dull throbbing noise in the distance, a noise which quickly grew to a deafening racket above the nursery.

He looked over at Nina Gundotter, the nursery supervisor. She was waiting by the telephone as if she thought William might ring up sooner or later to tell them where he was.

'Is that a helicopter?' he asked.

Nina explained, 'The police requested it. They couldn't get hold of any dogs, but they're going to fly over the forest now using thermal-imaging cameras.'

Jan nodded. He went over to the window to look at the thermometer; it was showing nine degrees. An autumn temperature – it wasn't bitterly cold out there, but it wasn't warm either. Unfortunately the wind had got up, but of course Jan knew that William was sheltered from the wind.

He had been standing fairly close to Nina when she had approached one of the police officers to ask about their strategy, but the response had been evasive.

'We'll search the lake, of course, but that won't happen until tomorrow, when it's light,' the officer had said, speaking very quietly.

All but two of the staff had returned to the nursery this evening. White candles had been placed on the tables and in the windows, which gave the whole place a church-like atmosphere.

After fifteen or twenty minutes the sound of the helicopter died away. Jan turned to his boss. 'I think I need to go home and try to get some sleep. I'll come back first thing; it's my day off, but I'll come in anyway.'

Nina nodded. 'I'm going shortly myself,' she said. 'There's nothing more we can do tonight.'

Since arriving at the nursery Nina had not uttered one word of criticism to Jan. On the contrary, she appeared to support him completely, blaming the whole thing on Sigrid, who had a different supervisor over at Brown Bear: 'She should have *checked*.'

Jan shook his head. The last time he'd seen Sigrid she had been lying on the sofa in the Brown Bear staffroom; she had been given some kind of sedative when they got back from the forest.

'Neither of us was really on top of things today,' he said, pulling on his jacket. 'It was pretty chaotic up there . . . We had too many children with us.'

Nina sighed. She looked over at the dark windows, then at the telephone. 'I think someone else has found him in the forest,' she said. 'Someone who has taken him home with them . . . I'm sure William is fast asleep in a warm bed somewhere, and the police will get a phone call first thing in the morning.'

'Absolutely,' said Jan, buttoning his jacket. 'See you in the morning.' With a final nod to Nina, he left the nursery.

It felt colder than nine degrees when he got outside, but that was probably just his imagination. It wasn't winter yet, far from it. A warmly dressed person just *couldn't* freeze to death, even if he was lying out in the open. Sheltered from the wind, behind a concrete wall, for example, he would be fine for several days.

Jan set off. As he passed the brightly lit windows of Brown Bear he caught a glimpse of the staff keeping vigil inside, along with William's parents. Jan could see the mother slumped in a chair, a cup of coffee in front of her. She looked terrible.

Jan wanted to stop and stare for a while, but he kept on going.

At the edge of the forest he stood and listened; he could hear nothing but the wind soughing in the trees. The sound of the helicopter had completely disappeared by now. It might come back later with its thermal-imaging camera, but that was a risk he would have to take.

Jan looked around one last time, then stepped over the little ditch by the side of the road and headed off among the trees. He powered up the slope.

William had been alone and locked inside the bunker for over four hours now. But he had warm blankets, food and drink, and toys; he'd be fine. And soon Jan would be there with him.

31

With each autumn evening that passes, St Patricia's grey façade seems a little colder and darker to Jan. As he cycles past the wall on this particular evening, the hospital behind the wall looks like a great fortress. Pale, shimmering lights are visible in many of the windows, but they do not convey a welcoming atmosphere. Shadows seem to be moving inside the rooms, gazing out with longing from behind the bars.

Is one of the windows ajar up there?

Is that guitar music he can hear in the night?

No. Just his imagination.

Jan quickly cycles on past the hospital and down to the pre-school, away from the wall. It is Sunday, and only two months to go until Christmas. He is free this weekend but has come down anyway; he and Hanna parted company four days earlier with a kind of promise to help each other. Or at least not to give each other away.

'You can't get into the hospital through the sally port,' Hanna had said in Jan's kitchen. 'Nobody gets in that way . . . I've never got past the visitors' room.'

'So your friend Carl . . . he lets you and Rössel meet up there?'

'No, Ivan stays in his room. I send him letters.'

More secret letters, Jan thought. But he merely asked, 'So how *do* I get in, then?'

'Through the basement,' Hanna said. 'I can show you the entrance, if you like.'

Jan definitely liked the idea. He remembered that Högsmed had talked about a way from the hospital to the pre-school through the basement. *But it's not a very pleasant route*, the doctor had said.

What does that mean? Are there rats in the basement? Or people?

He arrives at the Dell and cautiously opens the door, knowing perfectly well that he's not supposed to be there tonight.

'Hello?' he says quietly. 'Hanna?'

There's a brief silence, then he hears her voice from the kitchen: 'Come in . . . everything's fine.'

Jan steps inside and closes the door. 'All quiet?'

'Yes – I managed to get them off. But they were like little monsters this evening, running around and screaming, just pushing me to the limit all the time.'

Jan says nothing; he knows that Hanna isn't particularly fond of the children.

As he takes off his jacket he notices that it is almost half past nine. He keeps his shoes on and takes a couple of steps towards the kitchen and the drawer where the keys are kept, but Hanna holds out her hand.

'Here.' She has already taken out one of the key cards, and passes it to Jan.

'Thanks.'

'You haven't changed your mind?'

Jan shakes his head and goes over to the door leading to the basement. It feels a little odd to enter the code and open the door in front of someone else at this late hour.

He turns around. 'See you later.'

'No,' she says. 'I'm coming down with you.'

He has no time to object; she switches on the light and sets off down the stairs, and all Jan can do is follow her.

He uses the underground corridor every day to deliver and collect the children, and by this stage Jan is heartily sick of the pictures on the walls. The smiling mice seem to be sneering at him.

They won't be using the lift tonight. Hanna leads the way to the safe room. Jan hasn't been here for more than two weeks – not since he stood there and heard someone coming down in the lift in the middle of the night. Someone who turned out to be Hanna.

'So there's a secret passageway here?' Jan wants to know.

'Secret . . . Well, it's hidden.' She presses down on the handle and opens the steel door. Then she turns around and looks at Jan. 'Are you sure about this?'

Jan nods.

'Come on, then.'

When Hanna switches on the light and Jan steps into the safe room, he suddenly has a picture in his mind's eye of a frightened little five-year-old boy sitting on a mattress in there. His heart skips a beat – but the light comes on to reveal a completely empty room.

The mattress and the pillows are still there, just as he remembered them. And the steel door at the far end of the room is still closed.

Hanna walks over to the door. 'Here it is.'

'That door is locked,' Jan says. 'I've already tried it.'

'I mean the floor.' She is pointing downwards.

'The floor?'

Jan walks forward – and feels something uneven beneath his feet. He looks down at the blue fitted carpet, but he is standing on something underneath it, something small and narrow.

The carpet covers the entire floor, but it isn't stuck down. Hanna goes over to one corner and lifts it up. Together they pull the carpet back towards the middle of the room. It comes away easily, and Jan can see grey concrete.

'A bit further,' Hanna says. 'Nearly there.'

She seems eager now, urging him on. They carry on pulling at the carpet, and suddenly Jan sees a hatch in the floor, half a metre wide and made of corrugated metal.

'That's the way in,' Hanna says.

Jan looks at the hatch, then at her. 'The way into the hospital?'

Hanna nods. 'It goes right under the wall.'

'Where does it come out?'

'Haven't a clue.'

Jan pulls the carpet back so that the whole of the hatch is exposed, and notices that there is an iron handle. 'How did you find it?'

'I did the same as you down here, looking around, checking things out . . . and I've had more time than you.'

'Has Rössel been helping you?' asks Jan.

She shakes her head.

Jan bends down, grabs hold of the iron handle and lifts off the hatch cover. He puts it to one side and gazes down into a big, square hole. But this isn't a drain; it's some kind of electrical conduit with thick cables running beneath the basement floor. It isn't very deep, perhaps a metre, but it seems to be the beginning of a narrow passage under the concrete, leading towards the locked door. Everything is pitch black down there.

'Are you going down?' Hanna asks.

'Maybe.'

Jan hesitates. He kneels and peers into the passageway. The hole is so dark that he can't see how far it goes. There are some old water pipes next to the cables, and swirling balls of dust. There is a faint smell of mould, or perhaps mud, but the concrete in the tunnel looks dry.

Dry, and wide enough for him. There should be room to climb in and crawl under the floor.

Are there rats' nests down there? Maybe. He listens, his ear cocked towards the underworld, but all is silent. 'Hello?' he whispers.

There is no reply, not even an echo.

Jan gets to his feet. He carefully replaces the cover, but leaves the carpet as it is, and looks at Hanna. 'I'm just going back upstairs . . . I need more light.'

'From what?' she asks.

'From an Angel.'

32

Hanna stares at the equipment Jan has just taken out of his locker.

'What's that?' she asks.

'An electronic baby monitor. Have you never seen one before?'

'No.' She shakes her head as she contemplates the two plastic boxes. 'What are they for?'

Jan looks at her. 'It's obvious you haven't got kids . . . They enable you to keep a check on the children while they're asleep.'

'But why can't you just go and see if they're OK?'

'Not everybody has time . . . or it's a question of security, I suppose. If the children are safe, the parents feel secure.' He thinks about William Halevi, and adds, 'If the parents don't feel secure, they're unhappy.'

Hanna takes one Angel, but doesn't look convinced. 'So what are you going to do with them now?'

'I'm going to use one as a torch,' he says. 'And if I leave the other one with you, you'll be able to hear me.'

'And that will somehow make you feel more secure?'

'A bit.'

Hanna weighs the Angel in her hand and says, 'I can listen, but I can't do any more. I mean, if you need any help down there, I can't—'

'It's enough if you can hear me,' Jan interrupts her.

It would be a lifeline. A bit like going into a cave with a rope around your ankle.

'Are you afraid?' she asks.

'No. I left the fear in the pocket of my other trousers,' he says. He smiles, but doesn't relax. He doesn't know what is going to happen, he doesn't know if the guards patrol regularly, but if he meets anyone down there he had better hope it is Lars Rettig, or some friend of his. If they are to be trusted.

Five minutes later he is standing beside the hole in the basement floor. It is almost half past ten now, but down here there is a feeling of timelessness. In the underworld it is always night.

He holds up the Angel and switches on the lamp. 'OK,' he says into the microphone. 'I'm going in.' His voice echoes in the safe room, but he doesn't know whether Hanna can hear him or not.

Supporting himself with his hands, he lowers his legs to the bottom of the electrical conduit, just about a metre below the floor of the basement. Once he is in, it is easier to bend down and point the lamp into the passageway; he can see that it carries on straight ahead, into the darkness.

He kneels down, breathing in the dry, dusty air. 'I'm going in.'

He makes his upper body as flat and narrow as possible, bends his head and creeps along on his hands and knees. He manages it without banging his head. It's like crawling into a crypt, with immovable blocks of stone on all sides, and the thick ceiling pressing against his back.

Claustrophobia? He has to keep the fear away, not think about coffins and locked sauna doors. He can breathe, he can move. The passageway is wide enough for him to move forward without too much difficulty – he just can't turn around. All he can do if anything happens is to shuffle backwards.

But what could possibly happen?

Jan coughs, feeling a sudden desire for water. It's dusty, but he keeps on going. His shadow dances jerkily over the concrete in the glow of the lamp.

When he shines the light ahead of him, he can see that the passageway ends in a grey concrete wall some ten metres away – or perhaps it just bends to one side.

He speaks into the Angel again: 'I think . . . I think I'm underneath the door of the safe room now.'

He feels slightly ridiculous, talking to himself. And how certain is he that the security guards up at the hospital don't have the right sort of technical equipment to pick up every word he is saying? Not certain at all.

He lowers the Angel, grits his teeth and keeps on moving forward. He listens for scrabbling noises or squeaks, but he can't see any rats. Not yet, anyway. There are little black lumps on the floor that could be droppings – or dead flies. He doesn't want to look too closely.

First one leg, then the other. Crawl, just crawl.

Suddenly Jan notices something on the roof of the passageway, perhaps five metres away. He lifts up the lamp again and sees that there is another hatch cover up ahead, made of corrugated metal, just like the one behind him.

The sight makes him crawl faster, as best he can. His head and shoulders keep banging against the concrete, his hands and knees are growing numb as they press against the floor – but at last he makes it.

He puts down the Angel in front of him and reaches up, almost convinced that the cover will be locked or screwed down.

But it isn't. It is loose, and he places the palms of his hands against the metal and pushes upwards. There is a scraping sound, and the heavy cover moves. He is able to push it to one side, slowly and carefully. To his ears the screech of the metal is deafeningly loud as it moves across the concrete floor, bit by bit, but he keeps on going.

A black hole opens up above him; there is no light. The room above is pitch dark, and when he has finished shifting the cover, there is absolute silence.

Jan slowly gets to his feet with the Angel in his hand. He is now standing upright in a square hole in a concrete floor, an opening which is an exact copy of the one he climbed into – but behind him, by the light of the Angel, he can see what must be the other side of the locked door of the safe room.

He clambers laboriously out of the hole. 'It's worked,' he whispers into the Angel. 'I got through, I'm in . . . some kind of cellar.' Then he switches off the transmitter; it feels wrong to be talking out loud, or even whispering, down here in the silence. He raises the lamp, sweeping it around him like a sabre. But the Angel is not a weapon; Jan has nothing with which he could defend himself, and he feels a bit like a four-year-old who has been left all alone in a big, dark house.

The air is stale here. There are no carpets on the floor, no colourful drawings on the walls. Still, having got out of the cramped tunnel, he ought to be feeling better than he actually does.

He is standing in an empty corridor which leads straight ahead, then disappears into the darkness around a corner. When he moves forward and looks around the corner, he sees a dark doorway seven or eight metres further ahead, on the left-hand side.

Jan hesitates, then begins to edge silently and cautiously towards the open doorway. He is in a completely unfamiliar environment now, and he is totally alone. But he blinks into the darkness and manages to summon up Alice Rami's face – not as she looked when they met as teenagers, but as he has imagined she will look as an adult, the way he has imagined her during all those lonely nights. Beautiful, intelligent, experienced. Perhaps a little weary, bearing the marks of the years that have passed, but strong and smiling.

Rami, his first love, his only girlfriend.

He gropes for a light switch along the walls, but fails to find one. Without the light of the Angel he would be in total darkness down here, but the beam has grown noticeably less bright over the past couple of minutes, and he has no spare batteries.

At the end of the corridor he raises the Angel and peers into the room beyond. It is an enormous cellar which appears to go on for ever. Jan can see white tiles on both the floor and the walls. The floor is grey with dirt and dust, and black mould has spread over every pale surface.

Is it a shower room? No, he can see decrepit bookshelves and steel tables along the walls. Further away there are some yellow plastic curtains, half closed around rusting beds and low washstands.

This is some kind of laboratory; it looks as if it has been closed up and abandoned for decades.

Jan looks around the tiled walls and feels his heart pounding.

He has found his way into St Psycho's.

PART TWO

Rituals

*Madness is a sad, grim business. Loss of control is hardly romantic.
Instead of bringing a release from reality,
it becomes a more complex trap.*

Julian Palacios, *Lost in the Woods*

Lynx

Jan couldn't see much of the forest in the darkness, but he was surrounded by all the sounds of the countryside at night. His boots scuffed rhythmically over rocks and gravel, the night breeze soughed in the fir trees, an owl hooted down by the lake. And the drums kept on beating, but that was just inside his head.

It was almost half past nine and he was on his way out of the narrow ravine. The hillside looming up on his left was no more than a black, shapeless lump, but Jan had found his way easily.

He reached the path down below the bunker a few minutes later; he stopped and listened intently. He couldn't hear any shouting or crying.

He crept up the slope like a cat, silent and wary. When he reached the steel door he lifted away the branches, placed his ear to the metal surface and listened again. Not a sound.

Slowly he drew back the bolts, opened the door and looked in. He heard nothing, felt nothing. It was neither hot nor cold inside the bunker.

Nor was there the smell of fear.

Jan held his breath. Nothing was moving, but in the stillness he could just make out the faint sound of someone breathing.

He tiptoed inside. Slowly and carefully he took out his mobile and switched it on so that a weak white light illuminated the bunker. Roboman was in the middle of the floor, switched on, its little lights flashing away. Jan noticed a couple of empty drinks cartons in one corner, along with open packets of sweets and crumpled sandwich wrappers.

That was good; William had eaten and drunk during the evening. And if he had needed to pee, there was the bucket Jan had placed at the far end of the room.

A little body was lying on the mattress: William. He was moving very slightly in his sleep. At some point during the evening he must have felt tired, and settled down next to the wall. He was now sleeping peacefully beneath a thick layer of blankets.

Jan crept across the room, took the bucket outside and emptied it a few metres away. Then he went back inside and lay down on his back to listen to William's breathing.

At this particular moment Jan felt a fantastic sense of calm suffusing his body. He felt victorious, almost happy that everything had worked out so well today. William had been lured away and locked up, but no harm whatsoever had come to him.

Jan could do this, no problem. Forty-six hours would soon pass.

William's parents were in the worst position; Jan knew they would be suffering agonies right now. Anxiety would have turned into fear, then into sheer terror. They wouldn't sleep tonight, not for one minute.

Jan sighed and closed his eyes. All was well in the forest.

He would just lie here for a while and keep watch over William, even though he was under no obligation to do so – no adult had kept watch over Jan when he'd been locked up.

33

Jan takes short steps through the basement of St Patricia's, stopping frequently, like an explorer in an unfamiliar system of caves. Slowly he gropes his way through dark rooms and corridors turning this way and that, his only support a small torch. The Angel in his right hand has not gone out yet, but the light is growing weaker all the time.

The room he came to first doesn't appear to have any other exits, so he turns back and continues down the corridor. It bends to the right after a few metres, then right again, then left and into another big room with tiled walls and floor. Something crunches beneath his shoes: there is broken glass on the floor.

The Dell seems far away right now; a part of him longs to turn around and head back to the familiarity of the safe room. But instead he keeps on going.

The darkness around him remains silent, which is reassuring.

Jan can see four black doorways leading out of this large, tiled room. He walks over and shines his torch through them one by one, but beyond each opening there is only a dusty passageway leading to a rusty metal door. He decides to ignore three of these passageways, but there is less dust on the floor of the fourth, as if someone has walked on it fairly recently. The door also looks less rusty, so he turns the handle.

Behind it is another corridor, lined with a series of doorways. He peers into the first opening and sees a small, bare room with an old iron bed, but no mattress. When he steps inside and holds up the Angel, he can just make out faded and yellowing postcards pinned to the walls, and some illegible graffiti. It seems to be an old sick room, or a cell.

Jan remembers the Black Hole at the Unit, and quickly backs out.

He glances into each cell, but sees only more bare walls and old iron beds. His steps are getting shorter and shorter. He has never been particularly afraid of the dark, but he is beginning to feel more and more alone down here. The doorways gape at him like black mouths, ready to swallow him up. Are they really empty?

Eventually he switches the Angel's transmitter back on. 'I've gone further into the basement,' he begins, 'but I don't think this area is in use any more. The lights don't work.'

The Angel in his hand is silent, but he hopes Hanna is listening.

'OK, I think I'm going to turn back soon . . .'

Then he stops; he doesn't feel entirely comfortable with the idea of talking down here. With each word he utters, the sense that someone is listening grows stronger. Attentive ears, lurking somewhere in the darkness.

'See you soon,' he whispers, hoping once more that Hanna can hear him before he switches off the transmitter.

The corridor takes a sharp turn, and he edges along it. It leads to yet another large tiled room with steel benches and white plastic curtains; is this a different room, or has he been here already?

Just keep walking. One step, then two, three, four . . .

Jan had been a little bit scared of encountering rats when he crawled out from under the floor, but now he realizes that he is in fact the rat. He is the one who daren't let out a squeak as he cautiously moves across the concrete floor, alert to the slightest sound.

In the big room the shadows gather around him. Fear of the dark begins to creep up on him, so he turns to the right and tries to stick close to the wall.

At first glance these rooms also look as if they have been closed up for many years, but gradually Jan begins to discover signs of more recent visits. On a wooden shelf beside some dark-glass containers, he sees a rolled-up football programme from a local match, and when he opens it up he finds it is from the previous season.

There is more graffiti on the walls, in black felt-tip pen. Just below the ceiling someone has scrawled JESUS SAVE ME IN THY BLOOD, and on another wall nearer the floor are the words I WANT A HOT WOMAN! It looks as if both sentences have been written with the same pen.

It is chilly in the underworld, yet Jan is sweating.

He pulls a cracked plastic curtain aside and discovers an old desk. He tries to open the drawers, but they are locked.

He gives up and stares thoughtfully at the ceiling. Rami is somewhere up above him. There are two wards for the women in the hospital, according to Hanna. But how is he going to get up there?

And where is Ivan Rössel? Here in the darkness he feels palpably close; Jan recalls his smile on the computer screen. But Rössel and the other violent patients must be kept behind locked doors, surely?

Suddenly Jan hears a low, rumbling sound in the distance, followed by an extended cry, like an echo.

He doesn't know exactly which direction the sound is coming from; perhaps it is just his imagination, but it makes him stop and listen, motionless.

He hears nothing more, but eventually he turns around. It's a combination of the noise, the darkness, the isolation down here. The hour is late, and the light from the Angel is growing weaker and weaker. He shines the beam around the big room – but which of the doorways did he actually come through? He can't remember.

He chooses the one on the right. Beyond it there is a long corridor, and suddenly he can see light. He keeps on walking, turns a corner and finds himself in a fairly large hallway with subdued lighting. On the far side is a wide glass door with a green sign that says EXIT, and through that door there is a pale-stone flight of stairs leading upwards.

Jan believes that he has found the way up to the wards, and eagerly steps forward – then stops abruptly. There is a metal box with a black, staring lens up above the glass door.

219

A camera.

If he walks over to the door, the camera will pick him up. So he turns around, goes back into the big room, and chooses the opening on the left.

This corridor is only three metres long and ends in a closed steel door.

Jan is lost.

There is panic in his head and legs now, but he suppresses it, turns around and slowly makes his way back across the tiled floor. It's fine, he will find the way if he just keeps moving and tries every door. He sweeps the dying light of the Angel across the wall and chooses a doorway at random. This time the long corridor feels both alien and familiar at the same time; he passes two more closed doors, and this time the corridor ends in an ordinary wooden door.

He lowers the Angel and opens the door, to be met by a sudden brightness. Strip-lights on a low ceiling. Warm air smelling of bleach rushes towards him, and he sees large white machines with dials and flashing lights. Huge fans and electric motors are whirring and throbbing, and there are baskets full of bedlinen and clothes, as well as a rail attached to the ceiling.

This is a laundry, Jan realizes – St Patricia's Hospital laundry.

He is not alone. A tall, thin man in grey overalls is standing with his back to Jan only five or six metres away, folding sheets. The man has an Mp3 player attached to his belt, his earphones are on, and he hasn't yet noticed Jan. But if he turns around . . .

Jan doesn't wait for that to happen; he closes the door quickly and silently. Then he goes back down the corridor and into the tiled room, heading for the other doorways. He nearly got caught just now – and yet he feels calmer. There are people down here after all, ordinary people doing their jobs.

That is when he hears more sounds, much closer this time: someone is singing, chanting quietly. Several voices in harmony. It sounds like an old hymn, but there is too much of an echo in the tiled room to enable Jan to make out any words.

Staff or patients?

Jan doesn't want to know who is singing like this so late at night.

He moves cautiously forward, keeping close to the wall. Ready to run.

Eventually he finds the right way. He recognizes the very first corridor with the little cells, and from there he makes his way through the first tiled room and back to the safe room. He feels almost completely at ease now.

He doesn't need to crawl under the floor this time: from this side he can open the steel door and make his way back to the Dell.

He is in the warmth and the light once more, and Jan switches off the Angel.

It is almost midnight, but Hanna is still awake when he gets back. She stares at him intently; she seems almost excited, and for a moment he forgets Rami.

'I heard you,' she says, holding up the other Angel. 'Clear as a bell.'

'Good.'

'Did you see anything down there?'

'Not much.' He breathes out and wipes his forehead. 'It's like a labyrinth, with corridors and old wards, and I think I heard voices . . .'

'Did you find a way up to the wards? Or a lift?'

Jan shakes his head. 'I only got as far as the laundry . . . There were people in there.'

'People? Men and women?'

'A man. A member of staff, I assume – but he didn't see me.'

Hanna nods, but doesn't seem particularly interested. 'So it was a wasted visit.'

'No,' says Jan. 'I've learned my way around down there.'

The Unit

Jan could see the fence with its barbed wire every time he sat at the desk in his room. It was impossible to avoid; it was at least twice his height. First of all there was a lawn, then the fence, and beyond it a path disappearing in the direction of the town.

The fence kept him trapped inside the Unit, he understood that – but it also protected him from the rest of the world.

What had he done to end up in here?

He looked at the bandages around his wrists. He knew what he had done.

He asked Jörgen for paper and pens so that he could do some drawing. He drew a rectangle and started on a new comic strip. The Secret Avenger, his own superhero, was fighting the Gang of Four at the bottom of a dark ravine. The Secret Avenger was immune to everything but bright light, so the gang were trying to get him with laser beams.

Suddenly there was a knock on the door, and a second later it opened, before Jan even had time to answer.

A man in a grey woollen sweater looked in. Not Jörgen. This man had a beard, but his head was completely bald. 'Hello there, Jan. Good to see you up and about.'

Jan didn't answer.

'My name's Tony . . . I'm a psychologist here. We're just going to check you over.'

A psychologist. That meant they were going to start digging away at him.

Tony stepped aside and a young male nurse came over to Jan with a stethoscope and hard hands. He took Jan's blood pressure, listened to his chest, and pulled his bandages to one side to look at the sutured wounds along his wrists.

'He seems fine,' the nurse said over his shoulder. 'Almost back to normal.'

'In physical terms,' Tony said.

'Absolutely . . . You can take care of his soul.'

Neither of them spoke directly to Jan, and the nurse didn't notice his burn marks. He stood up without another word when he had finished.

'Will I be going home soon?' Jan asked.

No reply. Tony had already closed the door.

Jan stopped drawing after only five frames. He lay back down on the bed and stared at the ceiling. He would be stuck in the Unit until someone let him out. Other people were making decisions for him, but he was used to that.

He stayed where he was; he had no desire to go out.

The sound of guitar music was coming through the wall. The girl in the room next door was still practising her chords, over and over again, but she was getting quicker now. And she had started to sing along.

Jan turned his head to the wall and listened. The words were in English, but he understood most of them. Rami was singing quietly about a house in New Orleans they called the Rising Sun, which had been the ruin of many a poor girl. She sang the same lines over and over again, before admitting to God that she was one of those poor girls.

The more Jan heard, the more he wanted to go next door. He didn't just want to listen, he wanted to watch the girl singing as well.

He suddenly sat up and went over to the chair by his desk. It was made of wood with a thin seat, and he started drumming on it, keeping time with the chords of the guitar. It went pretty well and he managed to hold the beat – he had played the drums in the school orchestra. None of the boys in school had ever asked him to be in their rock band, of course, but at least he had played Swedish and German marching music for two years. It had been pretty good fun.

Jan had nothing to live for, but he was good at keeping the beat.

His drumming on the chair grew louder and louder. He was so caught up in the four-beat pattern that he didn't notice that the guitar in the room next door had fallen silent. He didn't stop until the door suddenly flew open.

It was the guitar girl. 'What are you doing?' She didn't sound angry, just curious.

Jan froze with his hands above the chair. 'I'm drumming.'

'You're a drummer?'

'Kind of.'

The girl was still looking at him, a thoughtful expression on her face. She was tall and skinny, Jan noticed; she was pretty, but she had hardly any curves.

'Come with me.' She turned on her heel as if it was understood that Jan would follow her. And he did.

They went into the empty corridor and turned left; the girl opened the second door on the left-hand side, marked STORE-ROOM.

'You can, like, borrow stuff from here,' she said.

The storeroom was small but packed with shelves full of different things. There were books, table-tennis bats, and piles of board games and chess sets.

There were pens and paper and notebooks too; this must be where Jörgen had got the drawing paper from.

'Do you write?' the girl asked.

'Sometimes . . . I draw as well.'

'Me too,' she said, picking up a thick black notebook. 'There you go . . . Now you can keep a diary.'

'Thanks.'

Jan had never written about himself, but he took it anyway.

224

There were musical instruments on a couple of the shelves, and the girl moved across to them. 'This is where I found the Yamaha.'

'The Yamaha?'

'My guitar.'

Beside the shelves stood a drum kit. It was very small, just one battered bass drum and one crash cymbal, but the girl picked it up. 'You can take this.'

She carried the drum, Jan took the cymbal and the sticks. The girl led the way back to her room. 'Come in.'

Jan hesitated briefly, then went inside. He looked around in amazement; whereas his room was white, this one was coal-black. It looked like some kind of studio; the girl had covered the walls with huge pieces of black fabric.

She sat down on the bed with her guitar. 'Shall we give it a go?'

'OK.'

'You start.'

Jan picked up the sticks and began to play. He started off with a steady four-beat tempo on the drum, tapping the crash cymbal on the first and third beats. After a while he really got into it; it sounded pretty good.

The girl was nodding her head in time with the music. She was listening – and that gave him confidence. He wasn't used to it. The girl opened her mouth and began to sing, in the same slightly hoarse voice as when she spoke:

> *There is a house in Nyåker*
> *they call the Rising Sun*
> *it's been the ruin of many a young life,*
> *and God, I know I'm one . . .*

It was obviously the only verse she had, because she sang it twice, then fell silent. Jan stopped drumming at the same time. They looked at one another.

'Good,' she said. 'Shall we do it again?'

'What's your name?' asked Jan.

'Rami.'

'Rami?'

'Just Rami right now. Does that bother you?'

Jan shook his head. Then another question popped out before he had chance to think about it: 'Why are you here?'

But Rami needed only half a second to consider and then answer, as if it weren't particularly important. 'Because my older sister and I did something . . . something stupid. It was mostly my sister. She took off and went to Stockholm, and she's keeping out of the way. But I couldn't go with her, so I ended up in here.'

'What did you do?'

'We tried to poison our stepfather. He's disgusting.'

The room fell silent. Jan didn't know what to say, but suddenly he heard someone calling his name.

'Jan? Jan Hauger?'

He jumped, but was relieved at the interruption, and opened the door.

It was the nurse who looked like Jesus, but whose name was Jörgen.

'Phone call, Jan.'

'Who is it?'

'Some friend of yours.'

Friend? Jan glanced at Rami.

She nodded. 'We'll carry on afterwards.'

The staffroom was at the other end of the Unit. Jörgen showed him the way, then closed the door. There was a bed, a table, a telephone.

The receiver was lying on the table; Jan picked it up. 'Hello?'

'Hauger? You wanker. You fucking loser . . .'

Jan recognized the voice. He didn't say anything; all the air went out of his lungs.

But the voice on the other end of the phone had plenty of air. 'So you're alive, are you?' it went on. 'You should have died . . . we thought you were dead. You couldn't even manage to die, could you?'

Jan was listening and sweating, just as if he were in a sauna.

226

His hands were the worst; his palms were so wet that the receiver almost slipped out of his grasp.

'Do you know what we've told everybody in school, Hauger?'

Jan didn't speak.

'We said we saw you standing in the shower *wanking*. Wanking and groaning . . .'

'That's not true.'

'No, but nobody will believe you.'

Jan took a deep breath. 'I haven't said anything. About any of you.'

'We know that . . . Because if you do, we'll kill you.'

'You will anyway,' said Jan.

The only response was laughter. It sounded as if there were several boys standing around the phone, with different laughs.

Then there was a click as the call ended.

Jan looked down at his trousers. There was a warm, damp patch just below his flies: he had wet himself.

34

Jan is tired when he gets home from the Dell well after midnight – not physically, but mentally. The visit to St Psycho's has used up all his energy.

But he sleeps peacefully for the rest of the night; he wakes at half past seven and sets off for work on his bike an hour later.

Everything looks perfectly normal in the playground. The swings are empty and there are a few plastic spades in the sandpit, waiting for the children.

But when Jan opens the door, he can see that something is wrong. Hanna and Andreas are standing in the cloakroom with some of the children – but Hanna isn't supposed to be here, she should have gone home an hour ago.

'Morning, Jan,' says Andreas.

Jan smiles at his colleagues, but neither of them smiles back. He asks, 'Everything OK?'

Andreas nods. 'I think so . . . but we're having a meeting shortly.'

'A staff meeting,' Hanna says.

'What, a feelgood meeting?'

'I don't know . . . I don't think so.'

Andreas doesn't sound remotely curious. Jan tries to look equally unconcerned, but as he is taking off his jacket he catches Hanna's gaze for a second. Her blue eyes are just as blank and unreadable as usual, and she quickly looks away.

*

Fifteen minutes later they are all sitting around the kitchen table. All except Marie-Louise, who is standing straight-backed in front of her staff. She adjusts her blouse, clears her throat and presses the palms of her hands together.

'There's something we need to discuss,' she says. 'Something serious. As we all know, the rules regarding security here at the Dell are particularly important, but unfortunately there has been a breach.' She pauses, then goes on: 'When I arrived at about seven o'clock this morning, the security door leading to the basement was open. More or less wide open, in fact.'

She looks at her staff, but no one speaks. Jan makes an effort to prevent his eyes from darting all over the place.

'Hanna, you and I talked about this before the others arrived,' Marie-Louise goes on, 'and you say you have no idea how it can have happened.'

Hanna nods. Her gaze is steady, shining with innocence.

Jan is impressed.

'No, it's really weird,' Hanna says. 'It was definitely shut when I went to bed.'

Marie-Louise stares at her. 'You're absolutely certain?'

Hanna glances sideways, but only for a fraction of a second. 'Almost.'

Marie-Louise sighs. 'That door must always be kept closed. *Always.*'

The atmosphere is oppressive. Jan is sitting next to Hanna, but he doesn't say a word. He gazes blankly at Marie-Louise, wondering if he was the one who left the door open when he came up from the basement.

Suddenly they hear a bright, cheerful voice: 'Good morning, fellow citizens!'

Everyone turns to look at Mira, who is standing in the doorway smiling at the adults, with a big gap in her front teeth. Jan knows that she learned the expression 'fellow citizens' a few days ago, and she seems determined to use it as often as possible.

'Good morning, Mira,' Marie-Louise says quickly. 'We'll be there soon! We just need to have a little chat . . .'

'But Ville and Valle want to go to bed! We need to get every-thing ready for them!'

'Jan,' Marie-Louise says quietly, 'could you go and put Mira's dolls to bed, please?'

'Of course.'

He is glad to leave the room. This staff meeting is no fun at all; he can feel the thin web of secrets and lies between himself and Hanna, and he is afraid that one of the others might catch sight of it.

'Good morning, fellow citizen!'

'Good morning again, Mira.'

She seems pleased that it is Jan who has come to help her. They sit down next to her bed, and he picks up her two dolls and tucks them in under the covers.

Jan is more relaxed in here. He sorts everything out, he makes sure that Ville and Valle are lying comfortably side by side, with their heads on the pillow, and he runs his hand over the sheet to smooth out any creases – but still other thoughts come crowding into his mind.

He is wondering about the open door, of course. *If* he was the one who forgot to close it last night, he will have to pull himself together. Otherwise a camera will be installed at the Dell, sooner or later.

'There you go,' he says. 'Is that OK, Mira?'

She nods and leans over the bed. Each doll receives a pat on the head, then she backs away.

She picks her nose and looks at Jan. 'What did the man want?' she asks. 'Did he come to take Ville and Valle?'

'What man?'

Mira removes her finger from her nose. 'The man who was in here.'

'There was no man in here.'

'Oh yes there was,' Mira says firmly. 'I saw him when it was dark.'

'Last night, you mean?'

230

She nods. 'He was standing *there.*' Mira points at the floor by the foot of her bed.

Jan looks but doesn't say anything for a moment; he doesn't actually know what to say. 'You were dreaming,' he reassures her eventually. 'You just dreamed there was a man here.'

'No!'

'Yes, you did, Mira. You do have dreams sometimes. You dream about things even though they don't exist, and you dream you're playing outside even though you're lying in bed. That's true, isn't it?'

Mira gives this some thought, then nods again. Jan has convinced her, even though he himself is far from convinced. A man in the children's room?

'Good,' he says. 'Let's leave Ville and Valle to get some sleep, then.'

They move out of the room, with Mira skipping on ahead; she seems to have already forgotten what she told him.

Jan does not forget. He goes back to the staffroom, but almost everyone has gone. Andreas is rinsing his cup; Jan pours himself a fresh cup of coffee and asks in passing, 'Is the meeting over?'

'Yup.'

'So what conclusions did you reach?'

'Nothing startling,' says Andreas. 'I mean, we all know the door is supposed to be kept shut. So we need to make sure that we close it properly behind us, and check that everyone else is doing the same.'

'Sounds good.'

Suddenly Jan hears the main door slam, and turns around. Hanna has just left; she is finally on her way home after her night shift.

Jan pulls on his boots and quickly runs after her. He catches up with her by the gate, and calls out quietly, 'Hanna!'

She stops and turns around, but her expression suggests that they don't even know each other. 'I'm going home,' she says. 'What do you want?'

Jan looks around; there is no sign of any adults or children in the playground, but still he dare not say too much. 'Mira's had a nightmare.'

'Oh?' Hanna's tone is cool and neutral.

Jan lowers his voice. 'She had a dream about a man.'

'Yes, well, she's had dreams before, it's . . .'

'He was standing in the bedroom last night, next to her bed.'

Hanna looks at him, her expression blank, and Jan lowers his voice even more, to a dull whisper: 'Hanna . . . have you let anyone out through the sally port at night? A patient who might have gone into the children's room?'

She looks down at the path. 'It's fine. It's a friend.'

'A friend? A friend of yours?'

Hanna doesn't reply; she just looks at her watch and sets off again. 'My bus will be here in a minute.'

Jan sighs and follows her. 'Hanna, we need to—'

She breaks in without looking at him. 'I can't talk about this any more. You'll just have to trust me . . . It's fine. We know what we're doing.'

'*We?* Who's *we*, Hanna?'

She doesn't stop; she opens the gate and closes it behind her. Jan stands there watching her as she crosses the road. He thinks about the old joke, which isn't particularly funny:

Who was that lady I saw you with last night?

That was no lady, that was my wife.

But he hears Mira's voice in his head as he walks back into the pre-school: *Jan, who was that gentleman I saw by my bed last night?*

And he hears his own voice answering her: *That was no gentleman. That was Ivan Rössel.*

35

On the way home after his day shift, Jan makes a decision: no more secret visits to St Psycho's. No more trips down to the basement, or to the safe room. After the staff meeting with Marie-Louise, that's it.

He doesn't think he was the one who forgot to close the door; it seems more likely that it was Hanna, but it doesn't actually matter. Hanna ought to put a stop to her nocturnal visits too.

Not ought to – she *must* stop.

But when he gets home and opens the door, there is something waiting for him. A large, fat envelope is lying on the hall floor – but of course it isn't addressed to him. He is only the courier; the envelope is marked S. P.

Jan sighs and steps over the envelope. He doesn't want to touch it, but it can't just stay there, and eventually he picks it up. Now he is holding it in his hand, he might as well open it.

Thirty-six letters, large and small. Jan slowly shuffles through them on the kitchen table. None is addressed to Maria Blanker, but eleven of the letters are for the same person: Ivan Rössel. He seems to have plenty of pen friends.

But what do they want?

Jan ponders for a few seconds, thinking about Hanna and the open door. Then he quickly picks up one of Rössel's letters. It's an ordinary white envelope, with no sender's name, and it isn't very well sealed. He fetches a knife and slides it under the flap, which opens almost at once.

Prying. Jan doesn't like that word, but he still inserts two fingers in the envelope and removes the contents. There are several thin sheets of paper, covered with neat writing in ink:

My dearest Ivan, it's Carin again. Carin from Hedemora, if you remember me. It just occurred to me that I forgot to tell you about my two dogs last time I wrote. One is a <u>dachshund</u> and the other is a <u>terrier</u>. Their names are Sammy and Willy, and they get on really really well, and I love being with them. It's wonderful when we all go out for a walk together.

It is so tempting to lose myself in dreams; I often get so <u>stressed</u> because there is just so much to do in my life. So much <u>responsibility</u>! There are always piles of <u>bills</u> and then there's my job which of course I just <u>have</u> to get right, I really can't take any more time off. And then I have to walk Sammy and Willy and feed them and take care of them every day.

But I think about you so much, Ivan. I send you all my love. The <u>heat</u> of my soul soars above the sky like a burning flame and descends into your room, into your heart. I feel so much <u>Love</u> and <u>Tenderness</u> for you, and I have read <u>everything</u> about you.

I know that those of us who live outside a prison wall can be trapped by life just as much as those of you who are locked up behind it, and I have thought a great deal about how we can learn to climb over all the walls that surround us. But you make me <u>free</u> and I just <u>long</u> to meet you . . .

The letter goes on for three more pages, with lengthy declarations of love to Ivan Rössel and dreams of a life together. A photograph is attached: it shows a smiling woman with two barking dogs.

Jan folds the sheets of paper and carefully puts them back in the envelope, then he fetches a glue stick and reseals the flap. He doesn't open any more letters.

A love letter to Ivan Rössel. Well, that's what it sounded like anyway. Jan has read that notorious violent criminals who have ended up in prison often get fan mail – piles of letters from people they have never met. Letters from women who want to help them become better people. Do all of these letter-writers want to help Rössel?

Then he thinks about Rami, and the letter he started writing to her. But his love is different. Completely different.

The squirrel wants to get over the fence, she had written. *The squirrel wants to jump off the wheel.*

That was almost two weeks ago, and he hasn't written to her since then. And he promised himself that he wouldn't smuggle any more letters.

In spite of this he gets out a sheet of paper. *If* Rami is in the hospital under the name Blanker, and *if* he were to write a letter to her – what would he write? He doesn't want to sound like some lovesick stranger, like Carin from Hedemora.

Jan wants to explain who he is. So he picks up his pen and begins to write:

Hi, my name is Jan and I think you and I met a long time ago in another town, in a place called the Unit. Your name was Alice then, but you were tired of it, I remember. You used to play the guitar, I played the drums, and we talked a lot. I liked talking to you.

And now you are in St Patricia's. I don't know why, that doesn't matter to me. What matters is that I want to help you.

I've been drawing pictures in the books I think you left in the Dell, but I want to do more. A lot more.

I want to find a way in life for the two of us, and I want to help you . . .

Jan stops and looks at the words. *To escape* – that's what he wants to write, isn't it? But he doesn't do it. He can't write something like that unless Rami herself wants it to happen.

In the Unit she had talked about running away virtually every day. She wanted to get out of that place, she wanted to go and see her older sister, she wanted to go to Stockholm – she was only fourteen years old, but she had big plans.

Jan had no big plans at all. He just wanted to be with Rami.

True love does not die of natural causes. It is murdered by those who rule over us.

He ought to write that instead; this letter is no good. He screws it up and starts again:

Maria, my name is Jan Hauger and I work at St Patricia's, but not in the hospital itself. I am a pre-school teacher, but sometimes I think I am a lynx. You have a new name and see yourself as a squirrel now, but when we knew each other you used to be called Alice Rami. Didn't you?

I am almost sure it's true, and that you are the person I met in another town in a place called the Unit; I had the room next door to you. We used to play music together, and we told each other secrets; we also promised that when we got out of there, each of us would do something for the other person. We had a kind of pact.

I would really like to see you again and to talk about our pact, because I kept my side of the bargain, and I think you did too . . .

The Unit

'Look!'

Rami's cry made Jan jump. He had been sitting on the floor, calmly and quietly drumming along to her guitar chords, almost lulled into a soporific state by the rhythm, but she had suddenly stopped playing. She had got up from the bed and gone over to the desk by the window.

She was pointing at something. 'Have you seen my guardian animal?'

Jan stopped drumming. 'What?'

'He's out there on the grass.'

Jan had no idea what she was talking about, but he got up and looked out of the window. He saw a small greyish-brown creature darting around on the lawn. Every so often it stiffened and looked around, then it was off again.

'It's a squirrel,' Jan said.

'Squirrels bring luck, according to my grandmother,' Rami said. 'I've conjured him up . . . I can send him off to freedom.'

And almost at that same moment the squirrel dashed off towards the fence. It jumped up and gripped the wire netting with its paws, then slipped through the barbed wire before taking an insane leap towards the branch of a tree outside the grounds. It grabbed the tip of the branch, swung itself inwards towards the tree and disappeared.

'There you go, freedom . . .' She looked at Jan. 'Those were my thoughts, escaping over the fence. Now they are free!'

Jan gazed at Rami, wondering if she was serious. She was. She wasn't smiling, at any rate.

He suddenly realized that he had leaned forward, and was standing very close to her now. He was aware of the smell of her, a mixture of grass and pine resin. It was beginning to feel slightly embarrassing. He had to say something. 'So your . . . your name is just Rami?'

'I used to be called Alice, but Rami is fine.' She went back over to the bed and picked up the guitar, played a couple of chords and glanced up at Jan. 'Do you know what we ought to do?'

'No, what?'

'We should do a gig. We'll practise a bit more, then we'll play for the ghosts.'

'What ghosts?'

'All those who are imprisoned in here.'

Jan nodded, but he didn't regard himself as a prisoner. For him, the fence provided protection from the rest of the world.

Suddenly Rami's door opened and a woman with black hair and big, shiny glasses poked her head in. 'Alice?'

Rami looked defiant. 'What?'

'Don't forget our counselling session today. Three o'clock.'

Rami said nothing.

'We're just going to have a chat,' the woman said. 'I know it will make you feel better.'

The door closed.

'The Psychobabbler,' Rami said. 'I hate her.'

On his fifth morning in the Unit Jan was sitting in his room working on his comic strip about the Secret Avenger and the Gang of Four. The sheets on his bed were in a heap. They were dry now, but they had been wet when he'd woken up.

The diary was also beside him on the desk, the one Rami had given him. He had stuck the Polaroid of himself on the front cover, and had begun to write in it. He had written about things that had happened over the last week, things that Rami had said or his own thoughts, and he had ended up with several pages covered with line after line of words. Weird.

Suddenly there was a knock on his door. He did what Rami had done and refused to answer, but of course it was opened anyway.

A bearded face appeared – it was the psychologist. The one called Tony. 'Morning, Jan. Time we had a little chat, you and I.'

Jan stiffened. 'What about?'

'About a boy called Jan Hauger, I think.' Tony smiled in the middle of his beard. 'Come on, let's go up to my office.'

Jan stayed where he was, sitting at his desk with his pen and paper; he remembered the warning on the telephone. He had no intention of telling Tony anything.

But the psychologist waited patiently, and in the end he won. Jan got up and went with him. They walked through the dining room, then up the stairs to a corridor lined with offices.

The psychologist led Jan into one of them. 'Take a seat.'

Then he sat down behind the desk and read through a folder for a couple of minutes. Jan sat in silence, staring out of the window. The sky was blue, the sun was shining on pools of melting snow and ice in the car park.

Suddenly the psychologist looked up at him. 'Where did you get the sleeping tablets from?'

Jan was taken by surprise, and answered automatically, 'They were my mum's.'

'And the razor blade – was that your dad's?'

Jan nodded.

'Should we interpret that symbolically in some way?'

'I don't know what you mean.'

Jan didn't understand, and Tony leaned forward to explain. 'Well . . . You swallowed your mother's tablets and slit your wrists with your father's razor blade; was that some kind of protest, perhaps? A protest against your parents?'

Jan hadn't thought of that. He didn't think about it now either – he simply shook his head and said quietly, 'I knew where they were . . . Where they kept them.'

'OK . . . But if we can just summarize what happened a few days ago: you took fifteen sleeping tablets, slit your wrists and jumped into the lake just below your house?'

Jan didn't say anything. He supposed that was correct. But the things the psychologist claimed he had done already felt incredibly vague, like a dream. Like a comic strip. *The Secret Avenger and the Pond.*

'It's a pond,' he said eventually.

'OK, so the lake is a pond,' Tony said. 'But a person can drown perfectly well in a pond too, wouldn't you say?'

'Mm.'

Jan didn't want to think about how it had felt down there when he couldn't get any air into his lungs. He looked at the carpet underneath the desk. It was green.

'Anyway, you were pulled out of the pond by a couple of kind people who happened to be passing, and you were taken to the local hospital in an ambulance. Then you were transferred here, to the Child and Adolescent Mental Health Unit. And now we're sitting in my office.'

'Mm.'

Silence.

'You wanted to die in that pond,' Tony said. 'Do you still want to die?'

Jan looked out of the window again. Beyond the car park he could see the huge buildings that made up the hospital complex, several storeys high and constructed of steel and glass. The sun was shining on the windows – it had felt like winter when he jumped into the icy water, but now it looked like spring out there.

This was a secure world. He was locked up, but he was *safe*.

'No,' he said. He knew it was true; here inside the Unit he didn't want to die.

'Good,' said Tony. 'That's excellent, Jan.' He wrote down a couple of sentences on his notepad. 'But things were different a few days ago. How did you feel then?'

'Bad,' said Jan.

'And why did you feel bad?'

Jan sighed. He intended to say as little as possible about this. He could have said a great deal about the Gang of Four and all the rest of it – he could probably have talked for several hours – but nothing was going to be improved by a lot of talk. 'No friends,' was all he said.

'You haven't got any friends?' Tony said. 'Why not?'

'Dunno . . . They think I'm stupid.'

'Why's that?'

'Because I sit and draw stuff.'

'You draw?' Tony said. 'And what else do you do in your spare time?'

'I read . . . and I play the drums a bit.'

'In a band?'

'In the school orchestra.'

'So haven't you got any friends in the orchestra?'

Jan shook his head.

'So you feel very lonely, Jan . . . as if you're the loneliest person in the world?'

Jan nodded.

'And do you think this loneliness is your own fault?'

Jan shrugged his shoulders. 'Suppose so.'

'Why?'

Jan thought about it. 'Because everybody else has got friends.'

'Have they?'

Jan nodded again. 'And if they can do it, then I should be able to do it.'

'Have you *never* had friends?'

Jan gazed out of the window. 'I used to have one friend, in my class. But he moved away.'

'What was his name?'

'Hans.'

'And how long were you two friends?'

'As long as I can remember . . . Since nursery, I think.'

'So that means you *can* make friends,' said Tony. 'There's nothing wrong with you.'

Jan stared down at the desk, and considered saying, *I wet myself at night, that's what's wrong with me*. But he kept quiet.

'There is *nothing* wrong with you, Jan,' Tony said again. He leaned back. 'And we're going to have lots of chats about how we can help you to feel better. OK?'

'OK.'

Jan was allowed to leave. On his way back to the stairs he passed other doors and read the names and long titles: Gunnar Toll, Clinical Psychologist; Ludmila Nilsson, Medical Practitioner; Emma Halevi, Clinical Psychologist; Peter Brink, Counsellor. None of the names meant anything to him.

Lynx

Jan woke up on his back on a hard floor, and wondered for a moment where he was. Not at home. He had lain down somewhere fully dressed in his thick jacket, hat and scarf. Then he had fallen asleep. But where?

There was a low ceiling above his head – a ceiling made of re-inforced concrete.

Then he remembered: he was inside the bunker in the forest. He had intended to have a little rest, that was all, but he was still here.

Stupid. Dangerous.

He looked down his legs and saw that the steel door was ajar, with his boots almost sticking out through the opening. Outside he could see the greyness of the forest, beneath an equally grey sky. The sun wasn't up yet, but it was on its way.

Jan was suddenly afraid that William had crept out into the darkness, but when he turned his head he saw a thick bundle of blankets half a metre away. He could hear the sound of soft, regular breathing: William was still fast asleep.

The air inside the bunker was cold, and there was no warmth in Jan's body either. His legs felt numb; he lifted them one by one, moving them slowly to try to get the muscles going. He sat up slowly. He didn't feel rested, just stiff and dirty.

Last night he had experienced a heady sensation of victory, when the plan worked and his fantasy became a reality. This morning everything felt completely wrong. He was lying in a bunker next to a child he had locked up the previous day – what the hell was he doing?

William shifted under his blankets, and Jan went rigid. Was he waking up? No, not yet.

Jan took Roboman outside and recorded three new messages, telling William that everything was fine. He set the toy to standby so that William's own voice would activate it. Then he crept back inside and placed it on the floor.

He heard a faint cough, then a little hand emerged from the blankets and groped around on the floor. Jan quickly backed away, slipped outside and bolted the steel door shut.

Forty-six hours, he thought, looking at his watch.

It was only ten to seven – which meant there were some thirty hours left before he would let William go. A long time.

Jan arrived at Lynx fifteen minutes later. No one else was there yet, but he had his own key and could let himself in.

The whole place was silent, with no children's laughter echoing through the rooms.

He switched on the coffee machine, flopped down in an armchair and closed his eyes. The image of William's hand groping around for someone to hold on to was still fixed in his mind.

Just before half past seven the main door opened and Nina walked in. They looked at each other wearily; Nina's eyes were shadowed with anxiety. 'The children aren't coming in today,' she said. 'We've placed them with other nurseries temporarily.'

'OK.'

'Have you heard anything? Any news?'

Jan looked at her and opened his mouth. He felt a sudden desire to tell her everything. He would tell her that William was locked inside a camouflaged bunker deep in the forest, that he was bound to be a little bit scared but that he was completely unharmed, because Jan had planned the whole thing meticulously.

And the most important part: he would tell her *why* all this had happened. It wasn't about William – not really.

It was about Alice Rami.

244

'There's something I need to tell you—' he began, but he was interrupted by a sudden rattling noise out in the hallway as the front door opened. A police officer walked in, a uniformed constable. He was the same man who had told Jan the previous evening about a horrible discovery on a forest track some years ago.

Jan closed his mouth and straightened up. He was a reliable classroom assistant once more. It was a difficult role, but it still worked.

The police officer's mobile started to ring. He moved into a side room to take the call.

Jan looked Nina in the eye. 'I'm going to volunteer . . . to join the search party, I mean.'

Nina simply nodded – and she never asked what he had been going to tell her.

The sun slowly rose above the roof of Lynx. A blue and white police van arrived and began to function as some kind of liaison unit out in the car park. More and more police officers, military personnel and civilians began arriving at the nursery; they would have a cup of coffee, then head out into the forest. Jan went along too.

The search party got under way at quarter past nine. Police, members of the local army defence unit and volunteers in a long line. Two dogs would be brought in after lunch.

Jan stood somewhere in the middle listening to a police officer outlining how the search for William would be conducted: 'Our approach is calm and methodical.' Crevices in the rocks, dense fir trees, areas where water had collected – everything was to be searched.

The chain of people was going to begin with a broad sweep along the lake, Jan realized. When would they start searching on the other side of the ridge, where the bunker was?

The mood was subdued as they slowly moved forward through the forest.

At half past eleven a whistle suddenly blew. Evidently the search had been called off, and immediately there was a buzz among the participants. Had the boy been found? Dead or alive?

Nobody knew, but the orderly line began to break up as people gathered in smaller groups. Jan stood alone among the trees until he heard a woman shouting: 'Hauger! Is there a Jan Hauger here?'

'Yes?' he shouted back.

It was a police officer; she came striding up to Jan through the undergrowth. 'There's a meeting down at the nursery,' she said. 'They want you there.'

It was an order, and Jan's blood ran cold. *They've found him*, he thought. 'Why?' he asked.

'No idea . . . Would you like me to walk you down?'

'No,' Jan said quickly. 'I can find my own way.'

Nina, Sigrid and three other classroom assistants were sitting in the staffroom when he got back to Lynx. Two uniformed officers were also there, along with a man in civilian clothes; Jan realized immediately that he too was a police officer.

Jan unbuttoned his jacket and sat down next to Nina. 'The search party is taking a break,' he said.

Nina nodded; she already knew that. 'Something's happened . . . They want to talk to the staff, one at a time.'

'Why?'

Nina lowered her voice: 'Apparently the parents got a package in the post today, with William's little hat inside . . . So the police think someone has taken him.'

36

There is one thing Jan loves at the pre-school, something he sees every day: the children's innocent faces. Their honest eyes. Children don't hide anything – they don't know how. They haven't yet learned to lie convincingly, the way adults do.

But when he arrives for a night shift, Lilian is also struggling to hide how she feels this evening. Her red hair is uncombed, her blouse is creased and her eyes are dark and tired. She feels bad.

'Everything OK, Lilian?' Jan asks.

'Brilliant.'

'Anything wrong?'

She shakes her head. 'No. I just want to go home.'

It is more likely that she is intending to go out, possibly to Bill's Bar. Jan thinks that she is looking more and more worn out with every passing day. Perhaps it's the autumn. Perhaps it's the drink. She drinks too much, he knows that. But it's not the sort of thing people talk about.

Thanks, but I've got problems of my own, he thinks.

When Lilian has left he goes to join the children in the play-room. Mira and Leo, the only children who are staying overnight, are sitting there among a sea of building bricks.

Jan smiles and sits down beside them. 'What a fantastic building!'

'We know!' Mira shouts.

As usual Leo looks less pleased, but at least he seems calm today.

Jan picks up a couple of bricks. 'I'm going to build a hospital.'

Three hours and many games later, it is night once more. Mira and Leo are in bed; they have had supper and a story, and all is peaceful. The children are asleep and Jan is sitting in the staffroom filling out the food order.

He carries on working; time passes. Hidden in his bag is the latest batch of thirty-seven letters which he will soon deliver to the hospital.

One of them is to Rami from him. Eventually, when he got going, he sat there and wrote her a five-page letter. He wrote about their time together in the Unit, the things they talked about. And he wrote about what had happened to him afterwards, how he had become a pre-school teacher and finally ended up here at the Dell.

He promised himself that he wouldn't deliver any more letters, but that promise has evaporated.

At the end of the letter he wrote that he had never been able to forget her. *I will never forget you.* It wasn't a declaration of love; it was simply the truth.

He looks up and catches sight of himself. He is sitting opposite the staffroom's only window, and he can see his reflection floating in the darkness. But suddenly he notices something behind it, slender shadows moving in the night.

Animals – or people?

He leans closer to the glass. If there are people out there they are close to the fence, in the darkest area between two lights.

Jan considers going outside, but decides against it. Instead he carries on with the food order.

Suddenly the doorbell rings, a harsh, long-drawn-out sound. Jan glances towards the door, but remains in the staffroom.

The bell stops ringing, and everything goes quiet. But three minutes later there is a loud bang right in front of him, on the window. He jumps.

A pale face is staring in through the glass. A tall, bony man with a shaven head is standing motionless out there. He is wearing a thick black padded jacket, and underneath it he is dressed in white hospital scrubs. Jan doesn't recognize him.

'Can you open up?' the stranger shouts.

Jan hesitates, and the man goes on: 'Are you on your own?'

Jan shakes his head.

'Who else is in there?' the man demands.

'Who are you?' Jan shouts back.

'Security – night shift. Can you open up?'

Jan doesn't move. He wonders if the man knows Lars Rettig, but instead asks, 'Have you got some ID?'

The guard takes out a plastic card and holds it up for a few seconds, just long enough for Jan to see that the face on the card resembles the guard's, then he puts it away. His voice is harsh and impatient now: 'Open up!'

Jan will have to trust him; he opens the window, letting in the cold, and asks, 'What's happened?'

'We're missing a four-four.'

Jan has no idea what this means, and shakes his head. 'I haven't seen anything.'

'Can you give us a call if you do?' The guard doesn't wait for a reply; he backs away from the window and disappears into the darkness.

Jan closes the window and the room is silent.

Almost silent; the clock is still ticking towards midnight, when he is due to leave the package up in the visitors' room. He ought to postpone it, but that is impossible.

He checks on the two children and goes back to the staffroom. He is waiting for something to happen.

Has someone really escaped?

What should he do?

Stay here. This is where he's supposed to be, after all – with the sleeping children. But he has to make one last visit to St Psycho's. He will have to be careful now that people are moving around the hospital complex, but he just has to do it. The things he has

249

written in the letter to Rami are too important; she must have the opportunity to read them.

He waits another twenty minutes. The only thing that happens is that he feels more and more tired, both physically and mentally. He is tired of sitting up in the middle of the night, next to a high wall.

It shouldn't be like this . . . so dark and lonely. But that's the way it is, and at ten minutes to midnight he goes to check on the children one last time. Then he fetches the key card.

One last delivery. He hangs one Angel in the children's room, and heads for the door. Everyone has been very conscientious about keeping it closed since the telling-off from Marie-Louise, but now Jan must open it.

All is dark and quiet, and Jan quickly makes his way along the underground corridor. He has become very efficient in his deliveries; this time it takes only four minutes to travel up to the visitors' room and back down again. His heart is pounding all the time, but no one disturbs him, and the Angel attached to his belt remains silent. At five past midnight he is safely inside the Dell, as if nothing has happened.

Time to sleep. He makes up the sofa bed, then settles down and thinks about his letter to Rami for a little while before closing his eyes.

A rattling noise wakes Jan.

He opens his eyes, but the room is in darkness. Has he slept? He must have done, because the clock by his bed is showing 00:56.

Something is still rattling faintly outside the window, creaking and clattering. It's the fence. Someone is climbing up the fence.

Jan sits up, blinking in the darkness. He pulls on his jumper and trousers. Then he opens the blind a fraction and peeps out of the window.

He can't see a thing.

It feels wrong, and at first he can't understand why. Then he realizes he is used to having a light outside – but the nearest flood-light has gone out.

As he peers through the glass he can just about make out some sort of movement out there.

The rattling continues. He leans closer, staring hard. The noise is coming from the metal fence, and he can see a shadow roughly the height of a man on the other side. Someone is trying to climb up.

The front door is locked, he knows that.

Shouldn't go out, he thinks. *Shouldn't leave the children.*

And yet he goes to the cloakroom and puts on his shoes and jacket. The wind has picked up outside in the playground, and it is much colder. Jan keeps his head down and quickly makes his way round towards the section of the hospital complex where the rattling is coming from.

When he reaches the wooden fence surrounding the Dell and looks up at the metal fence, the noise has stopped. But the shadow is still there, and as Jan looks up he sees it reach for the top of the fence – then suddenly lose its grip. It falls backwards in a short arc, landing with a dull thud in the darkness.

Jan heads over towards the hospital. He has almost reached the fence when a white light suddenly flares into life, shining straight in his face. It comes from a powerful flashlight.

'Who's there?' a voice barks.

'Jan Hauger . . . I work at the pre-school.'

'OK,' says the voice. 'I recognize you. You're my stand-in with the Bohemos.'

The figure takes a step closer, and Jan recognizes the man and his broad shoulders. It's Carl, the drummer, with the tear-gas canister and handcuffs hanging from his belt. Rettig's friend, and Hanna's contact at the hospital.

Jan would like to ask him about that, but Carl gets in first: 'Have you delivered it?'

'Delivered what?'

'The package.' Carl nods in the direction of the hospital and the visitors' room, and Jan understands. So Carl knows that Jan is part of the chain involved in smuggling the letters.

No point in denying it. 'Yes,' Jan says quietly. 'I've already been up there.'

'OK, I'll go and pick it up. When everything's calmed down.'

'What happened?'

'A four-four.'

'Does that mean someone's escaped?'

'Yes,' says Carl. 'But the fence stopped him, and we managed to bring him down.'

'What are you going to do?'

'We'll sort it. You go back inside. Go and get some sleep.'

Jan nods and is just about to turn away when Carl adds, 'We have to stop soon.'

He seems to be talking to himself, but Jan asks, 'You mean this business with the letters?'

'The whole thing . . . It's all starting to get out of control.'

'What do you mean?'

But Carl doesn't answer. He simply walks away along the fence and disappears into the darkness.

37

Jan is awake at five, long before the children. He has managed only a few hours' sleep, and has been troubled by unpleasant dreams; he was swimming in a lake and his legs got stuck in the mud at the bottom. He struggled and struggled, but was unable to free himself.

Marie-Louise arrives at half past seven, and he immediately tells her what has happened – or at least the little he knows.

'Someone escaped?'

She seems horrified by the news, so Jan says, 'Well, someone tried.'

His memory of the night's events is already woolly.

'I'll find out what's happened,' says Marie-Louise.

Then the Dell is open and the day's activities begin, but while the children are resting after lunch Marie-Louise calls a staff meeting.

Jan sits down at the table, ready for anything.

'We've received a directive from the hospital board,' Marie-Louise announces. 'It has been decided that the Dell will be closed at night.'

Everyone absorbs the news in silence, Jan included. But he is surprised – he's due to do two more night shifts later in the week.

'So we're only going to be operating during the day?' Lilian asks.

'That's right.' Marie-Louise doesn't seem particularly upset by the decision as she goes on: 'Having the children here overnight was never a permanent solution, we've always known that. After all, children should be living in a *proper* home, and now social services think they have found suitable families for both Mira and Leo. So everything will work out perfectly.'

Jan leans forward and asks, 'When is this going to happen?'

'Quite soon. We will be working days only from the middle of November.' Marie-Louise seems to pick up on some hint of anxiety in his expression, because she adds, 'But there's nothing for you to worry about, Jan – your temporary contract won't be affected by this. Nobody will be affected, really – we'll just have to redo the rota and allocate more day shifts.' She smiles reassuringly at her staff. 'It means more companionship and less lone working.'

Jan makes an effort to look pleased, but it is only superficial. He is waiting for an answer from Rami – how is he going to get hold of it now? He is also certain that the Dell is being closed at night for security reasons. Perhaps because of last night's attempted escape, or because Marie-Louise found the basement door open. Perhaps she no longer trusts her staff.

When the others have left the room, Jan hangs back. 'Did they say anything about what happened last night?'

Marie-Louise gives a brief nod, as if she would prefer to think about something else. 'Yes. It was a patient who had been sectioned; he managed to get out of the ward and made it as far as the fence. It happens from time to time. But they caught up with him there, and security has been tightened up . . . Stepped up a level, they said.'

'Excellent,' says Jan, in spite of the fact that increased security at the hospital is the day's second piece of bad news as far as he is concerned.

The telephone rings among all the furniture in Jan's flat that evening. He waits a little while before reaching in among the chaos and picking up.

He is expecting it to be his mother in Nordbro, but it is a younger woman's voice. It takes him a few seconds to realize that it is Hanna Aronsson.

Though today was Hanna's day off, she asks, 'Have you heard about the night shifts?'

'Yes,' says Jan. 'How did you find out?'

'Lilian rang me.'

'No more evenings for us, then,' he says. He knows that Hanna understands what he means.

There is a brief silence at the other end of the phone, then she asks, 'Can you come round to mine for a bit? Number five Bellmans gränd?'

'OK, but why?'

'Because I want to return your books and have a little chat.'

Jan puts the phone down. He thinks of Hanna's blue eyes and wonders if he has made a new friend, just like Rami fifteen years ago.

Hanna lives in a recently built apartment block close to the main square. She opens the door quickly and invites him into a light, dust-free apartment, decorated in shades of pink and white. 'Hi . . . come in.'

She isn't smiling; her expression is tense as she heads towards the kitchen.

Jan follows her, but stops in the living room. He envies her all this light and space. There is a bookcase in the corner, and when he moves closer he sees that she reads non-fiction books about crime. There are titles such as *The Worst Murders in History, Monsters in Our Midst, Charles Manson in His Own Words, The Confessions of Ted Bundy* and *The Serial Killers – A Study in the Psychology of Violence.*

Books about murderers – a whole shelf full of them. Jan can't see any books about Patricia or other saints, but he supposes nobody writes that kind of thing any more.

'Are you coming?' Hanna shouts.

'On my way.'

She is making tea. The kitchen is small and just as clean as the living room, with neatly folded towels and tea towels next to the cooker. On the table there are four books that Jan recognizes: *The*

255

Princess with a Hundred Hands, *The Animal Lady*, *The Witch Who Was Poorly* and *Viveca's House of Stone*.

Hanna passes them over to Jan. 'Thanks for the loan.'

'Have you read them?'

'Yes, but they're pretty violent. Like when the princess gets the beggars' hands to strangle the robbers . . . It's not exactly the kind of thing you'd want to read to the kids, is it?'

Jan agrees, but says, 'They're no worse than your books though, are they?'

'What books?'

'The ones in there . . . all those books about murder.'

Hanna lowers her gaze. 'I haven't read them all. But I wanted to know more after . . . after I made contact with Ivan. There are tons of books about murderers.'

'People are fascinated by evil,' Jan says. He pauses for a moment, then goes on: 'Rössel has other pen friends besides you. Did you know that?'

'No.' Hanna looks up at him with renewed interest. 'How do you know?'

'I've seen some of the letters he gets.'

'Were they from women?'

'Some of them, yes.'

'Love letters?'

'Maybe . . . I haven't read them.' Jan has no intention of telling anyone that he opens the letters and secretly reads them.

There is a pile of paper on the table in front of them, a computer printout. Hanna reaches out and brushes it with her fingertips. 'I wanted to show you this . . . Ivan gave me the manuscript of his book.'

'When he was down in the school?'

Hanna shakes her head. 'That wasn't Ivan . . . It wasn't anyone from the hospital.'

'So who was it, then?'

'I can't tell you that.'

Jan gives up. He looks at the manuscript and sees that the title is *My Truth*. There is no author's name, but of course he knows who it is. 'Rössel's memoirs,' he says.

'Not memoirs,' Hanna says with a quick glance at Jan. 'I'm just reading it now and it's a kind of hypothesis.'

'A hypothesis? On how the murders happened?'

Hanna nods without saying anything. The tea is ready, and she pours them each a cup.

They sit down at the table, but Hanna carries on staring at the manuscript, and in the end he asks, 'Are you in love with Ivan Rössel?'

She looks up and quickly shakes her head.

'So what's all this about, then?'

Hanna doesn't reply, but she leans forward, gazing at him with those clear blue eyes for a long time, as if she is considering Jan's appearance.

She wants me to kiss her, Jan thinks.

Perhaps this is one of those occasions when people kiss each other. But when he thinks about kisses he remembers Rami's mouth pressed against his own in the Unit, and everything feels wrong.

He must think about something else. About the pre-school. About the children. 'I'm worried about Leo,' he says.

'What?'

'Leo Lundberg . . . Leo at the Dell.'

'I know who Leo is,' Hanna says.

'Yes, but . . . I've tried to talk to him, tried to care about him, but it's difficult. He's not happy . . . I don't know how to help him.'

'Help him with what?'

'Help him to forget what he's seen.'

'And what has he seen?'

Jan shakes his head. The very thought of little Leo upsets him, but in the end he answers, 'I think Leo saw his father kill his mother.'

Hanna gazes blankly at him. 'Have you spoken to Marie-Louise about this?'

'A bit, but she's not really interested.'

'There's nothing you can do,' Hanna says. 'You can't take away someone else's wounds; they're always going to be there.'

Jan sighs. 'I just want him to be happy, like any other kid . . . I want him to know that there's a lot of love in the world.'

Even he can hear that this sounds ridiculous. *There's a lot of love in the world.* It sounds a bit over the top.

'Perhaps you're trying to compensate for that other boy,' Hanna says.

'What other boy?'

'The one you lost in the forest.'

Jan gazes down at the table, then looks up at her. A confession is forcing its way out, like some kind of compulsion. 'That's not exactly what happened,' he says eventually. 'I didn't lose him.'

'No?'

'No . . . I left him in the forest.'

Hanna is staring at him, and Jan quickly goes on: 'It wasn't for very long . . . and he was perfectly safe.'

'Why did you do it?'

Jan sighs. 'It was a kind of revenge . . . on his parents. On his mother. I wanted her to feel really bad. And I thought I knew what I was doing, but . . .'

'And did you feel better afterwards?' Hanna asks.

'I don't know, I don't think so . . . I don't give it much thought these days.'

'Would you do it again?'

Jan looks at her and shakes his head, trying to look as honest as possible. 'I would never harm a child.'

'Good,' Hanna says. 'I believe you.'

Those blue eyes are still gazing at him. He can't really work Hanna out. Perhaps he ought to stay, talk to her some more, try to find out how she really feels about him, and about Ivan Rössel.

No. He gets to his feet. 'Thanks for the tea, Hanna. See you at work.'

He heads out into the cold night air and goes straight home, with his rucksack full of Rami's picture books.

The Unit

The concert that would end with a kiss and a fight was to be held in the TV room in the Unit.

Seven o'clock was the advertised time, but by then only three people had turned up. The first was the woman in black who had stuck her head around Rami's door to remind her about an appointment – the one Rami had nicknamed the Psychobabbler. And Jörgen had brought in a little girl with timid blue eyes; Jan had never seen her speak to anyone. She was just as shy as he was.

Jan had set up his drums slightly to one side behind Rami's microphone, so that he would be heard but not seen. He was already regretting this whole idea.

At five past seven more people began to turn up – the ghosts, as Rami called them. They ambled in and sat cross-legged on the floor. Jan didn't know many names, but he was starting to recognize most of the Unit's inmates by now. There were fourteen or fifteen of them, all in their early teens – mostly girls, but a few boys too – some with spiky black hair, others with neatly combed locks. Some sat motionless, some kept on shifting restlessly, looking around the whole time. Were they drug addicts? Were they bullies, or perhaps the victims of bullying?

Jan had no idea why anyone else had been admitted to the Unit. He didn't know anyone except Rami. And when he saw a skinny young girl stare at her and then lean over to her friend and whisper loudly, 'Who's *she*?', he realized that Rami had kept even more of a low profile.

She waited silently at the microphone, her back straight and her face almost chalk-white as she clutched her guitar.

Jörgen went and stood beside her with his hands in the pockets of his jeans, gazing out across the room. 'OK, people, time for some music. Our friends Alice and Jan are going to play us a couple of songs.'

This introduction was greeted with nervous giggles, and a disappointed question: 'But what about the TV?' It was a tall boy in a denim jacket. Jan couldn't remember his name. 'There's ice hockey on tonight . . . Aren't we allowed to watch TV?'

'Of course – after the music,' said Jörgen. 'Quiet now.'

But the ghosts were not quiet; they nudged one another and giggled and whispered.

Rami was also suffering from stage fright. Not as badly as Jan, but he could see that she had closed her eyes and seemed to be trying to forget that there was anyone else in the room. And yet there was a clear connection between Rami and the audience – as soon as she opened her mouth, every single person sitting on the floor fell silent. They were all staring at her.

'OK,' she drawled into the microphone. 'This is an American song I've translated . . .'

She began with 'The House of the Rising Sun', which suited Jan; this was the drum accompaniment he knew best. Then she went on to her version of Neil Young's 'Helpless', followed by Joy Division's 'Ceremony', both of which Jan had also rehearsed with her.

Rami had begun to relax while she was singing, and there was more colour in her face. When 'Ceremony' ended she suddenly turned around, walked over to Jan – and kissed him on the lips.

He stopped playing. The kiss lasted three seconds, but the world came to a standstill.

Rami smiled at him, then walked back to the microphone.

'This last song is called "Jan and Me",' she said, nodding to Jan to signal a four-beat.

He had never heard of the song; he was off balance after the kiss, but eventually he managed to start playing, keeping time with her nods. Rami played a minor chord and began to sing:

> *I am lying in my bed*
> *with Jan by my side*
> *we know where we are*
> *and we know where we're bound*
> *we're bound for outer space*
> *where it's cold and it's dark*
> *but the darkness is so beautiful*
> *we forget everything*

She closed her eyes and went into the chorus:

> *Me and Jan, Jan and me*
> *every night, every day . . .*

Jan was so taken aback by the words that he almost lost the beat. It sounded as if he and Rami were *together*, but they weren't. He had been aware of the scent of her, but she had never even touched him.

When the song ended Rami went straight into a different chord, keeping the same beat. She leaned towards the microphone and looked straight at the audience for the first time. Jan could see that she was smiling as she said, 'This is a song about my psychologist.'

She played a loud riff on the guitar and nodded to Jan to join in.

Rami found the rhythm, closed her eyes again and began to intone the lyrics with a harsh, thrusting pulse:

> *You gave birth to a whip out of your mouth*
> *you give birth to the blade of a saw from your back*
> *you raised little leeches*
> *in the depths of your brain*
> *and hurled me down when I stood up to you*

Then she took a deep breath before starting on the chorus, almost spitting out the words:

> *Psycho, psycho, psychobabble!*
> *Stop talking, stop talking crap!*
> *Leave me alo-one!*

The chorus just went on and on. Rami stood there straight-backed; she wasn't even singing notes any more, she was just chanting the words *Stop talking, stop talking crap!* over and over again. No music was coming from the guitar, but Jan kept up a steady rhythm, beating time to the words.

He could see everyone in the Unit, inmates and staff, simply sitting there as if someone had cast a spell on them; the teenagers were all listening intently.

But the Psychobabbler had got to her feet over by the door. She didn't look happy, and with every word that Rami chanted she took a step closer to the microphone. Eventually she was standing half a metre away from Rami, and about a metre from Jan. Rami hadn't seen her; she had her eyes closed and was still singing, 'Stop talking! Stop talking crap!'

The Psychobabbler grabbed hold of Rami's shoulder; Rami opened her eyes, but ignored her and carried on singing. However, it sounded more like a battle cry now: 'Stop! Stop! Stop!'

The Psychobabbler seized the microphone stand and moved it away, but Rami carried on yelling without the microphone. She opened her throat and let out a piercing scream that made those sitting on the floor recoil in shock. 'Die! Die!' Rami bellowed, then hurled herself at the Psychobabbler like a wild animal.

They crashed to the floor in the middle of the audience, rolling around as if they were locked together. Two wrestlers. Jan stared at them, but carried on drumming. He could hear Rami's screams, he could see her scratching and tearing with her fingernails – not at the Psychobabbler, but at herself. She raked her arms until they bled, she smeared streaks of bright-red blood all over herself, over the floor, over the Psychobabbler's face and her black clothes.

'Calm down, Alice!'

Jan heard the sound of running footsteps as Jörgen and a colleague arrived and dragged Rami off. But still she carried on screaming, her arms flailing wildly.

'Stop drumming!' Jörgen bellowed at Jan.

He stopped at once, but still the noise continued. Rami screamed and screamed. The two men had her in a firm grip by now, and dragged her out of the room. Jan heard her cries disappearing down the corridor, and then there was near silence.

The only sound in the television room was of someone panting. The Psychobabbler. Slowly she got to her feet and adjusted her bloodstained jumper. A colleague passed her a handkerchief.

'Now do you see?' said the Psychobabbler. 'Do you remember my diagnosis?'

The concert was over, but Jan stayed where he was for a little while before picking up his drum kit. His arms were trembling.

The boy in the denim jacket looked around with a nervous smile, then went over and switched on the TV.

Jan walked out alone. He went and put the drums back in the storeroom. He was intending to go back to his room and do some drawing, but when he saw Rami's closed door he stopped, looked at it for a moment, then knocked.

There was no answer, so he knocked again.

No answer.

'She's not there,' said a voice behind him.

Jan turned around and saw a girl in the corridor. One of the ghosts.

'What?'

'They took her down to the Black Hole.'

'The Black Hole . . . What's that?'

'It's where they lock you up if you kick off or something.'

'Where is it?'

'Down in the cellar,' said the ghost. 'It's got a door with a whole load of locks.'

*

263

The Black Hole?

Jan crept down into the underworld, to the long, silent corridors. He found the right door and knocked. There was no answer this time either; the door was made of steel, and no doubt swallowed every sound. But there was a tiny gap at the bottom.

He went back up to his room and fetched pens and a piece of paper. He didn't know what to write to Rami, but he had to cheer her up somehow, so he wrote: GOOD GIG! JAN

He slid the paper beneath the door, and managed to push a pen under as well. After a minute or so of absolute silence, the paper reappeared. Just one sentence had been added: I AM A SQUIRREL WITHOUT TREES OR AIR.

He looked at the piece of paper. Then he sat down and began to draw a picture of a girl with a guitar, standing on an enormous stage in front of a huge audience, all with their hands in the air. He made as good a job of Rami's face as he possibly could, then he pushed the picture under the door and quickly crept away.

The following morning he heard noises out in the corridor. Heavy footsteps and loud voices, then the sound of Rami's door slamming shut.

When everything had gone quiet he went and knocked on her door.

'Who is it?' she asked tonelessly through the door, her voice lacking any hint of curiosity.

'Jan.'

There was a brief silence, then she said, 'Come in.'

He opened the door very slowly and carefully, as if it might break. The room was in darkness, but he was used to that.

'Thanks for the picture,' she said.

'You're welcome.'

Rami was lying on the bed staring at the ceiling, with the guitar beside her like some kind of pet. Jan couldn't see if she was restrained in any way.

He wasn't afraid, but he stayed by the door. 'It went well yesterday,' he said. 'Really well.'

Rami shook her head. 'I've got to get away from this place, they're going to break me in here . . . You want to get out too, don't you?'

She had raised her head and was looking at him. Jan nodded slowly, even though it wasn't true. He wanted to stay in the Unit until he was old enough to leave school; he wanted to eat, sleep, play table tennis with Jörgen and play the drums with Rami.

She looked up at the ceiling again. 'But first I'm going to get my revenge on her.'

'On who?'

'The Psychobabbler. She's the one who had me locked up.'

'I know,' Jan said.

'But that's not the worst thing,' Rami said, nodding in the direction of her desk. 'While I was locked up she came in here and took my diary. I just know she's sitting there reading it now. From cover to cover.'

Jan looked over at the desk. What Rami said might well be true, because the book that had been lying on the desk was gone.

'She's going to regret that,' Rami said. 'She and her family.'

38

Jan doesn't recall ever having spoken to a neighbour, not in all the years he has lived in apartment blocks. He might have said hello if he met someone on the stairs, but he has never stopped to chat. To him a stairwell is not a meeting place, it is just a no-man's-land where the only sound is the reverberating echo of doors closing.

But here in Valla there is one neighbour he has spoken to, and now he wants to see him again.

When he gets home after the evening with Hanna, he places Rami's picture books on the kitchen table. He sleeps well that night.

He is still tired when he wakes up, but there are things he must do, and after breakfast he picks up an empty coffee cup and goes down two flights of stairs to the door that says V. LEGÉN on it, and rings the bell.

It takes almost a minute before the door opens. An aroma of pipe tobacco and alcohol reaches Jan's nostrils as his grey-haired neighbour stares blankly at him, but he gives Legén a big smile.

'Hello there,' Jan says. 'Me again, from upstairs . . . I'm baking another cake, and I wondered if you could possibly spare a bit more sugar?'

The neighbour seems to recognize him, but doesn't bother to say hello. 'Ordinary sugar?'

'Any kind.'

Legén simply takes the cup and turns away; he doesn't invite Jan into the dark hallway, but Jan steps inside anyway.

There is no sign of the bag from St Patricia's that was lying on the floor last time; Jan follows Legén into the kitchen. There are plates piled high all over the place, little islands of bottles and cans on the floor, and the windows are covered in a grey film of dust and grease.

'I work at St Patricia's, by the way,' he says to Legén's back.

His neighbour doesn't react at all; he simply carries on tipping sugar into the cup.

'You used to work there too, didn't you?' Jan goes on.

There is no reply this time either, but he thinks he picks up a brief nod over by the worktop. So he tries again: 'Did you work in the laundry?'

This time Legén definitely nods.

'How long were you there?'

'Twenty-eight years. And seven months.'

'Wow. But you've retired now?'

'Yes,' Legén says. 'Now I just make wine.'

Jan looks around. It's true; that's what the bottles and cans are for. The fruity, alcoholic aroma is coming from the containers, not from Legén.

'But maybe you still remember how things looked up there . . . in the hospital?' Jan says slowly.

'Maybe.'

'Any secret passageways?' Jan says, smiling to show that this is a joke. Which it isn't.

Legén stops pouring sugar and looks at Jan, who adds, 'I'd really like to hear some of your stories, if you feel like talking.'

'Why?' asks Legén, picking up the cup of sugar.

'Well, I work there . . . I'm just curious about the place. I've never been up to any of the wards.'

'Oh?' says Legén. 'So where do you work, then?'

Unable to come up with a convincing lie, Jan replies, 'At the pre-school.'

'Pre-school? There is no pre-school.'

'There is now. It's for children whose parents are in St Patricia's.'

Legén simply shakes his head in amazement; he considers Jan's request for a moment, then hands over the cup of sugar. 'OK . . . A hundred, in that case.'

'A hundred what?'

'A hundred kronor and I'll tell you. You can try my wine as well.'

Jan thinks about it, then nods. 'If you talk to me I'll fetch the money afterwards.'

Legén sits down at the kitchen table; he doesn't speak for a little while, but eventually he says, 'There are no secret passageways. Or at least I've never seen one. But there is something else.'

He rummages among the newspapers and receipts covering the surface of the table, and finds a pencil and a torn piece of paper. He begins to draw squares and narrow rectangles.

'What's that?' Jan asks.

'The laundry.' Legén draws an arrow. 'You go to the drying room. There's a big, wide door. But you don't go through it, you use the door on the right, just here. That takes you into a storeroom' – he draws a thick circle around one of the squares – 'and in there, behind all the stuff, is the way up.'

'A staircase?'

'No. An old lift. It goes straight up to the wards . . . The whole place. But not many people know about it.'

Jan looks at the messy sketch. 'But there are usually people in the laundry. And plenty of security guards.'

'Not on Sundays,' says Legén. 'The laundry is empty on Sundays; you can operate the lift from inside, and go up and down as you wish.'

For the first time he meets Jan's eye, and Jan gets the feeling that Legén is talking about himself. All of a sudden there is some kind of understanding between them. *Twenty-eight years at St Psycho's*, Jan thinks. Plenty of time to learn about every square metre of the place, every door and every corridor.

And he must have met many of the patients. Seen them and thought about them.

'Did *you* use the lift?' Jan asks.

'Now and again,' Legén replies.

'On Sundays?'

'Now and again.'

'You used to meet someone up there?'

Legén nods. He seems to be remembering those encounters.

'A woman?'

Legén's expression is mournful. 'She was beautiful, really lovely . . . but she carried hell inside her.'

Jan doesn't ask any more questions.

Lynx

The detective inspector had bright-green eyes that stared and stared and never looked away. She was sitting at Nina's desk in the office and seemed completely at home, as if she were now in charge of Lynx. Jan was trying to appear equally relaxed – he was just one of the members of staff being interviewed by the police.

'Did you see anyone else out in the forest?'

'You mean . . . any other adults?'

'Children or adults,' said the officer. 'Anyone who wasn't part of your group.'

Jan pretended to think back. He could have come up with a shadow among the trees, a crouching male figure spying on the boys with greedy eyes, but he knew that the police were hunting for a kidnapper now, and he didn't want to link himself to such a figure in any way. He shook his head. 'I didn't see anyone . . . but I did hear some noises.'

'Noises?'

Jan hadn't heard any noises, of course, but he had to carry on now he'd started: 'Yes . . . creaking branches, as if something was moving about among the fir trees. But I thought it was an animal.'

'What kind of animal?'

'I don't know . . . A deer, maybe. Or an elk.'

'Something large, in other words?'

'Exactly, a large animal . . . But not a predator.'

The inspector narrowed her eyes. 'What do you mean by predator?'

'Well . . . there *are* predators in the forest. You don't see them very often, because they're so timid, but there are bears and lynxes and wolves . . . or maybe not wolves, not this far south.' Jan knew he had started to babble; he closed his mouth and gave a slightly strained smile.

The inspector didn't ask any more questions. 'Thank you very much,' she said, writing something down in her notebook.

Jan stood up. 'Will you be organizing another search party?'

'Not just at the moment. The helicopter is going out, and there will be a number of specific targeted initiatives.'

'I'd be happy to help,' Jan said. 'With . . . anything at all.'

'Thank you.'

When Jan left the room he looked at the clock. It was twenty past two. Soon it would be twenty-four hours since William had entered the bunker and Jan had crept up and locked him in.

It felt like a year.

Nina and the rest of his colleagues from Lynx and Brown Bear were sitting in the staffroom. They barely spoke to one another; they were just waiting. It felt like a funeral tea. Sigrid Jansson wasn't there – she had signed herself off sick after her interrogation by the police and gone home.

Because that was what they were doing, wasn't it? Interrogating people? That's what it had felt like, and Jan was exhausted after all the questions. He knew that the police had read the letter he had sent to William's parents, and that they were searching for the boy's kidnapper, but surely he wasn't a suspect?

He poured himself a cup of coffee, sat down with the others and tried to relax. There was no longer any sign of the sun outside the window. It was still too early for twilight, but it was on the way.

William's second twilight in the forest, followed by evening, followed by night.

'How are you feeling, Jan?' one of his colleagues asked quietly.

He looked up. 'Not too bad.'

'It wasn't your fault.'

'Thanks.'

Not his fault. Sometimes Jan actually thought this was true, and that William had just somehow disappeared. But then he remembered what had really happened, and he felt sick. He was tired, beaten. He wasn't strong enough.

The nursery was unbearably quiet without the children. Silent and still. Not much happened; uniformed officers came and went in the corridor, their expressions still grim, and Jan realized that William had not been found.

He finished his coffee and looked out of the window again. The forest up above the nursery loomed like a dark shadow.

Stop this, a voice said inside his head. *Do the right thing and stop this ritual now. Let him go.*

Jan got to his feet. 'I have to go.'

'Do you want to go home?' asked Nina.

'I don't know . . . I might take a walk up to the forest.'

He looked helplessly at Nina, but she turned and gazed sadly out of the window. She said quietly, 'They don't think he's there any more.'

'OK . . . But I might just wander up there anyway before I go home. I have to do something.'

Some of his colleagues gave him sympathetic smiles, but Jan didn't smile back.

39

The Dell looks so fragile from a distance, Jan thinks. It's only a wooden hut after all, built to function on a trial basis for a few years before it disappears without a trace. Winter is on its way, and one severe storm sweeping in from the sea could rip off the roof, smash the walls and race through the rooms.

St Psycho's is a different matter altogether. The grey-stone building has stood for more than a hundred years, and will doubtless stand for a hundred more.

It is Saturday, and Jan has a night shift at the pre-school. He expects to hear the happy voices of the children when he opens the door, but all is quiet. The only sound is a faint clinking from the kitchen, and as Jan is taking off his jacket Hanna appears. She is holding a knife in her hand, but it's only an ordinary table knife; she's in the middle of emptying the dishwasher. 'Hi,' she says.

'Hi. I thought Lilian was working today?'

'She's ill.'

Jan looks around. 'Where are the children?'

'They've gone to visit Mira's new foster family.'

'Oh, right . . . When will they be back?'

'Any minute now.'

Jan takes a step closer to Hanna, in spite of the fact that there is no one else in the building, and says quietly, 'Listen, all the stuff we've talked about . . . all those secrets. You won't mention anything to anybody else, will you?'

He feels really stupid, but Hanna merely shakes her head, her expression blank. 'Secrets bind us together.'

'You're right,' Jan nods. 'We have a pact.'

He has no time to say any more; the door bursts open and two small bodies dressed in waterproofs come hurtling in: Mira and Leo.

Mira shouts with joy when she spots Jan, and both he and Hanna automatically move apart. *Maintain the façade in front of the children.*

Mira and Leo are accompanied by a man in a blue cap, a light-brown jacket and sturdy boots. He looks calm and reassuring; he smiles and shakes hands, first with Jan and then with Hanna, introducing himself as 'Mira's second daddy'. They both smile back at her new foster father.

'It all went very well today,' he says. 'They're great kids . . . This is going to be fantastic.'

'Absolutely,' Jan says.

Now the children are back he can't talk to Hanna any more. She finishes at half past six, and goes home dead on time, with big hugs for Mira and Leo and a brief nod to Jan.

When he is alone with the children he makes supper and sits down at the table with them. 'Did you have a good time today?'

Mira nods. 'I'm going to live on a farm. They've got horses!'

'Wow,' says Jan. 'Did you get to stroke them?'

Mira chatters on, brimming over with excitement. Jan sees the look on her face, and it makes him feel happy too.

Then he glances over at Leo. He knows that Leo is also going to live on a farm outside the town, but he can see no trace of excitement in Leo's eyes. 'Have you had enough to eat?' he asks.

'Maybe . . . Can we have some sweets?' asks Mira. She knows it's Saturday.

The children have some chocolate, read two picture books, then go to bed at quarter past eight, after the usual protests.

Jan sits down in the kitchen to wait. The underground passageway leading to St Psycho's is calling to him, but he has no intention of going down there tonight. That can wait until tomorrow, when the laundry will be empty and security will be slightly more relaxed. Tonight he will just slip up to the visitors' room. He has to take that risk.

At half past ten he goes up in the lift. He opens the door a fraction at first, but the room is empty and in darkness.

Nothing has changed, but when he quickly goes over to the sofa and lifts up the cushion, he finds a new envelope. It is pale blue this time, and not as fat.

When Jan is safely back in the kitchen, he opens the envelope and discovers that it contains eighteen letters, but he is really interested in only one of them. It is addressed to him, to *Jan*, and he rips it open immediately, like a Christmas present.

Inside there is a small piece of paper, with a short message in spidery handwriting. But Jan reads it over and over again:

> *Jan, the squirrel remembers you like a dream,*
> *a poem or a burning cloud in the sky.*
> *I remember you, remember you, remember you.*
> *I am still waiting to escape from the zoo.*
> *But you can see me in there,*
> *I have marked out my nest.*
> *Come out of the forest and see.*

A reply. A reply from Rami. It has to be. Jan puts down the piece of paper; his hand is shaking. Through the window he can see the lights of the hospital, but he suppresses the urge to go straight out into the night to search for Rami's room.

40

'Keith Moon meets Topper Headon!' Rettig shouts. 'That's exactly what it sounds like when you play, Jan!'

Jan nods and plays one last roll. He has been sitting behind the drum kit for almost an hour, and the music has made him forget the letters from the hospital.

And now Rettig has paid him a compliment, which is kind; Jan isn't sure whether to pass on the bad news about the Dell. But eventually he decides to tell him. When only he and Rettig are left in the rehearsal room, he casually says, 'By the way, the pre-school is going to be closed at night.'

Rettig carries on packing away the instruments. 'From when?'

'Soon . . . next week. All the children have foster families now.'

'OK, thanks for letting me know.'

'But you realize what this means?' says Jan.

'What?'

'That none of the staff will be there at night . . . So it looks as if we'll have to stop playing postman.'

But Rettig shakes his head. 'Just think about it, Jan.'

'Think about what?'

'About the fact that the Dell will be closed at night . . . What does it mean when something is closed?'

Jan gets up and puts down the drumsticks. He has been hard at it, and he has blisters on his fingers. 'It means no one can get in,' he says. 'When something is closed, the doors are locked.'

'Absolutely,' says Rettig, 'but you'll still have a set of keys, won't you?'

'Well, yes.'

'And the most important thing is that the place will be *empty* . . . There won't be anybody there at night, will there?'

'Maybe not.'

'And if someone has a key to a place that's closed, they can just go in and do whatever they want, can't they?'

'I suppose so,' says Jan. 'As long as they don't have some kind of surveillance.'

'There's no surveillance at night. I'm in charge then, remember.' Rettig closes his guitar case and goes on: 'But we can take a break from the deliveries if you think it's a good idea. We're running a major security exercise at St Patricia's in a couple of weeks, and things usually get a bit tense up there until everything falls into place.'

Jan is thinking about everything that has happened over the past few weeks. About the strange noises in the corridors. 'The hospital basement,' he says. 'Is it completely empty at night?'

'Why do you ask?'

Jan hesitates. He doesn't want to give anything away. 'Dr Högsmed mentioned something about the corridors in the basement when he was showing me around,' he says. 'He said it was unpleasant down there.'

'Högsmed's the boss, but he knows nothing,' Rettig replies. 'He's hardly ever been down to the basement.'

'But is there anyone else down there?'

Rettig nods. 'The communal areas are down there . . . The patients from the open wards are allowed to spend time down there without supervision. There's a swimming pool and a small chapel and a bowling alley – a bit of everything, really.'

Jan looks at him. 'The open wards . . . so those patients aren't dangerous?'

'Not usually,' Rettig replies. 'But sometimes they get ideas, and then you have to be on your guard.'

Jan knows he has to be on his guard, all the time. But Rami

feels so close now, and he wants to ask Rettig one last question: 'And if you happened to find me down there, would you sound the alarm?'

The question doesn't go down well with Rettig. 'You'd never get in, Jan . . . And why on earth would you want to get into St Patricia's? Do you really want to know what an asylum looks like on the inside?'

'No, no,' Jan says quickly. 'I was just wondering, if I did get into the hospital, would you give me away?'

'We're mates.' Rettig shakes his head. 'You don't grass on your mates. So I wouldn't do anything . . . I'd leave you alone.' He looks at Jan. 'But I wouldn't be able to help you either, if someone else found you. I'd deny the whole thing, just like in that American TV series.'

Jan can't ask for anything more. 'OK. I'll just have to improvise.'

'Everybody improvises up there at night,' Rettig says.

'What do you mean?'

Rettig shrugs his shoulders. 'The days are well organized at St Patricia's; we have good, solid routines. But the nights aren't quite as peaceful. Anything can happen then.' He grins at Jan and adds, 'Especially when there's a full moon.'

Jan doesn't ask any more questions. He moves away from the drum kit; he didn't perform particularly well tonight, whatever Rettig thinks. He's not really a team player.

That night Jan dreams about Alice Rami again; but it's a horrible dream. He is walking beside her along a road, and he ought to feel good – but when he looks down, the creature running along and panting between them is no ordinary dog. In fact, it isn't a dog at all.

It's a growling, snarling wild animal, a yellowish-brown cross between a lynx and a dragon.

'Come along, Rössel!' Rami calls as she jogs off down the road.

The creature grins scornfully at Jan and races after her.

Jan is left alone in the darkness.

Lynx

It was time for the madness to end, Jan realized.

When he left the nursery he had definitely decided: he was going to let William go. Let him go *now*. The planned forty-six hours in the bunker would be only twenty-four.

He turned off and headed up into the forest, striding purposefully along.

The track had been trampled by hundreds of boots over the past two days; it had been widened and was easy to walk along. Jan was able to move faster, and when he got into the forest he could see how the undergrowth had been flattened. It wasn't dark yet; it was only quarter past three. But there was no sign of anyone, and he couldn't hear the helicopter.

He carried on into the ravine, quickly went through the old gate, and slowed down only when he had almost reached the slope leading up to the bunker. He had to be careful here.

The small metal door was just as well hidden as before, and when Jan moved the branches aside he saw that it was still firmly closed.

He let out a long breath. Time to assume the role of the innocent classroom assistant who goes into the forest and happens to do what no one dares hope for any longer: he finds the missing child. By pure chance.

He put his mouth close to the door and shouted, loud and clear, 'Hello? Anyone there?'

He waited, but there was no response.

Jan could have carried on shouting, but after waiting for a few more seconds he pulled open the door. 'Hello?' he said again.

There was no response this time either.

Jan wasn't worried yet, just puzzled. He bent down and stuck his head inside the dark bunker. 'Hello?'

It was messier in there this time. The blankets lay in a heap by the wall, and there were many more empty sandwich packs, drink cartons and sweet wrappers strewn around. Roboman was also lying on the floor, but he was broken. His head was cracked and his right arm was missing.

But there was no sign of William.

Jan crawled inside. 'William?'

He shouldn't really call out the boy's name, but he was worried now. The boy wasn't in there, and yet there was nowhere he could have gone.

Eventually he caught sight of the red bucket. The toilet bucket. It was standing right by the back wall, but it was upside down. Why?

Jan looked up at the wall and saw one of the long, narrow gaps that let in air – but it had somehow become slightly bigger. Someone had poked away the earth, branches and old leaves, and managed to clear the opening so that it was now between twenty and thirty centimetres deep. Not big enough for an adult, but big enough for a five-year-old.

William had found a way out. He had probably tried to take Roboman with him, but had dropped the toy on the floor.

Jan tried to remain calm. He knew what he had to do, and set to work. He spread the blankets out on the floor and gathered up everything he had brought into the bunker: the food and drink, the toys and the plastic bucket. Then he bundled everything up in the blankets and dragged them outside. He had now removed all traces of himself from the bunker. The old mattress was still there, but couldn't be linked to him.

He quickly carried the bundles down to level ground, took exactly one hundred and twenty paces away from the bunker and hid the lot under a dense fir. He would fetch it later, when he had found William.

Jan looked around. It was twilight now, but nothing was moving in the forest.

Where should he start?

41

Jan goes to work earlier on the Sunday; he wants to get to the hospital before the sun goes down. It is shining like a big yellow ball in a dark-blue sky this afternoon. Autumn days can be so fresh and clear sometimes.

The sunshine is perfect, because after the reply from Rami, he wants to see the hospital in daylight.

I have marked out my nest, the letter had told him. *Come out of the forest and see.*

The forest is at the back of St Patricia's, so Jan has to make a detour. This is not without risk – he must keep out of range of the cameras and alarm systems. But the slope leading down to the brook that runs alongside the fence is thick with undergrowth and dense fir trees, and he is able to remain hidden in the shadows.

He stops between two firs and gazes over the fence at the rows of windows. From the edge of the forest he spots something new on the stone façade: something is fluttering in the wind up there.

A white flag. It looks as if it has been made from a torn sheet or a handkerchief, and it is hanging down from one of the windows.

Now he understands what the squirrel meant when she said she had marked out her nest.

Jan counts silently, circling the window with the flag in his mind's eye, as if the façade were a map: *fourth floor, seventh window from the right*. He must remember that position.

There is no sign of anyone behind the glass; the room is in darkness, but Rami has shown him exactly where she lives.

All he has to do now is get there – but the only way is through the basement.

Before tea Leo and Mira are playing doctors. Their cuddly toys are poorly, and the children are going to make them better. Jan helps them to sort out the little beds, then he has to lie down and be a patient too.

After they have eaten they go outside for a while. Leo and Mira want to play on the swings, but Jan is somehow detached from their activities. He gives them both a push, then glances over at the fence. It is dusk now, and the floodlights have come on, shining on wet leaves and the sharp points of the barbed wire.

Fifteen years have passed, but Jan hopes that Rami will still be there. His Rami, that is. The Rami who was in the room next door to him in the Unit for a while. The girl who let him in and was the first person who seemed to think he was worth talking to. No, not *seemed* to think – she actually liked spending time with Jan. And the fact that she left him and ran away like a squirrel – well, that was because of something else altogether.

It is late by the time the children fall asleep – just before nine.

Jan should be able to relax now, but it is impossible. Leo had trouble getting to sleep, and shouted for Jan several times. Jan's nerves are already at breaking point, and tonight he has a long journey ahead of him. Long and uncertain – even if he knows his goal.

Fourth floor, seventh window from the right.

At quarter past eleven he checks on Mira and Leo one last time, then heads down the stairs to the basement with the Angel clipped to his belt. There isn't a sound; the children have been fast asleep for more than two hours now.

He opens the door into the safe room; the door at the far end is still unlocked. He walks into the darkness.

He is back in the hospital basement, but he is better prepared this time. The Angel has new batteries, and the little beam sweeps across the old tiled walls. He knows where he is, but he is still unable to relax. Last time Hanna was upstairs listening in, but tonight he is all alone.

He sets off, with Legén's primitive map in his hand: the arrows should help him find his way.

To make sure he doesn't get lost, he has something else in his pocket: white paper. Before he left he sat in the kitchen and tore up several sheets of paper into tiny pieces. As he walks along he drops them one by one, a couple of metres apart.

Marking out his escape route.

He eventually reaches the grubby tiled rooms, and tucks the Angel underneath his jumper so that the light won't show too much, just in case any patients are wandering around down here. He is getting close to the laundry now, and even though Legén maintained it was closed on Sundays, he doesn't want to advertise his presence.

He looks up at the ceiling. Thick, snake-like electric cables are intertwined up there. And somewhere above him are the rooms where the patients live. About a hundred, Högsmed had said. And he is hoping that one of them, on the fourth floor, is Alice Rami.

He has reached the laundry. The door is closed. And locked? He reaches out and pushes down the handle. The door is stiff, but it opens.

The last time he was here there was a light on, but now the room is in darkness. It is like a black cave, apart from the odd light on the electricity meter and the washing machines, glowing like the red eyes of animals lurking in the gloom. Fans are whirring softly in the background; the air is warm and heavy.

Jan steps inside, still clutching his map.

He is looking for a wide door, but doesn't want to switch on the light. Or rather he does want to, but dare not. He gropes his way forward, past rows of padlocked metal cupboards and a table littered with dirty coffee cups. Then he is in a smaller room with no lights at all, and he has no choice but to use the Angel.

The beam falls on an enormous washing machine with a metal

face and a round, gaping mouth in the middle. The walls are lined with long shelves containing bundles of laundry; up at the top there is a steel rail with a row of vests on coat hangers; they look like slender white angels.

Jan carries on searching, and eventually he discovers a broad, black steel door.

The door to the drying room, according to the map. A few metres to the left there is a narrower wooden door with a round knob; Jan goes over and opens it.

The rooms in the laundry have been getting smaller and smaller, and this is the smallest of them all. A storeroom with stone walls. There is an old light switch by the door, and he decides to risk it in order to save the Angel's batteries.

A dusty bulb illuminates a windowless room full of rubbish: old wooden crates, empty soap-powder boxes, a broken coat hanger. But next to one of the shelves is exactly what Legén promised: a lift door with an iron handle. A very small door – more of a hatch, really. It is barely a metre wide and not much taller, and when Jan goes over and opens it, he realizes that this is not a lift meant for people. It is a wooden lift built many years ago to send baskets of clean laundry up to the various floors in the hospital.

There isn't much room inside; it would be impossible to stand upright. Jan stares at the opening and hesitates. Then he stoops down and pushes his head and shoulders inside. It's like crawling into the luggage compartment on a bus. Or into a big chest.

It is seriously claustrophobic, but still he squeezes himself inside.

Fluffy dust balls swirl away from his hands and knees; he can't stand up, but with a little bit of effort he can move his legs and turn around.

Before Jan closes the hatch he glances down at the Angel. What will he do if one of the children wakes up and calls out to him now? But he can't think about that; he is too close to Rami.

Fourth floor, seventh window.

He switches on the Angel's torch. The wooden walls are pressing in on him, and his shadow is dancing on the ceiling. He sees a number of black circles in front of him. Seven buttons. They are old and cracked, they might even be made of Bakelite, and one of them is marked EMERGENCY STOP. The other six are not numbered, but he takes a chance and presses the fourth button from the right.

He hears a clunking sound somewhere above him, and slowly the lift begins to move. Upwards. The wall in front of him slides downwards as the lift shakes and rattles.

Jan is on his way up through the hospital. His destination is by no means guaranteed, but he hopes it is the fourth floor.

He closes his eyes. He doesn't want to think about it, but the lift feels like a wooden coffin.

The Unit

After more than a week in the Unit Jan started to talk about why he had jumped in the pond. Not to some psychologist, but to Rami. It was a long story, told behind the closed door of her room.

Rami was restless that evening. She jumped up on to her un-made bed, then lay down with the pillow over her face. Then she got up again, grabbed her guitar and stood right at the edge of the mattress facing the black curtains, as if she could see an audience out there in front of her.

'I love *chaos*,' she said. 'Chaos is *freedom*. I want to sing in praise of insecurity . . . as if I'm standing on the very edge of the stage, and sometimes I just fall off.'

Jan was sitting on the floor, but said nothing.

Rami didn't look at him, she just went on: 'If I ever get to record an album, it will be like a suicide note. But without the suicide.'

Jan looked at the floor for a while, then said, 'I've done that.'

Rami struck a chord on the guitar, fierce and dark. 'Done what?' she said.

'I tried to kill myself,' Jan said. 'Last week.'

Rami played another chord. 'People should die for music,' she said. 'A song should be so good that people want to *die* when they hear it.'

'I wanted to die before I came here . . . And I almost managed it.'

Now it was Rami's turn to be quiet; she seemed to be listening at last. She took a couple of steps backwards and leaned against the wall. 'You wanted to *die*? For real?'

Jan nodded slowly. 'Yes . . . I would have died anyway.'

'What do you mean?'

'They would have killed me.'

'Who would?'

Jan held his breath and didn't look at Rami. Talking about what had happened was difficult, even though the door was closed, even though the fence was protecting him. He felt as if Torgny Fridman were sitting on the other side of the wall, listening.

'A gang,' he said eventually. 'A gang of lads at my school . . . They're in the year above me and they call themselves the Gang of Four, or maybe that's just what everybody else calls them. They rule the place – in the corridors, anyway. The teachers haven't got a clue. They don't do anything about it . . . Everybody just does whatever these lads say.'

'But not you?'

'I was stupid, I didn't think,' Jan says. 'One day in the lunch queue, Torgny Fridman told me to move out of the way. He wanted to go in front of me, but I wouldn't let him in . . . I stayed put, and in the end one of the teachers came and spoke to him and sent him right to the back of the queue. He never forgot it.' Jan sighed. 'From then on it was just a campaign of terror; it was war between me and Torgny. He used to have a go at me every time he saw me, either by shouting out what a worthless little shit I was, or by knocking me over.'

Jan paused.

'So I kept away from the gang. I counted the days, and I thought I might just make it.'

Friday afternoon, a bitterly cold day in March. Jan's last lesson today was PE, and now it's over. It's the end of the school week, and it's actually been pretty quiet. No fights.

He is the last person in the boys' changing room. He might even be the last person in the sports hall. It is a few hundred metres away from the rest of the school, and everyone else has gone. All the boys in his class waited for their friends. No one waited for Jan.

It's OK, it's always the same.

He picks up his flimsy towel, winds it around his waist and heads for the showers, where the dripping water echoes in the four small cubicles. He hangs up his towel and goes into the cubicle next to the pine door of the sauna.

He turns on the hot water, stands under the shower and begins to rub shower gel over his body.

'I was just standing there in the shower; my legs were tired after PE, and my head was completely empty,' Jan told Rami. 'I wasn't thinking about anything at all . . . Sometimes when you're having a hot shower it's as if you're dreaming, you know what I mean? I might have been thinking about the weekend; I was going to be on my own at home because Mum and Dad were going away somewhere . . . When I finished and turned to reach for my towel, I suddenly smelled cigarette smoke in the air. And then I saw that someone was standing outside the shower. It was Torgny Fridman.'

Torgny is fully dressed, wearing jeans, a denim jacket, and boots.

He is standing by the shower cubicle, blocking the doorway. He looks at Jan and smiles.

Torgny is not the leader of the gang, but he is the one who most wants to impress Peter Malm. Peter is the leader; he has never bothered with Jan. But Torgny is dangerous.

He seems delighted to have a naked Year 10 pupil in front of him.

Jan stares back at him. He doesn't do anything else. He might possibly be able to straighten up and push his way past Torgny, but in that case he would have to be someone else, not Jan Hauger.

So Jan stays where he is, and smiles.

He always smiles in threatening situations, even though he doesn't want to. The more frightened he is, the more he smiles.

Torgny is actually smiling too, a victorious smile. He shows his teeth, grinning broadly at Jan. Then he turns his head to the right and calls to someone. He carries on smiling and calls out several names, and when he has finished there is silence for a few seconds.

Then the door of the sauna opens and his three friends emerge.

The pack, the Gang of Four. Each of them is holding a glowing cigarette.

Could he push his way past them and escape?

Too late.

'So they were sitting in the sauna?' Rami said. 'Why?'

'They were hiding from the teachers,' Jan explained. 'They were having a secret smoke. The sauna was turned off, so they sat in there smoking and waiting for the weekend to begin. There was Torgny, Niklas, Christer, and Peter Malm. And they all walked out of the sauna, and when I saw them I moved backwards.'

But where can Jan go? He is standing in a shower cubicle, naked, in a puddle of cold water. He can't back away through a wall.

Torgny says just one word: 'Hauger.'

His name sounds like an accusation.

'What are you doing here, Hauger? Are you spying on us?'

Jan doesn't reply; he just keeps on smiling at Torgny to show that he is completely harmless. And he is, of course. Four fifteen-year-olds against one fourteen-year-old. That's about the right level of opposition for the gang.

Torgny was the one who discovered their prey, and now he is the one who brings it down. He places his cigarette in the corner of his mouth, grabs hold of Jan's arm and delivers a sharp kick to his shin. Jan crumples on to the tiles. Into the cold water.

He tries to get up, but feels hands on his body, holding him firmly. Not Peter Malm – he doesn't bother – but all the others. Three pairs of hands are pushing him down.

Through the fear Jan knows that Peter is the leader. He is the master, the others are his savage dogs. Jan tries to make eye contact.

Don't let them loose, he thinks.

'What shall we do with him?' Torgny asks.

'Do something cool,' says Peter.

Torgny nods; he has an idea: 'We'll stub out our fags on him!'

Peter stands back and carries on smoking as his subordinates put out their cigarettes. One by one, on Jan's skin. It turns into a competition to find the best place.

Christer stubs out his cigarette on Jan's chest, between the nipples.

Niklas goes for a testicle. 'Did you hear that?' he shouts. 'It made a hissing noise! Did you hear it?'

Peter Malm nods and takes another drag on his cigarette.

Torgny smiles and takes his time.

Eventually he chooses the place where the skin is thinnest, on the throat.

At that point Jan closes his eyes.

'The worst thing isn't the pain,' Jan said to Rami. 'I mean, of course it hurts, it's a bit like a nail going through your skin . . . but that passes.'

'So what is the worst thing?'

'It's the smell. It kind of lingers. You can smell burnt flesh . . . and it's your own.'

As he talked about it the smell was there again, as if it were still inside his nostrils after a whole week.

He had known he was going to die there in the shower. Alone with the Gang of Four – there was no hope for him.

The cigarettes have been stubbed out. Jan has brownish-red circles on his skin, like fresh birthmarks. The hands holding him down loosen their grip slightly; the fingers are beginning to tire.

Soon. Soon it will be over, he thinks. They'll go in a minute.

But then Peter Malm issues a new order: 'Chuck him in the sauna.'

'Fanfuckingtastic!' says Torgny. 'We'll lock him in!'

'What are you talking about?' says Niklas. 'There's no lock.'

Disappointed silence. Jan keeps quiet too.

'Chuck him in there anyway,' says Peter; it is obvious from the tone of his voice that he is starting to get bored. 'Chuck him in and we'll get out of here.'

The grip on Jan's arms tightens once more. They are assuming he will fight back, and he does. This is the final battle, but he loses it in no time. Six hands drag him towards the sauna, and Peter holds the door open.

For just a second Jan's thigh presses against Torgny as they struggle, and he realizes that Torgny has a rock-hard erection.

Then Jan is hurled into the sauna. He lands on his back on the duckboards, and the door slams shut.

Silence.

The light is on inside the sauna, and a faint smell of cigarette smoke still lingers in the air.

Jan can hear their laughter through the door.

'Time to turn up the heat, Hauger!'

The light goes out. The Gang of Four have switched it off.

Torgny is still shouting. 'We're taking your clothes.'

Niklas chips in, 'We're going to chuck them in the pond, Hauger, so everybody will think you've drowned!'

Jan doesn't respond. He lies there like a mouse in the darkness. Silent, waiting.

He knows that the Gang of Four are holding the door shut, but they're bound to leave at some point. Sooner or later torturing a little Year 10 kid is going to get boring, it's going to start feeling like hard work, and then they'll give up. That's what he's waiting for.

The black metal heater inside the sauna begins to make a series of clicking noises, and he realizes they've actually done it; they've turned the control outside the door from OFF to ON. But how high have they set the temperature? Fifty degrees? Sixty? Or much hotter?

It doesn't matter. They'll go soon.

Eventually everything goes quiet outside the door, and Jan feels brave enough to move.

He gets to his feet. The sauna is already warmer. Not hot, but warm.

He listens again, places the palm of his hand against the door, and pushes.

'I couldn't open it,' he said to Rami. 'It should have just swung open, but it wouldn't move. They'd jammed it somehow. So I was locked inside the sauna, and the heater was clicking away . . . It was getting hotter and hotter.'

Lynx

Jan saw street lights shimmering up ahead of him, and knew that he was on his way out of the forest.

He had been wandering around in a state of rising panic for forty-five minutes now, searching among the fir trees and even down by the lake, but he had found no trace of William. A five-year-old shouldn't have been able to get this far, but then William could have gone in absolutely any direction.

Jan had lost control. He was tired, slightly angry, and increasingly desperate. Sometimes he thought the child was hiding from him, that he was standing behind a tree giggling to himself.

Why had William clambered out of the bunker? Didn't he realize he was safer in there than out in the forest? He had plenty of food and drink, and he would have been locked in there for less than forty-eight hours. Then Jan would have let him go, whatever happened.

His plan. His carefully thought-out plan.

Jan stopped in the middle of the undergrowth. His shoes were soaking wet, he felt empty and exhausted.

Locked inside a bunker – with only a toy robot for company. Jan looked around him and suddenly felt how *wrong* the whole thing had been. It had to stop now. There had to be a happy ending.

He stood there for a long time on the edge of the forest, wondering what to do. He felt safe there because nobody could see him, but eventually he moved out from among the trees and headed down towards the street lights. This was a residential area with long rows of apartment blocks and large, asphalt-covered inner courtyards, all ready for the coming winter. There were lights showing in many of the windows, but the streets were deserted.

Jan walked along the nearest pavement, looking around all the time. He felt the urge to call out William's name, but clamped his lips firmly together.

If I were five years old, he thought, *and the glow of the street lights had lured me out of the forest, where would I go?*

Home, of course. When you have been locked up and then you escape, you want to go home.

But Jan knew where William lived, and it was in a completely different part of Nordbro. It was unlikely that he would be able to find his way there.

A few hundred metres away there was a main road, and Jan made his way towards it. What he really wanted was to go home too, go home and go to bed, but then he would be leaving William. Not just leaving, but *abandoning* him.

Up ahead he could see a bus stop, with a few teenagers hanging around. On the same side of the road a family was out for a walk, a man and his two children going towards the town centre.

No, it wasn't a family. As Jan got closer he could see that the smallest child was actually a dog, a long-legged poodle on a short lead. And the other . . . the other child was a little boy with fair hair.

The man holding the boy's hand looked like his grandfather, a pensioner in a cap, ambling along between the boy and the poodle. The boy wasn't wearing a hat, but he was dressed in a dark-blue padded jacket with white reflector strips.

Jan recognized it, and broke into a run.

'William!'

His shout made the boy stop and look around. The man tugged at his hand, but the boy pulled away, wanting to stop and see who was calling his name.

Jan was out of breath by the time he reached them. He bent down. 'Do you remember me, William?'

The boy looked at him without moving. Everything had stopped dead. The man holding William's hand was staring at Jan in surprise, and even the poodle had turned around and was standing there motionless.

Then William nodded. 'Lynx,' he said, his voice slightly hoarse.

'That's right, William . . . I work at Lynx.' Jan looked up at the man and tried to sound trustworthy and totally in control of himself. 'My name is Jan Hauger, I work at William's nursery. He's been missing . . . We've been looking for him.'

'Oh, right. I see. My name is Olsson.' The man appeared to relax. He let go of William's hand and pointed back down the road. 'He just turned up here a little while ago, when Charlie and I were out for our walk. He seemed to be lost, so I said we'd go and look for his parents.'

Jan looked at William, who was staring at the ground. He seemed slightly listless, but healthy. Not undernourished. His left hand was clutching Roboman's plastic arm.

'Great,' Jan said. 'But they live quite a long way from here, so I think we'd better ring for some help.'

'Help?' said Olsson.

'I think we need to ring the police. They're looking for William.'

'The police?' The man looked worried, but Jan nodded and took out his mobile. He rang the emergency number, and waited.

The man started to move away with the poodle, but Jan held up his hand. 'You and Charlie need to stay here,' he said as firmly as possible. 'I think they're going to want to speak to you as well.'

Obviously. Jan was in no doubt about the man's intentions towards William, but he knew the police would look at things very differently. As a thank you for taking care of William, Olsson would presumably be interrogated on suspicion of child abduction.

'Emergency – which service do you require?'

'Police,' said Jan. 'It's about a missing boy – he's been found.'

As he was waiting to be put through he looked down at William. Jan smiled at him, trying to look calm and reliable. He wanted to reach out and pat the boy on the head, but resisted the impulse.

'All's well that ends well,' he said. 'I think we'd better stay away from the forest in future.'

42

The rattling ascent in the old hospital lift takes an hour – or at least that's how it feels to Jan. He holds the claustrophobia at bay by keeping his eyes closed and picturing Rami; he conjures up her face and remembers her eyes beneath that blonde fringe. She was the only one he could talk to about the Gang of Four.

But the floor and the walls are shaking, and he is constantly reminded of where he is. If one of the cogs were to break and the lift were to get stuck between floors . . . He doesn't want to think about that. The drumbeats reverberate inside his head.

Suddenly the lift comes to an abrupt halt. Everything falls silent.

Jan switches off the Angel's torch and reaches out to the door in front of him. At first it won't move. The fear sinks its claws into him immediately, but then the door slowly gives way and slides open.

It stops after about forty or fifty centimetres; there is something heavy in the way. Jan peers out. There is a faint light, but all he can see is grey metal.

Slowly he begins to manoeuvre his way out. It feels as if he has woken up inside a coffin in a big house, just like Viveca in Rami's book.

His upper body is out now, and he can see that there is a metal cupboard in the way. The room beyond it seems to be some kind of medical storeroom, with bandages and packs of tablets on the shelves. The light is coming in through a narrow pane of glass in the door.

There isn't a sound.

Jan tentatively lowers his feet to the floor next to the cupboard, then he stands up and looks over at the exit. Three steps and he is there, reaching out his hand.

The door opens from the inside. He pulls it three or four centimetres towards him, feels fresh air come pouring in, and listens carefully. He still can't hear a thing.

St Psycho's is sleeping.

Jan tugs the door further towards him. He sees a long, wide corridor with pale-yellow walls. The glow of the ceiling lights is subdued, perhaps because it is night time. There isn't a soul in sight. He can smell disinfectant, so there must be cleaners around somewhere.

And patients.

And security guards, of course. Rettig and Carl and their friends.

Jan pulls himself together and steps out of the storeroom. The corridor extends in both directions, with rows of closed doors on both sides. The black hands on a large, round clock above the door are showing quarter to twelve.

Jan tucks a couple of the pieces of paper he has left into the lock to keep the door open. Then he moves along the vinyl floor, as quietly as possible.

Suddenly he feels like a fourteen-year-old again, back in the corridors of the Unit. There is the same silence, the same cold walls and closed doors.

A surprising sense of calm descends on him. Being here in the Corridor of the Closed Doors is almost like coming home.

He looks to the right and begins to count the unmarked doors. The seventh looks just like the rest – but to Jan's eyes it seems to shine with a greater luminosity, and it is waiting for him just seven or eight metres away.

He moves along slowly, past all the other doors. On each one there is a steel handle, with a small metal hatch beside it.

He has almost reached his goal. Should he knock on Rami's door, or try to open it?

Jan makes a decision: he will knock.

'Excuse me? Who are you?'

The sound of a voice makes him jump.

He has been caught. A security guard has opened the door at the far end of the corridor, and is staring at him. But it isn't Rettig or Carl – this is a middle-aged woman.

She takes a couple of steps towards him. 'Where have you come from?'

Jan blinks, desperately searching for an answer. 'From the laundry.'

'You're not supposed to be here,' the woman says. 'What are you doing here?'

'I got lost,' Jan says.

The woman stares, but doesn't say anything else; suddenly she turns and hurries away. To fetch help?

Jan needs to get away.

He glances at Rami's door one last time. So close, but there is nothing he can do right now. There is nothing he can give her.

No – maybe there is one thing.

He opens the small metal hatch in the wall next to her door and peers inside. The box is empty apart from a couple of sheets of paper. A menu, and information about a forthcoming fire drill.

Quickly he unclips the Angel from his belt and slips it into the box, hiding it beneath the sheets of paper. Then he closes the hatch.

The corridor is still empty, and Jan rushes back to the store-room. He removes the pieces of paper that were keeping the door open, but pushes one of them right into the lock to hold the catch pressed in. As he silently closes the door he hears heavy footsteps in the corridor. The guards are on their way.

The lift is just as cramped as before, but this time he clambers inside without hesitation. He presses the button on the far right, and the lift clunks into life.

Jan keeps his eyes closed all the way down.

When the lift stops he quickly opens the hatch; he is impatient and less tentative now. It is well after midnight, and he wants to get out of the hospital.

He gropes his way along, out of the laundry and through the tiled rooms. He has no Angel to help him this time, but somewhere up ahead he can see a flickering light.

And he can hear singing – is someone singing hymns down here?

He fumbles his way forward, staring down at the tiled floor. Where are the bits of paper? He can't see them in the darkness.

The light grows stronger as he shuffles down the long corridors. Eventually he turns a corner and sees a doorway filled with light; there are candles burning in a couple of wooden sconces on the walls.

He is standing in a narrow room with a bank of wooden benches. A few grey sacks have been thrown on the floor. It's a small chapel, and right at the front he sees an altarpiece – an old, cracked image of a woman with a gentle smile. He moves closer and is able to read the name PATRICIA painted in angular letters on the frame of the picture.

Patricia, the hospital's patron saint.

He turns away – but the grey sacks have begun to move.

They are patients. Three men in grey tracksuits, with grey faces. One older man with heavy jowls, and two younger men with shaved heads. They are staring at Jan, their expressions blank and empty. Perhaps it's because of the medication.

The older man points to the altar. His voice is mechanical. 'Patricia needs peace and quiet.'

'So do we,' says one of the others.

'Me too,' Jan says quietly.

'Do you live here?' one of the patients asks.

'Yes,' Jan replies. 'I live down here.'

The older man nods, and Jan takes a step past the three men. Slowly and carefully. Rettig has warned him. But the patients remain motionless, and Jan goes back out into the corridor.

Eventually he finds one of his scraps of paper on the floor. And then another. They show him the way, and he hurries along, following the white trail. He hears voices in the chapel behind him – the men have started singing hymns again. Jan speeds up, heading towards the end of the corridor.

Into another corridor, around several corners in this labyrinth – and at last he is back in the safe room.

He shuts the steel door behind him, then scurries along the familiar corridor, past the animal pictures and up the stairs. His adventure is over.

The last thing he does at the top of the stairs is to listen for footsteps from down below. But no one is pursuing him.

He closes the door and breathes out, but he can't relax. He checks on the children, and has a terrible shock.

Only one head is visible in the beds. It is Leo's. Mira's bed is empty.

Jan is utterly panic-stricken; he can't move. *You let them down. Another child is missing. Missing, missing—*

Then he hears the toilet flush in the bathroom.

Mira is almost six; she has learned how to go to the toilet on her own, without calling for an adult. She emerges from the bathroom and walks straight past him, still half asleep. She hasn't even noticed that he wasn't there.

'Goodnight, Mira,' he says behind her.

'Mm,' she replies, and gets back into bed.

A few minutes later she seems to have dropped off, and Jan is gradually able to wind down. He removes the other Angel from the children's room and puts it in his locker. If things work out this will be his link to the hospital. A way of transmitting secret messages.

43

'Is everyone feeling OK?' Marie-Louise asks.

There are a few indistinct mumbles.

The response is muted. Winter is on its way. It is late autumn, a weary grey Monday morning at the Dell, with an excess of darkness and very little light.

Jan says nothing, but no one seems to notice his silence. His night shift actually finished an hour ago, but in spite of his tiredness he has stayed on to attend the morning meeting. He wants to know if his visit to the hospital has been discovered – if Dr Högsmed has sent over a report about an *intruder*. The security guard was quite a long way from him, she can't possibly have seen his face all that clearly, but . . .

Marie-Louise doesn't mention it. She is behaving exactly the way she always does, except that she is slightly more subdued. Perhaps it's because of the autumn darkness outside the window.

Lilian is positively drooping. Her head is bent over her coffee cup so that the red hair covers her face; she seems to be half asleep. When Marie-Louise turns to her, Lilian doesn't look her in the eye.

'Lilian,' Marie-Louise says tentatively. 'What's that?'

'Sorry? What's what?'

Lilian raises her head and Jan sees that she still has the snake on her cheek. Her weekend tattoo.

'On your cheek . . . Have you painted something on your cheek?'

'This?' Lilian runs her fingers over her face, and seems surprised when she notices that her fingertips are slightly black. 'Oh, sorry, that was for a party . . . I forgot to get rid of it. Sorry. I'm really sorry.' She coughs loudly and suppresses a belch, and the smell of alcohol spreads across the table.

Marie-Louise frowns. 'Lilian, could I have a word with you in private?'

Lilian closes her mouth. 'What for?'

'Because you are far from sober.' Marie-Louise's voice is no longer gentle.

Lilian looks at her for a few seconds, then she gets up and leaves the table, her lips tightly pressed together. She walks out of the room after pausing to address the others: 'I am not drunk,' she mutters. 'I am *hung-over.*'

Marie-Louise follows her. 'Back in a moment.'

Both women seem to have repaired to the cloakroom; that's where their voices are now coming from. The conversation begins as a quiet discussion, but the volume rapidly increases. Marie-Louise's voice remains controlled, but Lilian responds with loud questions.

'Can't a person go out and *relax* after work? *Wind down* a little bit? Or are we all supposed to *dedicate our lives* to the kids, just like you've done?'

'Calm down please, Lilian – the children can hear you . . .'

'I am fucking calm!'

Around the table you could hear a pin drop. Hanna and Andreas keep their eyes lowered, and Jan can't think of anything to say.

The tirade continues: 'You're sick, that's your problem! You need to get some help!'

Is that Lilian or Marie-Louise? Jan can't tell; the voice that is yelling is too shrill.

'And you're so fucking *perfect*! I just can't do it any more, I can't be like you . . . The nut jobs can look after their own fucking kids!'

That must be Lilian, Jan realizes.

Marie-Louise's response is cold and curt: 'Lilian, you're hysterical.'

Hysteria is no longer an acceptable term, Jan hears Dr Högsmed saying inside his head.

The quarrel is making Andreas look ill; he shudders and gets to his feet. 'I'll go and see to the children.'

He goes into the playroom and soon Jan hears jolly nursery rhymes from the CD player, drowning out the loud voices from the cloakroom.

But like most arguments, this one soon comes to an end. After a few moments the front door slams shut; there is a brief silence, then Marie-Louise is back, smiling once more.

'Lilian has gone home for the day,' she says. 'She's going to have a little rest.'

Jan nods without speaking, but Hanna asks softly, 'Is she getting any help?'

Marie-Louise stops smiling. 'Help?'

'To cut down on her drinking,' Hanna says calmly.

Jan can feel the tension in the air.

Marie-Louise folds her arms. 'Lilian is not a child. She is responsible for her own actions.'

'But the employer also has a certain level of responsibility,' Hanna insists. She sounds as if she is quoting from some legal document when she goes on: 'If an employee is drinking too much there should be a treatment plan for their rehabilitation.'

'For *their rehabilitation*,' Marie-Louise repeats. 'Well, doesn't that sound marvellous?'

Hanna doesn't look amused. 'Is there a rehabilitation plan for Lilian?'

Marie-Louise stares at her. 'There are many eyes on us here, Hanna,' she says eventually. 'Just bear that in mind.'

Then she turns and walks out of the staffroom.

There are only the two of them left at the table now. Hanna rolls her eyes at Jan, but he shakes his head.

'Now she'll think you're a troublemaker,' he says quietly.

Hanna sighs. 'I care about Lilian. Don't you?'

'Well yes . . . obviously.'

'So why does she drink so much? Have you given it any thought?'

Jan hasn't given it any thought. 'To get drunk,' he says eventually.

'But why does she want to get drunk?'

Jan shrugs. 'I suppose she's unhappy. But there's unhappiness everywhere, isn't there?'

'You don't know anything . . . you just don't understand,' Hanna says, getting to her feet.

Jan stands up too. It feels good to leave the table, and equally good to think that he can soon go home. This has not been a pleasant Monday morning; the feelgood meeting was more about feeling bad.

He just wants to go home and get some sleep. He wants to be normal. He wants to look to the future, make a life for himself.

Never to be shut in again, he thinks.

He has no one to make a life with. Perhaps that is the worst thing of all. Not having someone to listen.

The Unit

Rami had climbed off her bed and sat down on the floor next to Jan. In the end his story about the Gang of Four had captured her attention.

'Had they locked you in the sauna?'

'Not locked . . . there was no lock,' he said. 'But they'd jammed something up against the door. I didn't know what it was, but it wouldn't move. It was rock-solid.'

'So you were trapped in the heat,' Rami said.

He nodded.

'How did you get out, then?'

'I didn't,' Jan said. 'It was Friday . . . Everyone had gone home.'

The silence in the sauna goes on and on. No doors slam. No caretaker pokes his head around the door and shouts 'Hello?' into the empty shower room.

The door refuses to move.

And the sauna is hot now. The air could get hotter, but it is hot enough already. As hot as the desert. Forty degrees perhaps, or fifty.

All he can do is grope around in the darkness, feeling his way across the pine floorboards. His hand touches a plastic bucket; he hears the water lapping against the sides.

There is wood everywhere inside a sauna. Bare wood on the floor and on the walls, with long planks fixed to the walls at two different levels. That is where you sit when you are having a sauna, or a crafty smoke.

Jan sits on the lower plank for a while. He is sweating now.

Someone is bound to come.

Then he stops thinking for a while; his head feels kind of empty. The skin on his bottom is a bit sore, but he is calmer now. The Gang of Four have gone.

No one else comes. There isn't a sound outside the door.

And it just keeps on getting hotter and hotter.

Jan was sitting on the floor in Rami's room with his head bowed. She was holding his hand and he could feel her beside him, but in his mind he was alone. He was still inside the sauna.

'I was unlucky,' he said. 'It was Friday, and the gym wasn't due to open again until Monday.'

'So what happened?' Rami asked.

Jan looked at her. 'I don't know.'

He didn't really remember very much, but now he started to think back. What did he actually do? How do you survive several days in a hot sauna?

Bang on the door. Keep on banging and banging, until you are quite sure that no one is coming. Peter Malm and his gang won't be coming back. They have jammed the door and cleared off; they have already forgotten you.

Then you can try shouting and banging on the door for a little bit longer, until you eventually give up. Your hands are aching and smarting; they are full of splinters from the coarse wood of the sauna door.

Fumble around and realize that you can actually see a little bit in the darkness – a faint strip of light is showing underneath the door, and there is a tiny shimmering patch in an air vent just below the ceiling. So you are not completely blind. You can see your hands in front of you like patches of pale grey.

You reach out and climb upwards. The heat increases as you get closer to the ceiling. Suddenly your fingers are touching something, something cylindrical, with a smooth metallic surface.

A beer can. Here in the near darkness it is impossible to see what brand it is, but you can hear the liquid slopping about when you pick it up. It feels as if it is about half full, but when you bring it up to your nose a sour, disgusting smell emanates from the little hole in the top. Someone has left it on the bench in the sauna; it could have been there for days, or even weeks.

Put the can down. Sit on the top bench and think. Try to think. How are you going to get out?

Don't expect anyone in the Gang of Four to come back and open the door; that's not going to happen.

Don't expect your parents to come looking for you either. They were supposed to be going away with your younger brother, to stay with some aunt. They might ring you, but when you don't answer they will just assume you are at a friend's house – even though you don't have any friends that you might visit. They live in a dream world where their son is happy at school, and you don't want to wake them from their dream.

No. You just have to assume that you are trapped in here, presumably until Monday morning. At least it was meatballs with mashed potato for lunch in the school canteen today, and you sat at a table all by yourself and ate ten of them.

You won't get any more food until Monday.

You should be pleased that you don't have any clothes. Standing naked in the shower room was horrible, you felt like a little frozen piglet out there, naked and surrounded by the Gang of Four in their new sweatshirts and expensive jeans. But in here you won't miss your clothes at all.

It is pretty hot up on the wooden bench. Frying tonight. The heat rises, and you are sweating more and more.

Climb down and sit on the lower level with your feet on the floor. It's a little bit cooler down here.

Sit there and bow your head.

Don't think, just wait.

Close your eyes.

Carry on waiting.

Raise your head and wonder whether you might run out of air. It is difficult to breathe . . . is that because of the heat, or is there some other reason? You once read a story about someone who was buried

308

alive in a coffin, and almost died from lack of oxygen. A sauna is a kind of coffin.

You take a deep breath and sniff the air – does it smell bad? Not yet. Fresh air is probably coming in through the gap at the bottom of the door, and through the vent up by the ceiling. Not much, but you hope it will be enough.

Lie down on the bench.

Close your eyes.

Don't think.

Just wait.

Wait . . .

Wake up with a start!

Have you been asleep?

It is still dark. How much time has passed since they shut you in? You have no idea. You have a watch with a luminous face that your grandmother gave you for your tenth birthday, but it is in the pocket of your trousers in the changing room.

Unless of course the Gang of Four really did take your boots and clothes with them and chucked them in the pond.

The sauna is still switched on.

The sweat is pouring off your body in the heat. You are incredibly thirsty.

Slide down on to the floor and crawl over to the bucket; it is there so that people can throw water on to the hot stones and fill the sauna with steam. There is actually a little water left in the bottom.

Don't be too hasty. You have no idea how long this water has been standing here. Every explorer knows that stagnant water can be poisonous, but in the end you scoop up a little and have a drink. It's not good. It's lukewarm and it tastes stale, but you have another drink. And another.

Then you put down the bucket, because you need to ration your resources.

'Ration your resources': that sounds like an adventure story with a hero, but you are no hero. You are completely powerless, you cannot breathe. You curl up on the floor and wait and wait and wait. The

gym is a short distance away from the school, on the outskirts of town – nobody passes here by chance.

You cannot hear a thing apart from a slight rushing sound in your ears, and from time to time a faint clicking from the heater. You get to your feet and bang on the door anyway, you shout and bang and shout. The door is thick and solid; it doesn't move a millimetre.

Then you curl up again, but the floorboards are getting hotter and hotter. Underneath the benches there is a cement floor which should be cooler, but you don't want to crawl in there. You know how filthy it must be. Thousands of people have sat on the benches up above, year after year, their sweat trickling down on to the floor. They have spat through the gaps in the benches, dropped their snuff, shed hairs and flakes of skin.

But you have to get away from the heat, and eventually you crawl in there anyway. You are a naked little piglet, crawling in among the damp filth beneath the benches. And it is cooler. It's dirty, but you can breathe.

You wait on the cement floor, dreaming of a friend. A tough guy. A man who begins to realize that something is wrong. Perhaps you arranged to meet at a restaurant in town – why haven't you turned up? You don't know his name, and you don't have any paper to draw his picture, but you start to conjure up this man inside your head.

He is known as the Secret Avenger. The Secret Avenger chooses not to reveal himself, he blends into his surroundings. If you look carefully you will see him there, but in a crowd he is invisible.

You know that the Secret Avenger has grown tired of waiting. He gets up from the table, pays for his whisky and decides to go looking for you. He transforms himself. He becomes the Righteous Avenger, with burning eyes and fists of steel. You know exactly what he looks like. Be careful, Torgny!

You lose consciousness, then come round.

You are not sweating as much now, but you are just as thirsty as before. You crawl over to the bucket and drink a little more water. By the sound of it there are perhaps ten or eleven gulps left in the bottom of the bucket. You drink three, then lie down on the cooler cement once more.

You close your eyes, dreaming in the darkness. Time passes. Sometimes you raise your head and you really believe that the Secret Avenger is on his way, that he has somehow tracked down the Gang of Four and beaten them up in order to find out what they have done with his best friend – but most of the time you know that no one is coming to save you.

You sleep, and you have no control over your dreams this time. Afterwards you cannot remember whether they were peaceful out-of-body experiences or nightmares, but at least they can't have been any worse than lying awake in the darkness.

Sooner or later you are awake again, and totally dehydrated. You have no idea if it is morning, but breakfast consists of a little water from the bottom of the bucket. It is slightly gritty, with hairs floating around in it, but you drink it anyway. Every last drop.

Is that a rumbling noise? You put down the bucket and listen. No, it isn't the Secret Avenger opening the door. Perhaps it was a car driving past the back of the gym.

You are going to die here in the sauna. You know that now. There is no more water. It is a little bit like lying in a dark desert. A night of tropical heat. Your body is gradually drying out.

Is it possible to drink sweat? It doesn't really matter, because you are so dehydrated that you have stopped sweating – there is just a greasy film coating your skin.

Is it possible to drink urine? You are naked and you need to pee, so it isn't difficult to test the theory, all you have to do is let a little bit trickle into your hand.

It tastes bitter, but you drink a mouthful anyway. One mouthful. That's all you can get down.

You crawl over to the door. The gap at the bottom is tiny, but you push your face up against it and try to see out. The lights are still on. The shower room looks just the same as it always does, with its shiny tiled floor. Out there the whole world is going about its business as if nothing terrible has happened, as if the Gang of Four does not exist.

Eventually, at some point when you are almost unconscious, you slowly clamber up to the top bench and the beer can – the one that is half full of some unidentified liquid. And you drink that too. It

311

is warm and sour and slightly viscous, but you drink and drink and empty the can. You are too thirsty to care what is sliding down your throat.

When it is all gone you swallow again, hard.

Clamp your lips together, you mustn't be sick. You must retain the liquid in your stomach, otherwise you will die.

But by now you want to die. So why do you go on fighting here in the darkness, minute by minute?

You lie down on the floor again. Is it Saturday or Sunday? You have given up, you simply lie there.

'Perhaps I died right there on the floor,' Jan said. 'Perhaps the Unit is heaven.'

Somehow he had ended up lying on the floor, with his head on Rami's lap. He looked up at her, but she shook her head.

'You didn't die.'

She bent her head and opened her mouth. Jan saw the tip of her tongue and was expecting the second kiss of his life, but Rami was aiming for his eyes.

She closed his eyelids with her tongue, first the right, then the left.

And when his eyes were closed she pushed her tongue into his mouth. This kiss felt better than the first one, like a journey across the vault of heaven. He felt her upper body pressing against him. It was soft, not hard as he had expected.

Rami released his lips eventually, exhaled with a gentle sigh and looked at him. 'But somebody rescued you in the end?'

Jan nodded without speaking. He wanted to lie here for the rest of his life; he didn't want to think about the sauna.

At long last you hear noises through the wooden door; someone is moving around in the changing room.

You open your eyes. The sauna is still as hot, but you are shivering.

More noises. Shoes stomping across the tiled floor.

'Hello?' a man's voice calls out.

You try to stand up and manage to get to your knees, but then you run out of strength. You fall forward, straight into the door. Your arms and your forehead hit the wooden panel and you stay there, leaning against the door, trying to bang on it.

The door opens.

It happens so quickly that you lose your balance and fall down on to the tiles.

The air in the shower room is ice-cold. The shock is so great that you lose consciousness again in a dark wave of nausea; there is nothing you can do about it. It lasts for only a few seconds, because when you open your eyes the man is still standing there. The man who has set you free.

A tennis player. He has grey hair and a bushy grey moustache, and he is wearing a white tracksuit. He is holding a broom in his hand – gradually you realize that the Gang of Four must have jammed the door shut with the broom handle before they took off.

The man is looking at you in amazement, as if you have performed some kind of trick by popping out of the sauna. 'What were you doing in there?' he asks.

You cough and take great gulps of air, but you do not answer him. Your throat is too dry. You simply crawl past your saviour across the tiled floor, past his white shoes, and slowly drag yourself to your feet.

You appear to be alive.

You stagger over to the washbasin by the entrance and turn the cold-water tap with a shaking hand. Then you drink, and drink and drink. Five deep gulps, six, seven. In the end your stomach starts to hurt; the water is too cold.

'Did someone shut you in?' The tennis player isn't prepared to give up. He is waiting for an answer. Explanations.

But you shake your head and totter out of the shower room.

At last you are free. You are so cold you are shaking now, but you have no intention of going back to stand under a hot shower. You just want to see if your clothes are still here.

They are. Your jeans, T-shirt, jumper and jacket are still there in one of the lockers – the gang didn't take them. You pull on the thin cotton T-shirt first, then the woolly jumper.

Then you pick up your jeans. You will put them on in a minute and head out into the winter, but you want to find your watch first.

The tennis player has followed you into the changing room. 'What's your name?'

You don't answer that question either, but you look at him and ask in a hoarse voice, 'What day is it today?'

'Sunday,' he says. 'We've got a match shortly.'

You take out the watch. It is one thirty-five.

One thirty-five on Sunday afternoon.

Close your eyes and work it out. You have been locked in the sauna for almost two days — forty-six hours.

Lynx

Was it a happy ending for all concerned? Jan assumed so. William Halevi had been found, and his parents could relax after two days of torture.

The staff at the nursery were also feeling better. Everyone except Sigrid, who was still signed off sick a week after William's disappearance. Jan heard that she was having some kind of counselling for post-traumatic stress.

And he was interviewed again by the police.

They didn't actually come out with it in so many words, but they suspected something. The day after William had been found, two plain-clothes officers came to Jan's apartment and looked around; he let them carry on. There was nothing to see. He had been back in the forest the previous evening, cleaned out the bunker, and thrown away or burned everything that had been inside it.

Two days later he was asked to go down to the police station. The interview was conducted by the inspector who had spoken to him earlier. She was no more cheerful on this occasion.

'You were the last person to see the boy in the forest, Jan. And you were the one who found him.'

'That's not true,' Jan said patiently. 'That pensioner found him . . . I can't remember his name now.'

'Sven Axel Olsson,' said the inspector.

'That's it . . . anyway, he was the one who was looking after William. And I just happened to see them.'

'And before that?'

'Sorry?'

'Where do you think William had been before you and herr Olsson found him?'

'I don't know . . . I haven't really thought about it. I suppose he was wandering around in the forest.'

The inspector looked at him. 'William says he was locked up.'

'Oh? In what kind of room?'

'I didn't say it was a room.'

'No, but I assume . . .'

'Have you any idea who could have locked him up?'

Jan shook his head. 'Do you believe him?'

The police officer didn't reply.

There was an unbearable silence in the interview room. Jan had to make a real effort not to break it and start babbling and speculating about various theories, which would be interpreted as some kind of confession.

But his mind was wandering and he had to say something, so he asked, 'How's Torgny doing now?'

'Who?' said the inspector. 'Who's Torgny?'

Jan stared at her. He had said the wrong name. 'William, I mean William. How's he doing? Is he back with his parents?'

The inspector nodded. 'He's fine. All things considered.'

In the end he was allowed to leave, but the inspector didn't apologize. The only thing Jan got was one last long stare from her.

He didn't care. William was back with his parents, safe and sound, and he himself was free. He could leave the police station and go wherever he wanted, but he walked out into the fresh air with a feeling of disappointment.

It had all gone so quickly. He had intended it to last longer – for forty-six hours.

44

Legén is drinking yellowish wine out of a cracked coffee mug. He pours a generous mug for Jan too; they are sitting among the mess at Legén's kitchen table. 'There you go.'

'Thanks.'

Jan is thirsty, but not for lukewarm yellow wine. He takes the mug containing the liquid and wonders how he is going to empty it without his neighbour noticing.

Legén's apartment is filthy and chaotic, but Jan actually enjoys these quiet sessions. He rang his neighbour's doorbell after work because he wanted someone to talk to. But to what extent does he trust Legén? How much is he actually prepared to tell him?

'I think there's snow on the way,' he says.

'Yes,' says Legén. 'This is the time for chopping wood. We used to have a shed when I was little, but we kept all kinds of stuff in it, so there wasn't any room for the wood. But you could sit inside the shed and have a bit of peace and quiet . . .'

The wine is making his neighbour quite talkative.

But eventually he runs out of steam, and Jan ventures, 'I went down to the hospital cellar and had a look around on Sunday . . . I saw some of the patients.'

'I'm not surprised,' says Legén. 'There's always been a fair amount of activity down there.' He takes a deep swig of his wine. 'But I was never worried. We just got on with things in the laundry, for almost thirty years. The dirty laundry came down and we sent it

317

back up . . . We found all kinds of things. Wallets, bottles of pills, all sorts.'

'There's a chapel in the basement,' Jan says. 'Did you know that?'

'Yes, but we never went in there,' Legén replies. 'They kind of please themselves when the bosses have gone home.'

When Jan gets back to his apartment he tries to do some drawing; he wants to finish *The Princess with a Hundred Hands*. It is the last book without proper pictures, Rami's fourth book.

He completes four drawings and colours three of them in, then he gives up. Instead he takes out his old diary.

He leafs through it slowly, reading his teenage thoughts and almost remembering how things used to be in those days – and when he reaches the middle of the book he finds an old item that he cut out of a local newspaper.

He remembers the cutting too. He came across it six years after the events at Lynx. It is a picture from the sports pages; there had been a junior football tournament, and the winning team was photographed after the final. A dozen boys are assembled for the camera, and in the middle stands the goalkeeper with the ball under his arm, smiling at Jan beneath his fringe.

William Halevi. His name is mentioned in the caption, but Jan recognized his face even before he read it.

He gazes at the picture for a long time. William looks happy, relaxed and unmarked by any bad memories from his time in the forest. He was eleven years old when the picture was taken, he played football, he seemed to have plenty of friends. His life would turn out well.

Jan can't know that, but he hopes it's true.

He gets up. The Angel is sitting on the shelf in the hallway. One of the Angels – the transmitter. He left the receiver inside St Psycho's. The standby button glows brightly; he has put new batteries in. He has thought about switching it on from time to time, but he knows that the distance from the receiver is too great. He would need to get much closer.

Jan stares at the Angel and thinks things over for another minute or two. Then he fetches his rucksack and his outdoor clothes. Dark outdoor clothes.

He doesn't cycle tonight, nor does he catch the bus. He goes on foot. He chooses the same route as he took last Sunday: a long detour through the forest and across the stream that flows past the hospital complex, then round to the slope at the back, a couple of metres from the fence.

Clouds are scudding by above the hospital grounds.

Jan is close. It is dark now, the darkness of November, and there is no need to hide among the fir trees. He can go right up to the top of the slope, above the stream. Slinking along like a lynx.

The fence around St Patricia's is lit up like a stage by the floodlights, but deeper in the grounds he can see broad patches of shadow. Pale lights are showing in some of the narrow windows, but most have the blinds drawn. The patients are hiding themselves.

Jan feels as if he is being watched – but not by eyes. By the hospital itself.

St Psycho's immutable stone façade is staring coldly at him, and he shudders. He would like to retreat back into the forest, but continues along the edge of the slope to a large rock left behind by glaciation. There is a well-trodden path here, which means that people have been walking past the hospital for many years, perhaps stopping to wonder what kind of monsters are locked up in there.

'Haven't you brought any bananas for the monkeys?'

Jan remembers Rami shouting at a group of middle-aged men in suits who had come to the Unit one evening on some kind of study visit. Perhaps they were politicians. Every single one had looked at her with fear in their eyes, and scuttled off down the corridor.

The Angel's range is three hundred metres. Jan is less than three hundred metres from the hospital now, he hopes, but he is safe from the floodlights. The pre-school is to the left behind the hospital complex, but it is hidden by the fence and the conifers. Jan looks at his watch: quarter past nine. Time to get started. He puts down his rucksack and unzips it. He takes out the Angel and switches it from standby to transmit.

He leans against the rock and thinks. He doesn't know what to say, and he doesn't know if Rami is listening over there. And he can't say her name, in case the Angel has ended up in the wrong hands.

But at last he raises the microphone to his lips. 'Hello?' he says quietly. 'Hello, squirrel?'

No one replies. Nothing happens.

He looks over at the hospital, silently counting the windows. Fourth floor, seventh from the right. It is one of the windows with a light on, if he has counted correctly. A pale ceiling light. A bulb protected by some kind of mesh, so that no one can smash it?

He takes a deep breath and tries again: 'If you can hear me, give me some kind of sign.'

He looks at the window, expecting to see a figure step into the light behind the bars. That doesn't happen, but something else does – the light suddenly goes out. The window is in darkness for a few seconds, then the light comes on again.

Jan feels an icy chill run down his spine.

'Did you do that, squirrel?'

The light goes out again, this time just for a couple of seconds, then it comes back on.

'Good,' Jan says into the Angel. 'Turn the light out once for yes, twice for no.'

The light goes out again. He has made contact.

'Do you know who I am?'

The light goes off immediately.

'Jan Hauger . . . I'm the one who's been sending you letters. And I was in the room next door to you years ago. In the Unit.'

The light doesn't go off this time, but of course he hasn't asked a question.

'And your name is Maria Blanker?'

Yes.

'But you used to have a different name?'

Yes.

'Alice Rami? Was that your name?'

Yes.

320

At last. Jan lowers the Angel. He is speaking to Rami at long last.

What can he say now? He has so many questions, but none that can be answered with a yes or no.

The seconds tick by, the drums reverberate inside his head. Jan feels stressed by his own indecisiveness, and blurts out one more question: 'Rami, can we meet up again? Just you and me?'

Standing in front of a six-metre-high fence, it is a ridiculous question. But the light goes off for a few seconds, then flashes on again.

'Good . . . I'll be in touch soon. Thanks.'

What is he thanking Rami for? He looks over at the hospital, at all those glowing windows, and he feels chilled to the bone, but most of all he feels shut out. Right now he would like to be sitting in there too, together with Rami.

He sets off back through the forest. Back home, where he will try to finish the picture book so that he can show all four of them to her. When they meet.

Who is Rami now? She is the Animal Lady. She has created Jan so that he will find his way over the fence and help her to get away from the house of stone. Away from the Animal Lady's desert island, away from the forest where the poorly witch lies dying.

The Unit

Jan sat close to Rami and she held on tightly to his arm, just above the bandages around his wrist. They were holding on to each other. He had finished telling her about the days in the sauna, and about jumping into the pond. He didn't feel much better, but at least he had done it.

And Rami had listened, as if his story meant something. Then she had asked quietly, 'Have you told anyone else about this?'

He shook his head. 'But I'm sure *they* think I have,' he said. 'One of them . . . Torgny, he rang me three days ago. He was scared, I could hear it in his voice. They probably think I've told on them already, but I haven't.' Jan looked down at the floor and went on: 'I know they'll be waiting for me at school when I go back . . . They're just going to start on me all over again.'

He fell silent. He was sitting here feeling terrified at the mere thought of the Gang of Four. He was cowering behind the fence in the Unit, knowing that the gang were out and about on the streets, happy and free. They had each other, they had loads of friends. He had only Rami.

'And it would be OK,' he said. 'I sometimes think it would be nice if there was a button you could press so that everything just ended. I didn't really struggle much when they threw me in the sauna . . . I thought I deserved it, I suppose.'

'No,' said Rami.

'Yes,' said Jan.

The room was utterly silent for a moment, then Rami suddenly said, 'I'll take care of them.'

'But how?'

'I don't know yet . . . When I get out of here.'

'When will that be?'

'Soon.'

Jan looked at her. Rami was unlikely to be talking about being let out of the Unit – she was talking about running away.

'What are you going to do?'

'I know people.'

She got up and walked over to one of the black curtains. 'I found this in the storeroom,' she said.

She lifted the curtain, and Jan saw an old black telephone on the floor.

'Does it work?'

She nodded. 'Is there anyone you want to ring?'

Jan shook his head. He had no one to ring.

'I usually speak to my sister in Stockholm,' Rami went on. 'I can ring anyone I like.'

She sounded so certain, and it was catching.

'I've got the school yearbook,' he said. 'There are pictures of them, with names and addresses.'

'OK.'

Jan looked at her, wanting to say something honest and profound, but Rami went on: 'There's something *you* can do for me too.'

'What?'

'I'll show you . . . Come with me.'

She led him out into the corridor, looked around and headed towards the staffroom. It was six thirty; the day staff had gone home and the door was closed. Next to the door a series of colour photographs and names were pinned up, under the heading DEPARTMENT 16 – THE TEAM.

Rami pointed to a picture of a smiling woman with a fringe swept to one side, and big glasses. 'That's her.'

Jan recognized her; she was the woman Rami had called the

Psychobabbler, the one she had fought with in the TV room. Underneath the picture was her name and job title: *Emma Halevi, Psychologist.*

'She interrupted our gig,' said Jan. 'And she locked you in the Black Hole.'

'Yes,' said Rami. 'And then she took my diary.'

Jan nodded; he remembered.

'She *read* it,' Rami said. 'I had a book like the one I gave you . . . I'd filled fifty pages, but she took it.'

Jan looked at the picture. He could hear Rami's quiet voice in his ear: 'I'm going to run away tomorrow. When I'm gone, I want you to do something to the Psychobabbler . . . creep in and piss on her desk, scribble graffiti all over her door, or something. Make her feel scared.'

'OK,' Jan said.

'You'll do it?'

He nodded slowly, as if he were agreeing to undertake a secret mission. He would make the Psychobabbler feel really, really scared, for Rami's sake.

45

'Am I supposed to feel sorry for the patients?' Lilian says, laughing over her beer. 'They do a pretty good job of that all on their own, the lot of them. They sit up there behind the wall feeling sorry for themselves, insisting that they're *innocent*.'

'Do they?' Jan asks.

'Of course. Every paedophile and murderer is entirely innocent, you must know that . . . No one behind bars ever accepts responsibility for anything.'

Jan doesn't agree, but he says nothing.

He has gone down to Bill's Bar the evening after Lilian's quarrel with Marie-Louise. Lilian was sitting there, of course, at a table towards the back of the bar. And of course there was a large glass of beer in front of her, and the way in which her head was swaying over it like a cobra hypnotized by a snake charmer suggested that it wasn't her first.

She didn't notice Jan when he walked in. She was not alone; Hanna was sitting opposite her, with a glass of water in front of her. As usual they looked as if they were sharing secrets, whispering to each other with their heads close together.

The bartender tonight is called Allan. They are not friends – Jan hasn't managed to make a single friend here in Valla – but he has got to know the names of the bartenders.

Jan orders an alcohol-free beer. He wonders whether to sneak off and sit in a different part of the bar, but no doubt Hanna would spot him on the way. And why should he creep about?

He goes over to join his colleagues. 'Evening,' he says.

'Jan!' Lilian beams at him; she seems glad of the interruption.

Hanna's expressionless eyes reveal nothing. She gives a brief nod, and Jan sits down.

'What are you drinking?' Lilian asks.

'Alcohol-free,' he says. 'I have to work tomorrow, so I can't . . .'

'Alcohol-free?' Lilian gives a husky laugh and picks up her glass. 'There's plenty of alcohol in here!'

Jan doesn't raise his glass in return; both he and Hanna look on in silence as Lilian tips her head back and empties half the contents of her glass.

Then she lowers her head, and Jan can see that she's not in good shape this evening. Lilian stares into her drink, then embarks on the same tirade about the hospital that Jan heard the very first time they met at Bill's Bar.

She starts talking again about the 'luxury hotel', as she calls it. 'I was curious about the people in there when I first arrived, but I've never felt sorry for them. I mean, if a person claims he's innocent, says he didn't murder or attack someone . . . Well, how can you cure them, in that case?'

Nobody answers her. She has another swig. Jan thinks her expression is beginning to resemble the drugged eyes of the patients down in the basement chapel at St Psycho's.

Lilian puts down her glass. 'I need a wee.'

She has problems getting up – the edge of the table seems to be holding her back – but eventually she wobbles away.

Jan and Hanna watch her go.

'How many has she had?' Jan asks.

'No idea. She was already well on the way when I got here, but . . . She's had three since then.'

Jan merely nods.

'I feel sorry for her,' Hanna goes on.

'I feel sorry for lots of people,' Jan says. 'Leo, for example.'

'So you said.' Hanna looks at him. 'You think about the children a lot, don't you?'

'I care about them.' Then Jan remembers that he has told Hanna about William's disappearance, and is afraid that what he says might sound suspicious. He adds, 'We all care about the children, Hanna.'

'We do.'

'Oh? But you care more about Ivan Rössel, don't you?'

She shakes her head. 'No. Well yes, I mean I care about Ivan, but . . . You don't understand what this is about, Jan.'

'No. It's nothing to do with me, anyway.' He has already finished his beer, and gets to his feet. Perhaps he might as well go home.

But Hanna seems to make a decision. She leans across the table and lowers her voice. 'It's about Ivan Rössel . . . and Lilian.'

'Lilian?'

Hanna looks at him as if she is gathering strength before making some kind of revelation. 'I made contact with Ivan for Lilian's sake.'

Jan sits down again. 'Sorry . . . what did you say?'

'Ivan *knows* things. And I'm trying to get him to tell me.'

'Tell you *what*?'

'That's better!' a voice calls. 'Did you miss me, kids?' Lilian is back, with another beer. She sways and beams at them. 'There was a girl crying her eyes out in the toilets,' she says, sitting down next to Jan. 'There's always somebody howling in the Ladies, isn't there, Hanna? Why do they do that?'

Hanna has clammed up. She glances at Jan, then says, 'Time we made a move.'

Lilian looks surprised. 'Already?'

Hanna nods. 'I'm calling a taxi . . . We'll drop you off.'

'But . . . but what about my drink?'

'We'll help you.' Hanna reaches for the glass, takes a couple of swigs and passes it to Jan. 'Here.'

He's not keen, but he takes a sip of the bitter liquid.

'OK, Lilian, time to go.'

*

Fifteen minutes later they are helping their colleague into a taxi outside the bar. Hanna directs the driver to a small terraced house in an area just north of the centre; the lights are on, and Jan catches a glimpse of a man in his forties peering out at the taxi from the kitchen window.

Jan recognizes him; he is the man who walked Lilian to the pre-school one evening.

'You're so good to me . . . so kind . . .'

Lilian thanks them several times for bringing her home, hugs Jan, kisses Hanna on both cheeks and eventually totters off towards her front door.

'OK.' Hanna turns to the driver. 'Back to the town centre, please . . . to the Casino Bar.'

'Casino?' says Jan.

'It's not a casino. That's just the name.'

The Casino Bar is on a back street, in a less well-populated area than Bill's Bar, and the clientele consists mainly of men. Jan suspects that this is usually the case. A few men in their fifties are slumped in front of a widescreen TV by the bar staring morosely at an Italian football match, as if their team were losing. The remaining tables are mostly empty.

Hanna asks for two glasses of juice and sits down as far away as possible from the bar, in a corner where there is no one else around.

'Bill's Bar isn't . . . safe,' she says. 'I saw people from St Psycho's in there.'

'Oh? What do they look like?'

'Vigilant.'

There is a brief silence, then Hanna goes on: 'Ivan Rössel needs contact with someone . . . Is that wrong?'

'Maybe not,' Jan says. He suddenly remembers something that Dr Högsmed said about his patients, and adds, 'But if you follow someone who is lost in the forest, you can easily get lost yourself.'

Hanna clamps her lips together. 'I'm not lost. I know what I'm doing.'

'And what are you doing?' Jan asks. 'With Ivan, I mean.'

Hanna looks away. 'I'm trying to get him to . . . to tell me things.'

'What things?'

'Whatever he knows about John Daniel.'

'John Daniel . . .'

Jan vaguely recognizes the name. From some newspaper?

'John Daniel Nilsson disappeared six years ago,' Hanna explains. 'He went up in smoke after a school dance in Gothenburg, during his last year at high school. No one has seen him since, but Ivan has . . . has hinted that he knows something about John Daniel.'

Jan nods; he remembers now. He was living in Gothenburg at the time, only five or six blocks from the school where the dance took place. Rössel was suspected of being involved in his disappearance, but has never confessed.

'But what has John Daniel got to do with you?'

'Not with me. With Lilian. I told you.'

Jan looks at her. 'So Lilian is involved?'

'John Daniel was her younger brother. She took the job at the pre-school to try and make contact with Ivan Rössel. And she managed it in the end, once she asked me for help . . . But it's turning out to be the ruin of her.'

46

Jan stays up reading crime reports on the internet until half past two in the morning in order to find out more. He discovers that John Daniel Nilsson was nineteen years old when he disappeared from the school dance on the outskirts of Gothenburg. One of his friends had smuggled in some vodka, and John Daniel had got drunk and been sick. He had gone outside alone at about eleven thirty, either to try and sober up or to go home – no one knew for certain – and he hadn't been seen since. The family had searched for him, along with the police and lots of volunteers, but John Daniel had vanished without a trace.

It remained an unsolved mystery. Rössel was a suspect, but had stayed silent. Until now, when, according to Hanna, he had begun to hint that he had been the last person to see the boy alive.

Jan goes on reading until his eyes begin to smart, and he starts to see William Halevi's boyish face in front of him, instead of the missing nineteen-year-old. He shuts down the computer and goes to bed.

The following morning he goes to work with a heavy head. Lilian is already there, and they nod wearily to one another.

'Everything OK, Lilian?'

'Mm,' she mumbles.

She looks hung-over, and she probably is, but Jan looks at her differently today. Lilian is the sister of a missing boy. She is a victim.

He is about to broach the subject tactfully, but then he hears Marie-Louise shout from the kitchen, 'Jan? Could you go up and collect Matilda?'

'No problem.'

He knows the drill. Everyone must be kept busy.

He spends all day taking children up to the visitors' room in St Patricia's and collecting them, but these excursions down the stairs and along the underground corridor are just part of his daily routine now. He doesn't give them a second thought.

But with Leo it isn't just routine. Jan brushes the boy's shoulder with his fingers as they travel up in the lift for his hour-long visit with his father. 'What are you going to do?' Jan asks.

'Play cards,' Leo replies.

'Are you sure?'

Leo nods. 'Dad always wants to play cards.'

'Ask him to tell you a story.'

Leo looks uncertain.

Jan feels no sense of joy or confidence when he gets back to the Dell, and he doesn't get the chance to speak to Lilian today. She doesn't talk to him either, doesn't even look at him; she is always with the children. But she doesn't play with them, she simply sits and watches them with tired eyes, or pats one of them on the head with a limp hand.

Hanna also seems to be avoiding Jan, and spends most of her time in the kitchen.

Marie-Louise is the only one who wants to talk to him. 'It's a relief, isn't it?'

'What is?' he asks.

'Knowing we don't have to do any more night shifts. Knowing that the children are all taken care of . . . that we've found good homes for all of them. I'm so pleased.'

'Will they be OK?'

'Oh yes, I'm sure they will.'

'I'm just a bit worried about Leo . . . He's so restless.'

'Leo will be fine too,' Marie-Louise says firmly.

Jan looks at her. Will all the children really be all right? Most children are, but not all of them. Some children turn into adults with mental-health issues, some end up in poverty, some turn to crime. Those are the statistics; there's nothing anyone can do about it.

But does that mean their work at the Dell is pointless?

At quarter to six Jan is in the kitchen. All the children have been picked up, and he has put a final load in the dishwasher. The working day is over, and when he hears Lilian close her locker in the cloakroom, he rushes to finish off what he is doing. He turns out the light and manages to get away a minute or so later, just after Lilian has left.

He locks the front door and hurries after her.

It is November now, with a frost and a biting wind. Out in the street he can see a figure in a dark jacket heading towards the town centre. He breaks into a jog and catches up with her.

'Lilian?'

She turns around without stopping and looks wearily at him. 'What?'

His first impulse is to ask if she fancies going to Bill's Bar, but he stops himself. He doesn't want to go there any more. 'Could we have a little chat?' he asks.

'What about?'

Jan looks around. Over by the wall two figures emerge through the steel door; he can't see their faces, but assumes that they are security guards who are heading home after their shift. And there are several people waiting at the bus stop. Eyes watching, ears listening.

'Let's just walk for a bit,' he says.

Lilian doesn't look pleased, but goes with him anyway. They pass the bus stop, and after a little while he says, 'We could talk about the pre-school . . . about what we could do for the children.'

Lilian gives a tired laugh. 'No, thanks. I just want to go home.'

'Shall we talk about Hanna, then?'

Lilian doesn't respond; she just keeps on walking, so Jan asks, 'Or about Ivan Rössel?'

She stops dead. 'Do you know him?'

Jan shakes his head and lowers his voice. 'No, but Hanna's told me a few things.'

Lilian glances over at the hospital. 'I can't talk here,' she says after a moment. 'Not now.'

'We could meet later.'

She seems to be thinking things over. 'Are you free tomorrow evening?'

Jan nods.

'Come round to my place at eight.'

'Can we talk then?' Jan says. 'About everything?'

Lilian nods, then looks at her watch. 'I've got to get home, my older brother is waiting. My husband's gone . . .'

She starts walking, but turns her head. 'Do you want to know why we split up?'

Jan says nothing, but she carries on anyway: 'He thought I was too obsessed with Ivan Rössel.'

47

The first snowflakes of winter are big and wet, and start falling on the Dell after lunch on Thursday. They land heavily on the ground around the pre-school, covering the sandpit and the swings like a dirty-grey fluffy blanket.

Jan watches the falling snow through the window, but with none of the excitement he used to feel when he was little. These days the winter weather just means even more layers of clothes on the children: vests, woolly socks, snowsuits and hats with ear flaps – it takes longer and longer to get them outside. They end up looking like little barrels, or little fabric robots lumbering across the playground.

He helps them get ready and goes out. Andreas and Marie-Louise are still working as a team, joking and laughing behind him. Hanna and Lilian are already outside, and have stopped for a cigarette break. They are not laughing; they are whispering, their heads close together.

Marie-Louise and Andreas. Hanna and Lilian.

Jan feels excluded from both pairings, so he turns his attention to the children as usual.

'Look at me!' they shout. 'Look at me!'

The children want to show how clever they are, playing on the swings and jumping around and building fragile sandcastles in the middle of the sandy, snowy slush. Jan helps them, but glances over at Lilian and Hanna from time to time, wishing he could hear what they are talking about.

When Marie-Louise comes outside the conversation stops, cigarettes are stubbed out and Lilian and Hanna help to gather the children together. But Jan sees them exchanging looks as they go back inside, like conspirators.

Marie-Louise doesn't appear to notice anything; she stands on the steps with Jan, smiling at the children as they stomp back indoors. 'They're so good,' she says.

Then she looks over at the wall surrounding the hospital and stops smiling. 'Were you ever afraid when you were little, Jan?'

He shakes his head. Not when he was little. He was never afraid, not even of the atomic bomb, until he met the Gang of Four. 'What about you?' he asks.

Marie-Louise also shakes her head. 'I lived in a small town when I was little, and nobody bothered to lock their doors,' she says. 'There were no burglars or muggers in those days . . . no dangerous criminals at all. Well, nobody talked about them, anyway. But there was an asylum in the middle of the town, and the mad people were allowed out sometimes . . . They wore strange clothes, so you could always tell where they came from. They looked nice, and I thought it was fun to say hello to them on the bus; they were always so pleased to have someone to talk to. Everyone else used to sit there, stiff as pokers, staring straight in front of them when some confused old soul got on, but I thought they were nice.' She looks at Jan and adds, 'So I used to say hello, and the old men would cheerfully say hello back.'

'That's nice,' Jan says.

Marie-Louise gazes over at the high wall again, and almost seems to be talking to herself. 'But such terrible things happen these days . . . There are such dangerous people in the world.'

'Or we're just more frightened,' Jan says.

But Marie-Louise gives no indication that she has heard him.

*

That evening Jan makes another attempt to contact Rami. He pretends to set off home in the darkness at the end of the working day, but kills time walking around the nearby residential area instead, waiting for things to quieten down around the hospital. Then he goes up to the big rock above the stream. He puts down his rucksack, takes out the Angel and switches it on, keeping his eyes fixed on the hospital.

Fourth floor, seventh from the right. There is a light on, but no sign of anyone behind the bars.

Jan tries to make contact anyway. 'Squirrel?' he says quietly.

Nothing happens. The light stays on.

Jan speaks into the microphone several times, but there is no response. If Rami isn't there, or if she's asleep, then why is the light on? Is it always on?

In the end he switches off the Angel and makes his way back down the slope. He feels like a failure, rejected by everyone this Thursday evening. Perhaps not quite everyone – the children still like him, but if he plays with them too much, it looks odd.

Jan doesn't want to look odd. That would attract Marie-Louise's attention, just as Lilian has done.

He thinks about the quiet conversations between Hanna and Lilian over the past week, whispering voices that fell silent as soon as he walked into the room.

He heads back towards the town, but he isn't going home. He is going round to Lilian's tonight, to talk about Ivan Rössel.

48

Jan rings the doorbell and waits. He listens. He can hear the sound of voices inside Lilian's house, but it could well be the murmur of a television.

It is Lilian's older brother who opens the door. Jan doesn't know his name. The man greets him with a nod and calls over his shoulder, 'Minty?'

The television is turned down. Lilian's voice says something incomprehensible, and her brother continues: 'Your little friend is here.'

He turns and leaves the house without looking at Jan again.

'You're called Minty?'

'Sometimes.'

'Why?'

Lilian shrugs her shoulders. 'I eat a lot of mints. To keep my breath fresh.'

Her voice is lifeless, but at least she isn't drunk. She has led Jan into the kitchen, and opens the fridge. He can see green bottles inside, but Lilian takes out a carton of milk.

'Hot chocolate?'

'Yes, please.'

She puts a pan of milk on the stove, and Jan sits down at the kitchen table. Party-Lilian from Bill's Bar is nowhere to be seen; she looks more exhausted than ever as she sits down and hands him a full mug.

'So Hanna's told you about Ivan Rössel,' she says.

'Yes.'

'And she's told you he's in St Psycho's?'

Jan nods. 'I've read a bit about him too.'

'Of course you have – he's a celebrity.' Lilian sighs. 'But the victims never become famous . . . No one wants to talk to a person who just cries all the time, I expect that's why. So we withdraw and grieve, while the murderers turn into stars.'

Jan says nothing, but she goes on: 'Have you spoken to Marie-Louise about this?'

'No . . . only to Hanna.'

'Good.' Lilian seems to relax, and picks up her mug. 'That's good . . . Marie-Louise would inform the hospital immediately if she knew what was going on.'

Silence descends on the little kitchen.

'And what is going on?' Jan asks.

Lilian appears to be considering what to tell him. 'A meeting,' she says eventually. 'We're going to have a meeting with Rössel. Hanna has arranged it, along with one of the security guards at the hospital.'

'A meeting about what?'

'We want answers. We want to persuade Rössel to start talking. About John Daniel.'

'Your brother,' Jan says quietly.

Lilian frowns sadly. 'He went missing.'

'I know . . . I read about John Daniel too.'

She sighs again. 'We want to know why it happened,' she says, staring down at the kitchen table. 'But there are no answers. Everything is just . . . darkness. And you think you must be dreaming – I felt like that for months six years ago, when John Daniel first disappeared. And then when I realized that I was awake and he was still gone, I thought I'd get over it, but you don't get over it, it just gnaws away at you the whole time . . . And it's worse for my dad. He believes that John Daniel is still alive. He sits there waiting by the phone, every single day.'

Jan listens and lets her talk; he feels like a psychologist.

Like Tony. 'But Rössel hasn't admitted anything, has he?' he prompts.

Lilian shakes her head. 'Rössel is a psychopath. He lacks the capacity to feel guilt, so he admits nothing. He tells half-truths, then retracts them. The only thing he wants is attention . . . It's like a game to him.'

'Do you hate him?'

She gives him a sharp look, as if the answer is obvious. 'John Daniel died; his life lasted just nineteen years. But Rössel has never been punished. He is looked after, he gets free food and accommodation. Life is good over there in St Patricia's.'

Jan thinks of those long, empty corridors. 'Are you sure about that?'

Lilian nods firmly. 'Oh yes, especially for a celebrity like Rössel. He's cared for, and he has peace and quiet. Medication, therapy, every kind of support you can think of. The doctors want to bathe in the reflected glow of his fame. But John Daniel, he . . .' She looks down at the table. 'He was murdered and his body lies hidden somewhere. And my life has been shortened as a result . . . That's what grief and hatred do to you. You dry up.'

Jan almost asks, *Is that why you drink so much?* But he doesn't. He has an idea of what Lilian has been through and how she feels about Rössel – he has felt something similar when it comes to Torgny Fridman and the Gang of Four.

'So you're working at the pre-school because of John Daniel?'

'Yes. I thought I'd be able to make contact with Rössel myself, but I couldn't do it. In the end I asked Hanna if she would help me, and she was more successful.'

'But aren't you worried about her?'

'Because she goes up to the hospital? She doesn't actually meet Rössel, they just exchange letters. There's no risk involved.'

Jan doesn't say anything, and eventually Lilian goes on: 'Hanna is the only one who knows who I am . . . that I'm related to John Daniel. I never spoke to the press after it happened; my parents did all that. They posed for the media, holding up school photos and weeping straight into the camera. They begged anyone who knew anything to contact the police. But no one ever did. And now we've been forgotten.'

Jan thinks about everything Hanna has told him, and asks, 'So what does Rössel want? Is he hoping to escape?'

Lilian presses her lips tightly together. She has more energy now. 'Rössel will never be free. He might think so, but it's not going to happen. He's just going to talk to us.'

'When?'

'Next Friday evening, when there's a fire drill at St Patricia's. They're going to practise a full evacuation, so all the patients will have to leave their rooms. The corridors will be pretty crowded.'

Jan remembers the elderly patients down in the basement chapel. Their vacant expressions.

'And what will happen to Rössel?' he asks.

'Hanna's contact . . . Carl . . . he's going to let Rössel into the visitors' room.'

'Where you'll be waiting?'

'We're meeting him in there, and he's going to tell us where John Daniel is buried.'

'Do you really believe that?'

'I know it,' says Lilian. 'He's promised Hanna.'

Jan wants to say something, but he hesitates. 'Things can go wrong,' he says quietly at last.

'Yes, but we won't be taking any risks with Rössel,' Lilian says. 'There will be four of us, me and my brother and two friends. We've gone over every single thing. I've let my brother into the Dell a couple of times just to suss things out.'

'At night?'

Lilian nods.

'The children have seen him,' Jan says.

'Oh?'

'Mira saw a man standing by her bed one night . . . You're not being as careful as you think.'

'We're careful enough.' Lilian looks at him. 'So now you know. Are you with us?'

'Me? What do you mean?'

'We might need some help. Someone to keep watch.'

'Maybe,' he says eventually. 'I'll have to give it some thought.'

On the way home he thinks back to what Lilian said about the fire drill. *The patients will have to leave their rooms. The corridors will be pretty crowded.* And of course Rami will be let out of her room, just like all the others.

Jan has booked a slot in the laundry room in his apartment block the following morning. He puts a white wash in one machine and a dark wash in the other, and switches them on.

On his way back upstairs he stops by the sign that says LEGÉN. He shouldn't go bothering his neighbour any more, but Jan has realized that he actually likes the man. Legén is just himself.

He rings the doorbell and after a minute or so Legén appears.

Jan waves. 'Morning, it's only me. How are things?'

'Fine.'

Legén simply stands there; he doesn't invite Jan in, but nor does he close the door.

'Would you like a cup of coffee?' Jan asks. He feels as if it is time he returned his neighbour's hospitality.

But Legén just scratches the back of his neck as he considers the invitation. 'Is it a dark roast?'

'Er . . . I think so,' Jan says.

'OK.'

Legén picks up a plastic bag from the floor and walks straight out of the door, as if he has been waiting to be asked for a long time. Jan leads the way up the stairs and into his apartment.

'Bit crowded in here,' says Legén, looking with curiosity at all the furniture.

Jan sighs. 'It's not mine.'

He goes into the kitchen, and a few minutes later the coffee machine is bubbling away. Legén is sitting at the table, and Jan has even managed to produce some biscuits.

'How's the wine coming along?' he asks.

'Good . . . It's going to be pretty strong stuff.' Legén sounds pleased with himself.

Jan takes a sip of his coffee and wonders how old Legén actually is. Seventy, perhaps. After all, he retired from St Patricia's four or five years ago, so that should be about right.

They drink their coffee in silence, then Jan looks at the clock. It is five past ten – he's forgotten all about his washing. 'You stay there,' he says to Legén.

When he opens the door of his apartment, he sees an elderly lady on the landing. A neighbour. She is small and thin, and she is carrying an overflowing laundry basket. She has obviously booked the slot after Jan, and she doesn't look pleased.

'I'm really sorry . . . I wasn't keeping an eye on the time.'

The woman merely nods. Jan hasn't even managed to close his front door, but suddenly she says, 'So you're friends, you and him?'

'Him?'

'Verner Legén.'

'Friends?' Jan says quietly so that Legén won't hear. 'I don't know about that, but we've had the odd chat.'

'And you've been inside his apartment?'

'Yes . . . I borrowed some sugar from him.'

He smiles, but his neighbour doesn't smile back. She just stares at him. 'Did he have any weapons in there?'

'Weapons?'

'Knives, guns . . .' she says. 'I mean, that's the sort of thing you worry about, as a neighbour.'

Jan doesn't understand, but shakes his head.

'No, I suppose he's quietened down these days,' the woman says to herself. 'He's getting on a bit, after all.'

There is an awkward silence. The woman sets off down the stairs to the laundry room, but Jan doesn't move.

In the end he has to ask the question: 'Has Legén had weapons in the past?'

She stops. 'Not here, well not as far as I know, anyway.'

'But somewhere else?'

The woman looks at him closely. 'Haven't you heard what he did in Gothenburg?'

'No?'

342

'He murdered a whole load of people. Went crazy. Ran around and stabbed them out in the street, one after another.'

Jan listens; it's all he can do. He is incapable of moving.

'Legén? He killed people?' he finally brings himself to ask.

The woman nods. 'Everybody in the building knows about him.' She sighs and adds, 'Nobody wants him living here. They should have kept him in St Psycho's . . . That's where they locked him up.'

Jan stares at her. 'But he used to *work* there, surely? In the laundry?'

The woman nods again. 'Later on, yes. But they have former patients working there, as I understand it . . . They've got quite a mixture of nutcases and doctors up there.'

His neighbour sighs yet again, and carries on down the stairs with her laundry basket.

Jan follows her and quickly collects his own laundry. Then he goes back upstairs, and notices that his door is ajar. He forgot to close it.

Did Legén hear the entire conversation with his neighbour?

He stops in the doorway, wondering what to do, but eventually he walks in.

Legén is still sitting at the kitchen table; he has topped up his coffee cup. He looks at Jan. 'You're back, then,' he says.

He has also lit his pipe, but he doesn't look happy. 'I heard what the old bag said. The whole bloody place could hear her.'

Jan doesn't know what to answer; he can't stop looking at Legén's hands, holding the pipe and the coffee cup. The hands that held the knife when he ran amok in the street.

At last Jan opens his mouth to say something. 'Were you happy up there at the hospital?'

Legén continues to suck on his pipe, so Jan goes on: 'I mean . . . you were there for a hell of a long time.'

'My whole life,' says Legén, puffing on his pipe. 'But I didn't murder anyone. *No, nein, nyet* . . . I was in there because of my mother.'

Jan looks at him.

'My mother was immoral, as they said back then . . . in the

343

thirties she had children by several different men, and she liked to party in the street, if I can put it that way. And she wasn't ashamed of it. So she was the one they locked up; in those days St Patricia's was a mental hospital and a kind of general institution. I was a child, I was just taken in with her. And that's where I stayed.'

'So you never . . . stabbed anyone?'

'That's just gossip,' Legén says. 'People will always talk . . . there's no end to it.'

Jan nods without speaking. *Trust people*, he thinks.

He sits down at the table. 'I've got a question. If the fire alarm goes off up at the hospital, what happens in the laundry?'

'We've practised this,' Legén replies, as if he still works there. 'We know what to do . . . If the smoke doesn't kill us, we turn off the machines and go up to the main entrance.'

'You don't use the lift?'

'No one uses the lift. Not if there's a fire.'

After a brief silence, Legén puts down his pipe and takes a litre bottle of pale-yellow wine out of his plastic bag. He places it in front of Jan. 'Try this,' he says. 'It's not the best batch I've ever made, but it's not bad . . . And it all ends up as piss anyway.'

'Thanks.'

'Are you going to get someone out?' Legén asks after a brief silence.

'Not at all.' The denial is automatic. 'No, I just want to—'

'If you do,' Legén interrupts, 'choose someone who deserves it. Some of the people in there ought to be allowed to change places with some of the lunatics out here.'

The Unit

Rami's escape attempt didn't succeed – Jan knew that as soon as he heard screams and shouts and the sound of breaking glass out in the corridor.

He listened but did nothing; he just stayed in his room and carried on working on his comic strip about the Secret Avenger. The shouts and screams were followed by a huge crash further down the corridor, then the sound of running footsteps.

Jan went over to the door. He heard another door slam shut, then even more loud voices. A whole chorus of them.

Then silence.

Jan waited a little while longer before peering cautiously into the corridor. Everything was quiet and deserted, but when he went and knocked on Rami's door, there was no reply.

This time he knew immediately where they had taken her, so he went down to the cellar. To the locked door of the Black Hole.

'Rami?' he called.

He could just hear her voice through the door: 'Yes.'

'What happened?'

'One of the ghosts saw me and told on me. So I hit her.'

Jan assumed she was talking about the pale girls. 'So they caught the squirrel,' he said.

'They caught me straight away,' she said. 'I didn't even manage to get outside . . . I bit them, but there were four of them. Just like your gang.'

Jan didn't know what to say. *We can't win, Rami.* That was what he always used to think, at least before he met her.

'How long do you have to stay in there?'

'They didn't say. Years, maybe . . . But it doesn't matter, because I know what I'm going to do when they let me out.'

Jan didn't ask any more questions, because he knew that Rami would never give up. He sat outside the door and waited, just to provide support. Eventually he spoke again. 'If you do it again . . . I'm coming with you.'

'Are you?'

'Yes.'

And it was true – he didn't want to leave the security of the Unit, but he would go anywhere with Rami.

'Do you know where I'm going to go?'

'Where?'

'To Stockholm. That's where I have to go . . . my older sister lives there.'

'OK,' Jan said.

'We'll form a band when we get there. We can play in Sergels Torg in the city centre, and use the money we get to make recordings . . . and we'll never, ever come back here.'

'And what about the pact?' Jan asked.

Rami seemed to be thinking things over. 'You can fulfil your part of the bargain later . . . and I'll fulfil mine, if you give me your address.'

'OK. I have to go now, Rami . . . I've got a counselling session.'

'With your psychobabbler?'

'Yes . . . but it's OK, he listens.'

'I listen too,' said Rami.

'I know.'

'Will you come and see me tonight? If they let me out?'

'I . . .' But he couldn't go on. He could only say the last three words silently to himself: *love you, Rami.*

*

'Why do you lock us up?' Jan asked.

'Lock you up?' Tony said.

'Down in the cellar. There's a locked room.'

'It's only if someone is violent. For their own sake . . . so they don't harm themselves. They just have to stay in there for a little while, until things calm down . . . just as everybody has to stay in here for a little while.'

Jan didn't respond, so the psychologist leaned forward. 'How are you feeling now, Jan?'

'Fine.'

'Have you made some friends here?'

'Maybe.'

'Good. And what about those self-destructive thoughts you were having? Have they gone now?'

'I think so,' he said.

'So maybe it's time you went home, then?'

They wanted to get rid of him, Jan realized. He had been here *for a little while*. They probably needed his room for someone else. 'Don't know,' he said.

'You don't know. But you can't stay here, can you?'

Jan didn't answer.

But if Rami's escape plan didn't work, it was a tempting thought: to stay behind the fence for the rest of his life, never have to face the world again. Never have to face the Gang of Four.

'It'll be good to get home,' Tony said. 'You can go home, go back to school . . . make friends and start living. And think about what you want to be.'

'What I want to be?'

'Yes . . . what kind of job would you like to do?'

Jan thought this over. He had never really considered it, but he replied, 'Maybe I'd like to be a teacher.'

'Why?'

'Because . . . I'd like to look after children. To protect them.'

After the session Jan drifted around the corridors. It was almost time for dinner, and he could hear voices from the TV room. He went down to the cellar, but the door of the Black Hole was wide open. They had let Rami out.

Fifteen minutes later she came into the dining room, after everybody else, when Jan was already eating at a table by the window. But Rami went and sat on her own at a corner table. That's the way things had been over the past few days – the more time they spent together, the less often they ate together. It was as if their liaison had to be kept secret from everyone else in the Unit.

But she looked at him from time to time, across the tables. Both of them knew what they wanted.

Jan went back to his room after dinner and stared at the white wall.

You're going home soon.

But he didn't want to go home. There were no friends waiting for him at home, just the Gang of Four.

He heard the door of Rami's room open and close about half an hour later.

He waited a bit longer. At nine o'clock the lights in the corridor were dimmed, and at quarter past nine he crept out of his room to Rami's door. He could hear a low murmuring from inside; Rami was talking on the stolen telephone. Jan waited until everything went quiet, then he knocked.

She opened the door a fraction, saw who it was and let him in.

'Who were you talking to?' Jan asked.

'My sister. She says she's waiting for me. She needs me.'

'So you're off to Stockholm?'

'You already know that.'

'When?'

'First thing tomorrow . . . Are you coming with me?'

Jan nodded, and took out a piece of paper. 'This is my address,' he said. 'They're saying I have to go home, so just in case . . . I'm not allowed to stay here.'

Rami tucked the piece of paper in the pocket of her jeans. 'Do you *want* to stay here?' she asked.

'Sometimes . . . Everything's so calm in here. And you're here.'

She held out her arms, and he went to her.

'We'll take care of the Psychobabbler and the Gang of Four,' she whispered in his ear. 'I promise.'

49

CRAZED ATTACK BY MOUNTAIN LAKE.

Jan is sitting in his apartment reading the headline in an old newspaper cutting; he reads it over and over again.

Crazed attack. He thinks about the term. An attack carried out by a crazy person. Someone else. Not the person who writes the words, and not the person who's reading them.

Someone else. But who?

It's Friday evening and he's back from work. There is exactly one week to go until the fire drill, and Lilian is still determined to go ahead with her plan to take Ivan Rössel to task in the visitors' room. She and Hanna have started whispering to Jan as well now, not only to each other. Now he knows what is going on, they obviously want to be sure he is with them.

Jan has only promised not to tell on them, nothing else.

As he was cycling past the hospital on his way home, he saw Dr Högsmed striding along by the wall. The doctor recognized him and raised his hand; Jan waved back with a smile, and watched him disappear through the steel door. Perhaps he was going up to his office to try out the hat test on someone.

Högsmed is probably a good psychiatrist, Jan thinks, but he has no idea what goes on in the hospital at night. He doesn't know about the secret route from the pre-school, or the secret letters and the meetings in the visitors' room. Högsmed thinks that everything at St Patricia's is ticking along nicely, just the way he and the board have planned it.

But Jan believes the desire to kick against routine is part of human nature; both children and adults are constantly tempted to bend the rules.

A week to go. Time cannot be stopped.

Jan feels stressed by the ticking clock, just like when he was at Lynx.

He takes out the old diary again – the one Rami gave him in the storeroom at the Unit. He looks at the picture on the front, the Polaroid Rami took the very first time they met. He is surprised at how young and healthy he looks, bearing in mind how close to death he had been the day before the picture was taken. First almost completely dehydrated in the sauna, then drugged with sleeping tablets, bleeding from wounds inflicted with a razor, and almost drowned in a pond. And yet he is staring straight into the camera, with his head up.

The diary contains not only his own memories and thoughts. There are also some folded newspaper cuttings, and perhaps they are the reason why he has kept the diary. He has taken them out and read them from time to time, late at night.

The first is an entire page, with a big black and white picture of a rock jutting out several metres above the shining surface of a lake, with that headline, CRAZED ATTACK BY MOUNTAIN LAKE, followed by a subheading: *Two boys killed on camping trip.*

Jan has read the article time and time again over the past fifteen years or more, and he practically knows it by heart at this stage.

Two boys aged fifteen and sixteen were attacked and killed last night by an unknown assailant. The boys were camping on a rocky outcrop above a mountain lake twelve kilometres outside Nordbro when they were attacked.

According to the police the murderer appears to have slit the tent open with his knife, then inflicted multiple stab wounds on both boys before rolling them up in the tent and pushing it into the lake. *The severely injured boys were unable to get out of the tent, and drowned.*

The article continues for two more columns, with comments from a detective inspector and a certain amount of speculation.

There is another cutting from the following day:

THIRD VICTIM FOUND
Teenage boy with severe head injuries discovered by roadside

It seems likely that a hit and run driver is responsible for the condition of a 16-year-old boy who was found in a shallow ditch outside Nordbro early on Wednesday morning. The boy was unconscious and was suffering from head injuries, multiple lacerations and several broken bones. He was taken to the emergency department at the Western Hospital, but has yet to regain consciousness.

The police are not ruling out a connection between this tragic event and the double murder of two teenage boys near a mountain lake just a few kilometres away.

'Evidently these three boys were on an overnight camping trip together when someone attacked them with a knife,' says Inspector Hans Torstensson.

He was not prepared to comment or speculate on the suggestion that the same person might have murdered the two boys, then deliberately driven into the third boy as he tried to flee from the scene of the crime along the main road.

'The investigation will continue until all the outstanding issues are resolved.'

Did anyone else remember those events after fifteen years, Jan wonders? The families of the boys would remember, of course, but they have probably moved on by now. Parents and siblings have gritted their teeth and gradually come to terms with their grief – unless they are like Lilian, of course. The police will definitely have put the investigation on the back burner, in spite of the inspector's assurances. They will have put the final details of the unsolved crimes in some file and archived the whole thing.

Perhaps it is only Jan who still wonders what happened.

Two murdered, one severely injured.

But by whom?

The questions about the identity of the perpetrator have been in Jan's mind all these years, long after the sense of relief faded away.

Jan has not written in the diary for about a week now, so he turns to a clean page and begins to write a situation report to himself. He writes about the Dell, about the staff and about his secret excursions to the hospital. Finally he writes:

I came to Valla to make contact with Rami again – but that wasn't the only reason. I wanted to work with vulnerable children, and to make them feel better about themselves.

I also came here to try to create a life for myself, and to make friends. But that hasn't happened. Perhaps it's Rami's fault. Perhaps I have used her as a kind of shield, protecting me from the rest of the world . . .

He could never confess these thoughts to Rami face to face. But he wants to talk to her, as soon as possible.

He looks at the clock. It is quarter past nine. Not too late for a little outing on his bike.

Lilian has her preparations to make before the fire drill, and so does Jan.

50

Black clouds have gathered in the night sky, hovering above the hospital and releasing a fine drizzle over the forest. Jan wipes the ice-cold drops of water from his forehead, crouches down in the undergrowth and tries to find some shelter under a birch tree.

He takes out the Angel. The hospital looms up in front of him; Jan has a friend in there, so the rain and cold don't matter at all.

'Are you there, squirrel?' he whispers into the microphone, his gaze fixed on the forbidding façade. Fourth floor, seventh from the right.

The light goes off, then comes back on again.

A clear signal – Rami is back in her room.

Jan slowly exhales, and asks, 'Do you still want to get out?'

The light flashes off and on. *Yes.*

'As soon as possible?'

Yes.

Both responses are instant, with no hesitation. The woman who is answering him is definitely not drugged or confused.

'I want to see you too, I want to hear what happened after you left the Unit. I waited for an answer from you, but it never came . . . I just know you fulfilled your part of the pact. You stopped the Gang of Four.' Jan pauses for a moment, gathers his thoughts, then goes on: 'But *how* did you do it? You told me you knew people who could take care of them, and I've wondered all these years . . . Who was it?'

The Secret Avenger, he thinks. But who was the Secret Avenger?

There is no answer, of course. The light stays on.

'I didn't feel sorry for Niklas, Peter and Christer. I just couldn't. And now there's only one member of the Gang of Four left. His name is Torgny, Torgny Fridman. I told you about him fifteen years ago. He owns an ironmonger's shop back in Nordbro, where I grew up. And he's got a wife and a child and a successful life . . . but I find it difficult to forget what he did.'

The light in the window doesn't go off, but he believes that Rami is listening.

'There's something else I need to tell you . . . I qualified as a classroom assistant ten years ago. And in one of my first temporary posts I was looking after a little boy called William . . . When I saw William's mother, I recognized her. She was the Psychobabbler from the Unit, your psychologist. You remember her, don't you? You asked me to do something to her. To punish her.'

Silence. Jan has reached the heart of his confession. He had meant to sound triumphant, but his voice lacks strength, as if he were apologizing. 'So . . . so one day when we were in the forest, I lured William away from the rest of the group and locked him up in an old bunker. He was fine in there, as far as possible, anyway. It was much worse for his parents . . . for the Psychobabbler. She was worried for a long time.'

The confession is over, but Jan has one thing left to say: 'Your escape route, Rami. Listen carefully.' He keeps his eyes fixed on the window, and goes on: 'During the fire drill next Friday evening, all the patients will be let out of their rooms. I presume you already know about it?'

The light flashes.

'You need to move away from the others. There's a storeroom on your floor, not far from your room. The door won't be locked – I've jammed the catch with a bit of paper. And inside the storeroom, behind a cupboard, there's an old laundry lift. It goes straight down to the basement.'

The light flashes. Rami understands.

'I'll be waiting for you down there,' Jan says. 'Then we can make our way out together.'

Can he really make that promise? He doesn't want to think about the things that could go wrong; he is just waiting for an answer.

And it comes: the light flashes one last time.

'Good . . . See you soon, Rami.'

Jan switches off the Angel. He is glad to leave the forest; it is a lonely place. But soon he won't be lonely any more.

Twenty minutes later he is ringing Lilian's doorbell. This time there is no sign of her brother. Lilian lets him in, but only as far as the hallway. She is on edge, and not in the mood for small talk.

'Have you made up your mind?'

Jan nods, with the memory of Rami's light flashing off and on still in his mind. 'I'll do it.'

'You're with us?'

He nods again. 'I can stand guard inside the pre-school,' he says. 'When you go up to meet Rössel in the visitors' room, I'll wait there.'

'We need a driver too,' Lilian says. 'You've got a car, haven't you?'

'I have.'

'In that case we'd really like to use it to get everyone there at the same time, and to get back home afterwards,' Lilian says.

She is focused now, and sober. Jan hears footsteps upstairs; someone is moving around up there.

'And you're going to talk to Rössel about your brother?' he says. 'That's all?'

'That's all.'

Lilian looks him in the eye. Jan suddenly remembers what Dr Högsmed said about how difficult it is to cure psychopaths.

'Why do you think Rössel has agreed to meet you? Does he want to confess in order to make himself feel better? Because he's become a good person?'

Lilian lowers her head. 'I don't care what Rössel has become. Just as long as he tells the truth.'

*

356

At the feelgood meeting Marie-Louise reminds everyone about Friday's fire drill. 'It's going to be quite a big thing, with the police and rescue services involved,' she says. 'But it's in the evening, so it won't affect us. The pre-school will remain closed, as usual.'

Not completely closed, Jan thinks.

He catches a quick glance from Lilian across the table. She looks tired and tense this Monday morning, and she smells of strong mints.

The working week begins, crawling by one day at a time, and suddenly it is Friday.

The last child Jan collects from the visitors' room is Leo.

From the lift, Jan catches a glimpse of the father: a short, burly man in a grey hospital sweatshirt who glances over at the lift before he goes back through the door leading to the hospital. The last thing he does is to raise his arm to his son, and Leo waves back.

The boy is calm and quiet on the way back to the Dell.

'Do you like going to see your daddy?' Jan asks as they step out of the lift.

Leo nods. Jan places a hand on his shoulder and hopes that St Patricia will watch over him when he grows up. The saint, not the hospital.

Marie-Louise smiles at Jan as he hands Leo over to his foster parents.

'You do a really good job with the children, Jan,' she says. 'You never get nervous, like the girls.'

'Which girls?'

'Hanna and Lilian . . . they're always on edge when they have to go up to the hospital, but I suppose it's hardly surprising.' She smiles at him again. 'None of us is used to that sort of person.'

'That sort of person . . . You mean the patients?'

'Exactly. The ones who are locked up in there.'

Jan looks at her smile, but can't bring himself to smile back. 'I'm used to them,' he says. 'I know them.'

'What do you mean?'

'I was locked up too, when I was a teenager.'

The smile disappears. Marie-Louise raises her eyebrows, and Jan goes on: 'I was in the child psych unit. We used to call it the Unit, short for Child and Adolescent Mental Health Unit. But it was a secure institution, just like St Patricia's. Those who were dangerous and those who were afraid were all locked up together inside the Unit.'

Marie-Louise manages to close her mouth; she seems to be having difficulty working out what to say. 'But why?' she asks eventually. 'Why were you in there?'

'I was one of those who was afraid,' Jan says. 'I was afraid of the world outside.'

There is an awkward silence in the kitchen.

'I didn't know,' Marie-Louise says at last. 'You never mentioned it, Jan.'

'It just never came up . . . but I'm not ashamed of it.'

Marie-Louise nods understandingly, but he feels she is looking at him with new eyes. He catches her glancing at him several times with a wary expression. It seems as if Jan has destroyed her confidence in him – he has let her down by revealing the cracks in his soul.

But it doesn't matter any more. Cracks let in the light.

The last thing he does at the end of the working day is to take Rami's picture books and his own diary out of his rucksack and put them away safely in his locker. There isn't much room in there among his jacket, umbrella and books, but he manages to squash them in.

When Rami comes out of St Psycho's tonight he will open the locker and show her all the picture books. And the new ink drawings.

Because Jan *is* going to help her escape from the clinic. This time it's going to work.

The Unit

Jan knew there was only one way out of the Unit that wasn't locked: the window above the cooker in the kitchen. The staff wanted to be able to air the room to get rid of the smell of cooking. The kitchen was at the back of the building and had no internal door, but there was almost always someone there during the day, so if you wanted to escape, you would have to be up early.

Jan woke at six. He had set his alarm, and when it started to buzz and he opened his eyes, he felt a long, slender body beside him.

Rami was lying there, her eyes wide open.

Jan quickly pushed his hand down to feel the sheet underneath him, but it was dry.

Rami kissed his forehead. 'Stockholm,' she said.

Jan just wanted to lie there, to forget about running away. But he nodded, and they got up.

They didn't switch on the light; they got dressed and crept out into the corridor like two grey shadows. Jan was carrying a little bag containing a few clothes and his diary, with his bedspread tucked underneath his arm; Rami was behind him with her own bag and something large and black. The guitar case, Jan realized.

'Are you taking *that* with you?' he whispered.

She nodded. 'I told you . . . We're going to sing and play on the streets of Stockholm to make some money.'

Jan couldn't sing, but he didn't say anything. All the doors were closed, including the door to the staffroom at the end of the corridor. Jan looked at it for a long time as they crept past. The kitchen was empty and in darkness.

Rami put down the guitar case and slid back the bolts securing the window. She pushed it wide open, and the icy morning air swept in.

She took a deep breath. 'Stockholm,' she said again, as if it were a magical place.

She quickly climbed up on to the hob and jumped out of the window. Outside there was a paved patio area with a wooden table and chairs.

Jan watched as Rami picked up one of the chairs and carried it across the grass to the fence. Halfway there she looked back over her shoulder and he nodded to her – but remained standing by the window.

Shit, he thought.

Then he spun around without even thinking and raced back into the corridor. He ran to the right, towards the bedrooms, but stopped outside the closed door of the staffroom. He raised his fist and banged on the door, three times.

He didn't know if anyone was in there, and he didn't wait to find out. He went straight back to the kitchen.

Rami was waiting for him outside the window. 'Where have you been?'

'I went to the toilet,' he lied.

Then he climbed up on to the windowsill and jumped out.

'The table,' he said.

Jan and Rami had gone over their escape plan in advance; they each grabbed one end of the table on the patio and carried it across to the fence. Then Rami put the chair on top of the table, and Jan climbed up and hurled the brown bedspread at the top of the fence. Twice he missed, but the third time the thick fabric covered the barbed wire and stayed there.

It was bitterly cold by the fence, but Jan was sweating. He quickly glanced back at the Unit and saw that all the windows were in darkness except one: the light had just been switched on in the staffroom.

He could make out two figures in the room: a young female auxiliary whose name he didn't know, and Jörgen, who was pulling on his shirt. They must have slept together, just like Jan and Rami.

Jan looked at her again. 'You first.'

She was lighter than him, and leapt up at the fence from the chair. Rami was a squirrel now, and got a good grip on the wire through the bedspread. She got one leg over the barbed wire, swung the rest of her body over the top and landed on the other side.

They looked at each other through the fence. Jan picked up the guitar and managed to throw it over to her.

She nodded. 'Your turn.'

Jan jumped up. He was no squirrel, but he managed to hang on through sheer willpower. The barbs had begun to poke through the bedspread, scratching the palms of his hands, but he managed to clamber right up to the top.

At that moment he heard the sound of banging on the window behind him – they had been seen.

A door opened, someone shouted at them.

Jan swallowed nervously but didn't look around; he swung himself over and dropped to the ground.

They were on the other side of the fence. They gathered up their things and set off along the path, side by side. It was ten to seven; there wasn't anyone around, but the sun was just beginning to rise.

From this point their plan was less sure – they had just wanted to get away. Jan had hardly any spare clothes, and only fifty kronor in his pocket.

'We're free!' Rami said, then she yelled, 'Stockholm!' at the top of her voice.

This was the first time Jan had seen Rami excited, almost happy. Her cheeks were rosy; he smiled at her, and suddenly knew what it meant to enjoy being with one special person.

He was fourteen years old, and head over heels in love.

*

The staff from the Unit caught up with them only ten minutes later. The paths in the surrounding area were deserted; the search party had no problem spotting Jan and Rami.

The sound of an engine broke the silence of the morning.

A small white car appeared from the back of the Unit, swung around and picked up speed.

Rami stopped smiling. 'It's *them!*'

The cumbersome guitar case was slowing her down, so Jan took it off her and they broke into a run. The path curved to the left and followed a small stream; tarmac and water meandered along side by side for another hundred metres, then there was a narrow wooden bridge.

'This way!' Rami shouted.

On the other side there was a grove of trees, and beyond the trees they could just see the town centre.

Jan didn't need to say a word – he and Rami ran towards the bridge, then across it.

She was faster, and was halfway to the trees by the time the car pulled up on the other side of the water. Jan was slower; he had too much to carry. He turned his head and saw Jörgen leap out of the driver's seat. The girl was getting out of the passenger seat; she looked more hesitant.

The Secret Avenger would have blown up the bridge, but Jan didn't have any dynamite.

Jörgen was already halfway across, and his strides were twice as long as Jan's.

It was all over, they weren't going to make it. Jan had known it all along, really.

'Rami!'

She didn't stop, but she did slow down and look at him. A slim figure in the morning light, the love of his life.

Jan's lungs were hurting. He had hardly any strength left, but managed another ten or twelve loping steps towards her.

'Here!' he panted, handing over the guitar case. He shoved his hand in his pocket and pulled out the fifty-kronor note. 'Take this . . . Now run!'

There was no time, but Rami leaned forward, pressed her cheek against his and whispered, 'Don't forget the pact.'

Then she flew across the grass with a fresh burst of energy and disappeared among the trees. The guitar case seemed weightless in her hand.

Jan took a few steps after her, but he had lost the impetus, and a couple of seconds later two hands seized him by the shoulders.

'OK, that's it.'

Jörgen was also out of breath after the chase, but his grip was firm, and Jan made no attempt to resist. They walked back across the bridge, back towards the Unit.

'Are you going to lock me up in the Black Hole?'

'The Black Hole?'

'That place down in the cellar . . . where you lock people up.'

'No, I shouldn't think so,' said Jörgen. 'It's only those who bite and scratch who end up down there. And you're not going to start fighting us, are you, Jan?'

Jan shook his head.

'Was it you who banged on the door just now?'

Jan nodded.

'Why did you do that?'

'Don't know.'

Jörgen looked at him. 'Why? Did you want to get caught, Jan?'

He didn't reply.

They walked towards the car, but Jan kept looking over his shoulder. Jörgen's colleague had disappeared among the trees.

Once he had settled Jan in the back seat of the car, Jörgen went back across the bridge, shouting to her.

It was quiet in the car; Jan could hear the sound of his own breathing.

Did you want to get caught? he wondered. *Did you want Rami to get caught?*

After a minute or so he saw the auxiliary emerge from the trees, shaking her head at Jörgen. They stood talking by the bridge for a little while; Jan saw Jörgen take out his phone and call someone. Then they returned to the car.

'OK, let's go,' said Jörgen.

They drove back to the Unit. Back to safety inside the fence.

Jan was locked up, and he was happy.

He knew that Rami was equally happy to be free.

51

Waiting in the darkness, fifteen years after their flight from the Unit.

Jan is alone, but not for much longer. He is standing down in the hospital basement, waiting for Rami. He has made his way in via the laundry, and is by the old lift in the little storeroom.

It is twenty past ten on Friday night, and Jan is really supposed to be up in the Dell. That is where Lilian thinks he is, but he has left his post and entered the hospital through the safe room. He knows his way around down here now, and the laundry was completely deserted when he arrived, just as Legén had said it would be. The only unusual sign was a series of small yellow lights flashing on a panel on the wall; perhaps they were something to do with the impending fire drill.

Jan listens for the sound of shuffling steps behind him, or voices raised in song from the chapel. But all is silent in the underworld.

He is the only one here – and soon Rami will be here too. At least he hopes so, and if he closes his eyes he can hear her singing: *Me and Jan, Jan and me, every night, every day . . .*

He blinks and gives himself a shake; he must remain alert.

The drums had been pounding inside his head when Jan drove Lilian and three men to the Dell half an hour earlier.

One of the men was Lilian's taciturn older brother. The others didn't introduce themselves, but they looked as if they were a few years younger than Lilian. Jan assumed they were friends of her missing brother, John Daniel.

Hanna wasn't around this evening, and without her Lilian seemed even more tense than usual. She had put on some make-up, Jan noticed: red lipstick and dark eyeshadow. It looked ridiculous, and who was it actually for? Was it for Carl, the security guard, or for Ivan Rössel?

Jan parked in the shadows beneath a large oak tree, a short distance away from the pre-school. Well away from the hospital's CCTV cameras.

No one spoke as they got out of the car.

Lilian quickly smoked one last cigarette in the street, then she unlocked the door and led the way into the darkness of the pre-school. She didn't switch on the light, but turned to Jan. 'So you're staying here, Jan? Is that OK?'

He nodded.

'Ring me straight away if anyone comes.'

Jan nodded again, and Lilian managed a strained smile. She fetched a key card from the kitchen, opened the door and disappeared down the stairs. The three silent men followed her, and Jan closed the door behind them.

So four people will be meeting Ivan Rössel in the visitors' room. That means he will be at a disadvantage when Carl smuggles him out of the secure unit. Jan hopes that Lilian and her family will be able to establish some kind of rapport with Rössel, get him to talk – but there's nothing he can do to help.

He has his own meeting to think about.

Once Lilian and the men had gone, Jan waited for fifteen minutes in the cloakroom by the door leading down to the basement. Nothing whatsoever happened. He went over to the window and gazed up at the hospital. The lights were on, but there wasn't a soul in sight.

Eventually he went into the kitchen and picked up the second key card. He opened the door; the light was still on down in the basement.

It was time.

*

Jan stands motionless in the laundry, thinking about what he will say to Rami when the lift door opens.

Hi Alice. You've escaped from the Black Hole – welcome.

And then what? Should he tell her that he's been thinking about her all these years? That he fell in love with her during those very first days in the Unit? He was so in love with Rami – but so scared of the outside world that he tried to get the staff to stop them the morning they ran away.

Jan had been caught, but Rami made it. She must have managed to catch the train to Stockholm and her sister, because she didn't come back to the Unit during the week Jan remained there.

And nobody mentioned her either – she was no longer their problem.

The following week Jan was discharged. He hadn't spoken to his psychologist after the escape attempt, but abracadabra – Tony must have decided he was fit to leave.

'You're going home,' Jörgen had said when he opened Jan's door. All Jan could do was pack his clothes, the diary Rami had given him, and the comic strip he had started about the Secret Avenger and the Gang of Four.

He had to put the drum kit back in the storeroom, of course, but he took the sticks with him.

Jan walked out of the Unit with his little bag and was picked up by his father, who wasn't smiling. 'So they've finished taking you apart, have they?' was all he said.

Jan didn't reply, and they drove home in silence.

The next Monday Jan went back to school. He hardly slept the night before; he lay awake thinking about the school corridors and the Gang of Four. He could see himself scuttling along the walls like a little mouse.

He walked to school alone, just like before. He still had no friends. It didn't matter.

His classmates stared at him, but nobody asked how he was feeling or where he had been for the last few weeks.

Perhaps they all knew. That didn't matter either.

367

Sooner or later Jan would run into the Gang of Four in the corridor, he knew that. But somehow the fear had gone. It was spring, late April, and the end of the school year was in sight. Jan took one day at a time. In the evenings he got out his drumsticks and played quietly on a telephone directory, or carried on with his drawing.

There was no sign of life from Rami – no phone calls or postcards from Stockholm.

The last week in May was traditionally given over to a range of activities, and the older students went out on trips and excursions.

On the Thursday morning when Jan got to school he saw groups of pupils standing around in the corridors. He heard whispered conversations about something terrible, *a crazed attack*.

'Is it true?' people were asking. 'Is it really true?'

Nobody spoke directly to Jan, but eventually he picked up the fact that something had happened in the forest outside the town. Someone had died. Had been *killed*.

Then a teacher told the class that two students had been murdered, and after that there were even more rumours flying around, and several newspaper articles about the *crazed attack*. The buzz continued until the summer holidays.

Jan took in everything that had happened with a kind of bleak astonishment. He couldn't quite believe that the Gang of Four had been virtually obliterated, that Torgny Fridman was the only one left.

It was their pact. Somehow Rami had managed to fulfil her side of the bargain.

But Jan never heard from her again, and it was over five years before he saw the name RAMI in the window of Nordbro's only music shop. Her debut album had just been released, and when he went in to buy a copy he saw that one of the songs was entitled 'Jan and Me'.

It was a sign from her – it had to be.

He had started working at the Lynx nursery by then, and that August when he saw the psychologist Emma Halevi and her son

368

William walking across the playground, the Unit and the Psycho-babbler were the first things he thought about.

And the next thing was the pact.

Memories of his teenage years make Jan realize something down in the laundry room: not once during the autumn has he wondered *why* Rami is locked up in St Psycho's.

What has she done to end up here, on a secure ward?

He doesn't know, and he doesn't really want to think about it now. All he can do is wait for her.

A noise breaks the silence – a wailing sound. Sirens approaching the hospital. The sound is coming from the road and is getting louder and louder through the thick walls.

Fire engines?

Jan notices that a different light has started to flash over on the panel: a red dot below the yellow ones. Some kind of alarm?

He looks at his watch. The fire drill seems to have started early.

Suddenly his mobile starts to buzz in his pocket. Jan gives a start, but quickly takes it out.

'Hello?' he says quietly, expecting to hear Lilian's voice. What is he going to say to her?

But it is a different voice, and it sounds worried: 'Jan . . . it's Marie-Louise.'

'Hi,' Jan says, clutching his phone tightly. 'Is everything OK?'

'Not really . . . something's happened. I'm trying to ring everyone, but hardly anyone is answering . . . I was just wondering, have you seen Leo? Leo Lundberg?'

'No . . . why?'

'Leo has run away from his new family,' Marie-Louise explains. 'He was playing out in the garden before dark, but when his foster parents went out to call him in, he wasn't there.'

Jan listens, but he doesn't know what to say. He finds it difficult to think about the children right now, but he has to say something. 'Leo is my favourite.'

Marie-Louise doesn't say anything at first; it's as if she doesn't understand. 'The most important thing is to find him,' she says after a moment. 'Where are you, Jan? Are you at home?'

Jan feels as if he has been somehow caught out, and lowers his voice even more. 'Yes. Yes, I am.'

'OK, well at least you know what's happened. The police are looking for Leo too; get in touch with them or with me if . . . if you see anything.'

'Of course I will. Speak to you soon.'

Jan ends the call and is able to relax a little. He thinks about Leo, about the boy's anxiety and restlessness. It's unfortunate that he's run away, but the police are involved and there is nothing Jan can do. All he can do is wait here, for Rami's sake.

And just a few minutes later he hears a different noise: a dull clanking in the underworld, a noise that gets louder and louder.

It's coming from the mechanism of the laundry lift.

Jan's pulse rate increases and he takes a couple of steps towards the hatch in the wall. It doesn't move, but the clanking keeps on getting louder. The lift is on its way down.

It stops behind the hatch with a thud, then everything goes quiet. Slowly the hatch begins to move. There is someone inside the lift, someone who wants to get out.

Jan's heart is pounding; he steps forward. 'You've made it,' he says. 'Welcome.'

He sees an arm appear, then a denim-clad leg. But they don't move. The arm and the leg simply dangle there, apparently lifeless.

'Rami?'

Jan takes a final step towards the lift and reaches out his hand – but suddenly everything is moving too fast for him. The hatch flies open with a crash, and Jan doesn't have time to get out of the way. It hits him in the chest; the pain is instant and crippling.

Something hisses, the air is suddenly full of white mist. And Jan can't breathe.

He closes his eyes and coughs and jerks back, but his legs give way and he falls backwards on to the floor.

Tear gas, someone has sprayed tear gas in his face.

A body is shoved out of the lift, heavy and inert, and lands next to him like a sack of potatoes.

Jan's eyes are streaming but he blinks and tries to look up. He sees the body beside him, the staring eyes.

A man. A security guard. There is a wide gap in his throat; it has been cut. Jan touches him, and his hand is covered in warm blood.

He recognizes the guard: it's Carl. The drummer from the Bohemos and Ivan Rössel's escort – but he's dying.

'Carl?'

Or perhaps he's already dead. Carl isn't moving, and he's bleeding heavily from the wound in his throat. The blood looks black; it has poured down over his T-shirt.

Jan blinks again, trying to see clearly in spite of the tear gas. In the laundry lift something is moving. A shadow.

There is another person inside the lift, he realizes; someone who has managed to squeeze in and travel down to the cellar along with the dying guard.

The shadow slithers out into the storeroom and straightens up: a tall figure dressed in hospital clothes – a grey sweatshirt, grey cotton trousers and white trainers.

A patient.

But this is not Alice Rami. The body is too tall and broad, the hair is too dark.

This is a man.

He leans over Jan in a miasma of smoke, tear gas and something else – lighter fluid, or petrol.

He makes a sudden movement towards Jan, twists his hands and pulls. 'Relax,' the man says quietly.

Jan is unable to move his arms. There is a plastic loop around his wrists, some kind of handcuff.

The man slips a canister into his pocket and hauls Jan to his feet. His face is in shadow, but Jan can see that he is armed with something more than tear gas. In his right hand he is holding a short knife.

No, not a knife. It's a razor, with a jagged edge.

'I know who you are,' the man says. 'I've heard you talking to me.'

His voice is hoarse, but calm and clear. It is only his movements that are rapid and jerky as he tugs at Jan.

'You're going to help me get out of here.'

Jan blinks at him. 'Who are you?'

The man quickly brings his left hand up beneath his chin, and there is a click. 'Look.'

A white beam flashes on in the darkness, lighting up his face – and Jan recognizes him.

It is Ivan Rössel, with the other Angel in his hand. He is several years older than he was in the newspaper pictures, with dark furrows lining his long, narrow face. The curly hair is halfway to his shoulders, and is dark grey now.

Jan coughs. 'Rami,' he whispers, looking at the Angel. 'I gave that to Alice Rami.'

'You gave it to me,' Rössel says.

'Rami was supposed to come down in the lift and—'

'Nobody else is coming down,' Rössel interrupts him. 'There's just you and me.'

Then he gives Jan a shove and holds the razor blade against his throat. 'Come along, my friend,' he says. 'We're going to get out of here . . . and we're going to hide that in the lift.'

Rössel points to Carl's body. 'Grab hold of his arms.'

Another shove, and Jan begins to move, as if he were in a trance. He reaches out with his bound hands and manages to get a grip on the dead guard's upper body. He bundles it back into the laundry lift.

'Push him in.'

Jan leans into the lift, struggling with the heavy body. Lifeless arms, dangling legs. It all has to go in.

He notices Carl's belt. The clip for the tear-gas canister is empty, but next to it there are a number of white plastic loops, ready to slip over someone's wrists.

As Jan pushes the body into the lift, he removes a couple of these from Carl's belt and tucks them under his jumper, without

Rössel spotting anything. He steps back, and Rössel slams the hatch shut.

'Let's go.'

There is nothing Jan can do. He is forced to walk ahead of Rössel, out of the laundry, through the tiled rooms. It is impossible to stop; Rössel keeps shoving him hard in the back, and he can feel the razor blade against his throat every time Rössel moves his right hand.

Jan moves through the basement like a sleepwalker. His eyes are hurting, his hands are covered in blood.

What has happened? How can this have happened?

Ivan Rössel was squeezed inside the lift along with Carl. And Carl was dead, slaughtered by Rössel.

And Rami? She was the one who was supposed to come down in the lift, but . . .

'Don't get lost,' Rössel says as he pushes Jan through a doorway. 'Follow the bits of paper if you don't know the way.'

But Jan does know the way. They carry on along the corridors without meeting anyone. Then straight through the safe room, and out into the corridor leading back to the pre-school, where the lights are still on.

Jan stops by the lift. He turns his head. 'They're waiting for you in the visitors' room,' he says. 'You do know that, don't you? A family . . . They want to talk to you about their missing brother, John Daniel . . .'

Rössel shakes his head. 'They don't want to *talk*,' he says. 'They were going to kill me up there, that was the plan. Carl sold me down the river.'

'No, they just want to know where—'

'They were going to murder me, I know it.' Another shove, and Rössel moves him away from the lift and over towards the stairs. 'You're the only person I trust right now, my friend. And we're going to get out of here.'

Rössel's voice remains quiet and clear. A teacher's voice, accustomed to giving instructions and providing explanations.

He nudges Jan up the stairs to the door of the Dell. 'Open it.'

Jan hesitates, but takes out the key card and opens the door.

They walk past the staff lockers, where Rami's picture books lie hidden. And Jan's diary. He was going to show them all to her tonight; he had been so looking forward to it.

Andreas has left a cap and a raincoat hanging on a hook; Rössel puts them on. Then he kicks open the front door and leads Jan outside. The night air is cold, colder than before, but it soothes Jan's eyes.

He blinks away a few tears and looks around. Red and blue lights are flashing over in the hospital car park. Police cars, fire engines, ambulances. The fire drill is well under way – if it is actually a drill, of course. Rössel does smell of smoke.

Rössel doesn't stop; he doesn't even glance across at the vehicles. 'Have you got a car?' he asks.

Jan nods. It is parked within sight of the pre-school, and it isn't locked.

Once they reach the Volvo Rössel pats down Jan's trousers and removes his mobile phone. It disappears into the raincoat pocket.

A swift slicing movement with the razor blade, and suddenly Jan is able to move his hands.

'Into the car, my friend.' Rössel opens the driver's door, bundles Jan behind the wheel and chucks the Angel on the seat next to him. He slams the door and climbs into the back seat, behind Jan.

The stench of Rössel – smoke and petrol and tear gas – is acrid within the confines of the car.

'Drive,' he says.

Rami? Jan thinks, gazing at his hands on the wheel.

'I can't drive. I can't see a thing.'

'You can see the road. Drive away from the hospital. Just keep going straight ahead until I tell you otherwise.'

Jan makes one last effort to understand what has happened: 'Where's Rami?'

'Forget her,' says Rössel. 'There is no Rami in the hospital. It was me you were talking to. All the time.'

'But Rami must have—'

Rössel presses the razor against his windpipe. Jan can feel the blade trembling.

'*Drive.* Otherwise you'll end up like Carl. Ear to ear.'

Jan doesn't say another word. He starts the car and puts his foot down.

Rössel keeps the razor just below Jan's chin, and it is this threat that takes Jan away from St Patricia's, away from the wall and the Dell. Away from the chance of ever seeing Alice Rami again.

Away from the lights of the town, and into the darkness.

52

Jan is driving a murderer through the night. A murderer who is holding a razor to his throat. But a murderer who somehow cares about him, Jan realizes: Rössel reached out and turned up the heat, then asked, 'Too hot?'

'No.'

The gentle hum of the heater is quite soporific. Out on the streets it is bitterly cold, but inside the car it's as warm as a summer's day. The razor blade is still in place.

'Turn right here,' Rössel says.

Jan turns right. His eyes are still smarting, but his vision is gradually improving.

There are few cars out and about; the only vehicles they meet are a couple of taxis.

'Straight on,' Rössel instructs. Jan drives straight on.

They head away from the centre and through the middle of a deserted industrial estate. Jan doesn't attempt to think, he just drives, and eventually they are on the motorway that leads to Gothenburg. That too is almost deserted.

'Put your foot down.'

A lorry thunders past on its way out of town, and the lights of farmhouses are visible among the trees on both sides of the road, but these are the only signs of human life tonight. It is Friday, and people are at home. There is no police surveillance on the motorway.

'We're out of town now,' Rössel says. 'Out in the country.'

Jan doesn't say anything. He maintains a steady speed, but after ten minutes Rössel leans forward with a new order: 'Pull in over there.'

Jan sees the entrance to a lay-by and picnic area, illuminated by a couple of lights but with no sign of any other cars. He pulls in and brakes immediately; he wants to keep the car close to the lights, and Rössel doesn't object.

'Switch off the engine.'

Jan obeys, and there is silence inside the car. Total silence.

Rössel lets out a heavy sigh, then says, 'The smell has gone now . . . The hospital smell.'

But Jan is still aware of the acrid stench of tear gas and lighter fluid from Rössel's clothes, and asks quietly, 'What happened back there?'

Rössel takes a deep breath. 'There was a real fire,' he says. 'I'd managed to smuggle some thinner out of the paint shop, and a lighter. I poured the lot on the floor in the corridor and set fire to it.'

The razor moves away a fraction when Rössel is speaking, so Jan asks another question: 'Then what?'

'Chaos, of course. It wasn't a drill any more. It's always chaos when their plans don't work. But I kept calm and went to the storeroom. It wasn't locked, so all I had to do was walk in. But I had to change my plans at the last minute.' He sighs again. 'Someone tried to stop me.'

'His name is Carl.'

'I know that. But he doesn't need a name now.'

Jan keeps quiet. It occurs to him that Rössel hasn't used his name either. Not once.

Rössel shuffles in his seat. 'There is no smell, not any more. It's the loneliness that smells in a hospital . . . Long corridors of loneliness, like in a monastery.' He leans forward. 'And you, my friend? Are you lonely too?'

Jan looks out at the empty lay-by. He resists the impulse to move his head – the razor is too close to his throat again. 'Sometimes.'

'Only sometimes?'

Jan could say anything, but he tells the truth: 'No . . . often.'

Rössel seems satisfied with the answer. 'I thought so . . . You smell of loneliness.'

Jan turns his head slowly. No sudden movements.

'I was waiting for someone else tonight,' he says. 'Her name is Rami. Alice Rami.'

'There is no Rami in the hospital.'

'She calls herself Blanker in there . . . Maria Blanker, on the fourth floor.'

Rössel sounds irritated. 'You know nothing,' he says. 'Maria Blanker is *not* Rami. She's her sister. And Blanker's room is on the third floor.'

'Rami's sister?'

'I know *everything*,' says Rössel. He sounds very certain, sitting behind Jan. 'I listen, I read letters, I put the pieces of the puzzle together . . . I know everything about everybody.'

'I wrote letters to Maria Blanker. And she replied.'

'Who knows where letters end up? You wrote letters, but it was me you were writing to. I gave Carl some money, he let me read the letters, and I read and read . . . Your letter was different, I was curious. So I wrote back and told you my room was on the fourth floor. You left that little machine in my letter box, and you called out to your squirrel. I replied with the light . . . Off, on, off, on. You remember?'

Jan remembers. Rössel's words are beginning to sink in.

No Rami. Only Rössel, all along.

What did he put in the letters? What did he tell him via the Angel?

Everything. Jan thought he was talking to Rami, so he talked about everything. He had so much to tell her.

'So it's all over now,' he says.

He is empty and exhausted. But he doesn't move; he can still feel the razor against his skin just below his right ear.

'It isn't over at all,' Rössel says. 'It just goes on and on.'

Suddenly he lowers his arm. The razor disappears and Jan hears

Rössel let out a long breath, then say quietly, as if he is talking to himself, 'That feeling just now, an open road in the darkness . . . The feeling of freedom. I've had walls and fences around me for five years. And now I've left it all behind.'

Jan turns his head a fraction. 'And all those people who wrote you letters . . . have you left them too?'

'Of course.'

'Including Hanna Aronsson?'

'Ah yes, Hanna.' Rössel sounds smug. 'She's not here, is she? She's somewhere else tonight.'

Jan understands. Rössel has fooled everyone.

He's a psychopath. He lacks the capacity to feel guilt, Lilian had said. *The only thing he wants is attention.*

Jan tries to imagine Rössel as a teacher. With such a soft voice, he must have inspired confidence in the classroom. And not only there; many people he encountered in the street, on his camping holidays, out in the country, must have thought he was trustworthy. Totally harmless.

Hi, my name's Ivan; I'm a teacher making the most of the summer holidays . . . Listen, I don't suppose you could help me carry this table into my caravan? It's that one just over there, on its own. Yes, a coffee table, it would be brilliant if we could get it inside . . . I know it's late, my friend, but perhaps you've got time for a cup of coffee afterwards? Or something stronger? I've got beer or wine . . . Of course, you go in first. Careful, it's dark in here, you can hardly see a thing. That's it, go straight in . . .

Jan shivers, in spite of the heat inside the car.

He hears Rössel moving behind him, then his voice very close to Jan's ear: 'We'll be on the move again soon, driving down the open road . . . We're going on a trip together, you and I.'

Jan has only one thought in his mind, and in the end he has to come out with it: 'We ought to go back to the hospital.'

'Why?'

'Because . . . because the people up there will be worried if they know you're out.'

Rössel lets out a cough, or perhaps a chuckle. 'They've got other

379

things to think about right now.' He pauses, then goes on: 'But this is what I'm talking about, the freedom of the open road. I want to do things out here. Write books, confess my sins . . . You know I promised to show everyone where a missing boy is hidden? That would be a good thing, wouldn't it?'

'Yes,' Jan says. 'That would be a good thing.'

'Or . . . or we could do other things. Things nobody wants to talk about. The things you think about all the time.'

Jan's mouth is dry; he listens to the soft voice and feels Rössel's words crawl inside him. But he turns his head and faces the back seat. 'You don't know me.'

'Yes, I do. I know you. You told me everything. And that's good. It's nice not to have any secrets.'

'I haven't—'

But Rössel interrupts him: 'So now you have to choose.'

'Choose what?'

'Well, you want to do things, don't you?'

'What things?'

'There are fantasies you want to be a part of,' says Rössel, pointing to the Angel on the front seat. 'I heard your dreams . . . Someone hurt you deeply when you were young, and you have dreamed of revenge ever since.'

Jan gazes at the empty road, with Rössel's voice in his ear: 'If you could choose between good and evil . . . between saving a family and taking revenge for the hurt that was inflicted on you, which would you choose?'

Jan says nothing. The car feels very cold now, and the darkness comes crowding in.

'It is opportunity that creates an avenger,' Rössel goes on. 'But before the opportunity comes along, the fantasies must exist . . . fantasies like yours.'

'No.'

'Yes. You dream of locking someone up. A boy.'

Jan quickly shakes his head, but doesn't speak.

The darkness is complete, and the road and the night are calling.

'Not a boy,' he says.

'Yes,' Rössel says. 'The fantasy runs through your mind like a film, doesn't it? We all have our favourite fantasies.'

Jan nods; he knows.

'Fantasies are like a drug,' Rössel's soft voice continues. 'Fantasies *are* a drug. The more we fantasize, the stronger they grow. We want to hurt someone. Carry out an evil ritual. You can never escape from those thoughts. Not until you do something about them.' He leans forward again. 'Which would you choose?' he asks. 'Would you choose to do good or evil?'

Choose?

Jan lowers his gaze. 'I can't choose.'

'But you must,' Rössel says. 'Atonement or revenge? Look out at the road; soon we will come to a fork. You have to choose now.'

Jan blinks.

He looks out at the dark road. He closes his eyes.

Choose now, he thinks.

53

Jan hardly needs to press down on the accelerator or move the steering wheel – the Volvo obeys him anyway. It glides along on the crown of a black highway. Away from St Psycho's. Heading east along the open road.

He and the Secret Avenger sail past Swedish towns and villages that sound a bit like a nursery rhyme: Vara, Skara, Hova, Kumla and Arboga. The coniferous forest grows denser on either side of the road.

During the journey Jan tells the Secret Avenger about the revenge he wreaked on the Gang of Four. He thinks he knows what happened now.

It was early summer, fifteen years ago . . . you had gone off with your caravan, travelling around the inland forests. You were looking for a good place to camp . . . A fairly remote spot, as usual. And suddenly you came to a small lake deep in the forest. The only sign of human life was a little tent on the other side of the lake.

You went for a walk to get to know the area, then settled down inside your caravan. Perhaps you had a few drinks as twilight fell. A few more drinks, and you started to feel curious about who actually was in the tent. So you took a stroll over there.

It turned out to be three boys celebrating the end of the school year. You told them you were a teacher, in order to try and establish some kind of rapport. They laughed at you, called you a paedo. So you lumbered back to your caravan and drank even more. And after midnight you went back to the tent, but this time you were carrying a knife . . .

The Secret Avenger doesn't say anything. He merely listens as Jan describes his attack on two of the boys, and how the third boy tried to get away along the road – but the Secret Avenger got into his car and eventually caught up with him.

'I don't remember any of that,' says the Secret Avenger, 'but you could well be right.'

'Yes.' Jan nods to himself. 'But one of them is still around.'

'Still around,' says the Secret Avenger, brandishing the razor. 'For the time being.'

Jan drives and drives; he doesn't stop until they are approaching Nordbro. He pulls into a car park and switches off the engine, and they sleep in the car for a few hours. No one disturbs them.

The light slowly creeps over the horizon. It is dawn, then morning.

Jan wakes behind the wheel; he rouses the Secret Avenger and starts the car.

It is half past nine when they reach the town where Jan grew up. The streets are icy and deserted. It is Saturday morning.

The car heads towards the town centre, until Jan brakes and steers left at a sign marked NORTH. He knows where they are going; he turns the wheel and the car glides through the town as if it were on rails. No one can stop them now.

And then they have arrived. A sign says, CAUTION – CHILDREN PLAYING! This is an ordinary residential street, and this is where Jan's enemy lives with his wife and his little boy.

Number seven. A brown box just like all the rest.

Jan pulls up on the opposite side of the street. From here you can see in through the kitchen window of number seven. There is a light on, but the only person visible is a woman in a dressing gown. She is sitting at the breakfast table with her head bowed.

Torgny Fridman's wife knows nothing about fantasies. She carries on eating, alone.

'We missed him,' the Secret Avenger says.

Jan starts the car again, and this time he follows the signs to the town centre. Inside his head he can hear the pounding of drums.

They park on a side street close to Fridman's shop. Jan does everything right; he buys a parking ticket, then adjusts his jacket and runs a hand through his hair so that he will look neat and tidy.

The Secret Avenger pulls his hat down over his eyes and reaches out his hand. 'Give me the car keys . . . Just in case we need to make a quick getaway.'

Jan hands them over. Together they walk along the street, around the corner and into the ironmongery. The doorbell jingles cheerily as they walk in, but no one turns to look at them. It is still early, and there is only one customer in the shop.

And an ironmonger. Torgny Fridman is standing behind the counter showing the customer a range of leaf rakes. He picks up the rakes one by one and makes ridiculous little movements to demonstrate how they should be used.

Jan silently heads off to the right, towards the bigger tools made of iron and steel. They are weapons, every single one of them. Out of the corner of his eye he can see the Secret Avenger walking towards the hunting knives.

There are seven large axes left; the wooden shaft on this one is almost a metre long. Jan reaches out and picks it up. He feels the weight of the steel.

The fantasy about the final battle against the Gang of Four has been played out so many times inside his head, but the Secret Avenger has always taken the leading role. Until now.

Jan walks up to the counter with the axe and waits calmly while the other customer pays for his rake and leaves the shop. It takes a minute or so, then at last Jan is standing in front of Torgny with the axe in his hand. Torgny smiles, just as he would at any customer.

Jan is not smiling. He has spent enough time kow-towing to Torgny in his life.

'I've gone for this one,' he says, placing the axe on the counter.

Torgny nods. 'Good choice,' he says. 'Are you planning to chop some wood before the winter sets in?'

He doesn't have time to say any more, because suddenly there is the sound of feet running across the floor behind Jan. Small feet.

'Daddy! I've finished the cats, Daddy!'

Jan turns his head and sees the little boy, Torgny's son, racing towards them with a colouring book in his hand.

'Good boy, Filip,' Torgny says. 'Daddy won't be long!' He nods to Jan again, and asks the usual question: 'Will that be all?'

'No.' Jan places one hand on the axe. 'Don't you remember me?'

Torgny looks unsure. 'I don't think I—' he begins.

But Jan interrupts him. 'Jan Hauger.'

Torgny shakes his head. 'That will be three hundred and ninety kronor, please.'

He has picked up a bag for the axe, but Jan keeps his hand on it.

'I wanted to die rather than face you and your friends again.'

A kind of mask begins to fall from Torgny's face as Jan goes on. The shopkeeper's mask is disappearing, and behind it there is confusion. Jan wants to lure out the fifteen-year-old Torgny, the bully who must still be in there somewhere.

He carries on talking, as if he were addressing a child. 'You and your gang burned me with cigarettes.'

Torgny listens, but says nothing.

'Then you locked me in the sauna and turned up the heat.'

The shopkeeper opens his mouth at last. 'Are you saying *I* did that?'

'You and three others.'

'But why?' Torgny asks.

Jan doesn't answer the question. The drums are pounding.

'I know you remember me,' he says instead. 'It was you, Peter Malm, Niklas Svensson and Christer Vilhelmsson.'

Torgny nods, and Jan continues: 'Your friends . . . the ones who died in the forest.'

'I remember,' Torgny says. 'I know what happened.'

Jan glances sideways. He senses that the Secret Avenger is standing somewhere behind him.

'Christer stabbed Niklas and Peter to death,' Torgny goes on quietly. 'In their tent.'

Jan stares at him.

Torgny raises his voice slightly and begins to speak more quickly. 'They'd gone camping during the last week of the school year. I wasn't with them so I don't know everything, but there was some sort of quarrel. Peter started it; he always wanted to push people, try to break them. Christer couldn't handle it . . . In the end he snapped, and he had a knife with him. He killed Niklas and Peter while they were asleep, then Christer took off through the forest and ran straight in front of a car.'

Jan shakes his head. 'It wasn't Christer Vilhelmsson who killed them. It was . . .'

'It *was* Christer,' Torgny insists. 'He always hung around with us, but he got picked on the whole time. He was right at the bottom of the pecking order.'

'*I* was at the bottom of the pecking order,' Jan says.

'No.' Torgny shakes his head. 'You were nothing to us. You just happened to get in the way.'

Jan opens his mouth to speak, but suddenly turns around. The Secret Avenger has disappeared.

Torgny is also looking around the shop. 'Filip? Where's Filip?' he asks.

Jan lets go of the axe and backs away from the counter. He bumps into someone, another customer, but he doesn't stop. He breaks into a run.

Out into the autumn chill. There are more people on the streets now, with unfamiliar faces.

Jan spots his Volvo as it pulls out of its parking space. He can see the Secret Avenger sitting behind the wheel, and a little head is sticking up on the seat beside him. A five-year-old boy.

Jan picks up speed. He races across the road, shouting and waving, but the Secret Avenger doesn't even glance in his direction. The car moves out into the traffic and away from Jan.

'Rössel!'

The child in the passenger seat seems to hear Jan's shout; he turns his head and looks back, but the car doesn't stop.

Jan knows where the Secret Avenger is heading: to the bunker by the lake. He is taking the boy to the room with the concrete walls, and he is going to lock him up inside it. Not for two days this time, but for much longer. Weeks, months, perhaps for ever. This was what Jan had fantasized about, wasn't it? The final revenge on the Gang of Four: stealing away one of their children.

'Rössel!' he yells. 'Stop!'

People are looking at him, but he doesn't care. He runs along the pavement as fast as he can. He sees the Secret Avenger slow down and stop, but only for a red light. The Volvo is indicating right; soon it will turn off and disappear for ever with Torgny's son. Without a trace.

There is nothing Jan can do, and now he is regretting everything. Regretting everything he has been fantasizing about for so long. He closes his eyes, with just one thought in his head: *wrong choice.*

54

Jan is driving the car, looking out at the motorway through the windscreen. He has fantasized about one route through the night, but he has made a different choice. He will not go back to Nordbro with Rössel, he will not go and see Torgny, he will not take away his son.

It was a fantasy that he allowed to play out to its conclusion, but all desire for revenge has left him now. He knows that every violent fantasy ends in the same way when it becomes reality: with fear and regret and loneliness.

He and Rössel have been travelling along the motorway for almost an hour, and they have reached the suburbs of Gothenburg. Rössel has directed him here, and when Jan chose the route the razor was removed from his throat.

'I knew you would make this choice,' Rössel says. He is still sitting in the back seat like a king; then he leans forward. 'We're on the right road. We're going out into the forest . . . we're going to find a grave there. That's what I promised.'

'Yes,' Jan says. 'But what about afterwards? Are you going back to the hospital?'

'Absolutely.'

'I mean, there are psychologists at St Patricia's, aren't there? They can help you.'

Rössel bursts out laughing. '*Psychologists*,' he says, sounding as if he is talking about vermin. 'Psychologists want answers they can't have. They ask about my childhood, whether there's a history of mental illness in the family . . . They want to find a good reason why I used to travel around with my caravan in the summer picking up teenagers, but there are no reasons. The world is incomprehensible . . . So do you know why I did it?'

'No,' says Jan. 'And I don't want to . . .'

'I took them because I was evil, of course,' Rössel goes on. 'Because I am the son of Satan, and I want to be the master of life and death . . . Or maybe it was just because the ones I chose were defenceless and drunk, while I was strong and sober. Or then again, maybe I'm innocent, who knows? Only time will tell.'

Jan wants to stop this, and looks in the rear-view mirror. 'Were you ever in the forests around Nordbro?' he asks. 'Did you ever camp up there?'

'Nordbro? No, I never went that far north.'

Jan wonders if Rössel is lying. Probably not. Perhaps the truth lies in the simple answer that came from Jan's subconscious, put into words by a fantasy figure; perhaps one member of the Gang of Four killed two of the others.

The world is incomprehensible, and dark. So Jan keeps on driving, his hands gripping the wheel. But the petrol gauge is dipping into the red zone – he didn't think of this before they set off. He sees a Statoil sign beside the motorway, and points to it. 'We need petrol.'

There is no reply from the back seat. When he looks in the mirror he sees that Rössel is leaning back with his eyes closed; the razor is beside him, and he has one hand on the tear-gas canister.

Jan turns off for the service station, slowly pulls in between two HGVs and stops by a pump under the stark neon light.

He takes his credit card from his wallet and steps out into the cold. As he moves away from the car he feels the plastic loops pressing against his stomach. The restraints he took from Carl and hid under his jumper – they're still there. Would he use them on Rössel if he got the chance?

And if a patrol car slid into the petrol station now, would Jan alert the police? If he did, Rössel would be taken into custody and Jan would be free.

But Lilian's brother would never be found.

And that is why they are here.

Jan unhooks the nozzle and tries to think, glancing into the car every few seconds. Rössel's head and face are hidden by the roof of the car, but he can see the body in its grey trousers on the back seat. It is completely motionless. Has Rössel really fallen asleep?

He carries on filling up the car and looks around. The ranks of shiny petrol pumps are standing to attention in the neon light, and a short distance away a lorry is moving off with a muted hissing sound.

The pump clicks. The tank is full, and Jan replaces the nozzle.

Another quick glance into the car – but the back seat is empty.

Rössel is gone, along with the razor and the tear gas.

Jan looks around. The parking area is deserted. There isn't a soul in sight, but there are plenty of HGVs ten or twelve metres away, parked so close together that they form a labyrinth on the tarmac.

Has Rössel sneaked in between them?

Jan leaves the car and moves cautiously towards the trucks. He crouches down and tries to look underneath them, but he can't see any grey trousers moving on the other side.

He has a bad feeling in his stomach as he slowly walks back to the car.

'Here I am,' a voice says behind him.

Jan stops dead and turns around.

'Did you think I'd done a runner?'

Jan shakes his head. He and Rössel understand one another. They are going to the grave now, and neither of them is about to pull out. Whatever happens afterwards.

'Where were you?'

Rössel is holding a couple of spades with sharp edges under one arm, and something shiny in his other hand. A bottle. 'I was doing a bit of shopping,' he says. 'I bought the spades, then I went over to the trucks. They've come from all over Europe . . . and sometimes the drivers are carrying booze. So I bought a bottle.'

He holds it up, and Jan sees that it is vodka.

'And what did you use for money?'

'I used yours.' Rössel is offering Jan a small object – his own wallet. 'You left this in the car.'

Jan takes the wallet. 'I don't need alcohol.'

Rössel opens the bottle and takes a swig. He isn't smiling. 'Yes, you do. Tonight we need both spades and spirits.'

They drive on through the night. Rössel is more subdued now, but he is still giving directions from the back seat. He points: 'Left here.'

A roundabout, then a narrower road. Gothenburg is a big place and this is a part of the city Jan is not familiar with, but he can see a chain of jagged hills in the distance and thinks they are somewhere north-east of the centre, around Utby.

'Turn right here,' Rössel says, taking a swig of vodka. 'Then right again.'

Jan obeys. He finds himself driving along a long, straight road where both the lights and the houses become more and more sparse. A white road sign flashes past: TRASTVÄGEN.

The sign is the last indication of their proximity to the city; after that there are no more buildings, only the road. It turns into a forest track leading upwards, climbing steep slopes covered with dark bushes and trees.

'Here,' Rössel says quietly. 'We can't drive any further . . . park here.'

Jan stops the car. He switches off the engine and turns on the interior light.

In the rear-view mirror he sees Rössel drinking deeply from the bottle, closing his eyes as he swallows.

'Medicine,' he says, passing the bottle to Jan.

Jan takes a small sip, no more. He looks down at the side pocket on the car door and sees pens and a few sheets of paper. He has an idea, and reaches for a pen and a sheet of paper. He shows them to Rössel. 'Draw a map,' he says.

'A map?'

Jan nods. 'We can leave it here . . . just in case we get lost in the forest.' He remembers how he memorized the area around the Nordbro lake nine years ago, and says, 'You do remember the way to the grave, don't you?'

This is the first time he has asked Rössel to do something. He waits in silence.

But Rössel shakes his head. 'I can't . . . I can't draw.'

'I can,' Jan says. He draws two parallel lines on the paper and writes *Trastvägen*. 'This is where we are now . . . So where are we going?'

Rössel hesitates. 'Draw a path,' he says eventually. 'Up to the left.'

Jan begins to draw. The line winds its way onwards, and Rössel explains about the differences in level, streams and large rocky areas. Jan was right – the entire landscape is preserved inside Rössel's head. He has thought about this place a great deal.

'There, put a cross there on that ledge.' Rössel seems more eager now as he points at the map. 'And write that . . . I just happened to meet the boy on a park bench, and I took him into the forest and buried the body up in the hills.'

The confession, Jan thinks. A written confession for Lilian and her family, at long last.

Jan finishes writing and shows the map to Rössel, who looks at the piece of paper and nods.

'Good,' Jan says quietly, and places the map on the passenger seat.

'Let's go,' Rössel says. He climbs out of the car and Jan does the same. Their night's work is waiting.

The spades are waiting too. Jan opens the boot and takes out an old blanket. He also has the Angel with him; it will be their only source of light in the darkness.

Rössel straightens up; he seems resolute now. He leads them over a ditch, away from the track and up through the undergrowth, between rocky outcrops and towering firs.

The last of the light is left behind. The wilderness begins.

After perhaps three hundred metres of moving between the trees they reach a chaotic mass of angular shadows. Jan holds up the Angel and sees shining blocks of granite, polished by glaciation thousands of years ago and piled up at the bottom of a sheer rock face. Somewhere in the darkness he can hear the sound of rushing water.

'Are we climbing up there?'

'No, it's impossible.' Rössel shakes his head. 'We have to go round . . . It's not as steep.'

They find a small path that snakes around the blocks and heads upwards at an angle. Rössel leads the way; he appears to be moving through his memory map, and shows no hesitation as he leans forward to climb the steep slope.

Jan follows a few metres behind him. The image of Carl's dead body is in his mind, and he prefers to have Rössel in front of him while the razor is still around.

After twenty metres Rössel stops to catch his breath. 'I carried the boy all the way up here,' he says. 'That was hard work.'

'Was John Daniel still alive then?' Jan asks. 'Did you kill him here?'

'I didn't kill him.' Rössel turns to face him; he sounds tired now. 'He died in my car, because of all the booze he'd knocked back during the evening. He threw up and choked on his own vomit in the boot. It wasn't my fault.'

Jan looks at him. 'He would have lived if you'd left him alone. Like the others.'

Rössel shrugs his shoulders. 'He could have stayed sober.'

He doesn't say any more, but as they continue their ascent Rössel's head is constantly moving to and fro in the darkness, as if he is searching for enemies.

There is a ledge a few metres higher up and Rössel disappears behind it. Jan makes a final effort and follows him. The ground levels out here. They have reached a broad plateau high above the forest, part of a longer chain of hills.

Rössel is standing there waiting for him, with a spade in his hand. He looks over at a solitary pine tree growing on the plateau. 'This is where I came that night,' he says. 'I'd done some walking around here . . . I knew the area. The last time was after a terrible winter storm, and I noticed that a small pine tree had been blown over up on the top of the hill. It had been torn out by the roots, leaving a gaping hole underneath.'

Jan holds up the Angel and sees that the hilltop is some fifteen or twenty metres wide. On the far side it falls away sharply, down to the spot where the granite blocks are piled up at the bottom.

There is plenty of undergrowth and low bushes up here, and the pine tree. Its roots have somehow managed to re-establish themselves. The pine is growing tall and straight, although the needles at the top don't look very healthy. But there is no hole where the roots were originally torn out.

'Where is he?' Jan asks.

'Here.' Rössel walks over to the tree, his voice flat and mechanical now. 'I carried the body up here and dumped it in the hole underneath the roots. Then I managed to push the tree back upright, and the body was nowhere to be seen.'

Jan shines the beam of the Angel at the top of the tree. 'It's dying.'

'It is now.'

Jan doesn't say any more; he merely watches as Rössel takes a step away from the pine and opens out the blanket.

'Start digging there . . . Right next to the trunk.'

Jan looks at the uneven ground. He is thinking about roots and secrets and different choices.

Then he picks up the spade, drives it into the ground and begins to dig. His body is full of energy now; he needs energy, because the ground is so hard. There aren't many stones, but the spade must hack its way through tightly packed earth and tough root systems.

Rössel is still holding the other spade, but he is staring at the ground on the far side of the tree.

Jan keeps on digging, building up a pile of earth next to the trunk; a wide hole is opening up in front of him. From time to time he picks up the Angel and directs its beam at the hole, but he can see nothing yet.

'Keep going,' Rössel says.

Some of the roots are so thick that Jan can't chop through them, so he digs out the earth around them and carries on downwards.

When he finally stops for a rest and looks at his watch, it is quarter to one. His arms are aching, but he keeps on digging.

Another slender root is sticking out of the earth – at least that's what he thinks, until he sees that it is something else.

A yellowish bone.

The spade stops in mid-air as Jan stares down. He picks up the Angel again, and in the light he sees more bones. Bones and scraps of frayed material.

Rössel also sees the find, and nods. 'Good . . . keep going.'

Jan hesitates. 'I might damage him.'

'*It*,' says Rössel. 'It's only a body.'

Jan doesn't answer; he bends his back and carries on. As carefully as possible he clears away the earth from around the bones; more and more pale fragments begin to appear. Slowly he reveals the shape of a skeleton, but the roots of the tree have grown during the passing years, and many bones have been broken or are missing.

After perhaps half an hour a large grey stone comes away from the damp wall of earth and rolls down into the bottom of the hole.

No, not a stone, Jan realizes – it's a skull. He doesn't want to look any closer, but he can see that bits of skin are still attached, like old paper.

Rössel says nothing; he simply climbs down and begins to gather up all the loose bones. He passes them up one by one, and Jan carefully lays them on the blanket. The round skull is placed there too.

Eventually there are no more bits to hand over.

'Is that it?' Jan asks.

'That's it,' Rössel replies, taking a last swig from the bottle. 'We just need to finish this off now.' He clambers out of the grave, leans on the spade and smiles at Jan.

'Finish this off?'

There is no answer to Jan's question, but suddenly he hears the sound of rustling in the undergrowth behind him.

Boots.

Rössel glances in the direction of the noise. 'Welcome,' he says.

'Hi, Ivan,' a subdued voice replies in the darkness. It's a woman's voice; she sounds tired and out of breath.

Jan turns his head, holds up the Angel and sees someone he recognizes coming up the slope.

'Hi, Jan.'

It is Hanna Aronsson, and she is moving slowly. She is carrying something: she has a small, limp body in her arms. With a blind-fold around its eyes.

A sleeping child, or perhaps a child who has been drugged.

A boy.

55

Fifteen seconds later Jan is lying slumped on the ground.

Rössel has knocked him down, and it happened very quickly. One whirling blow with the spade in the darkness as Jan was staring at Hanna Aronsson, trying to understand why she was here. And who is the boy?

Rössel stepped forward and aimed at Jan's right leg. The steel spade hit him just below the knee, the leg gave way and Jan went down in a flash of pain and nausea.

He loses consciousness.

Seconds pass, perhaps minutes.

'Did everything go OK up there?' He can hear Rössel's voice.

And Hanna's reply: 'Yes, but I had to wait a while until he was outside on his own.'

'Good,' Rössel says.

The voices and the cold slowly bring Jan round, and when he looks up he can see a faint light. The Angel is lying in front of him, switched on, and in its glow he can just make out Rössel and Hanna like two shadows, a few metres away.

'And he didn't see you?' Rössel asks.

'No. Nobody saw me.'

Rössel has lowered the spade; he seems to be relaxing. He takes three steps towards Hanna and kisses her on the cheek, touches her blonde hair. 'I've wanted to do that for so long,' he says.

But his movements look stiff. His hands are unused to intimacy.

Jan has also recognized the boy: it is Leo. Leo Lundberg. Five years old, missing and the focus of a police search – Jan remembers Marie-Louise's call, telling him that the boy had disappeared from his foster parents' garden.

The blindfold covering Leo's eyes is wide and black. He is breathing, but doesn't appear to be awake; his body is heavy and inert in Hanna's arms.

Jan watches as Rössel takes Leo and lays him down next to the hollow by the pine tree. 'This is where he will lie,' Rössel says. 'Down here.'

It is like watching a shadow play. Jan feels dazed and somehow distant, but the pain in his leg is beginning to ease. He tries to sit up.

Rössel notices and turns to him. 'Don't move.'

Jan slowly shakes his head and sits up anyway. He tries to get Hanna to meet his gaze. 'What are you doing?' he asks. 'Why have you brought Leo here?'

'We didn't bring him,' Rössel says. '*You* did.'

Jan stares at him. 'Me?'

'This is the scene of the crime, this is where it all ends,' Rössel says. 'You even drew a map . . . A map with a confession, admitting what you'd done. It's in the car, waiting for the police.'

Jan listens and looks at Hanna again, still trying to make eye contact. 'What are you doing here, Hanna?'

But she merely glances at him, then looks away; in the light of the Angel her expression is blank, her eyes empty. 'Sorry,' she says, lowering her gaze. 'But you were a perfect fit . . . You can save Ivan if you take the blame for the crimes he's suspected of.'

'I'm not taking the blame.'

'Yes, you are. You've abducted boys in the past.'

Jan understands. Hanna has chosen him; he is a murderer who will be found dead next to an old victim and a new victim, while she and her Ivan disappear into the night. Rössel can be back at the hospital in an hour, and with a bit of luck no one will have noticed that he's been gone.

Folie à deux. Shared psychosis. Or love over the wall. Jan recalls

398

Dr Högsmed's warning about getting too close to a psychopath, and looks at Hanna. 'You got lost in the forest,' he says.

She shakes her head. 'I know what I'm doing. I'm here to set Ivan free . . . and you would do exactly the same for your Rami.'

Jan doesn't answer.

Leo, he thinks. How is he going to save Leo?

'Do it now, Hanna,' Rössel says, offering her the spade. 'Show me how strong you are.'

Hanna looks at the spade for a long time, then she closes her eyes. She doesn't move. 'I can't,' she says quietly.

'It's only a body.' Rössel is still holding out the spade. 'It can't feel anything.'

'I can't do it.'

Only Jan is looking at Leo. He is still lying on the ground by the hole, but Jan suddenly notices that he is moving. The little boy can't see because of the blindfold, but whatever Hanna has used to knock him out, chloroform or something similar, is starting to wear off.

But not quickly enough. Jan must keep talking: 'There's no way Rössel is going to be released, Hanna. He killed a guard tonight during his escape . . . He slit Carl's throat.'

She looks sharply at Rössel. 'Is this true?'

'I did what I had to do,' he replies. 'And now it's your turn.'

Hanna stays put; she is staring at the spade. 'No.'

'Yes,' says Rössel in a louder voice.

Jan can see Leo stretching in the shadows on the ground; he isn't fully awake, but he's getting there.

A metre or so from Jan's leg is the Angel, the only light on the hillside. And even closer, right next to him, he can see his spade.

Rössel sighs and gets out the bottle again. He takes a swig and nods. 'I'll take care of it.'

Jan reaches out and closes his fingers around his spade as Hanna looks at Rössel once more.

'Ivan, we don't need to—'

He cuts her off abruptly. 'I'm going to do it now.'

But Jan's time has come, and he finally takes his chance. In one single rapid movement he is on his knees, raising the spade with both hands like a long, slender club.

'Leo!' he yells to the boy. 'Run! Just get away from here!'

Leo is on his feet. He has begun to move.

Jan strikes. The spade comes crashing down and there is a crunching noise from the Angel. The light goes out.

The autumn night sweeps in; it is almost pitch dark now. The only discernible light is coming from the buildings far below. Jan has already dropped the spade, and he shouts again, 'Run towards the lights, Leo!'

The drums are pounding inside his head, several beats per second. There isn't much time now.

He sees a small body disappearing into the darkness, running away. Leo has torn off the blindfold.

'Run!'

Jan gets to his feet, using the spade for support.

'Don't move!' Rössel bellows.

He is standing in front of Jan like a black shadow, with his own spade raised high above his shoulders. And then he strikes, two hard blows that shake the handle of Jan's spade; the third blow knocks it out of Jan's grasp, and it clatters away across the stones.

But Rössel's spade is also useless – the handle has split and cracked in the middle. He tosses it away and takes something else out of his pocket, holding it up in front of him.

Not the tear gas, but the razor.

'Jump,' Rössel says.

Jan backs away holding his hands up in front of him, but his leg is still hurting and won't obey him properly. He stumbles over a stone or a root, dangerously close to the sheer drop. He tries to pretend that there is solid ground everywhere, but the dizziness is taking hold.

Rössel moves forward with the razor at the ready. He makes a rapid swiping movement and the back of Jan's hand burns with pain and begins to bleed. Several veins have been slashed.

Rössel holds the blade up even higher. 'Jump,' he orders again. 'You might survive.'

But Jan doesn't move any further backwards. He looks at Rössel's outstretched hand, the hand holding the razor, and fumbles under his jumper. He has no weapon, of course, but he does have the plastic loops he took from Carl. Thin, strong loops that can catch something and hold it fast.

He removes one of the loops and reaches out.

Rössel isn't fast enough. Jan grabs hold of his hand and manages to slip the loop over both their hands. All he has to do now is pull, and his own wrist is firmly attached to Rössel's. Jan can now control the razor, and keep it away from him.

Rössel is breathing hard in the darkness, tugging and jerking. He tries to transfer the razor to his left hand so that he can cut himself free, but Jan grabs hold of that hand too.

They are holding on to each other like a couple about to start dancing, and there is no escape: Jan is trapped by Rössel and Rössel is trapped by Jan.

Rössel keeps on fighting, but Jan won't let go.

He closes his eyes. He hopes that Leo got away. That he heard Jan's shouts and ran down the slope, heading towards the lights.

'Give up,' Rössel says. 'Before you die.' He is breathless and his voice has lost all trace of softness. The predator has emerged, the beast that has been hiding behind the self-possessed teacher.

Jan is finding it impossible to regain his balance, and Rössel cannot let him go. Jan opens his eyes. They are moving inexorably towards the sheer drop. He and Rössel, bound together in a macabre embrace. They are both panting, breathing in time with one another.

'Your turn, my friend!' Rössel shouts.

Jan is losing the battle, he is on the point of being hurled out into the void. And there is nothing to hold on to. Only Ivan Rössel.

He turns to look for help. Leo has gone, and there is just one lone figure by the pine tree. Hanna is standing motionless in the undergrowth, watching them. She is frozen to the spot; she can do nothing.

But Leo got away. He fled from the predator, out of the forest. He is strong, he will make it.

Jan is happy with that victory.

He feels the edge of the solid ground beneath his feet, but he does not hesitate. Just one small step backwards into the darkness.

One step, and he takes Rössel with him over the edge.

56

'Is everyone feeling all right?' Marie-Louise asks.

No one responds to her gentle query.

Hanna is as quiet as her colleagues this morning. She has no words. She has come back to work and is trying to look calm, even though she can hardly breathe. So much has gone wrong. She feels as if she is sitting in the middle of a storm, with no idea of when it will pass.

It is Wednesday now. The Dell has remained closed since the chaotic fire drill, and meanwhile the rumours about St Patricia's have been growing. There have been newspaper articles about what happened, reports on the radio, and the TV news has shown pictures of the closed hospital gates.

Marie-Louise doesn't ask any more questions. She turns her head. 'Dr Högsmed is here today to give us an update and fill in one or two gaps. I think we all need some kind of . . .' She falls silent, unable to find the right words. 'Doctor,' she says.

'Thank you, Marie-Louise.'

Högsmed has been sitting at the table with his head bowed, as if he has hardly slept over the past few days. But now he straightens his back and begins to speak: 'So . . . We had rather a dramatic start to the weekend. Dramatic and tragic. As you know we had scheduled a major fire drill for Friday night, but it became rather more complicated than we had intended. This was because a real fire was discovered on the fourth floor, just before the actual drill was due to begin.'

The doctor pauses. There is absolute silence around the table. Hanna looks out of the window at St Psycho's.

'As a consequence of this fire,' Högsmed goes on, 'a certain amount of confusion arose with regard to the dividing line between the actual emergency and the drill. This meant that we had very poor control over some areas, and the patients were able to wander around freely. Possibly as a result of this chaos there was a fatal attack on one of the security guards on the fourth floor, followed by the escape of the man who started the fire. One of our most dangerous patients.'

Ivan, Hanna thinks. Was he dangerous? Yes. But he was also loving and considerate. She sits quietly at the staffroom table with Andreas. They are the only two who have turned up today. The chairs on either side of Hanna are empty.

One of them is Lilian's, of course, but she has been signed off due to ill health.

The other chair was Jan Hauger's.

Hanna had seen Jan fall over the edge of the precipice high above the forest, along with Ivan – two dark figures locked together, neither of them prepared to let go.

She had stood there frozen to the spot; she had closed her eyes and waited for the dull thud of bodies hitting the rocks, and after a second or two the thud came.

The forest was silent. Then Hanna heard something in the darkness: the sound of whimpering from down below.

'Ivan?' she had shouted over the edge.

The whimpering continued, but the voice sounded like Jan's. Then it stopped.

Hanna had turned and fled. Leo was gone; he had already run off into the night, and she decided to let him be. Kidnapping him and trying to put the blame on Jan Hauger had been Ivan's idea, not hers. She was glad Leo had got away.

She had stumbled down through the trees to her rented car, then driven back to Valla on the motorway.

By three o'clock she was home. She had locked the door, then flushed the gloves, the syringe and the empty ampoule of Valium down the toilet; anything that could link her to Leo's abduction had to go. Then she had gone to bed, repeating the same mantra over and over again in her head.

Nothing. She knew nothing. Nothing about the fire. Nothing about Ivan Rössel. Nothing about Jan Hauger and his obsession with Alice Rami.

But what was going to happen now? The lack of certainty almost drove her mad.

She had called Lilian on Saturday morning.

Lilian's voice was subdued when she answered the phone. Hanna tried to sound perfectly normal, and asked what had happened on Friday night.

'Nothing,' Lilian said. 'Nothing at all. Rössel never came to the visitors' room. Nobody came . . . so in the end we went home.'

'What a shame,' Hanna said.

She didn't know what else to say. She didn't really want to speak to Lilian at all, but there was one question she had to ask: 'Have the police called you?'

'No,' Lilian said. 'Why would they do that? Do they suspect something?'

'I shouldn't think so,' Hanna said quickly.

But of course that was exactly what she thought. After all, the grave that had contained the remains of Lilian's brother was open now. When the police found Ivan's and Jan's bodies, they would also find John Daniel, and his family would be informed. They would know, at long last. Hanna cared only about making sure she wasn't involved.

Nothing, she knew nothing.

Lilian was quiet for a moment, then she went on: 'But Marie-Louise called last night; did she speak to you as well?'

'Yes.'

'So you know Leo Lundberg was missing.'

'Yes.'

'And what about you? Do you have anything to tell me, Hanna?'

'No, nothing,' Hanna said. She quickly put down the phone and let out a long breath.

Nothing.

She had gone back to her lonely bed and thought about Ivan. She had been obsessed with him for months, dreamed of helping him, getting him out of St Patricia's at any price. But they had managed only a few brief conversations in the visitors' room, supervised by Carl, who was always ready to accept a bribe. They had made love once, on the mattress down in the safe room.

Now Ivan was gone. She missed him.

But she realized that she actually missed Jan Hauger too.

Högsmed has paused in his account of the weekend's events. He takes a deep breath and continues: 'So we had a number of incidents on the same night. But eventually we managed to bring the situation under control, and all the patients are now accounted for . . . with the exception of the person who escaped. He was found dead, in the company of' – the doctor glances sideways at Marie-Louise – 'the person we suspect of helping him to escape. I am talking about your colleague, Jan Hauger. He is being treated in hospital; his injuries are severe, but he will live.'

No one speaks. Everyone seems to be holding their breath – including Hanna.

Jan is alive.

She hears the doctor sigh heavily, then he adds, 'Staff recruitment falls within my remit, and of course I take full responsibility for the appointment of Jan Hauger.'

Marie-Louise looks down at the table, and chips in with a comment: 'It wasn't easy to tell. Jan seemed reliable in many ways, but there were a number of . . . warning signs. He recently told me he'd had mental-health issues in the past. He had apparently spent some time in a psychiatric unit when he was a teenager.'

Dr Högsmed continues his account. He tells them about Leo Lundberg's disappearance from his foster family's garden on Friday evening, and the ensuing police search – until he suddenly appeared at a farmhouse outside Gothenburg late that night. This meant that he hadn't run away; he had been abducted in a car.

Finally Högsmed explains that the police found Jan Hauger unconscious at the bottom of a sheer drop in the forest, not far from the location where Leo turned up. The patient Jan had helped to escape was lying underneath him, dead. They had left Jan's car down on the track, together with a written confession.

'We are assuming this was a kind of suicide note,' the doctor says. 'Hauger and the patient had dug up a grave in the forest, but they let the child go . . . before throwing themselves off the precipice together.'

Silence once more. They probably all knew this already, but they still seem shocked. Andreas looks utterly devastated, and Hanna hopes her own expression is equally sorrowful.

'How's Leo?' Marie-Louise asks.

'He is unharmed. He doesn't remember much, and perhaps that's just as well,' Högsmed says. 'He only remembers that someone came up behind him in the garden when he was playing on the swing, and grabbed hold of his arms. The doctor found a needle mark on his arm, so no doubt some kind of sedative was involved, but he's feeling fine now, under the circumstances.'

Hanna's fists are tightly clenched under the table. What has Leo told the police? What does he remember about what happened in the darkness above the forest? He was drugged and blindfolded – so surely he won't remember *her*? And if Jan recovers, will he be able to talk? Will anyone believe him?

She has to say something, and leans forward. 'I've just remembered something.'

Everyone is looking at her, and she goes on: 'It was just something Jan Hauger told me ages ago, and I don't know if it means anything . . . but he said he took a group of children out on an excursion in the forest one day, and he separated one of the boys from the rest and left him out there.'

'Oh?' Högsmed says quickly. 'And when was this?'

'It was when he was working at some nursery or other . . . it sounded as if it was years and years ago.'

Marie-Louise stares at her for a long time. 'You should have spoken to me about this, Hanna.'

'I know, but I thought . . . I thought it was some kind of weird joke. I mean, Jan always seemed so reliable, didn't he? And the children really liked him. Didn't they?'

Högsmed looks at her and clears his throat. 'This is highly confidential,' he says, 'but the police went to Hauger's apartment over the weekend. They found a number of suspicious items, including a large number of drawings depicting extremely violent incidents and revenge fantasies. And one of Hauger's neighbours used to work in the hospital; apparently Hauger had been asking questions about various escape routes.'

Hanna bows her head. 'Poor Jan,' she says quietly.

The others are looking at her oddly.

'I just mean . . . he should have got some help. We should have been more vigilant.'

'Disturbed antisocial tendencies are very difficult to spot,' Högsmed says. 'Even we professionals sometimes miss the signs.'

A final long silence.

He looks down at his papers. 'Well . . . that's all I wanted to say, really.'

'Thank you so much, Doctor.' Marie-Louise clasps her hands together and smiles at Hanna and Andreas. 'I'm sure you must have questions, but we can deal with those later. Time to look forward. The children will be here soon.'

Hanna quickly gets to her feet. She pretends that this is an ordinary working day.

And it *is* an ordinary working day, an ordinary day at the beginning of the long winter. Apart from the fact that Jan and Ivan are gone, and Lilian is off sick.

As Hanna leaves the room she hears the front door slam shut.

The children, she thinks, and prepares to continue playing the role of the conscientious pre-school teacher.

Little Josefine has arrived, dressed in a warm dark-green snowsuit and with a foster parent in tow.

Josefine gives Hanna a big smile; she has lost yet another front tooth over the weekend. 'It's snowing!' she shouts.

'Is it?' Hanna looks out of the window. Josefine is right; big white snowflakes are swirling through the air. Perhaps the snow will lie for a while this time.

'Good,' she says, smiling at Josefine. 'In that case maybe we can go out and play in the snow when the others arrive. We'll make snow angels! But perhaps you could go into the playroom in the meantime?'

Josefine takes off her outdoor clothes and scampers off.

Hanna begins to relax.

'Excuse me . . .' a voice behind her says. 'Have you seen any handmade books around here?'

Hanna turns around. 'Sorry?'

She realizes that it is Josefine's foster mother who has asked the question. Or her legal guardian, perhaps. The woman seems to be in her thirties; her grey woolly hat is pulled well down over her forehead, and she is wearing narrow, black-framed glasses.

Hanna looks at her with curiosity. She has only seen this woman on the odd occasion in the past; Josefine is usually brought to the Dell and picked up by an older man.

'I left some books here last summer,' the woman goes on. 'Four slim books . . . I wrote them for my older sister, but she wasn't allowed to have them.'

Hanna knows exactly what she is talking about – Jan's picture books. But she shakes her head. 'Sorry. I don't think I've seen them . . . but you're welcome to have a look.'

'Really?'

'Of course. Come on in.'

The woman takes off her shoes and unbuttons her jacket.

Hanna has to ask, 'Is your name Alice Rami?'

The woman nods and straightens her back, but her expression is wary. Her gaze is very direct. 'How do you know that?' she asks.

'Because . . . I've heard of you.'

'Oh?'

The woman is not smiling, but Hanna goes on anyway: 'You were a musician, weren't you?'

Alice Rami grimaces. 'For a little while, many years ago.'

'What happened?'

Rami sighs. 'A lot of things happened. My sister was ill; she just kept on getting worse and worse, and I wasn't feeling too good either. So I stopped playing.'

She is talking about her older sister, Hanna realizes. Maria Blanker.

'But she's getting the care she needs now?' Hanna asks.

Alice Rami nods, and Hanna wants to ask why her sister is locked up inside St Patricia's. But that would probably be too intrusive. Instead she asks, 'Do you think she'll be out soon?'

'We're hoping so,' Rami says quietly. 'For Josefine's sake.'

'Good.' She nods to Rami with a sympathetic look on her face. 'I know what it's like to wait for someone.'

'Are you waiting too?'

'I was. I was waiting for a man . . . a very special man.'

There is a brief silence, then suddenly Hanna hears voices behind her. Marie-Louise and Dr Högsmed have emerged from the kitchen. Högsmed is asking something about a staff locker, and Marie-Louise replies, 'Yes, he did have one . . . But we keep a set of spare keys.'

Hanna looks at Rami again. Here she is – the woman Jan Hauger has been waiting for all through the autumn. But in the wrong place, which is slightly ironic.

Jan was never in contact with Alice Rami. He never got the answers to his questions, but perhaps Hanna can try? If she and Lilian aren't friends any more, perhaps Rami could be her friend? She feels lonely now. Abandoned.

'We can look for the books together, if you like.'

Hanna hears a rattling sound behind her and looks around. Marie-Louise has opened Jan's locker; it was stuffed full, and several things have fallen out on to the floor: a raincoat, a small bicycle pump and a number of books.

Hanna doesn't want to look at Jan's possessions. She turns back to Alice Rami, and goes on: 'We can check in the book boxes in the playroom.'

But Rami is no longer listening to her. Her gaze is fixed on a point to Hanna's right. 'There they are,' she says.

Hanna looks around. Rami is looking at the picture books – they are lying on the floor in front of Jan's locker. And when Hanna looks more closely she recognizes them, of course: *The Animal Lady*, *The Witch Who Was Poorly*, *Viveca's House of Stone* and *The Princess with a Hundred Hands*.

Four stories about loneliness.

Hanna is still standing in the hallway, and before she can stop her Rami goes into the staffroom and over to the locker. She bends down between Marie-Louise and Dr Högsmed and picks up the books, one by one.

She leafs through them. 'Someone has been drawing in these,' she says quietly. 'Do you know who's done these drawings?'

Rami looks up, but Hanna cannot say anything. She can only shake her head, even though she can clearly see Jan Hauger's face in front of her.

There is a fifth book on the floor; it was lying underneath the others, and Hanna hasn't seen it before.

An old, black notebook with a picture on the cover: a faded Polaroid that has been stuck on. The photograph shows a boy with blond hair, staring into the camera from a hospital bed.

Rami picks up the notebook. She straightens up and looks at it for a long time. 'I recognize this too,' she says eventually. 'I was the one who took this picture . . . a long, long time ago.'

She opens the book and reads a name: *Jan Hauger*. She looks up. 'Does he work here?'

Marie-Louise looks troubled. 'No,' she says quietly. 'Unfortunately he isn't with us any more . . . Did you know him?'

Rami nods, without saying anything further.

Hanna can feel the panic welling up in her stomach. She wants to say something, but Rami just keeps looking through Jan's diary, staring at the drawings and densely written pages with a look of incredulity on her face.

She keeps hold of the book, and smiles affectionately.

'Oh yes, I knew him. We were friends, Jan and me.'

Acknowledgements

Thanks to Kajsa Asklöf, Roger Barrett, Katarina Ehnmark Lundquist, Ann Heberlein, Rikard Hedlund, Kari Jacobsen, Cherstin Juhlin, Anders Parsmo, Ann Rule, Åsa Selling and Bengt Witte, who directly or indirectly helped with this novel.

Johan Theorin's first novel, *Echoes from the Dead*, won The Swedish Crime Academy's Best First Novel award in 2007, and went on to win the CWA John Creasey (New Blood) Dagger in 2009. His second novel, *The Darkest Room*, won the Best Swedish Novel 2008, and the CWA International Dagger in 2010.